AGAINST THE TIDE

AGAINST THE TIDE

JOHN F. HANLEY

Matador
9 Priory Business Park,
Wistow Road, Kibworth Beauchamp,
Leicestershire. LE8 0RX
Tel: (+44) 116 279 2299
Fax: (+44) 116 279 2277
Email: books@troubador.co.uk
Web: www.troubador.co.uk/matador

This is a work of fiction.
Apart from well-known historical figures and events, the names, characters and incidents
portrayed in it are the work of the author's imagination. Any resemblance to actual persons,
living or dead, events or localities is entirely coincidental.

ISBN 9781780882987

British Library Cataloguing in Publication Data.
A catalogue record for this book is available from the British Library.

Typeset by Troubador Publishing Ltd, Leicester, UK
Printed and bound in the UK by TJ International, Padstow, Cornwall

Matador is an imprint of Troubador Publishing Ltd

In memory of Marjorie Evelyn Hanley (nee Renouf) 1920 - 2009.

"Love is all truth, Lust full of forged lies."
Shakespeare: *Venus and Adonis* 799-804

Preface

July 1939

Jersey: Population 50,000. Largest of the Channel Islands at forty-five square miles (1,000 times smaller than New Jersey), lies ten miles from France and 100 miles from England. Extensively fortified to resist French invasion, it has been a British Crown Possession for over 800 years.

Shaped like the hide of a cow pegged out on its four extremities it declines from 400 feet in the north to sea level in the south. Because of this sunny angle, it is ideal for agriculture and produces thousands of tons of early potatoes for the British market each year. Sheltered in the bay of St Malo, caressed by the Gulf Stream, it enjoys an even more benign tax regime. It has become a haven for the wealthy who love new potatoes almost as much as counting their money.

1

He had me by the balls. Surprised, angry, I tried to twist away but the Dutchman laughed, gave another tweak then pulled me under. I thrashed back to the surface and snorted out seawater. It had amused a section of the crowd closest to us. Most of them didn't understand water polo, but appreciated a good tussle.

Miko stood up and shouted to Phillips, the referee, trying to draw his attention to the fouling at this end of the pitch. He was wasting his time but it distracted my marker enough for me to wriggle free and shout for the ball. Nelson spotted me and lobbed it so high it crossed the sun, blinding me as I followed its arc. I fumbled the catch and was jerked underwater again. Surely Phillips had seen that blatant foul. I surfaced and reached for the ball to take the penalty but he had raised the blue flag. He tapped his sandal with the flagstick, indicating that I had pushed off my marker and committed the foul. So now, Phillips, honorary policeman, dishonest butcher and pompous fart, believed he could see underwater.

The Dutchman took the free shot, paddled back behind me, rubbed his unshaven chin into my neck and scratched my ribs with his nails. 'You are quick, my friend, but you must play fair.'

Nelson swam the ball up and shouted at me to clear the goal area. I stretched to my left but the *salaud* grabbed my trunks and pulled me back. I threw up my arms theatrically, sucked in a good breath and ducked underwater. When I surfaced, the ref was pointing his white flag. I retrieved the ball and passed it for a quick return but the Dutchman was already on me. Nelson flipped the ball into the perfect position. As I grabbed it, pain seared through me. The bugger was crushing my testicles.

Over the whistle's screech, I heard the Dutchman calling out, 'He has, how you say – cramp.'

Phillips laughed. 'Help him out but no substitution for the white team.'

Cookie left his goal and towed me to the concrete wall that marked one side of the pitch. 'Careful, Jack. He's a tough nut. Want me to have a word?'

Big-hearted Joe Buesnal, Cookie to his friends, was quite capable of knocking the tulips out of the Dutchman. Six foot four, eighteen stone, fists like shoulders of mutton, he was playing for the island's defence. I had been given a chance to lead the attack on his goal in a warm-up match for our annual battle with Guernsey. I shook my head. I didn't need his protection.

He rolled me onto the warm, pitted surface. I slithered across to the side and dangled my legs in the sea, trying to fight off the spasms. The tide was receding, but wavelets still splattered against the granite retaining wall. A cormorant popped up yards away and twisted its long, oiled neck in my direction. With a wink of one liquid eye, it ducked under, in search of a late lunch. I vomited mine into the water, conscious of Phillips' fat legs as he scurried up and down the wall policing the game. The Blues scored twice while my team was reduced to six men.

Someone hissed at me. Miko had worked his way through the crowd on the concrete steps. Now for a lecture in broken English. I sighed and shuffled towards him.

'*Te idióta.*' He spread his hands in exasperation. 'Why, you let him hold? You remember nothing? *Spuma!*'

I knew the last part meant "make white water" in Hungarian but that was impossible against someone whose sprint was equal to mine. I shrugged. 'It's only a practice match.'

He spat foreign words in his rusty voice. They sounded like broken tools in a metal bucket. Their meaning was clear but I still threw him the sort of dumb look I'd perfected on my Latin master.

He shook his head and spoke slowly in English. 'You clown. Is only practice match?' he sneered. 'How you make senior team if that your belief? Huh?'

He was right. I was on trial and, so far, I hadn't done very well. I knew the older players had their doubts about selecting someone just for their speed but Nelson had persuaded them. Perhaps they were right, I should stick to racing. I started to untie my cap.

'No, Jerk.' He couldn't even pronounce my name. A couple of spectators laughed.

'So what do you suggest?'

He pulled his right arm across his chest, slapped his elbow, dropped his shoulder, and rotated it backwards. '*Nincs fék a kezemben.*'

I stared at him in disbelief but he nodded and slipped back into the crowd.

Phillips' whistle shrilled – half-time.

I hobbled towards the rest of team. They were arguing but stopped as I reached them.

Nelson turned to me. 'How do you feel?'

Just then, I heard my name and glanced up to catch Caroline's wave. After her diving display, she had swapped her white Jantzen costume for a low-cut yellow dress that left even less to the imagination. I waved back. She must have seen the treatment I had been getting. Did she care, or was she just hoping for some blood in the water to relieve the tedium? Higher up in the wooden stand, Saul reclined in a white linen suit. He doffed his hat and raised two fingers before nudging Rachel. She smiled but didn't wave.

Caroline mouthed something to me then caressed her hair with her hand. The look and gesture were almost as effective as the Dutchman's grip and I started to ache again.

The timekeeper blew his whistle and Phillips waddled back to the halfway marker, his white plimsolls slapping through the puddles.

Nelson tapped me harder. 'Yes or no?'

I looked from Caroline to Rachel and noticed that Miko had squeezed onto a seat below them. He glared with about as much sympathy as the cormorant, and mouthed "*spumá*".

'Jack, wake up. I need an answer.'

I sucked in a calming breath and grunted, 'I'll do my best.'

3

Fletcher, who fancied Caroline, snorted, 'Fat lot of use that'll be. Best place for you is in the stands with your Jew friend.'

I lurched towards him but Nelson blocked me off. 'That's enough, you two. Save it for the opposition.' He shoved me hard towards the water. I attempted a somersault, but landed on my back with a stinging splash and surfaced to ironic applause.

Nelson swam up. 'Forget Fletcher, he's just jealous. Best way to shut him up is to score a goal.'

Nelson's misplaced faith did little to slow my heart rate.

Phillips blew his whistle and tossed the ball into the centre of the pitch. I got there first, flipped it back to Nelson, surged on towards the goal and straight into the Dutchman's fist. Again, the ref ignored the foul.

'You have played this game much? It is good fun, no?' He laughed and jabbed his knee into my backside. 'In Holland it is only the men who play. Ya, only the men.' As I turned, he pinched the skin under my armpit. I jerked my shoulders back in reflex pushing into his chest. 'Ah, so, we are learning, no?' He dug his knuckle into my spine.

Play was getting closer. I squirmed and wriggled, trying to rise in the water for a flick-on shot. The whistle went. Fletcher had been fouled.

Everyone froze in their positions like floating statues. Free throw to Whites. Fletcher looked around and, with a wicked grin, threw the ball straight at me. No chance to flick it on. I felt fingers reaching between my legs again as the ball flopped in front of me. It floated free, out of reach of the Dutchman, but his hand threatened to wring my balls if I stretched out.

Caroline's screech cut through the tableau. 'Do it, Jack!'

The Dutchman's voice grated in my ear. 'You don't have the guts, boy.'

Fire shot through my body and into my brain; the blood roared in my head. I exploded forward, rolled my shoulder and flung my elbow back into his face. Released from his iron grip, I scooped up the ball and hurled it into the net. Goal!

The crowd roared. The goal judge waved his flags and I turned back to face the team in triumph. The whistle shrieked – not the congratulatory looping blast for a goal – but the long sharp screech of disapproval. I looked at Phillips.

He jabbed his white flag at me, spat out his whistle and bellowed, 'White seven. Permanent exclusion for brutality – leave the pitch and this area immediately.'

I grabbed the ball, pulled it back and aimed at him. 'You bast–'

Cookie snatched it from me and pushed his nose into my face, cutting off my words, 'Don't make it worse. Just get out and get changed.' He shoved me to the side then helped Nelson to drag the Dutchman to the wall. Blood streamed from his nose. The crowd was silent.

I levered myself out. My arms were trembling and I scraped my thigh on the rough concrete. Brewster, the club manager, studied his hands as I stumbled to my feet. My face was burning. I untied my cap, crumpled it in my fist and dropped it onto the table. One of its long wet laces whipped onto the match sheet. I turned and marched towards the granite steps, up and away from the silence of the arena.

'Jack, wait.' Saul bustled through the crowd. I stopped, praying he wouldn't add to my embarrassment. He spat his cigarette into the sea. '"*O, vengeance, vengeance! A very excellent piece of villainy,*" Jack. If you were a *kaffir*, I'd have to cut your balls off.' He roared something in Afrikaans and slapped me on the shoulder.

Everyone could hear him. I remembered a line from our play where Bassanio curses Gratiano for his noisy friendship. I blurted it out now. '"*Thou art too rude, too wild, too bold of voice.*"' If I pushed him into the water, I might regain some credibility with the crowd.

He must have sensed my thought as panic flickered in his golden eyes. He edged towards the steps. I moved closer, feinted with my right hand and flicked his hat off with my left. This drew an appreciative laugh from the gallery as it spun into a puddle, but his freckled cheeks flushed with anger. Perhaps he did deserve a swim. I reached out, but he scooped up his hat and darted off towards the diving boards, chased by the laughter from above. I shrugged and moved away.

'Jack.' Rachel's voice.

I paused and looked back. Saul was showing her his soggy hat.

5

She grinned at me over his shoulder. Behind her, I saw the Dutchman sprawled on the concrete while Brewster administered first aid. Caroline was standing in the group surrounding him. Well, she'd got her blood. I willed her to look in my direction but she seemed focused on the casualty.

Rachel beckoned me towards her. I couldn't. I was in enough trouble already. Exclusion meant that I had to leave the pool area without delay. A cold shower wouldn't do any harm.

2

I was still shivering as I entered the men's open-air changing room. Saul never came into this high-walled arena even though he was now eighteen and entitled to a privilege all the juniors craved. From our experience at school, I suspected that he found the casual nakedness uncomfortable. Unlike Saul, I'd never been teased or even asked about my circumcision. During our brief and embarrassing conversation about the facts of life, Father had explained that it had been for medical reasons. Ironically, with his bright copper hair, Saul looked far less Jewish than I did with my dark curls and prominent nose.

I wasn't surprised to find Nutty prostrate on the central wooden platform, barbecuing himself in the sun. I crept in, wrinkling my nose at the smell of olive oil and vinegar, with which he had smeared his old body. Fortunately, he was toasting his back this afternoon. As I reached my clothes, I heard him stir.

'Ah, young Jack, I thought you were playing that infernal game.'

'I was.'

'Where are the other savages then?'

'It's just me. I was thrown out for brutality.'

'Well, perhaps you'll stick to swimming now.'

I didn't answer, just sat on the bench in the sun and contemplated his prone figure.

'You want to tell me what happened? A balanced view, mind, and don't blame the ref, even though it was our beloved centenier.'

'I thought you hadn't watched the game.'

'I slipped in here after the diving, as soon as I saw him sucking on his whistle. I say, young Rachel has improved, hasn't she?' His

7

eyes were shaded under his arm but there was conspiratorial twinkle in his voice.

'Yes, she's got more rotation now, sharper entries.' I didn't bite on his bait.

'It would seem your mutual trainer, Miko Pavas, has been more successful with her than he has with you then.' He laughed.

'How do you know about that?'

He tapped his nose. 'It's a small island, Jack. A foreigner; is he Hungarian or Romanian?'

I shrugged. 'Romanian, I think, though he says he used to coach the Hungarian team.'

'Well his methods are working.' He grinned. 'She'll soon be up to Miss Hayden-Brown's standard.'

Another little dig. Caroline's father had paid almost as much in coaching fees for her diving as he had for her piano lessons. His money hadn't been wasted on either.

Of course, Miko had not been accorded the privilege of entry to the open-air; his membership application had been "awaiting processing" since the beginning of the season, so he paid a daily rate each time he walked down the bridge that separated the pool from the promenade.

I kept quiet.

'Come on, tell me what happened.'

'Nothing. I was being fouled by that guest player, you know, the Dutchman?'

Nutty had been there when we changed before the match and I was sure that introductions had been made. I was also sure that my opponent had given me an odd look as I changed into my trunks.

He nodded. 'And?'

'I retaliated.'

'Jack, getting a story out of you is like milking a bull. What happened?'

'Okay, I lost my temper, used my elbow. Miko calls the move *nincs fék*, or something.'

'That sounds painful.'

'It's meant to be a rotation and follow through. It's just that his nose got in the way.'

'I suggest that you don't use that phrase when you explain yourself to the committee.'

'Oh shit. You think it'll be taken that seriously?'

'Of course it will, if Centenier Phillips has anything to do with it.'

'I don't understand him at all. He used to be so friendly. I was in his swimming class when I was eleven or so. He even gave me extra lessons, got in the water with me, showed me how to get the right shape for front crawl.'

He raised himself up an elbow and peered at me. 'You don't know, do you?'

'Know what?'

'Oh, nothing.'

What was he trying to tell me? 'Why doesn't he come in here? Change with the rest of us?'

He smiled. 'Probably doesn't want to show us his war wounds.'

'Seriously? Was he badly shot up?'

He laughed. 'Only thing damaged was his arse.'

'How?'

'He sat on it for so long. No wounds, Jack. He was in *Ally Sloper's Cavalry.*'

'Can't imagine him on a horse.'

'Neither can I. It was a nickname for the Army Service Corps. ASC, get it?'

'You got me there.'

'Yes, our beloved centenier spent his war years procuring livestock for the troops to eat.'

'So that's the connection with his butcher's shop?'

'His family had that before the war. But that's not the reason he got the cushy job. He was fit enough for the front line but volunteered his expertise.'

'I still don't understand why he seems to hate me so much.'

'I don't think it's you in particular, but it's not for me to tell. You need to ask your father, or your uncle.'

'Oh, that business in his shop. Mum mentioned something about a fight a long time ago. Phillips sacked someone. Uncle Fred went to see him and they had a big argument. I didn't know Father was involved.'

'No, everyone knows about that.' He paused, considering. 'I mustn't speak out of turn, but there was a water polo match back before the war – must have been the summer of 1911 or 1912. All I can say is your uncle had to jump in to separate them.'

'What? My father and Phillips fighting in the pool?' I couldn't imagine it. Not much of a contest. My father was a great bear of a man.

'I know what you're thinking but Phillips wasn't always that shape. It was a good fight whilst it lasted. The funny thing was that Fred came off worst and got bashed by both of them.'

'I'll ask Uncle Fred about that. I'm sure you're making it up.'

'Oh, no. It happened. They were both suspended. None of us really knew what it was about, though we suspected that a girl was involved. Anyway, that was a long time ago.'

'Hey, come on. Don't leave me in suspenders.'

'Right, but you will have to promise you didn't hear this from me.' He waited.

'Okay, I promise.'

A secretive smile crossed his face. 'I believe her name was –'

'Renouf, you little shit.' A wet polo cap slapped my face. Fletcher jumped onto the platform, towering over me. 'We lost that because of you and you can't even look after the kit. You should have rinsed it along with your stupid little brain!'

'What the hell is wrong with you, Fletcher? What have I done to upset you?'

'Apart from break his swimming records and steal his girl? Probably not much,' Nutty answered.

His languid tone provoked a fit of the giggles, which I couldn't contain. I tried but had to surrender to insane cackling.

'Shut up, farm boy. It's not funny!' Fletcher boiled over, thrust forward and grabbed my throat.

Trapped between the bench and the platform, unable to use my legs, I flapped uselessly at him. Dimly, I heard Nutty protesting. Unable to breathe or speak, I pleaded with my eyes. Light faded, leaving an image of his smile as I drifted into a roaring darkness before his face disappeared, and I collapsed onto the concrete floor.

Cookie materialised to lift me back into the sun. I rolled onto the platform, still in a daze.

'You all right, Jack?'

I blinked, tried to cough. Nutty pressed a bottle of lemonade into my hand. I looked around and saw Fletcher, slumped on the bench, holding his head. The drink was warm but I managed to gulp some of it down.

I smiled my thanks to Cookie, then turned to Nutty, sure that he had been telling me something important before Fletcher arrived. 'What were we talking about?'

He rubbed his chin. 'Ah, your mother –'

'Is Renouf here?' Nelson's voice cut through the chatter. He spotted Fletcher first. 'What happened to him?'

'Slipped,' was Cookie's reply.

'Disappointed in love,' was Nutty's.

'Clumsy lump. Renouf, we need to see you in the manager's office. Get dressed and cut along.'

Nutty rolled his eyes at me and mouthed "later" as I struggled into my clothes.

3

Patrick Brewster had been secretary/manager of the club for the past two seasons, after a long career in the Royal Navy. As I stood before his desk, he spoke to Nelson.

'You know my feelings on sportsmanship, Jim. Water polo is not a game for hooligans; it was devised by gentlemen and should be played in that spirit. What happens in the harbour in Guernsey, once every two years, should not influence the way the game is played here, in our pool.' He stroked his beard. 'That great spirit, which drives our amateur sport, is indeed fundamental to the Olympic Movement, and should not be subverted by those from Europe,' he waved towards the east, 'who believe sport is a form of warfare and not a game.'

There was more to this than throwing a leather ball around a floating pitch. I felt a flush spreading to my cheeks, sensed Nelson's discomfort behind me. Where was this leading? Were they going to throw me out of the club for defending myself?

Brewster leant back in his chair and sucked on his pipe. 'We are competing against the crew of HMS *Jersey* next week. Shall we send them back to sea with broken teeth, cut lips and fractured noses?'

Nelson cleared his throat. 'It was my fault. I should have replaced Jack at half-time when I realised what was happening. The Dutchman –'

'He has a name you know.' Brewster fumbled around for the scrap of paper. 'Kohler, that's it, Rudolph Kohler. He's here on holiday, staying at the Palace Hotel. The manager asked me to find a game for him. Seems he plays in the Dutch league. Fine hospitality we've offered.' He scratched his head. 'Now, what to do, eh?'

Phillips spoke up. 'Well, Mr Secretary, under the club rules, exclusion for brutality should be reported to the full committee and the player suspended until a meeting has been convened.'

'Quite, thank you. Yes, that's clear enough. Tell me, do we have any discretion in the matter –'

'Really, Mr Secretary. We can't ignore the rules. That, that –'

'Yes, thank you, Centenier Phillips.' He looked up at me. His tone was formal now and I stiffened. 'Jack Renouf, following your actions this afternoon, I have no option but to suspend you from water polo until next Sunday, when this incident –'

'Just water polo? Surely he must be suspended comp –'

Brewster continued over Phillips' interruption. 'Just water polo, gentlemen. That is sufficient penalty. Renouf will miss the match against the Royal Navy and, I believe, the league match next Friday. Is that correct?'

Nelson nodded. 'Yes, but –'

'Well, gentlemen, thank you for your time. I'd like a few private words with Renouf, if you don't mind.'

Phillips clearly did mind but left, trailing indignation.

'Now, Jack.'

'Sir, you saw what happened. It's not fair. He was fouling me all the time and the referee ignored it. I had every right –'

'That's enough. Now calm down.'

I was seething with frustration and determined to have my say. 'He broke every rule in the book. He even tried to drown me and I'm the one who gets punished. It's bloody ridiculous.'

Brewster laughed. 'Oh, for God's sake, Renouf, it's not about right and wrong. You were stupid enough to retaliate where everyone could see you. What do you expect? Of course you have to be seen to be punished. You can't elbow someone in the face in front of hundreds of witnesses and be applauded for it.'

'But, he –'

'It doesn't matter what he did. If you are going to play the game with adults then you have to learn to take responsibility for your actions. You were in the wrong and you know it.'

I sighed. He was right, Fletcher was right; they were all bloody right. 'Yes, I'm sorry, sir. I apologise. Thank you for dealing with me –'

'That's sufficient. You will still be able to swim in the match. Get some training in. Try to get that qualifying time. Now get out of here before I change my mind and feed you to the fish.'

I started for the door.

'And, Jack, a word of advice. We all make enemies in life, that can't be avoided, but one of the secrets of happiness is to be very careful who you pick as friends.'

That wasn't the advice I wanted. I was about to challenge him when I spotted my reflection in the window. I was nearly nineteen, going on ninety, if some of my friends and relations were to be believed. Perhaps this was a lesson to be learned, but I'd damn well pick who I wanted as friends – not who my father, my uncle, or any other busybody adult felt was appropriate. I swallowed my retort and left.

Phillips was waiting. 'What did he say?'

'Mind your...' I bit my tongue. 'Not much. Just some advice about controlling myself.'

'Stand up for yourself, Renouf, but don't lose your temper like that. If that had been against Guernsey, we would have been stuck with only six men. For God's sake, we could have lost the match and the donkeys would have laughed their hind legs off.'

I wasn't sure if he really was angry, but we were in the shade so his face wasn't flushed from the sun.

'Don't believe everything your Hebrew friend tells you. Mr Brewster is right; there is another way. You have to play to the rules; without them, we're lost. Be strong, but play like, like...' he struggled to complete the analogy, 'an Englishman.'

So there we were, two Jerseymen, whose aspirations should be to act like Englishmen, and one of us was a Jew hater. That explained a lot about Saul's treatment, and about Miko's.

My impulse was to snap back, call him a fascist, spit some of Shylock's lines at him: "*Hath not a Jew eyes...*" Instead, I mouthed the Kipling poem on my bedroom wall. "*If you can keep your head when all about you are losing theirs and blaming it on you*"; is that what you mean?'

He grabbed my elbow and leant closer, his fetid breath in my ear. 'The trouble with you, Renouf, is that you spend too much time with your head up Shakespeare's arse.'

He turned and waddled off, shaking his head. A Strauss waltz floated from the speakers, soothing the ranks of sun-seekers sprawled in deck chairs, reading their Sunday newspapers. Enjoy your holiday – it might be the last for some time, or so the headlines implied.

Saul approached with Rachel. She stopped and peered at me in the shadows. The sun was in their eyes and she had to squint. In contrast to Saul's pale features, her face was tanned. Normally, her eyes were a rich coffee; now, after several dives from ten metres, they were tinged with pink. She fluttered her thick charcoal lashes and smiled.

'We're wandering along to the beach café for an espresso. Want to join us?' she asked.

I smiled back, noticing that Saul's eyes were still bright with anger. 'Thanks, Rachel, perhaps later.'

She hesitated. I felt that she wanted to talk to me alone, but Saul tugged her arm. She shrugged, mouthed 'see you' and followed him towards the bridge. They paused at the kiosk and Saul doffed his hat to me.

Someone punched me from behind. I spun, arching my elbow to strike back.

Caroline gasped in surprise. 'Christ, Jack. Don't hit me as well.'

I exhaled sharply and turned to face her, my pulse racing.

She twitched one of the blonde tresses from her forehead. 'Well, have you been suspended for your brutality, my little angel, or have they given you a medal for thumping the poor foreigner?'

I shook my head. I needed to get away, needed some distraction. A few hours with Caroline would be good. I also needed to start taking it less seriously. 'He deserved it. If he'd carried on marking me like that, we'd have had to get married.'

'How splendid. Do tell me more.' She looped her arm into mine. 'You can give me all the sordid details on the way.'

'Way? Where?'

She dragged me along the bridge. 'To the hospital, silly. I've arranged to pick up our friend and take him back to his hotel and you're coming along to apologise.'

Why should I apologise to the Dutchman? It was his bloody fault

15

anyway. I jerked her arm back as we reached the gate and pulled her into the rail.

'What's wrong, Jack?' There was concern in her voice now as she looked enquiringly at me.

I stared out over the beach, seeing only shades of grey, oblivious to the sprawl of near naked bodies and children screeching about on the sand.

I felt her hand on my cheek. Her voice was soft. 'I think you're feeling a little guilty, aren't you?'

I sighed and nodded.

'You're also realising that you are not as innocent as you were a couple of hours ago.' Her hand caressed my ear. 'That was brutal, Jack. Cold, calculated, murderous even.'

I didn't respond.

She turned my head to face her. 'I think you've grown up a bit this afternoon and it frightens me.'

I stared back. We might only be eighteen but we had shared so much, had been as intimate in body and thought as I believed possible. How could she know me so well when I didn't really understand myself? I shrugged, helpless for words, desperate for her to change my mood.

Her light blue irises, also red-rimmed, from plunging fifteen feet underwater, expanded as she smiled. 'Do you remember when we stood on this bridge before that first party at Saul's and you made me pour that decent bottle of claret into the sand?'

I grimaced.

'Yes, you bastard. I can't believe I let you. I should have hit you over your thick head with it. And all because you don't approve of drink.'

'We didn't need it. Of course, you didn't know Saul then. If you had, you would have realised that his parents keep enough alcohol in their apartment to float the *Queen Mary*.'

'I really didn't understand you then. I'm not much wiser now. Jack Renouf, you are a bloody puzzle.'

I grinned. She had lifted my mood. 'Come on then, Florence Nightingale, let's get this over with.'

4

Feeling more relaxed, I hugged her, conscious of the soft warmth under her thin dress and the seductive power of her perfume. Sometimes, when we were alone in the house, Caroline raided her stock and amused herself by making me apply *eau de cologne* and *parfume* to various intimate parts of her naked body. This testing of my "nose" was one of her favourite games. I usually had difficulty identifying all the ingredients, but I could recognise jasmine and guessed this was her current favourite, Coco. Whatever its composition, it was sufficiently powerful to shift thought processing from my brain to a less inhibited part of my body. *Get the Dutchman out of the way,* it pleaded.

She'd left her father's Bugatti, a 57C drophead coupe, in Roseville Street, just across the main road.

'Come on, Jack. I'll make sure he doesn't eat you.' She jumped into the scarlet roadster, pressed the starter and had the eight cylinders roaring a fortissimo chorus in bottom C before I could close my door. She dropped the clutch and bounced onto the crown of the road, jerking me back into the cream leather seat.

I gritted my teeth. The bonnet was long and the front mudguards so sensuously rounded that even I had difficulty seeing the road. She was a good six inches shorter than me and her Ray-Bans, with their rose-coloured lenses, couldn't have helped as we charged through the empty streets to the General Hospital.

She pulled up alongside the entrance in Gloucester Street and pointed towards the granite façade. I started to protest but she shoved me out and ordered me to get the "casualty" while making her only use of the rear view mirror so far, to reapply her make-up and fiddle with her hair.

I returned a few minutes later, struggling to keep the grin off my face. 'He's already been collected I'm afraid. The hotel sent a car.'

'Damn!' Caroline thumped the wooden steering wheel. 'Get in. We'll go and see him at the Palace, then.'

'But why? Why do you want to drag me up there?'

She looked up at me, the bright spots on her high cheekbones shining through the rouge, crimson lips pouting in disdain. 'Jack, you know you have to apologise to him. I saw you smiling as you got out of the water. You didn't lose your temper. You planned that and you must make amends.'

'What?' I kicked the tyre in disbelief. 'You were the one who shouted out "Do it!" You wanted me to hit him.'

'Don't be so bloody stupid. I most certainly did not. You must have imagined it. Perhaps it was someone else who called out. Rachel, perhaps?' She looked witheringly at me. 'You are so crass sometimes, I almost despair of you. I thought you sportsmen were supposed to be gentlemen. Now, are you coming with me or do I have to go and apologise for you?'

My friends wondered why I put up with her. Perhaps they were right, but she was so different, exciting, unpredictable and challenging. Yet, she was surprisingly vulnerable. I never bragged about how far we went, in contrast to my friends who kept a score of their, often imaginary, successes. That was private, between the two of us, besides which, no one would have believed me.

'Dear Jack, you look like one of your precious cows waiting to be milked. Are you coming with me or are you walking home?'

We glared at each other – my anger threatened to overwhelm what little sense remained. I looked away. There was an iron cannon in the park across the road. Perhaps I should go and kick that instead. It was probably more malleable than her self-belief. Sod it. Did I really want to end it here, now, over a bloody Dutchman? I turned back. She was still staring at me but her lips curled into a hint of a smile. Was it triumph or understanding? I was sure that, before the end of this crazy day, our relationship would be resolved, one way

18

or another, but not here by the side of the dusty road. I clambered into the car and stared straight ahead.

'Oh for God's sake, put your brave face on and stop sulking.'

We found the Dutchman stretched out in a rattan chair near the eastern end of the sun terrace. He seemed to be asleep and bore few marks of my attack. Caroline coughed. Kohler's eyelids fluttered but there was no other reaction. She nudged me with her elbow.

I grimaced at her and croaked, 'Excuse me.'

The Dutchman slowly opened his eyes and, for a fleeting second, I saw confusion, bordering on panic, in their grey depths, then he was awake. His lips spread wide in a friendly grin and he raised his arms above his head.

'I surrender. Please, no more.'

The voice was relaxed, only the slightest suggestion of an accent. He turned to Caroline and opened his eyes in a rather obvious gesture of appreciation. A cold wave of apprehension sucked at my insides.

Caroline cued me. 'We've come to apologise, Mr Kohler.'

He looked surprised. 'Rudi, call me Rudi. But there is no need.' He shrugged his shoulders. 'It is only a game. There is little damage.' He pointed at his left eye. 'A slight swelling and a cut inside my lip,' he rubbed his jaw, 'a little soreness –'

Caroline interrupted. 'But you were unconscious. We were all worried.'

Kohler leapt up. 'Look, no damage. Fit, as you English say, as a fiddle. I was only briefly stunned. The team needed a replacement so I stayed "injured".'

I knew I had knocked him out and that he must still be in some pain. If he wanted to pretend otherwise to impress Caroline, what could I say?

'Anyway, enough of this nonsense, I was more in danger from the cold water.'

Caroline laughed. 'That wasn't cold. You should start training in May when its only fifty-five degrees – that would make your teeth chatter and your testicles tremble. Isn't that what you told me, Jack?'

I mimicked Kohler's relaxed tone. 'Fortunately, my dear, that's one pleasure you will never have – trying to warm up your frozen balls.'

He smiled through her silence. 'Well this is all very jolly – perhaps it is time for you to join me in a drink and tell me all about yourselves. I must say, I am honoured by your company.' He caught the eye of a waiter hovering in the distance and signalled him to approach.

We found comfortable cane chairs by the side of the pool. Caroline and Kohler sipped overdressed cocktails. I nursed a Coke.

'So you have just finished school, Jack. What do you do now?'

'He's got a place at Wadham College, Oxford, haven't you, dear?' Caroline patted my arm in imitation of my mother, though there was irony in her tone.

Kohler looked puzzled.

'Nothing has been decided yet,' I snapped at her.

'Ah, I see. You are, perhaps, reluctant to leave this lovely young lady, for the trials of university?'

'Don't be silly. He can hardly wait to get away. It can be hell, cooped up on this little island.'

'Only for foreigners. Some of us...' I trailed off, realising my gaffe.

'I understand. After all, this "foreigner" is only here on holiday. It is a beautiful island but it could become, how you say, claus...'

'...traphobic.' Caroline finished the word for him. 'Yes, very, but only if you are used to wide open spaces. Jack's family have been here since before the last ice age.'

'Ah, I see. What do they do?'

'Farm. We have sixty vergees in St Martin.'

'Don't confuse him with your silly measurements, Jack. That's about twenty-five acres in proper English.'

Kohler laughed. 'Vergees, acres, I know little of land. I am a city Dutchman. But is that a large farm?'

'It's big enough to be called a farm but there are at least fifty larger than us. About the size of this hotel site.' I waved my arm over the gardens, which swept down to the bay. 'Somewhat steeper in places though.'

Caroline laughed at the understatement – only Jerseymen farmed cliffs.

'We grow potatoes for the early season, some broccoli and we

20

have twenty-two cows.' I realised my enthusiasm must sound rather naïve to the "city" Dutchman.

'Don't forget the bull, Jack.'

I groaned. 'Yes, and a bull.'

She laughed. 'This bull is so big, Rudi, that all the men are frightened of him. Isn't that so, Jack?'

'What she wants me to tell you is that *Marcus Piavonius Victorinus,* or Victor, to those who don't read the Herdbook, weighs over one hundred stone and is probably the most vicious monster that's ever been bred. And yes, only my mother, who is five feet two and weighs a mere seven stone, has the courage to go anywhere near him. Satisfied, Caroline?'

'For God's sake, Jack, don't be so touchy. I think it's quite funny, especially his silly name. Haven't you read that book on bull fighting I gave you?'

'*Fiesta?* Yes, of course I've read it. I like Hemingway's style but I'm sure Victor would see off any of his *toreros.*' We glared at each other – a little like matador and mad bull.

'So, you don't farm on Sundays?' Kohler interjected as Caroline started to paw the ground.

'No. I mean yes, but we have some Breton workers. Alan and I help out during the holidays but Father prefers us to study or take part in sport.'

'Alan? This is a brother?' Kohler seemed interested.

'Yes, Jack. Where is the *dear* boy today?'

Alan hated the sight of her and couldn't understand my interest in the "stuck up bitch". 'He's at Crabbé, practising.'

Kohler looked mystified and Caroline, losing patience with my monosyllabic responses, intervened. 'He's sixteen, a pain in the arse and he shoots at pieces of paper. Apparently, it's a sport.'

'Ah, target shooting. I understand. He is good?'

'Good enough. He's representing the college at Bisley next week. It's the annual public schools' shooting competition in England. Our team stands a good chance this year. He normally swims on a Sunday but today –'

'I understand now. I, too, shoot, during the winter. What weapon does he use?'

'It's not a weapon, it's a rifle, an Enfield 303 adapted for target shooting.'

'Ah, yes. I know this gun. It is very accurate.'

Caroline yawned. 'I'm sure it's all very fascinating to those who like shooting holes in paper, but I don't see the point.'

We both looked at her in surprise. Didn't she read the newspapers or listen to the radio?

'There are many riflemen in Jersey, Jack?' Kohler ignored her attempt to close the conversation.

'It's a big club. Then there's our cadet force and, of course, the militia and...' I stopped. 'Why are you so interested? You're not a spy, are you?'

Caroline hooted. 'Jack, you are really strange at times. I'm sure Rudi is just being polite.'

'Of course. You must not think I am too much of a nosey foreigner.'

'Not at all.' I did though, and let the silence hang.

Caroline leant towards Kohler. 'And what about you, our friendly "foreigner", what do you do?'

'As little as possible.'

Caroline laughed.

'I too am a student, but I study life –'

'No seriously, we're interested.'

I was far from interested. I was beginning to dislike the arrogant bastard even more but Caroline was clearly intrigued.

I surveyed the terraced gardens, choked with colour, sloping to the meadows and the rich summer barrier of woodland, which seemed to dip into the bay. I closed my eyes, dimly aware of their conversation, which washed over me like the oscillation of a poorly-tuned wireless. Kohler came from Rotterdam and was doing post-graduate work on economics. I sensed that even Caroline found this talk of economics less than exciting and my hope that she would soon become bored rose. It was burning in the sun now and the sparkling water looked inviting.

'Anyone fancy a swim?' I interrupted Kohler's discourse on fiscal discipline and the new Europe.

Caroline brightened. 'Yes, my stuff's in the car. Be a dear, Jack, and get it.'

22

I scowled. With me out of the way, perhaps the talk might turn to more enticing matters than monetarism. Kohler couldn't really be that much of a bore. Handsome young men who swam and played dirty water polo couldn't be obsessed with such dry ideas, especially with expensive perfume from seductive blondes breezing over them.

I hurried back but they had disappeared. Sod them. I dropped her bag onto a chair, got changed and threw myself into the fresh water to work off my anger in some quick, twenty-five yard lengths.

I was gasping on the side when Caroline placed her foot on my head and tried to push me under.

'Where have you been, then?' I asked.

'Oh, Rudi has been showing me his room and some photographs of his home. He has a lovely view, with his own bathroom. This really is a super hotel.'

My stomach somersaulted again. She had slipped into her crimson costume with the plunging back and the clinging low cut front. Kohler stood beside her. He was taller, had a better body, was probably fitter and was certainly more attractive than me – even after my attempt to rearrange his face. They made a striking pair.

She winked at me, executed a perfect dive and swam a length underwater.

He plunged in and surfaced behind her.

She spun towards him, giggling.

I heard his laugh, not the mocking tone he had used to needle me in the match, but the genuine hoot of pleasure.

No. Bugger you, it's not going to be that easy. I sprinted towards them. Head up for the final few yards, I splashed between them and wrapped my arms around her, daring him to fight for possession.

She didn't resist, in fact she seemed to enjoy it, and even leant forward to kiss me lightly on my lips.

I tensed, waiting for Kohler to grab me from behind. I felt his breath on my neck then heard a splash as he swam away.

I turned Caroline in my arms to watch as he spun against the wall and started sprinting hard for the other end. It was his turn to burn off some anger.

She peered into my eyes. 'I think you've made your point.'

'Yes, I hope I have. Let's get out of here. We need to talk.'

She laughed and ran her hand down my chest. 'Talking can come later, there's something more important we need to do first.'

The blood rushed to my face. Her power to reverse my emotions with a look, a touch, was beyond my comprehension.

She squeezed my arm as I helped her out. 'Manners, though. We have to say goodbye, thank him for his hospitality.'

I wondered if another blow on his nose would be sufficient.

We walked over and she reached down to stop him as he sprinted in for a turn. He looked relaxed, though he was breathing heavily.

I offered a terse thank you for his hospitality and told him that we had to go. He insisted on shaking hands with both of us, though he clung on to Caroline's rather too long for my liking and complimented her on her choice of Coco Chanel as her perfumer. Bastard.

She brought my towel to me and started to rub me dry. 'Come on, get changed. We can go to my house. Father is away until next week.'

The hollowness inside me had changed to a tingling anticipation.

'Shit. The bastard is back.' She spun off the driveway to Les Routeurs, their converted farmhouse, and pulled up, out of sight, around the corner.

'How do you know?'

'Didn't you see his silver Jag? He must have flown in lunchtime. Fuck.' She looked around. 'Open the gate to the field, Jack. I'll drive in.'

The large field was full of high grass, densely planted. It sloped gently down to Grands Vaux Valley. It was good land and I knew that her father let it out to a local farmer who used it for winter hay.

She parked, grabbed a blanket from the boot and ploughed through the crop, leaving a trail of destruction in her wake. Satisfied that she was far enough in, she dropped the blanket, kicked off her sandals, shrugged out of her dress and stood there, hands on hips, naked as the day she was born. She couldn't be bothered with underwear. Her face was as flushed as mine.

'Now, Jack, let's forget about fighting, Dutchmen and other distractions.' She tugged my shirt out of my trousers and ran her fingers up my belly to my chest.

I tried to speak but she pressed her cool, soft lips onto mine and dragged me down. My mind, still seeking resolution of our earlier conflict, fought my body for control and lost.

The sun pressed us into the grass. I struggled to match her urgent rhythm, far more intense than I had felt before. She had taught me well though, and I decoupled my mind to divorce my thoughts from the pulsing ache. I thought of the questions I wanted answered. Why was the wave I caught when surfing always smaller than the one behind? Why did Caroline never let me use a *French letter*? Who was that woman my father and Phillips were fighting over all those years before? How could I hate her and love her at the same time? I stopped.

'What? What's wrong, Jack. My God, you haven't –'

'No. It's okay. I haven't but I can't go on.'

She pushed her hands into my chest and stared at me. Her eyes were frightened. 'Why? What am I doing wrong?'

'It's not you. The sun's burning my bum. I have to roll over.'

I eased out of her and lay on my back, grateful for the cool grass underneath. In truth, I could have suffered a bit longer but it didn't seem right. Her flirtation with the Dutchman; her domineering behaviour had turned my anger to acid. It felt like indigestion – this jealousy. It had a vicious grip and now it seized my tongue. I rolled onto my elbow and studied her flushed face. Her eyes held mine, a challenge.

I dared. 'Who were you with just now? It wasn't me, was it?'

She blinked and her eyes moistened.

Bile surged from my stomach and my temples pounded as she slowly sat up and pulled her dress towards her. She twisted away from me, bent over and stepped into the creased garment. Without a backward glance, or a single word, she walked away, through the grass, towards her house.

It was so still, so quiet, I could hear my heart thudding through my chest. What I'd just said could not be unsaid. It would be a long, lonely walk home.

5

Monday 10th July 1939

God she looked beautiful. I was entranced by her presence, the power she exuded.

'Wake up, stop dreaming,' Alan hissed from the corner of his mouth and I blinked in surprise.

'Fix – '

I fumbled with my scabbard, tilting it forward to get a grip on the hilt before the end of the command.

Knowles ran his eye along our line then barked. 'Bayonets!'

We froze in position as the Royal Militia line opposite completed their preparation. I focused on the warship as she swung through her final arc in the narrow harbour. HMS *Jersey* had crept through the pier heads minutes before at high tide. Dressed overall with only a smidgen of smoke from her single stack, her 4.7-inch guns trained fore and aft, she looked magnificent. This was her first voyage and our own destroyer, largely paid for by public subscription, had come to offer her thanks. I'd read everything about her and longed to explore once this ceremony was over. Unlike the new 10,000 ton cruiser HMS *Sheffield*, which had anchored a mile offshore two weeks previously, our destroyer was actually in the harbour.

Her crew was now making its final assembly before her captain was piped ashore to meet with the official party waiting restlessly off to my left. I re-gripped the stock above the sling, trying to ensure that, when the next series of orders were delivered, I wouldn't let the island down by dropping my rifle as I had in training. Alan was alongside me. As the squad sergeant, I was the right-hand marker and could sense the whole line of twelve tensing for the order.

Captain Knowles, the OC of our Officer Training Corps, turned to face his opposite number and the militia soldiers, in their dress blues and peaked caps. We were clad in scratchy khaki, and, in the blistering heat from the midday sun, sweat trickled down my neck. I wanted to adjust my black beret to stop the itch and could feel a line of moisture beginning to slip from my brow, but I held steady. I had no choice, thousands of islanders were watching. So was Fletcher, who was standing directly opposite in the militia's ranks. His rifle's eighteen-inch bayonet glinted menacingly at me.

Knowles stiffened as the gangway was finally secured and I spotted the militia officer nod at him. They had agreed before that, even though Knowles was now only a classics teacher, he would give the final orders. His chest of decorations, and the MC with bar on its purple and white ribbon that was pinned to his chest ensured there was no argument.

The lieutenant governor, representing King George, and the bailiff took a step forward together.

Knowles' shoulders tensed then he screamed the order. 'Honour Guards – Royal Salute – Present – Arms!'

All twenty-four of us, in both guards, crashed our boots in unison. There was a slight pause before the drums rolled and the band struck up "God Save The King".

Tears of pride pricked my eyes as I held position. I thought of the sleek warship, gently breathing against the granite wall, her thin sides protected by bundles of old tyres. We'd been too busy preparing to watch her sweep across the bay but I pictured her ploughing through the waves as she hunted down submarines or raced in to fire her ten torpedoes at enemy capital ships. I knew there was only room for 200 men on her cramped decks, and she must be hell in a heavy sea, but I would love to be part of that fighting machine.

The anthem had finished and the crowds were cheering above the sirens every boat and ship was sounding.

'Honour Guards – Slope – Arms! – Order – Arms!'

Thankfully, I brought my rifle down to the normal attention position. The official party moved off.

Knowles turned to face us. 'Squad – Stand – At Ease!'

We exhaled together. We had done it and not let the side down. I was able to look around at last. The contingent from college had assembled behind the white railings. Two masters shielded their charges from rubbing shoulders, or anything else, with the representatives from the Jersey College for Girls.

Saul was edging towards their human barricade seeking a means to subvert authority, as usual. Even if he found a way through, the girls would throw him back. He just wasn't the sort of fish they'd take home for supper. As he looked like a sack of spuds in uniform, he'd been excused service in the Training Corps.

One of the masters, sensing his intent, prodded him back into the panting herd, which pinned him to the railing where he spotted me and waved. I waggled my bayonet in response but drew a stern look from Knowles.

Earlier, I'd felt sure I'd seen Caroline on the top level of the Victoria Pier and now I scanned the crowd for her as people started to move back towards the town.

Knowles interrupted my reverie and dismissed us. We broke ranks and walked to the side to look more closely at the ship. The militia marched off behind us.

I loitered, conscious of my sore neck, trying again to catch sight of Caroline. Alan had noticed the bruising around my throat as we washed that morning and had teased me that Caroline was turning into a vampire. For once, I was grateful for the usually hated collar, which hid the marks of Fletcher's attack. I certainly wasn't going to tell him the truth about that or my later encounter with Kohler and Caroline.

I tried again to unravel the puzzle. Caroline and I had been so close when we were apart. During the year she was travelling through America, Italy, and France, studying with Schnabel and other piano maestros, we had exchanged letters nearly every week. We'd had the thinking time to explain our feelings and explore our new relationship, and we'd been frank with each other. Now we could see each other every day, we seemed to clash most of the time. Perhaps it was easier to manage a relationship by post. I just didn't know what I wanted anymore. I knew we needed to talk though. I couldn't leave it like this.

I started to follow the others when I sniffed Shalimar in the air. I turned and there she was, descending the granite steps. She looked straight through me as though I didn't exist then brushed past on her way to the pier side. My stomach turned a ragged somersault and the question, which had plagued me all sleepless night, was answered in an instant.

The dark grey destroyer was the perfect backdrop for her golden brilliance and I shuddered in a mixture of delight and frustration. A loud wolf whistle from somewhere on the destroyer's upper decks made her turn. She smiled to acknowledge the compliment and work stopped on the ship.

The Dutchman followed her down the steps. He held her hat and cardigan in one hand and a camera in the other. He grinned, then dropped her hat onto the muzzle of my rifle before standing back to snap her with the ship behind. I felt the bile rising again. Had she been discussing us with this bastard? Of course she had. Was it just revenge? Why had she brought him here? Was it to punish me, make me jealous? I wanted to lash out, but not at her. I realised my rifle, with its floppy hat over the muzzle, was trembling in my hand. My bayonet would make short work of that and him.

Alan nudged me and raised his eyebrows. He nodded towards Caroline, who was now behaving like a fashion model, posing outrageously while Kohler captured her from all angles with his camera. I watched, trembling in confusion, as a man in a crumpled suit, sporting a red and white striped armband, approached Kohler. The Dutchman probably wouldn't realise that he was an honorary policeman.

'Excuse me, sir, but we would be grateful if you didn't take any more photographs, eh. We have posted notices about cameras and such like, eh.'

Kohler looked startled, as much by the man's curious accent as his request, but smiled engagingly. 'I am sorry, I was not thinking. Only the girl is so beautiful, I could not resist.'

Caroline was furious. 'What do you mean no photographs? Who says so? This is a free country, isn't it?' She tapped the unfortunate man on the shoulder. 'I know you, don't I? Yes... it's... you serve in Voisins, don't you, Haberdashery?' She sneered at him.

'Why don't you get back to your counter and leave us alone, you, you busybody.'

The haberdasher flushed, tipped his hat at her and stepped back.

Caroline continued the attack. 'You haven't told me who made up this ridiculous order yet. Do you think we are spies? Why can't we take photographs of our ship, you silly little man?'

The altercation had drawn the interest of two uniformed policemen, commonly known as Bluebottles, who were observing with some amusement from a little distance away. I was fed up with feeling confused and angry at the way she was treating the man who was only doing his duty. I needed to act. I flicked the hat away, thrust my rifle at Alan and moved forwards.

Kohler was aiming his camera at Caroline and her prey when I reached out and grabbed his arm. 'I think it would be wise if you stopped now, Mr Kohler.' I lifted the camera out of his hands.

Caroline turned to confront me but I strode off towards the two policemen, leaving her fuming in my wake.

She caught up with me and tugged my arm. 'What the fuck are you playing at, Jack? How dare you embarrass us like that.'

I ignored her and carried on walking. Several people had turned to stare at her and one lady clucked her disapproval of Caroline's language.

She grabbed at my uniform. 'Give me the camera, you shit. Stop when I'm talking to you.'

I shrugged her off, but knew that she wasn't going to give up that easily. I stopped, conscious of the growing interest of the crowd. 'Leave it alone, Caroline. I will return the camera. Now calm down.'

'Calm down? Calm down? Don't you fucking well tell me to calm down, you bastard. Give me that camera now.'

'Disgusting! Your language is disgusting, young lady. Behave yourself immediately.' The piercing voice of one of the girls' college teachers slashed at Caroline.

She froze then turned slowly to face the woman, who had detached herself from the crowd and was waving a parasol at her. 'Go impale yourself, you barren old cow.'

Even the seagulls stopped screeching. In the distance, faint traffic noises, but on the Victoria Pier, only the sound of granite breathing could be heard. The teacher's eyes narrowed as she strode across the gulf that separated them. She looked Caroline straight in the face. 'Apologise now, or I shall call the police.'

Caroline snorted and leant towards her mockingly, her voice controlled and languid. 'You do, sweetie, and I'll ram that brolly up your fat arse!'

The white-gloved hand blurred as it slapped into Caroline's cheek. 'You little madam. How dare you!'

Caroline lifted her arm to hit her back but I grabbed her waist to lift her onto my hip, stepped to the low granite kerb and dropped her over the edge.

The crowd surged forward as she splashed into the water twelve-feet below. They waited until she surfaced then they roared their approval and treated me to a round of applause. I was turning to apologise to the stunned teacher when I felt the Dutchman's breath on my neck.

'The camera, Jack, please, unless you wish to join our friend.'

I attempted to pull away but, with a speed which shocked me, the Dutchman twisted my wrist up between my shoulder blades and applied vicious leverage against the joint. I choked on the pain as he yanked the camera from my hand. He propelled me to the edge, balancing me with the pressure on my wrist. I stared down at Caroline, who was paddling to the iron ladder. He let me free to clutch vainly at the air.

A khaki arm reached out and pulled me back from the brink. I twisted and collided with Alan as he tripped over a hawser, then I regained my balance. Three of the honour guard had hold of Kohler while a fourth held out the camera to me. The Dutchman offered no resistance but glared with such venom that I stepped back defensively. The crowd was watching this tableau with considerable interest, expecting even more excitement as the Bluebottles started to race the honorary policeman towards the centre of the public disturbance. I reached out for the camera and offered it to the Dutchman.

'Let him go. It was a misunderstanding, that's all. I'll sort it out with the police.'

'Are you sure? Don't you want us to give him a ducking as well?'

Alan seemed to be enjoying himself and the others nodded enthusiastic agreement.

'No. Thank you for your help but enough is enough. Let him go, please.'

The Dutchman accepted the camera, shrugged free of his guards and managed a rueful smile. 'Today, you have the army, Jack. Tomorrow...?' He lifted his shoulders and spread his hands to punctuate the unfinished sentence then backed away.

The policemen stumbled through the crowd but, before they could start their enquiries, there was a bellow of displeasure from the top of the ladder as Caroline's dripping head appeared. She shook her matted hair like a crazed dog, spraying us with seawater and slime. Holding her once-white Italian shoes in her left hand, she advanced on the nearest uniformed bobby. Her thin cotton dress clung to her breasts and hips. Her bohemian disregard for underwear brought further clucks of disapproval from the women in the crowd. The policeman, uncertain where to look, examined the blank page in his notebook until her hair dripped onto his arm.

She cleared her throat and raised her chin to stare at me. 'Take this down, officer. I wish to swear a complaint against this lout for attempted murder and...'

While everyone edged forward to hear the evidence and offer their testimony as witnesses, I noticed Kohler casually strolling away towards the town.

6

I looked at my watch. Nearly four o'clock. We had been cooped up in this anteroom for over two hours and hadn't even been offered a drink, let alone lunch. Alan paced up and down, kicking the door at each end. The other three sat on the floor, their backs against the wall. My brother glared at me every time he passed. Typically, our officer had disappeared before we were arrested. That was another of life's little puzzles: why officers were always there when not wanted, but invariably missing when needed. The police had forced us to hand our rifles to other squad members before they marched us off to the town hall. We still had our belts and bayonets though. We'd been told to wait until the duty centenier had finished his lunch. I supposed this was part of the punishment.

The door squeaked open. 'You're for it now, you young hooligans.' The poor haberdasher seemed more amused than angry as he ushered us out into the corridor.

'Wait. Come on you lot, smarten yourselves up.'

'Oh for Christ's sake, Jack. It's a bit late to start playing the sergeant, isn't it?'

'Shut up, Lance Corporal Renouf, and do up your buttons. Let's try and retain some dignity here, shall we.'

They looked disparagingly at me but started to tidy their uniforms.

I barked, 'Squad – Ten – Shun!'

Our boots crashed in the narrow corridor, making the honorary policeman jump.

'Left – Turn – Quick – March!' I fell in alongside and marched them to the glass-panelled door at the end of the corridor. The haberdasher rushed after us and opened it wide. I wheeled them in and we clattered to a halt in front of a large, highly-polished desk.

Centenier Phillips looked up. I silently mouthed several words, which would not have disgraced Saul at his worst. I should have expected it, even though there were several centeniers in this parish. Too late, I'd have to see it through. I'd rehearsed the moment and couldn't back off.

'Squad – Off – Caps! Reporting as ordered, sir!' I'd planned to demonstrate our discipline and hoped that the duty centenier would let us off with a short lecture. No chance with Phillips. It would be the rulebook, the whole rulebook and nothing but the bloody rulebook.

He looked at us with not the slightest hint of amusement on his fat face. 'I'll not have weapons in my office. Take them off immediately.'

I hesitated. 'Are you sure, sir?'

'Don't be impertinent, you young pup. Take them off now.'

I looked at the others. There was a little smile playing about Alan's lips. We'd practised grounding arms but never bayonets before. As our belts were attached to their scabbards through loops, they would have to come off. 'Squad – ground – belts!' The movement was almost synchronised as we flicked the heavy brass buckles on our leather belts. The weight of the scabbards and bayonets dragged on our battledress trousers and gravity did the rest. They clattered to the floor. Phillips would have found himself staring at five pairs of khaki underpants had Alan not decided to stay cool and discard his that morning.

A crimson flush suffused Phillips' face. His mouth opened and closed like a starving fish before he found the words he needed. 'I suppose you find that amusing, but I can now add insulting behaviour and one case of indecent exposure to your catalogue of crimes.'

'We were merely following your orders, sir. I did get you to confirm them.'

Phillips thumped his fist onto the metal desk, scattering paperweights, pens and paper onto the floor. 'How dare you. You insolent, stupid boy! Take your scabbards off your belts and get dressed before I have you thrown into the cells. Help them, man, don't just stand there!'

The poor constable's officer collected the bayonets and laid them carefully on the desk while we pulled up our trousers and re-buckled our belts. We were in deep manure, but I didn't care anymore. I glared at Phillips, determined to find out about the fight he'd had with my father. I fought an urge to grab my bayonet and stick it up his fat arse, but I'd just have to dream on for the moment. He glared back then turned to his clerk, who was biting his lip, clearly trying to suppress a giggle or two. 'The charges, please.'

The man coughed, and in a dry voice, just on the right side of hysterical, read out the list of complaints from various members of the public. There was no mention of the Dutchman. In the excitement, he had been overlooked.

Phillips listened, made notes and showed his disbelief. He tapped his pen on the desk, weighing his words. I expected a gale of outrage but was surprised when he spoke softly.

'I will need to consult with the constable on this before I summon your parents and your headmaster. This sort of behaviour has to be stamped on firmly and I do not wish any *technicality,'* he stared directly at me as he stressed the word, 'to influence the correct course of action. However, I will say this. If I were your parents, I would thrash you until you begged forgiveness and, if I were your headmaster, I would seriously question your right to wear those uniforms.'

He let his final words hang in the air then stood up and nodded to the clerk. 'Dismissed, for further reports.'

'But, sir. Don't you want to hear our side of the...' I spluttered at his retreating back as he waddled out of the room.

Alan and the others bounced out into the street. I followed more thoughtfully. To Alan it was all a huge joke. He didn't realise how vindictive someone like Phillips could be. At best, there would be serious embarrassment for the family. At worst, we could all be expelled or even birched, or both, and all because of my bloody-minded former girlfriend.

Released into the sunshine and the clatter of traffic at the busy intersection, the remnants of our honour guard could contain themselves no longer. They slumped against the ornate granite wall, their chests heaving with laughter.

'Well, I think my clever brother should treat us all to some grub and an espresso. You lot coming?' Alan had brushed down his uniform and was admiring his reflection in the arched window.

I tugged some coins from my pocket. 'Here, you treat them. I'm not in the mood.'

'Oh, I suppose you're going off to mope about your bloody girlfriend. Come on, man, forget the bitch. Come and drown your sorrows in some of Luigi's finest.'

'No, thanks. I'll just wander about a bit... perhaps pop in for a cup of tea with Uncle Fred.'

'What, "Red" Fred? You bonkers or something, man? He'll bore the pants off you. Besides, if Dad finds out, he'll lose a wheel. You know how he feels about him.' Alan seemed horrified. Our mother's elder and only living brother had been disowned by the family, not only for his extreme politics, but also for the fact that he was living in sin with a Spanish woman at least twenty years his junior.

'I'll take the chance. Meet you at Snow Hill at six and, Alan...'

'Yeah?'

'Don't forget to pack tonight. I'll get you up at half-five and down to the boat by half-six. I'm training at seven so I'm not going to wait for you.'

'Okay, Mummy.'

The others laughed.

'And, Alan, try not to get arrested again if you can possibly help it.'

He chased me across the road and halfway up Old Street, studded boots echoing off the walls, before he collided with a pram, which appeared from a doorway. He tumbled into the gutter, much to the amusement of the cadets, who had trotted after him.

While he apologised to the startled woman, I turned into Union Street. Stopping outside one of the three-storied terraced houses, less dilapidated than its eighteenth-century neighbours, I knocked on the blood-red front door.

7

Malita peered at my uniform. She wore no make-up and her thick black hair, pulled back in a tight bun, pinched an already tired face into a caricature of resentment. It softened when she saw my face.

'Yak, *buenos tardes*. Come in, you are most welcome.' Her voice was much deeper than her slender figure suggested and heavy with a Spanish accent. However hard she tried, she couldn't pronounce my name, so I was forever a hefty Siberian ox to her Spanish tongue. She hugged and kissed me on both cheeks then, with a broad wink, ushered me into the kitchen.

Rachel looked up and laughed at my startled expression. 'Don't worry, I'm just about to leave.'

'Nonsense, you stay, talk to Yak. You say you have thing to tell him.'

Rachel's face reddened.

'Not now, Malita. I have to go. My parents will be expecting their tea.'

'Ah, you too soft with them. They have hands. They make own food.' She sounded exasperated as though this was an old argument, often repeated.

'Why aren't you two at work?' I asked.

'We're surprised as well. They closed the workroom so we could watch the ship arrive. I suppose we'll have to make the time up later. You looked very smart, Jack,' Rachel answered as she got up and held her chair for me.

I brushed against her as I moved to sit down. The chair was warm from her body and a faint scent, more simple than Caroline's exotic perfumes, hung in the air. She looked tired and her eyes were puffy, as though she had been crying. I knew that she and Malita worked together in the dressmaking department at de Gruchys, but hadn't realised they were this close. I felt like I'd broken into an intimate conversation. Malita led her to the door.

She paused and smiled back at me. 'I would like to speak to you sometime, Jack. It's not important though. When you have a moment...' her voice tailed off as she turned away.

I was intrigued. We'd been friends for years but she'd never spoken like that before, as though she were frightened of me. What had I done? Should I go after her? I got up as I heard the front door close.

Malita blocked my way. 'Not for now, Yak. She need time, alone.' She shrugged and motioned me to sit. Grabbing a ladle from the range, she banged it against one of the copper pans hanging above. Once they'd stopped reverberating, I heard movement from the basement, followed by footfalls on the wooden steps. Uncle Fred, wearing overalls, covered in sawdust, appeared from the passageway.

'Jack, *coumme est qu' tu'es ?*' He limped over and grasped me on both shoulders. '*I, y,a Iongtemps qu, je n,vos avais pon veu.*'

It hadn't been that long but I had neglected them since Caroline had returned from her travels. I had brought her round to meet them. I wouldn't repeat that mistake.

'*Tch'est qu'en s'ait d'eune tassee d'thee?*' Fred motioned me to sit at the pine table while Malita turned to the kettle.

'Yes, please, Uncle, if you're having one.' I watched as Malita rattled the teapot out of the cupboard.

'Well, young man, what have you been up to then – playing at soldiers?' In sharp contrast to his use of our Jèrriais language, Fred's English accent was guaranteed to raise eyebrows, if not hackles. It was pure home counties, languid yet piercing, its contorted vowels a superb counterfeit of the aristocratic disdain which he so despised. He derived great amusement from mimicking his "class" enemy.

'Doing one's duty, Uncle.' I put on my own best accent.

Fred's lined face creased into a wide grin. 'From the look of you, not a labour of love, I vow.'

'It was a bit hot, Uncle, in fact, someone had to jump into the harbour to cool off.'

I told the story while Malita served the tea, reducing both of them to fits with my impersonation of Phillips.

'You need to be careful, Jack. His self-importance has cleansed his veins of any dint of kindness. Like all bullies, he's vulnerable to ridicule and won't forgive anyone who bests him.'

'He's married, isn't he?' I asked.

'Yes, poor Doris. She's the living proof that love is indeed blind.' Fred chuckled.

'Do they have any children?'

He peered at me. 'Interesting question, Jack. What prompted that?'

'Well I was talking to Nutty about him –'

'Hedley Pallot? And what did the old gossip have to say?'

'Not much but he did hint at a few things.'

He smiled. 'I bet he did. Did he tell you that Phillips does a lot of charity work with children?'

'Why?'

'*Entre nous,* and not to be repeated. He was posted to Palestine, caught something nasty – probably from a camel. Can't have any children of his own.'

'And that should make me feel sorry for him?'

'Perhaps. It changed him. He used to be a bit wild but now he's obsessed with rules, hence the refereeing and busybody policing. He's always been a bit of a loner but he's stubborn and well-connected, though not overly blessed with intelligence. That makes him potentially dangerous.'

'He didn't go to college, did he?'

'No. Not enough brains and the family didn't have the money. That's something else that grates on him.'

I sucked in a breath. 'What do you know about a fight he had with Father?'

He stared at me, measuring how much I knew, then laughed. 'Where did you hear that?'

'Oh, at the club. Is it true?'

'Hedley again, I suppose. I'm afraid you'll have to ask your father about that.'

'Oh, come on, Uncle, spill the beans.'

He considered for a moment. 'Alright, but you didn't hear it from me. Which fight are you talking about?'

'There's more than one?'

'Oh, yes. Your father isn't a forgiving person either.'

Didn't I know that. 'The one during the water polo match. The one over the girl.'

He coughed and sprayed tea over the table. 'My sister, you mean?'

'Oh, God. Not my mother? She didn't, you know, with Phillips?'

'No, no. Phillips let his interest be known, as they say, and Mary used that to encourage your father to be more forceful. He was very shy then. Phillips misread her interest and thought Aubin was trying to steal her. They had words, which turned into fists. It was very embarrassing at the time. The committee had to sit in judgement and banned them both from competitions for a couple of weeks. Sound familiar, Jack?'

How did he know? Of course, Rachel must have told them. 'Was there another fight?'

'Yes, but you'll need to ask your father about that. I wasn't there and no one else saw it. I heard that Phillips' face looked as though it had been used to mop the sawdust off the floor in his butcher's shop.'

'Did Father fight with him there?'

'No, that was me. I was trying to persuade one of his employees to join the union. Phillips found out and sacked him. I confronted him in the shop. I was arrested.' From his tone, it wasn't a pleasant memory. 'I'll get even one day, when he isn't hiding behind the parish police.' He smiled to hide the bitterness in his voice. 'Anyway, what are you going to do about the fragrant Caroline?'

'Apart from give her another bath you mean?'

They laughed.

'Not much I can do. I've messed up there. It's not all her fault. In fact, I think I've behaved like a pig.'

'"*Chein q'nou n'a jamais veu, et jamais n'vairra, ch'est un nid d'souothis dans l'ouotheille d'un cat.*"'

I translated, 'What one has never seen, and will never see, is a mouse's nest in a cat's ear. Is that right?'

'Exactly. Mistress Caroline has you by the nose, young man. You must find her company very...' a strange smile flickered across his face, as though a distant memory had been disturbed. He paused, searching for the right word. 'Stimulating.'

'He is lucky young man, she is strong and honest lady. I like.' Malita beamed at me. 'I like also much Rachel. Is difficult choice, no?' Her grin widened. I felt my cheeks colour.

'What do you mean, Malita?'

She laughed and turned to Fred. 'He is, how you say, making a pull of my leg, no?'

Fred chortled. 'No, Lita. He doesn't understand what you mean.'

'Si, Yak, you come here. Look in mirror.'

Amused, I followed her round the table and stood in front of the tarnished mirror. 'You look and tell what is you see.'

'Humour her, Jack.'

'Okay, I see my mother's curls, though they need a cut. Uncle Fred's broken nose.' I ducked as a lump of cake flew towards me. I scrutinised my face. 'My father's eyes, without the wrinkles of course. A chin in need of a shave, some cuts from this morning's hurried effort –'

'What else, Yak?' Malita moved closer to me.

'Dusty uniform, too small round the shoulders, collar too tight.' I turned to her. 'What am I looking for?'

Fred laughed. 'I think she means that you might have a problem with girls, Jack.'

'Problem, you say *problem*. Is no problem for him. Is, how you say, big battle for girls.' She grinned, teasing me, digging her hand into my curls.

'That's nonsense, Malita. I think I'm quite shy.'

'Shy. What is this "shy"? I see you on the stage.' She clapped her hands together in delight. 'You make the yoke, eh, *shy* for Shylock.' She poked me in the ribs. 'This is clever, but you lie. Girls, they love you with your curls, your hot eyes, your smile, even with silly beard. You fill the hall with your voice, your charm. Even when you lose, and the Christian is saved, they cry for you, these girls.'

'But, that's acting, Malita, only acting.'

'You no shy. I think you know who you are, my Yak.'

'That's enough, Lita, you're embarrassing him. He's eighteen, leave him some innocence.'

I felt very self-conscious as Malita moved closer and placed her hands on either side of my face. 'Is too late. The war has begun.'

I pulled away, retreated to my uncle. 'I'm sorry, Malita. You're wrong. Rachel is just a friend.' I shrugged. 'And after today, I think Caroline and I are finished anyway.'

'Just as well.' Fred sounded more serious.

'You no listen, Yak, he is old man, no understand how it is now.'

'Not so old that I can't recognise trouble when I see it; wilful, self-opinionated, arrogant.'

'Yak, that is what he no like –'

'Her father is nothing more than –'

'Please, Uncle, she can't help her father.' I was somewhat surprised to find myself defending her but I wanted to divert Fred before the floodgates of his obsession opened wide.

'It's bastards like him who will destroy us. Capitalists, greedy pigs, feeding fat in the trough whilst the workers starve.'

'Uncle, you sound like a pamphleteer.'

He looked startled then smiled. 'Do I now? I didn't know you read that sort of literature.'

'I don't as a rule, but you sound so one-sided –'

'I suppose you have discussions at school, do you? Weigh all the evidence, look at *both* sides, come out with a balanced view, eh?'

It wasn't quite that simple. My classmates didn't care for political discussion. 'You've told me about what happened in the war and I think I understand –'

'Oh, that's good, then. You think you understand what it's like in the trenches.' He was in full flow now, his sarcasm tearing at me. Like a toppling wave, I could dive under it, ride it ashore, let it swamp me or throw myself straight into it and risk a heavy bruising.

'For God's sake, Uncle. You know damn well, I can't understand. I used the wrong word. I've listened to you. I try to understand. I'll always listen, but only if you don't bloody shout!'

He laughed. 'Good for you. That's my Jack, *nil carborundum*, or haven't you been taught that one yet?'

'It's my personal motto. I won't let the *bastards grind me down*. Not that I see you as –'

'Quite, though perhaps sometimes I act as one, eh?'

Over 800 Jerseymen had not returned from the war. Three of them would have been my uncles. 'I'm sorry. It's just that I find it difficult to understand. I've never seen a dead body, never been in a real fight.' Though my neck felt like it had. 'How could I understand what happened to you in Belgium or Russia? I've never even seen snow.'

'Well, I never want to see any again, I can tell you.' His eyes misted over and he swallowed with difficulty. 'The problem with snow is that it shows up the blood, Jack. I never knew there was so much blood until they sent us to that wasteland. 200,000 of us to save the Tsar. Save him? I wanted to kill the fucking bastard!'

His eyes blazed now with an anger I didn't want to touch. His vile words echoed in the small room. Whatever had happened to him in those frozen wastes was way beyond my understanding.

We supped our tea in silence, Malita and I conscious of Fred's inner battle with his emotions.

Eventually, the resonance subsided. He turned to me. 'How's your training with Mr Pavas going?'

'How do you know about that? Christ, are there no secrets in this island?'

'Don't be silly, Jack. Of course there aren't.' He stroked his nose. 'I've still got a few though, despite my friends at the town hall. Take your Mr Pavas – you call him Miko, don't you?'

'That's what he asked us to call him.'

'Now, he is a very interesting man and I bet you know nothing about him, do you?'

'Enough. He knows what he's talking about and he's improved my swimming.'

Fred laughed. 'He could improve your mind as well. He won't have told you, but he was a lecturer in physics in Timisoara, in Romania, before the fascists expelled him from the university.'

'Physics?' I was trying to reconcile my image of a university teacher with the picture presented by Miko but failed. He always wore the same khaki shorts, white polo shirt, blue cotton cap and brown sandals. He looked more like a beachcomber than a professor. Even when he was dressed up as a waiter in his penguin suit, with his shaven head, he looked anything but an academic.

'Yes, he's desperate to get back to a university. He claims it's an interesting time in his special field of transmutation, whatever that means.'

'I know he's trying to get to England but he can't get a permit. Why's that, Uncle?'

'Why do you think? They're trying to limit the number of Jews, that's why.'

'Even clever ones?'

'Especially clever ones. Never mind, their loss is our gain.' He winked and I realised that he would be working on Miko to turn him into a Communist. Fred had some murky connections.

'No, he's never mentioned physics but he has a scientific approach to training though I sometimes find his explanations hard to follow. Do you know that water is 800 times more dense than the air and that to double your swimming speed you need to increase your effort by eight times?'

'Ah, that would be Newton's third law of action and reaction.'

'How the –'

'I do remember some things from my school days, obviously more than you. Do you just daydream in science lessons?'

'Of course not. I think constructively and sometimes work out how I'm going to beat you at chess.'

'Aha, so you are dreaming.'

'I bet you didn't know that, though a man can outrun a horse over a short distance, he will never outswim a fish.'

'I know you won't. It seems you have difficulty outswimming a Dutchman.'

Sometimes our conversations were a bit like our games of chess. One day I would win one. I knew Malita held the same forlorn hope. I smiled, acknowledging defeat.

He slurped his tea. 'How's your mother?'

No query about my father then. One day I'd find out why they hated each other but not from either of them.

'She's fine, Alan's as tall as me now, still mad on shooting things.

Dying to join the army. Excuse the pun. The farm's doing well. Father's okay. We speak. Well, I listen. I think Mum misses you.' Big mouth, had to let it slip out.

He glanced at Malita. 'I miss her too.' He grabbed my hand and squeezed it. I felt the emotion he couldn't put into words. 'Anyway, one day, we'll pop out and see them all, won't we, Lita?'

I knew there was a greater chance of snow falling in July than those two turning up on our porch.

He rattled the teapot. 'What did you think of the destroyer then? Would you want to go to war on it? Or would you prefer your cousin's command.'

'*Sheffield*? Oh, come on Uncle, Ed doesn't know me. He must be at least six times removed. I didn't even get an invite to look her over. Did you go?'

'Strange thing, Jack. You know every boat going out to her was "full" when I tried – no room for undesirables on one of His Majesty's ships.'

I hadn't realised. 'Anyway, there isn't going to be a war, Uncle. Hitler isn't a complete idiot. How can he take on two empires? How could he attack the Maginot Line?'

Fred picked up the breadbin and grabbed several cups. He plonked the bin down on one edge of the table, turned the cups upside down and placed them at roughly six-inch intervals on the surface so that they formed a line from the bin to the other edge. Finally, he filled the gap from the last teacup to the edge of the table with a tea towel.

'*Voilà*, the Maginot Line.' He thumped the bin. 'Swiss border – mountains.' Reaching across, he ruffled the tea towel. 'Belgium border – no mountains.'

He inspected his model then got up and returned with a scrubbing brush. He upended it and placed it between two of the cups. 'Ardennes Forest – impenetrable. Huh. In between, forts with interlocking fields of fire.'

He looked up at me. 'Right, Jack, how do you defeat this?'

'Go round it? Over the tea towel?'

He thumped the table. 'Yes. If you can see that, why can't the French?' Before I could answer, he continued. 'The Germans won't stay on the chessboard, you know. Anyway, Maginot's plan created employment so it satisfied the socialists. It was designed to be defensive, so it satisfied the pacifists and it gave the army somewhere to put its soldiers. As a defence against Hitler, it is as much use as a sand castle.'

He sighed. 'I suppose you discuss this at school, read the *Evening Post*, listen to the BBC? Do you also listen to the German Radio or read their papers?'

'Of course not.' I felt rather uncomfortable at the suggestion.

'Yak, take no notice – he worry too much. Look.' She bent over and pulled two cardboard boxes from a cupboard. Their shape looked familiar. She opened one and pulled out a gas mask.

'We've all got those now, Malita. Father collected ours last week. Mum even sent him back to get one for Victor.'

'Oh, Yak, you silly.' She giggled.

It wasn't far from the truth though. I sometimes thought that Mum cared more for that bloody bull than she did for us. I picked up the mask and examined it. 'This isn't one of ours, is it?'

'No. Fred no want ours. He get these from France. Say they safe. He get from town hall, he think they put pin holes in and he choke.' She mimed him collapsing from a gas attack.

Fred wasn't amused and said something in Spanish, which bought a flush to her cheeks. 'That's the one sensible thing the government's done. That and conscription.' He looked fierce. 'It's time to prepare. Those bastards won't stop at the Channel once they've carved through the French.'

'Oh, Uncle. Isn't that just scaremongering? Hitler isn't that daft. The French army is twice the size of his and –'

'Twice as stupid. *Igitur qui desiderat pacem, praeparet bellum.*'

'If you want peace, prepare for war – *Vegetius.*'

'So you haven't been asleep in your Latin lessons, even if you have in physics.'

'No, Uncle. And I do read the newspapers.' I hesitated. 'If Hitler's going anywhere – its east. It's Stalin who should *praeparet bellum.*' That was a bit below the belt as he was always trumpeting the achievements of the Soviet Union.

He shot back. 'What about Poland? Do you think that Danzig is

46

safe? He's very cunning, Mr Hitler. He absorbed Austria, Czechoslovakia and the Rhineland without firing a shot. And now Mussolini has joined him in the Pact of Steel – may they both rust in hell.' He wagged his finger at me. 'All the countries between him and Russia are fascist either openly or secretly. And what of us? What of the Great British Empire, bastion of democracy? What of Albion? Rotten at the core, that's what.'

He was on his soapbox again.

'Our leaders are in the pockets of big business rascals like Hayden-Brown – fascists, all of them. They keep their boots on the workers' necks whilst lining their silken pockets. Mosley and his Union of Fascists – some think he's just a crank, you know, but he's well-connected. He's in with the establishment. They want to accommodate Hitler –'

'Uncle, you're sounding like Churchill.'

'And what's wrong with that?'

'I thought he was class enemy number one.'

'Of course he is, and he'll never be forgiven. But, Jack, in a time of war, my enemy's enemy is my friend.' He looked thoughtful. 'You know, if Hitler does swallow Poland, Churchill will be back in government and Chamberlain will be finished. We have to watch out for that toff Halifax though. He's in Mosley's circle.'

'What? The Foreign Secretary?'

'The Foreign Appeaser more like.'

'How do you know all this, Uncle? It's never been reported in the news.'

'Newspapers, and who do you think runs those?' He waved my response away. 'Let's just say I know what I know and leave it at that.'

'Hah. That's a master's response when he doesn't know the answer.'

'Well, I don't know the bloody answer, either. All I know is that we've appointed ourselves Poland's guardian angel. As soon as dear Adolph crosses her borders, we'll be at war and no one is going to stop the bloody house painter from that adventure. He'll crush her in months and then roll up the rest of us so that he can create his Fascist European Union. America will sit it out in splendid isolation and those of you who survive will have to learn German and how to goosestep.'

'What about *you*, though, Uncle?'

He fiddled with the mask and looked at Malita. 'There won't be a future for me or Lita, even if these work. Socialists, Jews, Freemasons, Gypsies, Jehovah Witnesses, the mentally ill...' he dropped the mask. 'Everyone who isn't Aryan is for the chop, Jack. But don't take my word for it, read his bloody book. It's all in *Mein Kampf.*'

'Leave him, he is too young.' Malita stared at Fred. 'He does not understand.' She waved her arm around to indicate the island. 'How could he?'

'Too young? How old were your brothers when the Falangists asked them questions, huh? How old were the boys who fought with us at Ebro?'

'Enough. *Es una chorrada!*' Malita slammed her fists on the table and leant over Fred, her face contorted with rage. She screamed at him in rapid Spanish, gesturing obscenely with her hands as she berated him. She paused for breath then turned to me. 'Is best, Yak, you go now.'

'No. *Hujer perdida.* You go. You leave us alone. I must talk with Jack. Go!' Fred towered over Malita, his anger overpowering.

She bowed her head and muttered something before backing towards the door. She turned to speak but dropped her head instead and started to climb the stairs.

8

We listened to her footsteps, heard the bed springs creak then waited until the house echoed with her silence. Fred slumped back into his chair and reached for the teapot. He poured another cup for both of us. I wanted to leave but couldn't.

'What have your parents told you about me?'

'Very little. Mum told me about what happened at Ypres, your posting to India and Russia, but Father has never said anything.'

'Apart from "stay away from him".'

'I'm afraid so.'

'Do you know why?'

I recalled Nutty's words, but that was trivial. I thought I knew the real reason for my father's dislike of his brother-in-law.

'One reason, Uncle Ralph has said so as well, is that you're a Marxist.'

'Red Fred, eh?' he laughed.

'Yes, I'm afraid it's your nickname.'

'I know, but I have worse names.' He leaned forward. 'Do you want to know why they call me that, why I believe in Marxism, why I believe that Hitler means what he says?'

I swallowed then nodded. I did want to know. I wanted to know why my fifty-year old uncle looked seventy, why his face was scarred with worry, his hair white, and why he lived with a woman who was barely in her thirties but looked older than my mother. Most of all, I wanted to know why they were all so frightened of this man and his ideas.

He told me. He used words like weapons, describing horrors

which made my flesh crawl. How could men do these things to each other? I felt sick. I'd drunk far too much tea and had to leave the room and seek relief in the toilet in the yard. The physical and mental relief was incredible as I emptied my bladder and some of my mind. I couldn't cope with much more, though I had wanted to know, to understand.

When I returned, the room was empty. I heard him shuffling about in the front room. Soon the sound of a tenor singing filled the house. It was Gigli or Bjorling – his Caruso records were more scratchy. It was from a Puccini opera, though I didn't know which one. The Italian composer was one of his few passions. Caroline preferred Beethoven but I couldn't help but feel moved every time I heard this music. If I could get a gramophone outside, I might try to sooth Victor with it.

Fred returned and slumped over the table. Devoid of expression, he seemed unaware of my presence. I looked at him with a sense of overwhelming sadness. I felt something for my father as well and now appreciated why he refused to talk about the war. I looked at my watch, it was time to go, but I couldn't leave him like this. I wanted to put my arm around him.

I got up but stopped as I heard Malita's feet padding on the stairs. He looked up and listened. He waited until the door creaked open, got up and walked over to her, put his arm around her shoulders and kissed her on the cheek. He led her to the chair, sat down beside her and whispered in Spanish. She nodded then they both looked at me. We sat listening to the music until it died away and the needle started clicking.

Malita left to attend to it and Fred leaned towards me again. 'What is your greatest fear, Jack?'

I hesitated. I was sure it wasn't drowning that terrified me. I saw it. 'I think I'm frightened of losing control, of showing fear itself. Does that make sense?'

He nodded. 'It's a good question to ask people, though don't expect an honest answer. Not many have experienced real fear.'

'What of you, Uncle?'

He looked across at Malita, who had returned and was now

brewing another pot of tea. 'That particular reservoir is empty. There's a limit in each of us. I exceeded mine years ago. I'm still full of other emotions though; especially hate for Hitler and all his beliefs. You read his book but understand that, evil as he is, he is just a servant.'

No wonder I couldn't beat him at chess. He was full of surprises. My puzzled expression must have been sufficient.

'Oh, yes. He's the Pope's general.'

'Uncle, that's crazy. You don't mean that.'

'He mean it, Yak. He think Hitler will destroy all Communist for Pope. He think Catholic big enemy of the people.'

She shrugged, in that peculiar way of hers – why argue with someone who won't listen? She shoved the teapot at him. 'Here, you drink. Keep quiet.' She looked at the clock above the dresser. 'Is time Yak go.'

'But I haven't told him about England or Spain yet.'

'Good. You save for another day. Yak think you mad old man.' She waved her hand at me then touched her finger to her lips. 'You drink tea. Then you go home.'

We supped in silence.

After she had cleared away, Malita decided that it was too late for me to catch the bus from Snow Hill and suggested that Fred take me back on his motorcycle. I'd helped Fred rebuild the bike and knew how special it was to him, but felt brave enough to suggest that I might be allowed to borrow it to ride myself home.

'Bugger me, you cheeky sod. Borrow my bike? I suppose you want my hat as well. Here, take my shoes and socks if you want –'

Malita grabbed his arm and laughed. 'Yak, *tiene cojones;* he help mend this beast. Why no let him ride her?'

'Ride her? Ride *Boadicea*? She'll buck him off and leave him bleeding in the gutter. He's too young to handle a machine like that.'

'Stupid man. It is you she buck off. You scared he ride her better. Yak is man now and he has *cojones* as big as yours.' She moved towards Fred, her hand stretched out in a claw. 'Perhaps bigger.'

He edged away, keeping the kitchen table between them. 'Right, but remember the history of this bike.' He sounded very concerned.

'Yak, he is stupid. He believe silly story when he buy this bike of bits. Is nothing wrong with bike – just man who ride it.'

51

Though I'd longed to, I'd never asked to ride *Boadicea* before and was somewhat deflated by uncle's dismissive response.

'It's okay, Malita, Uncle is right. It's better if I don't. I'll walk.'

Fred dodged round the table, clasped my shoulders and pulled me towards the door. 'Why do I listen to her? You wouldn't ask unless you were sure, would you?'

'No, I wouldn't. I know every bit of her, from her Norton box, through her Castle forks, to her JAP heart. I've polished every part of her, listened to her breathe. I think she knows me as well –'

Malita giggled. 'He has made choice. He love her, not Caroline.'

Fred sighed in resignation and pulled me into the yard. Together we lifted the tarpaulin away from the 1933 Brough Superior SS100. Her black nickel-plated paintwork gleamed in the shadows as we manoeuvred her out of the yard and into the road. I held the machine on the front brake and caressed my left hand over the stainless steel petrol tank between my knees.

'I suppose you want my goggles as well as my shoes, socks, pants and bike?'

'Just the goggles will do, Uncle.'

Fred extracted a pair of well-worn flying goggles from the saddlebag and slid them onto my head.

I began the complicated procedure of starting the Brough from cold. Eventually the long chrome twin exhausts spat out behind my right leg as the engine throbbed into life. I let it settle into a steady beat, almost as fast as my heart's.

Fred clapped me on the shoulder and mouthed, *mêfi-ous* – take care.

I smiled over my shoulder at Malita, then nodded goodbye to them.

Boadicea was ten times more powerful than *Bessy,* my little 250cc BSA, and much heavier. I pulled in the clutch lever with my left hand, took my right off the twist throttle and nudged the gear lever forward into first, released the clutch and stalled.

I expected Fred to complain but something had distracted him. He grabbed Malita's arm and cocked his head towards the end of the road. She turned to look and I followed her gaze.

A black Jaguar was parked about fifty yards away. The sole car in the road gleamed in the evening sunlight. Two men, wearing hats, sat in its front seats. Fred mumbled something to Malita. She shrugged.

Fred waved me away. I was curious about the car but didn't want to ask any more questions. I'd had enough for a while and *Boadicea* beckoned more enticingly than one of Fred's mysteries.

I kicked her into life again and this time managed to slip the clutch and bounce down the street with only a seductive wobble from her rear tyre to indicate her displeasure as we turned right into Dumaresq Street.

9

Once I was out of their sight, I relaxed, though it occurred to me that my third-party insurance certificate was insufficient to pay for any damage should *Boadicea* and I have a falling out with each other. The airflow began to tug at my jacket until I summoned the courage to take my left hand off the handlebar, undo the buttons and let it flare out behind me as I leant forward into the thirty miles per hour wind.

I turned into Pier Road, opened the throttle and let her surge forward up the hill until we were rattling windows as we passed. The acceleration was fantastic, almost jerking my arms from my shoulders. I swung her up the steep slope to Mount Bingham and twisted the throttle to the stop. The sound was glorious as it echoed off the granite walls on either side.

I pulled across the road and slipped into neutral. Below was the harbour with HMS *Jersey* tied up alongside the Victoria Quay. There were still crowds of people standing about admiring her sleekness. This was arrow-like, compared to the *St Patrick* mail boat berthed at the adjacent Albert Quay, which would be Alan's transport to Southampton the following morning.

What a bloody strange day. I still couldn't believe that I'd thrown Caroline over the quay. What did I feel about her? There were so many competing emotions, so many contradictions, that I just didn't know. Was it lust that had held us together or was it love? I realised that Jack, the great observer, the clever scholar, didn't have a bloody clue.

I looked down at HMS *Jersey* again and remembered the sound as she'd hit the murky water. Whatever I felt was now irrelevant. Our relationship had drowned amongst the weeds in the harbour.

Malita had also said something about Rachel – *is difficult choice, no?* Choice for whom? Rachel and I were friends, talked at lot, but we'd never shared any intimacy. She was the opposite of Caroline in almost every respect: she was kind, considerate, undemonstrative, unsophisticated but also very pretty in an intense way. She was slim, almost thin, and carried herself with purpose. She didn't swing her hips like Caroline, didn't play to the crowd. Yet she was just as good a diver, better in many ways, though she didn't risk the high tariff twists and rotations. She was a far stronger swimmer and we'd splashed alongside each other many times in deep-sea training before my scare. She'd never given me any visible sign that she saw me as more than a friend but, now I thought about it, she always seemed to be there. She'd been watching me during the match. Perhaps it had been her who had called out and not Caroline.

'*Is difficult choice, no?*' What had she meant? Had Rachel confided in her, or was she just guessing?

I looked across the bay to Noirmont Point. The headland and wedge of coastline to St Aubin was in silhouette now as the sun dipped towards St Ouen. Its late evening rays still dazzled and, through the glare, I spotted an insect-like shape rising up from the airport. Seconds later I heard the twin-engined buzz as the de Havilland *Rapide* turned towards me and set a course for France.

Fort Regent stood sentinel over the dozing town and I thought I could hear the bark of orders as the militia drilled in the parade ground beyond Glacis Field. It was a beautiful evening and I was sitting astride the most wondrous machine. I should fire her up, steam off towards the sun and blast along the five-mile road. I wanted to test George Brough's claim that she could reach a hundred miles per hour. Yet I felt unsettled and couldn't find the enthusiasm. I needed to clear my head of girls but they wouldn't disappear. Caroline was such an enigma and Malita had intrigued me with her sly comments about Rachel.

I knew she wanted to talk to me though. Whether it was about her feelings or something more urgent, I had no idea. I kicked

Boadicea into life. Feel the rush and roar of *Boadicea's* bloodlust for speed, or try to unravel the puzzle Malita had set?

Sod it. I'd had enough talk for one day. I turned the handlebars towards the sun, pushed her into gear and aimed her nose towards the harbour. She picked up speed but wobbled as I reached the crest then, of her own accord, she leant right and I was riding downhill towards the east and the pool. I shrugged – my fate was now in *Boadicea's* handlebars.

We trundled along Havre des Pas, past the holidaymakers stretching their legs after dinner. Fred had mentioned that her previous owner had a connection with the area but refused to tell me more. It was a riddle, a teaser, as he called it. He loved little mysteries. It was a bit too deep for me, though I assured him I would solve it one day.

Turning up Roseville Street, I weaved towards the imposing granite house where the Vibert family lived. Dark green shutters covered the windows on the ground floor but the sash window of Rachel's bedroom was half-open. Her net curtains danced over the sill. I pulled *Boadicea* out of gear and coasted to a halt opposite the stern-faced front door, the very image of its master.

Rachel rarely mentioned her parents, though I knew the relationship was strained. I'd never seen them at the club, even though it was a mere hundred yards from their house.

I couldn't see any movement in her room. Of course, she could be clearing up after dinner or helping her mother in any number of household chores. She might even be reading the *Evening Post* to her father, whose eyesight was deteriorating. This much she had told me of her daily routine. She also told me her father refused to have the new fangled electricity in his house and had never been to the cinema, believing it to be the invention of the Devil. He seemed to have a limited sense of humour and I didn't feel like testing it by knocking on his door at eight-thirty in the evening. The talk would have to wait.

I blipped the throttle, startling myself as the exhaust note bounced off the pink granite. Feeling guilty, I engaged gear and started to ride off. A quick glance and I caught a shadow moving behind the curtains in her room. I shrugged, defeated, opened the throttle in a farewell salvo and charged towards the sea.

I sped round the block, revelling in the snarl of the twin exhaust pipes as I accelerated out of corners. I did another circuit of the town but it was deserted, just the shop windows to impress. I felt drawn back to Havre des Pas.

A few minutes later, I passed the ornate Ommaroo Hotel, pulled up outside the club and parked up on the wide pavement at the top of the bridge. The gate was closed and locked. I sat there watching the tide, on the turn now. Seagulls screeched as an old woman emptied her bag of crusts onto the beach by the seawall, where the shadows were creeping in with the tide. How different it was when the club had a dance evening and the terraces thronged with life. You could hear the band for miles, when the tide was up. There would be an aquatic show soon, the climax of which would be the torchlight parade around the quarter-mile circumference of the pool, flickering flames shining off the black water. Thanks to Brewster, I would still have my chance in the spotlight on Thursday, in the swimming match against the Royal Navy. A good opportunity to achieve the qualifying time I needed for selection for the Southern Counties.

What I needed now, apart from divine guidance on my love life, was some sleep. I'd missed training with Miko this morning because of the destroyer. Whether I slept or not, I would have to turn up at seven o'clock tomorrow or I'd never find the speed I needed.

I was contemplating how to shave a few more tenths of a second off my somersault turn when a black blur shot across the beach below me. The little cocker spaniel was chasing a stick and scurried as though the fires of hell were scorching its tail. It looked familiar as it ploughed to a halt in the soft sand and snatched the bleached twig. It lifted its head and accelerated towards its master, tail wagging at the successful retrieval. Mine wagged too as I recognised Rachel bending now to take the gift from little Bobby's mouth. She glanced up, saw me, smiled and started to walk towards the wall.

'Fancy seeing you here,' she called as she climbed the granite steps, Bobby trailing behind. 'That's not your bike, is it?'

'No, it's Uncle Fred's, he's lent it to me to get home as I missed the bus. We did a lot of talking after you left.'

'Not about me, I hope?' She look worried as she approached.

'No, don't fret. We discussed war, the last, the next, and religion.'
I wondered if Malita had ever said anything to her.

She was in front of me now, the spaniel panting by her leg, a shy
smile on her face. Her upper body was illuminated by the fading
sun, almost cutting her in half. She was wearing an old cardigan and
tweed skirt, her bare legs attractively shaped in high-heeled sandals.
She towered over me as I sat on the low saddle.

'Are you alright?' she asked.

'Yes, I think so, why?'

'Well you look rather confused, sad even.'

If she'd listened to Fred and Malita, she'd look sad as well but it
wasn't something I wanted to share with her. 'It's been a strange day.'

She prodded the front wheel with her toe. 'Is this a noisy bike?'

'Why?'

'Well, about twenty minutes ago I heard this throbbing sound
outside my house and then this almighty roar. I just caught a glimpse
of a motor-bike speeding down the road – it wasn't you by any
chance?'

I felt my cheeks redden. 'It might have been.' She was playing
with me.

'Was it?'

I held my hands up in surrender. 'I confess, it was I and my
trusty steed – *Boadicea.*'

'That's a dramatic name. Did you christen her?'

'No it was Fred. He claims the previous owner called her *George
VII* but he felt she was female so he's started a new dynasty.'

'And is she?'

'What?'

'Female?'

My cheeks were burning again.

She smiled. 'After all, you're sitting in a good place to know.'

Even Bobby was looking up at me, waiting for an answer.

'I think she might be but perhaps,' I hesitated. 'I need a second
opinion.'

She laughed, bent over, picked up the spaniel and placed him
on the pillion seat. 'Well what do you think, Bobby? Is this bike
female?'

'I was rather hoping *you* would give me the opinion.'

She arched her eyebrows. 'How bold of you. Do nice girls sit on little seats like that?' She pointed at the small leather pillion, an afterthought on such a sleek machine. 'Where would I hold on?'

The answer was obvious. I felt my stomach turn hollow. We'd just crossed an invisible barrier. Her slender figure focused on me, yet was distant and teasing at the same time. More riddles. I wanted to feel her weight on the saddle behind me, her long fingers clutching my waist as I fed the power through the rear wheel and flung us into the distance.

'Well there's one way to find out but –'

A car screeched to a halt in the road alongside us. Startled, we turned as Caroline's Bugatti settled on its springs. She swung her door open and thrust herself onto the pavement. Ignoring us, she strode to the boot and heaved it open. Emerging with a length of towrope, she marched towards us. She stopped and looked down at me. Her expression was inscrutable. Anger, betrayal? What thoughts were pounding away in there.

She held the rope out in front of Rachel. 'Here, you skinny bitch. Either tie yourself to him with it, or hang yourself.' Dropping the rope at Rachel's feet, she turned back to the car, slid into the seat, gunned the engine and snarled away. Through the cloud of exhaust, we could see that she was not alone. Kohler turned and waved his arm in mock salute. Bobby barked.

Rachel and I looked at each other open-mouthed, then at the rope. As we looked up, our eyes met and we started to giggle; quietly at first, in disbelief. This quickly turned to relief, and then to uncontrolled amusement. Caroline was way beyond being a puzzle. At times like this, she seemed insane. If Caroline and I were finished, as her daft theatrical response and closeness to Kohler would seem to confirm, why should she confront Rachel in such an over-dramatic fashion?

Rachel touched my arm. 'Don't even try to work it out, Jack. Even Caroline doesn't know why she acts like she does.' She withdrew her hand. 'Anyway, I suppose I had better take Bobby home.' She moved away, tugging the spaniel with her.

'Wait, Rachel.' Still trapped on the saddle, I couldn't reach out to her with my hands but the pleading was clear in my voice. 'Please, wait.'

She stopped and turned back, her face completely in shadow now.

'I still want you to try the pillion. Come on, be a sport, come for a ride. It won't be long, just around the block. Come on. I need your company. I want to be with you.' There, I'd said it, committed myself.

She stared at me for a long moment. 'No. It's too dangerous. I've never been on a motorbike before. What if I fall off?'

'You won't.' I reached behind my neck and unclipped the chain. I held it out and the small silver charm danced in the fading sun. 'My Saint Christopher, patron saint of travellers. Here, wear it.'

Shock turned into a shy smile. 'I can't take that, Jack, it's your lucky charm. I bet your mother gave it to you.' She giggled.

'Please wear it, and please come with me.'

She took a deep breath and shut her eyes as if holding an internal debate with whatever demons had spooked her. She opened them slowly, reached out for the chain and nodded. 'Alright. I'll take Bobby home, put on some slacks and shoes, then come back to you in five minutes.' She held my gaze. 'Please don't hurt me.' Then she turned and hauled Bobby across the road and ran up the street.

I sat, dazed, my stomach somersaulting like a high diver plunging into the dense water below. Perhaps I should have taken *Boadicea* for that speed run instead – at least her needs were simple.

10

Five minutes dragged into ten, then fifteen. I could have swum from the Dicq Rock to Green Street slip and back while waiting. By the time she returned, it felt as though I'd swum around the island.

She'd changed into black tailored slacks and a thick woollen jumper, sensible flat shoes and white socks. She had tied a bright red silk scarf round her chestnut hair and looked better prepared for a brisk ride than I felt in my khaki battledress.

She moved gracefully to the handlebars and took my face in both her hands. 'You will be very careful, won't you?'

'Don't worry.'

'No violent movements, no hard braking and definitely no speeding. Understand?' She tilted my face up to hers revealing that she had spent her "five" minutes applying a little lipstick and some eye shadow.

'Trust me, I'm a fighter pilot.' I prodded *Boadicea* back into life.

She chuckled, moved round behind me and swung her left leg over the saddle. I felt the bike jiggle on its sprung frame and waited for her to find the only hand holds available: around my waist. Her touch was tentative as she held the rough serge in both hands.

I turned my head to her. 'Better hold tighter until we get balanced.'

She poked me in the ribs, shuffled closer, slipped her hands under the jacket and gripped my sides.

'Ready?'

She nodded her chin into my shoulder.

'We'll ride to Gorey. Lean with me when we turn.'

I felt her stiffen in fright.

'It's okay. We'll only be going slowly.'

I felt her trembling as she moved closer, almost hugging me now. I released the brake and let out the clutch. We wobbled alarmingly. Fred had warned me that *Boadicea* could be skittish and, with the extra weight over the rear wheel, the front was now very light. I would have to be extra careful.

Once past the Dicq, I accelerated smoothly up to fifty miles per hour along the coast road, the exhaust note rippling along behind. Rachel shifted forward and soon her arms encircled my waist as she pressed into me.

I risked a glance behind and saw that her eyes were still squeezed closed.

'Open your eyes. Enjoy the moment!' I screamed above the wind.

Past Greve D'Azette, *Boadicea* cantered along towards the dusk. She snuggled closer and shouted in my ear. 'This is fun, but slow down so I can look.'

I eased back and felt her cheek on my neck as she turned her head to look at the sea. I felt warmth glowing inside me even as the cold air dissolved my eyes and squeezed tears down my cheeks. I blinked and realised I would have to put on the goggles if we were to ride much further. Perhaps this was far enough. I slowed to a walking pace then turned smoothly right, off the main road and onto the slipway at Green Island. I coasted to a halt and splayed my feet to stabilise the machine and its passenger. One blip and the engine coughed into silence. Above the ticking of the cooling metal, I could hear Rachel tunelessly singing to herself.

'Slide off and I'll park up.'

She released her grip and swung herself off the pillion while I pulled *Boadicea* up onto her stand.

'That was quite frightening, but quite amazing as well.'

She stood waiting as I clambered off then darted down the slip towards the beach.

I caught up with her at the end of the granite outfall and stood behind her. She was trembling again. I hesitated then slipped my left arm around her waist and felt her shivering under her jumper.

'Come on. Let's sit in the bus shelter and watch the sun go down.'

I took her hand and led her up the slipway and across to the wooden shelter. We sat on the bench and turned towards the west as the sun sank over the pool in the distance. We'd both swum there from the slipway the previous summer, a mile and a quarter in a straight line, forty minutes in the chilly water.

We stared in silence, still holding hands.

Her grip was firm but soft and I felt her fingers moving slowly against mine.

I swapped hands so that I could slip my left arm around her shoulder and pull her into me. She didn't resist but didn't turn her face to me either. The excuse for closeness had gone now we weren't on the bike. I knew she was worried about something important. She was obviously vulnerable. How to be receptive but not romantic? I was too used to Caroline and our barrier-free physical relationship.

I really cared for Rachel. She had asked me not to hurt her, but how should I respond if she did cross the divide? I was determined not to cross it myself. I just had to keep my body under control. Perhaps talking would help.

'A penny for them?' I tried to make my voice light.

She sighed. 'Jack, you are so sweet and I am so fond of you –'

'But?'

She eased her hand out of mine and turned her face towards me. Her eyes reflected the soft yellow rays of the sinking sun, though her expression was guarded. 'But you know so little about me. And there's Caroline to consider.'

'Caroline and I are finished.'

'You know that's not true. You've had a difficult day but she's still very keen on you –'

'What? After that exhibition?'

'Yes, especially after that *exhibition*.' She smiled. 'I don't think you really understand, do you?'

I tried to keep the sudden disappointment off my face.

She spotted it. 'Don't be sad. It's just not the right time, yet.'

I tried to speak but she lifted her mouth and touched her lips gently to mine, brushed them tenderly then slid them onto my cheek before whispering in my ear.

'It's not right. We can't, until you...'

'Yes?'

'Until you *both* believe it's over.' She hugged me and dropped her head into my neck.

Holding back now was the hardest thing I had ever done. Her brief kiss had melted something, released an emotion I didn't understand. I wanted to kiss her again but I kept my head up and held her tightly. I let her burrow into me, felt her body heave, as her sobbing increased.

Embarrassed, I clung on helpless, uncertain what to say or do. I realised that there was nothing to be said. All I could do was comfort her and so I held her and rubbed her back while she cried in my arms.

I waited for what seemed longer than that Green Island swim until she had exhausted her tears. The dusk settled like a blanket around us and still I waited. She couldn't be this upset about Caroline, could she?

Eventually she raised her head and I was ready with my handkerchief.

'A gentleman to the end.' Her voice was unsteady. 'I'm so sorry, Jack. I should have kept it inside. You didn't deserve that. It's not fair.' She blew her nose and sniffled, clutching the piece of cotton in her hands.

'It's me who should be sorry. I shouldn't have presumed –'

'No, Jack, this isn't about you.' She shook her head and splattered the remaining tears over her wrists. She took more deep breaths and looked away towards the sun's final pink ribbon, which still streaked the western sky. She slumped back into me and rested her cheek against mine. 'It's been a strange day, for both of us.'

'Do you want to tell me about it?'

She kissed my cheek. 'Of course I do but I don't know if I'm ready yet. It's too soon. I have to tell someone and I want it to be you but it's still too painful.'

I wanted to know this secret, even though I realised that it was not about me. It was breaking her heart but I couldn't push, would have to wait. I pulled her closer and enveloped her in my arms. 'I think I understand. I can wait until you are ready –'

Suddenly she pulled away, sat upright and turned to look directly at me. 'Jack, you are too good to be true at times.' Her tone had changed and she was almost fierce with me. 'You are easy prey. I don't want to be mean about Caroline but, despite what she believes, this is not a competition. You are not a prize. You have to be yourself, but first you have to know who you are. When you've worked that out then we can be...' her voice tailed off.

'Friends, or?' I tried to finish her sentence but my voice faltered.

She smiled. 'Only time will tell.' She squeezed my hands. 'Please take me home now. Slowly.'

11

She seemed more relaxed on the ride back, leaning into me, her arms tight around my waist as we cruised through the velvet night, the feeble Lucas headlight illuminating little more than the mudguard on the front wheel. I could feel the vibrations as she hummed tunelessly into my back. As we reached Havre des Pas, she began to tense up and pull me back towards her.

I turned into Roseville Street but she whispered urgently, 'Stop. Don't take me any further.'

I pulled up and let the engine idle. It burbled, almost soothingly.

She dismounted. 'I don't want to go home. I can't face them yet.' She sounded worried, almost frightened. She rested her hands on my shoulders and pressed her forehead into mine. 'Can we walk for a bit?'

I tried to focus on her eyes but they were too close. What was troubling her? Was it really about me not knowing myself, or was she also struggling for an identity? I couldn't abandon her now but I couldn't abandon *Boadicea* either.

'I'll turn around and park at the top of the bridge. You join me there, okay?'

She lifted her head and nodded.

I risked a feet-up turn and propelled the big bike across the road and onto the pavement again, yards from where Caroline had confronted us earlier. It was still warm, balmy even, and I slipped my jacket off and slung it over my shoulder.

She joined me and reached out for my right hand. 'Let's sneak into the pool.' She sounded more cheerful as she squeezed her palm into mine. 'Come on, no one will know.'

'Someone will spot us if we climb over the gate. We'll have to go along the beach and over the back by the stands. I reckon we've got about an hour before the tide cuts us off. Time enough for you to tell me what's wrong?'

'Perhaps.' She pulled me towards the steps and hurried me across the sand and onto the rocks behind the terraces. We clambered up the bank and underneath the stands until we were in the shadows of the diving stage.

'Let's go up to the Blue Terrace. I feel like a dance.'

She was becoming even more unpredictable than Caroline. She'd be wanting to go for a swim next.

'Okay, but you'll have to make the music.'

We climbed the steep granite steps, past the lookout and surveyed the empty terrace. The deckchairs and tables had been scooped up and piled in the shadows alongside the buffet.

The fairy lights, strung along the promenade, seemed brighter in the encroaching gloom as I dropped my jacket and held out my arms to invite her to dance. She eased herself into position and began to hum "Stardust" softly. We moved comfortably together, though I was careful where I placed my hobnailed army boots. Those lessons in the Plaza ballroom above West's Cinema hadn't been entirely wasted. She relaxed and moved with me as I responded to her increasing tempo until we twirled in a crescendo, spinning dizzily, almost out of control. We grabbed the buffet counter and held on while the world steadied itself.

'That was fun, Jack. I needed that.' She threw her arms around my neck and kissed me firmly on the lips. Before I could react, she was gone, running off towards the cabins. 'Come on, let's play hide and seek. You stay there and count to ten and then come and find me.'

Her disembodied voice echoed from the dark somewhere in the middle of the ladies changing area.

'Count out loud so that I can hide.'

'Never mind counting, I'm coming now and I'm going to tickle you until you scream for mercy.'

She didn't respond, so I started off on the quest, uncertain what she expected me to do when I found her. Was this just a teasing game for her, or was she hiding from more than just me?

I tiptoed along the line of cabins, pausing at each to look over the top of the three-quarter length door, my eyes adjusting to the gloom. I heard her shallow breaths but passed on. Two could play at this game. I made a little more noise so that she could follow my progress then slipped into one of the cabins, sat down on the slatted bench and waited.

I strained to listen. Was she stalking me now?

The cabin door burst open and she flung herself at me, wrapped her arms around my neck and kissed me hard. This time she stayed and allowed me to kiss her back. Her lips were cool and moist, her breath sweet and her tongue teased mine as she melted into me. We held the kiss, moving through urgent passion to quiet tenderness, then eased apart.

She sat on the bench beside me and grabbed my wrists. 'If I tell you my secret, will you promise me that you will share it with no one, ever?'

I had no idea what she wanted to say but I had to hear it.

'Are you sure you want to tell me? Can you trust me when I don't know myself?'

'Don't be cruel, Jack. I trust you probably more than you will ever know.' She reached out and ran her fingers over my face, touching my eyes then my lips.

A shiver wriggled down my spine. 'Alright, I promise.'

She took a deep breath then let it out slowly.

'Yesterday, I discovered that I'm not who I thought I was.'

The shiver froze. I tried to speak but she pressed her finger to my lips.

'Just listen, I need to explain this. My parents are difficult. You haven't spoken to them but you've seen them. They live in a different age. Mother is kind and generous but never ever disagrees with Father. He is fierce, frightening at times, stubborn beyond belief and will never entertain an opposite point of view. They never discuss things with me. I was told to leave school, told to go to work, given my tasks; there was no debate. I tried to question him once and he roared me into tears.'

She hesitated, reliving the moment, her voice catching with sadness. 'I think they love me but that would be the last thing they would ever say. They are quite alone. There were some relatives we used to visit but there was a big argument and now only one of Mother's cousins ever calls. They are both Viberts, you know, though they aren't related. They did tell me that once.'

She paused again. 'Yesterday evening I overheard Mother talking to Cousin Enid. They didn't realise I was in the hallway. They were talking about Enid's daughter, who has a prolapse.'

She sensed my question but squeezed it off with her hand. 'That's a woman's problem with her womb. Apparently, it's pretty awful and she is in considerable pain. I'll spare you the details. Anyway, they were discussing whether she should follow the doctor's advice and have a hysterectomy. She's thirty-five now, which is quite young for such an operation. Enid reminded Mother that she had the same problem when she was thirty-three and wanted to know what went through her mind before she had the operation. Mother is sixty-one. I'm eighteen. You can do the arithmetic. It means that I was born ten years after her womb was removed. You see, Jack, I am a little miracle.'

She swallowed. 'I crept away and sneaked into his study, where he keeps his desk. There is a little hidden compartment. He is very clever with his hands and he made the desk. It probably has other secrets as well. He was out collecting rents so I opened the compartment and pulled out the small bundle of papers wedged in there. One of them was in French – you know, the legal Norman version. It was a letter from Jurat Le Brocq. I didn't understand all of it but it referred to an agreement between my father, Edward Vibert, and two other parties, a George Vibert and Louisa Mahrer who were resident in Caen. It was about the adoption of a sixth-month old infant girl.'

I gasped but she pressed her hand over my mouth before I could speak.

'I remembered Mother and Father arguing about his young cousin who had stayed in France after the war – how he was good for nothing, indolent, a ladies' man. I didn't understand what they meant at the time and he wasn't mentioned again in my presence. I do remember another time when they had received a letter and were talking about a Louisa who lived in France.' She stopped.

I felt her stiffen, could feel the tension gripping her. I waited.

'Mother said "it was only to be expected." Father was very angry and slammed the table before ripping the letter to shreds. He turned to Mother and said, "What else could you expect from the Jewish bitch?"'

I reached out and pulled her into me.

'You see, Jack, I've been living a lie for eighteen years – I'm not me.'

I didn't know what to say but had to speak. 'Do they know?'

'Not yet. Oh, Jack, where can I get the courage to tell them?'

'Do you need to?'

She stopped sniffling. 'You're right. Why do they need to know – what can I gain by confronting them? Father will see my searching his desk as a betrayal. No, it's not worth it. Unless they're willing to tell me about my real parents and why they kept this from me. Tell me that I'm more than a purchased servant. Tell me they love me. Because they never have. Not once. Not ever.'

Silence, then a small voice. 'I'm sorry, Jack. This must be very tedious for you. You wanted some fun, not my sordid little story.'

'That's cruel, Rachel. Of course I'm interested. I just want to help you find the best way of dealing with this.' I turned away, hurt.

'Don't sulk, Jack.' She turned with me and ran her hand over my cheek. 'You have been wonderful. Don't you understand that you are the only person I wanted to tell? She reached up and kissed me again. My heart raced as she pulled my head towards her, crushing my lips with a force and passion I had never experienced before. I felt helpless, and, again, she was the first to break away.

'I'm too hot. Let's go for a swim,' she said

'What? You're mad. We haven't got any costumes, or towels – we'll be seen.'

'Shush, stop being so...' she sought for the word, 'conventional. Come on. It will cheer us up.'

She stood up, removed her shoes and socks and pulled her jumper over her head, revealing a white bra, which she shrugged out of in one movement. Almost innocently, like a young child, she undid the side zip on her slacks, stepped out then kicked them away. Without pausing, she rolled down her white knickers then stood, hands on hips, looking at me. 'Come on, slow coach. I'm ready.'

I couldn't believe it. Was this Rachel or Caroline in front of me? The speed with which she had shed her clothes and the matter of fact way she now stood naked, almost challenging, was a complete surprise. Naturally, I'd examined her shape, surreptitiously, through her wet costume before. Now, I admired her well-rounded, firm breasts and prominent nipples, the slender waist, which curved into almost boyish hips, and the dark triangle between her legs. She was beautiful, but quite mad.

Impatient with me, she started to tug my shirt out of my trousers, reached for my belt and started to struggle with the buckle. It had been easy enough to release in the town hall, but I hadn't had the chance to tell her about that yet.

'Come on, Jack, you've been swimming without your trunks before.'

I batted her hands away, released the buckle myself and let gravity take over. There was no way I could control the erection and she giggled when I eased my underpants over it before I dropped them to the concrete floor.

'My, my – I think that little rudder will slow you down.'

'What do you mean *little*?'

But she was gone, running off down the alleyway, her feet pattering softly as she weaved her way to the terrace. I struggled furiously with the laces of my boots and gaiters, tripping over the jumbled clothes and almost fighting my way out of the cabin. When I reached the top of the steps, she was dancing about on the concrete starting blocks twenty-feet below.

'Wait, Rachel. Don't dive, you'll make too much noise.' But it was too late. She had plunged in and disappeared under the black water.

I hurried after her. There was no way I was going to jump or dive in this state so I waded down the short flight of steps, gasping as the cool water rose to my waist. I could hear her splashing about as she surfaced.

'Quiet,' I hissed, 'swim slowly to the raft.' I stepped lower, enjoying the tingle on my skin as the sea sucked me under, took a deep breath and swam breaststroke along the sandy bottom towards the closest moored raft. It felt very strange without a costume and she was right about the rudder effect. The water bubbled away as I let out a silent laugh.

I surfaced once for air but she was nowhere in sight. I dived again and propelled myself to the wooden platform. I'd once been too frightened to dive under and surface into the pocket of air, yet it was a fascinating experience once I had plucked up the courage.

I had to go quite deep to avoid the empty copper tanks, which provided the flotation, before I popped up with barely enough room to keep my head above the inky water. The club had purchased the large rafts from the company which had scrapped the RMS *Mauretania* for seven pounds each – a bargain, we'd been told. They were certainly well made and it was fun hiding under there and listening to the swimmers jumping about on top.

There was still no sign of Rachel then, suddenly, she slid up behind me and clasped me round the neck.

'This is fabulous.' She sounded so carefree, as if the last thirty minutes had never happened. Would I ever understand women? I felt her nipples rubbing against my back and was suddenly aware of my rudder again.

The raft had drifted closer to the bridge and I could stand on tiptoe. I spun around and wrapped my arms around her, pressing her breasts into my chest. My former patron saint of travel now dangled round her neck, a silver shield between us. She gasped as the top of her thighs brushed against my stiffness then giggled again.

'I apologise. It is not so little. Not that I have any experience of rudders. For all I know, amongst rudders, it might be considered a very small one indeed.'

Before I could reply, she found my mouth and pressed her salty tongue into mine.

Despite the cool water, I was burning. I couldn't tell whether it was with desire or embarrassment. I felt awkward, guilty. I shouldn't be doing this, yet I wanted to caress her, run my hands along the curve of her spine and down to her firm buttocks. I wanted to lose myself in her but instead I broke off the kiss and turned myself so that I pressed into her side and away from the danger area of her thighs. She moaned but I hugged her and kissed her forehead, trying desperately to subdue the evidence of my arousal. I had to start behaving like the gentleman she believed me to be rather than taking advantage of her emotional confusion. While this sounded good to my thinking brain, the other one didn't agree so I thought of frozen rivers of blood and the despair in my uncle's voice. That worked.

I let her rest against me, felt her heart beating. We stayed in a comforting embrace for a few more minutes but I was losing the battle. She stirred against me, her hand moved slowly south. I shuddered then she kissed me with such completeness that those frozen rivers turned into hot springs and I eased myself into her.

It was a strange sensation – the cold water sucked around us as she moved freely. I lost myself in her rhythm but tried to detach myself to prolong the moment as Caroline had taught me. But Rachel was so genuine, so absorbed in me, so determined, that I couldn't. The heat shot through me and into her. We both shuddered but she kept her lips tight to mine, grabbed my buttocks and pulled me deep into her. Her heart thudded against my chest and our breathing echoed against the metal barrels.

Eventually she eased away and I ducked my head under, luxuriating in the coldness. She joined me and tried to kiss my lips but bit my nose instead. I could feel the bubbles from her giggles tickling my chin.

We broke the surface and even though it was pitch-black, I could sense her smile.

'I feel much better now. Thank you, Jack. Thank you.'

My laughter exploded, shaking the planking. She joined in until we shivered with the release of tension and of the awareness of the chilly water and the reality of what we had done.

She spoke softly, 'Should we swim back now and try to dry ourselves?'

'Of course, I know where I can find a towel.'

We ducked under the raft and swam side by side until we reached the steps. Her body glistened in the reflections off the water as she mounted the steps. She paused and turned to me. 'It'll be alright won't it? With the cold water, nothing could happen. Could it?'

My stomach lurched. Caroline would have known, wouldn't

have asked. Old wives' tale? How many old wives made love under cold water? I forced my words up from the depths. 'You'll be – I mean, we'll be fine.'

I was about to reach out and pull her back for a reassuring kiss when our world exploded in a blaze of light. The beams from three torches pounced on our heads.

'Now, what have we here?

I recognised Brewster's voice and felt like a bucket of ice had been thrown over us. Rachel splashed back to hide behind me, modest now in front of the two policemen and the club manager.

Brewster handed two towels to me. He turned to the policemen. 'I'm sorry about this. These two are club members. This was obviously a silly prank. The woman who telephoned you must have been mistaken about burglars breaking in. Please let me handle this now. I'm sure they have an explanation for their behaviour. If not, I will want to talk to their parents about their state of undress.'

'Oh God, no. Please, Mr Brewster, please don't tell my parents. It would kill them.' Rachel's voice crackled with fear.

'Good night then, sir.' The policemen grinned then swung their torches onto the granite steps and climbed up to the terrace. Brewster waited for us to wrap the towels around ourselves then led us to his office.

As we followed him, I was sure I could see a Bugatti parked outside the telephone box opposite the Ommaroo Hotel.

12

'Sorry.'

'Uh. Sorry?'

'Yes, about yesterday.'

'*Sajnos,* eh? Words cheap. You say "sorry". I want you swim "sorry" – now work apology. You think I have nothing better to do than stand and watch you? *Fereg!*'

I assumed *fereg* wasn't a compliment in either Romanian or Hungarian and lowered myself into the pool. I'd never seen Miko angry before. I felt guilty about not turning up yesterday and being late again this morning. He was doing this for nothing, after all. I'd swim off my apology but I felt so tired.

I'd fallen asleep just before I was meant to wake Alan. We were then too late for me to drive him to the harbour, get back and collect *Boadicea.* Father had driven him instead, insisting I follow behind. After we'd seen Alan up the gangplank and onto the steamer, he'd turned on me and given me a lecture about responsibility, arriving home late at night, fouling up his morning and riding Fred's bike. Rather than argue, I'd let his anger wash over me, keeping my clenched fists hidden behind my back. Puzzled by my silence, he'd stalked off, kicked the car's tyres and driven away. I'd heard some clapping from the deck above and turned to see Alan and a few of his friends applauding ironically. When he returned on Friday, I'd warm his ears for him.

Now Miko was acting like my father. Bugger the lot of them. Instead of warming up slowly, I sprinted the first four lengths and worked off my frustration.

Exhausted, I hung my arms on the poolside, gasping for breath.

'So, this is good training, eh? You finish before you start. Why I bother with you? Why I waste my time?'

I glared at him.

He glared back at me. '*Fereg!*'

There was more to this than being late for training. God, he didn't know about Rachel, did he? It wasn't possible. He couldn't have seen her yet, not at this hour.

'What's this *fereg*, an insult?'

'No insult. Just truth. It mean "useless worm"– like you – useless worm. Now swim, or go home.'

I spat out a mouthful of water just short of his sandals, turned and swam another four lengths at half-pace, plotting revenge.

'Better, now you ready to train?'

'Yes.'

'We begin. You swim ten lengths feet only, ten lengths arms only.' He threw the cork float at me.

I hated this type of training

'Whatever you say, Doctor Pavas.'

That got his attention. He squatted down so that our faces were inches apart. His ice-blue eyes pierced mine. 'You speak to your uncle? I see. You wish to talk more, waste more time, or swim?'

That's it. No more sarcasm. I snapped. 'I'm fed up. Do this, do that. No argument. You know best. But you don't even swim yourself. You're just an academic. It's all talk.'

He peeled his cap from his head and rubbed it across his brow then smiled as though he had been expecting my outburst. 'So, Jerk, you need lesson. You think I all talk, perhaps cannot swim? How fast you swim twenty-five yards?'

'You know bloody well. You're the one with the stop watch.'

'Yes,' he dangled it in front of me, 'it say twelve seconds with dive. You slow after that and make one minute one second for the race. Too slow.'

'I'd like to see you do better.' I'd made the challenge. He could smell my feet if he accepted.

'Out. We race. One length.'

I hauled myself out and stood next to him. He was at least three inches shorter and twenty years older. This could be embarrassing for both of us, but I'd committed myself now.

'Aren't you going to change?'

He looked at me in surprise. 'Why? This is not difficult race.'

He must be mad. Polo shirt, shorts with pockets. He'd sink. I watched as he kicked off his sandals, removed the stopwatch and some bits and pieces from his pockets, then tightened his belt.

He stepped to the side to take his marks.

'How much start do you want?'

'I no need start, Jerk. You go when ready.'

This had to be a bluff. I was the fastest swimmer over this distance on the island. He was old and wearing clothes. He'd wait for me to dive in then stand and laugh at me. I realised that would be the best result and took my position.

As soon as he crouched, I launched myself into a shallow racing dive and applied maximum effort. He was on my blind side and I was conscious of some movement alongside. I thrashed the water like a mad man, held my breath and reached for the wall. He was sitting on it. He'd beaten me by a body length, wearing clothes. Thank God no one had been watching.

I fought for breath. He patted me on the head. His breathing seemed normal. His shirt, with the red ILSA logo, clung to his back. His shorts dripped onto the concrete but he didn't seem to be out of breath. He dried his face on my towel.

The sun caught his back and, through the wet shirt, I could see the outlines of deep scars. I gasped.

He turned in surprise. 'What?'

I pointed to his body. 'Your back, Miko. What happened to your back?'

He motioned me out of the pool and pressed the towel into my hands. 'You do not want to know.'

'I do, Miko.'

'And so do I.' Rachel stepped from behind the hut and my stomach somersaulted. She looked so attractive standing there, without make-up, in a simple frock, hair loose and natural.

So, she'd seen my humiliation.

'I'm sorry. I shouldn't have been spying. I came to see Miko. I thought you'd be gone by now. Jack, you look like a stranded fish. Close your mouth.'

I studied her. Eyes red-rimmed and puffy. She'd not slept either. I wanted to hug her, kiss her. Instead, I closed my mouth.

Miko looked at both of us and grimaced. 'This is not story for sunny morning. You not want to hear this.'

Rachel looked at me. I nodded. She spoke softy. 'I think we do.'

'Once this is told, it cannot be unsaid, you understand.' There was a sorrow in his tone which made me hesitate.

'Please, Miko.' I looked at Rachel and she nodded again.

'So be it. You have been warned. It will hurt me to tell. You still wish this?'

I was no longer sure but Rachel moved closer and touched his arm. 'Please share this hurt with us. We are your friends. We won't tell anyone else.'

He sighed in resignation and slowly peeled his shirt over his shoulders and turned his back to us. The sun was still low and it highlighted the devastation. Ridges of weals and welts criss-crossed his spine. Interspersed with these were blackened pits where the skin had scarred over. Rachel pulled her hand over her mouth. She looked sick.

'Is not pretty but does not hurt and I have good movement – enough to beat Jerk.'

'Who did this to you?' Rachel reached out tentatively to touch his abused flesh.

'The "Iron Guards" at Makó.'

We must have looked puzzled.

'On the border, between Romania and Hungary, after we leave Timisoara.'

'We?' Rachel glanced at me.

'Yes, me and Elena, my wife. We queue with thousands. Hours and hours, we shuffle forward to border post. We try to cross, we have papers. Payment is expected from Jews. This is no problem but the guards are beating an old man. I, stupid, try stop them. They club me, search my case. They find books written by Jews – physics texts, you understand. This is forbidden by the fascists. They throw them on bonfire. I try to rescue. They laugh and drag me behind fence.'

He swallowed. His tone had been matter of fact but, now he was reliving the moment, his voice softened and I strained to hear. 'They tie me to post, spread me.' He demonstrated, shaping his body into an "X".

I shuddered at the picture. I'd read about floggings in Nelson's navy but couldn't imagine the true horror.

'I do not see what they use but there are two of them. They grunt and swear. I stop counting at thirty blows. I stop thinking. I am only pain.' He stopped.

We were feet apart but I sensed his mind was a thousand miles distant. 'They leave me hanging. I learn after, some brave men in queue cut me down during night and carry me to my wife. She doctor – real doctor, Jerk, not silly academic.'

I hung my head in shame.

'She patch my wounds, give me water. We decide to cross away from guards. We wait for days until I am strong again, then we walk. We walk forever. Across Carpathians, around Slovakia until we reach border with Poland. There are no guards, just the Vistula.'

He paused again, lowered himself to the ground and sat, his wet shorts still dripping around him. He hugged his knees. I wanted him to stop, dreading what he still had to tell. Rachel grabbed my arm and pulled me down alongside him. Miko, my man of steel, who had just thrashed me in the pool, shrivelled in front of us. He was quivering and it wasn't with cold.

We waited. 'Is broad river, this Vistula. Elena is weak swimmer. We try twice but current is strong. We are pushed back. We are weak, hungry. My back bleeds. We hear dogs barking. We rest, decide one more try – at night.'

He stopped; his mouth moved but no sound came out. Rachel reached out, put the towel around his shoulders and hugged him. I felt tears prick my eyes.

He forced himself to continue. 'Is bright moonlight. We reach midstream. Is one hundred metres to Poland. We hear dogs behind, see torches. We cannot return. I hold Elena, but she very weak, cannot swim. I try for both of us but we are dragged under. Is very cold. I fight to surface. I tow her, try to keep her head above water but it is rough, the wind increase, there are waves. My fingers are numb. Elena is unconscious. She slips away. I swim after but cannot reach. I chase until I see her no more. I awake on shore. I never see Elena again.'

We waited. I held my breath.

His eyes had misted over. 'Why this happen? Is because we are Jews?'

I felt like ice. Did Miko know Rachel's secret? I daren't look at her.

'You leave now. Training finished for today. I warn you. Once you hear story, you cannot unlisten. I'm sorry – *sajnos*. It is sad but that is the past.' He pulled himself up. 'You have future. Yes, there will be war but you two will survive. Be strong. Remember, sometimes is better not to fight all the time. Better to swallow pride, turn aside, wait. I learn too late.'

He took Rachel's hands. 'You are strong, brave. You know what you want but do not know who you are.'

She gasped.

'You will find this knowledge. When you do, what you want will come to you.'

He turned to me, tapped me on the head. 'You learn something today?'

'Yes, I did.'

'You will not win through training now. You must win in here.'

He tapped my forehead again. 'I beat you in there – not in pool.' He looked across at Rachel but spoke to me. 'You know who you are but you do not know what you want. One day, soon, you will.'

He stood back. 'I leave now, have to serve the breakfast. Perhaps I find guest to discuss particle acceleration.' He shrugged. 'Perhaps not.' He picked up his polo shirt and sandals and walked towards the hotel.

We watched him in silence. I felt a terrible sadness. I also felt shame for the way he had been treated by the club. I would swim for both of us from now on.

Rachel and I were alone, but I didn't know what to say. I felt powerless to break the silence. She'd made it clear that she'd come to see Miko and not me. Perhaps she didn't want to talk. Miko had said some profound things to us. Things we needed to think about before we tried to discuss them.

'Jack, talk to me.'

Would I ever understand women? 'I don't know what to say. I'm stunned.'

'It puts our little problems into perspective, doesn't it?' She sighed then looked at her watch. 'I'm going to be late for work.' She turned away then stopped.

Did she want to talk now? She'd just said she was late for work. I tried to read her shoulders. 'I'll run you down there on the bike.'

'But you'll be late as well.' Her shoulders slumped.

'That doesn't matter. They can't expel me now.' I hadn't looked at it like that before. They could give me a poor reference but I'd finished my exams and was just hanging around now until term finished.

She turned to look at me again; the sort of smile I sometimes used on Alan fixed on her face.

'Don't be silly. I think you're in enough trouble already. I'm alright. Don't worry about last night. I'm fine.' She winked, hesitated, a slight flush on her cheeks. 'Do you want to meet later, after work?'

I wanted to spend the rest of the day with her, didn't want to go to school.

'Yes, I'd like that. I've got to take the bike back. How about meeting me at Fred's – what time do you finish?'

'Five o'clock.'

'Okay, I'll see you at five-thirty at his house.'

She stepped forward and pecked me on the cheek. 'Tell me. If he'd worn his sandals, do you think you would have beaten him?'

'Cheeky cow. You'll pay for that later.'

'If you can catch me.' Before I could delay our parting any longer, she dashed off, skirt swirling around her tanned legs, hair splashing across her shoulders. I watched until she was out of sight, chewing my lip, trying to make sense of the strange feelings coursing through me.

'Ground – Belts!' As soon as I entered the prefects' room, I faced a line of my friends standing to attention with their trousers around their ankles. Nutty was right – you couldn't keep secrets in this island.

'Nice one, Renouf.' Beresford, the school captain, slapped me on the back. 'I wish I'd been there. Short arms inspection, sir. Want to check the dirt on my barrel?' They hooted and started bounding round the room like kangaroos. Their juvenile insanity was infectious and I joined in, glad to escape into boyhood again, at least for a few moments.

Exhausted, we slumped into the battered leather chairs. Beresford went off with the official slipper and a couple of prefects to see if they could catch any juniors who had been stupid enough to arrive after the bell. I sat around with the others hatching our plan to borrow the Head's car, disassemble it and crane it onto the roof again.

There was a commotion outside. I looked up to see Saul thrown through the doorway by two of the larger prefects.

'Desist thou foul and pestilent knaves!' Saul stumbled to gain his footing in front of us. Needless to say, he hadn't been appointed as a prefect and thought the whole business neanderthal.

'For Christ sake. What do you want, you Yiddish creep?' Surcouf pushed himself up from the sofa and stood in front of Saul.

'Ah, the fishmonger squeaks.' Saul gave Surcouf a withering look. I could sense a dusty reference on his tongue. He smiled and looked around the room. '"*Some report a sea-maid spawn'd him; some that he was begot between two stock-fishes. But it is certain that when he makes water his urine is congealed ice.*" Flop back on your slab, Surcouf, I'm not here to inspect your scales. I have a message for Jack.'

'Renouf, do we have to put up with this indignity? Can't you two meet for your Jew boy rituals after dark somewhere?' Surcouf was a shade over six-feet tall. Surprisingly, for a fishmonger's son, albeit one with four shops, he was a snob. He was also a racist and, at that moment, he sounded like a border guard. A red mist enveloped me. I lifted my foot, planted it on his behind and shoved as hard as I could. He shot across the room, caught the edge of the scarred oak table with his thighs before ending up spread-eagled over it.

I bounced up, grabbed the bat he had been fiddling with and rushed towards him. All I could see were the Iron Guards wielding bloodied whips. As I raised the bat to exact vengeance for Miko and Saul, pain tore through my shoulder. I twisted around to find Beresford's angry face inches from mine.

'What the hell are you playing at, Jack? What's going on here?'

I was panting with anger, my face on fire. I held his stare but dropped the bat. When its echo had died away, I pointed at Surcouf, who was still splayed across the table. 'Ask him.'

He turned to the other prefects. 'Well?'

'It's nothing, Beresford. He called Marcks a Yid.'

'Get out.' He kicked Surcouf's leg. 'And take your filthy Nazi tongue with you. I don't want to see you in here again.' He turned back to me. 'And you should know better. Control yourself. If you want to fight, take it to the gym. Not in here. Understand?'

'Well, thanks for the entertainment.' Saul's sardonic tone brought me back to the reason for the attack. 'It's jolly kind of you, Jack, but a little bit excessive. He's just an uncouth lout. I don't think he meant any harm.'

'Saul, you amaze me.' I wanted to tell him that there were more uncouth louts out there than he realised. That many of them would enjoy cutting him to pieces just because he was a Jew, but now wasn't the time. 'Why did you want to see me?'

'Oh, it's nothing secret. I'm not asking you to join the world conspiracy against bigots or anything dramatic. I've got a message. Grumpy wants to see you, in his study, now.'

13

'Well, Renouf, just what am I going to do with you?' Mr Grumbridge – Grumpy to all his students – tapped his pipe against the leaded window and gestured at the two juniors who had dared trespass on the hallowed lawn outside of his study.

Recognising the rhetorical question, I stood across the desk from the headmaster, hands behind my back in respectful silence.

In silhouette the master looked liked a raven, his wings folded, his balding head nodding in time with the stem of his pipe. As if conducting some hidden orchestra, his shoulders twitched to an internal rhythm. The shaking stopped and he was motionless. He whirled and his gown swished, settled, then enfolded him. His black sleeved arm stretched out and dangled a letter across the massive desk, proffered it to me then let it slip from his fingers and flutter onto the green blotter.

'You'll have to apologise. Firstly to Centenier Phillips, then to Mr Brewster and...' the words seemed to freeze on his lips, 'to both girls' parents.'

I squeezed my hands together and lifted my chin, trying not to blink.

I was very fond of old Grumpy, admired him, had been inspired by his love of Shakespeare, Keats and Byron. I thought he was the perfect teacher, though many of my classmates didn't care for his passion for literature and chose to make fun of him behind his back.

I could sense the pain behind the outrage. All I had to do was nod acquiescence. But I couldn't.

Grumpy slumped into his chair, the folds of his gown draping themselves over the padded arms. 'Well?'

I moistened my lips and tried to speak but my throat was too tight, my tongue beyond control. I felt the heat rising in my cheeks.

'Hell's teeth, boy. Damn your eyes. Your silence will choke you.'

My hands twitched behind my back as the master leant forward, his hands thrusting out from his gown, almost in supplication.

'I'm very sorry, sir, but I will not apologise to Mr Phillips. I will to Mr Brewster. I won't –'

'That's enough, Renouf. You will not dictate the terms of your apologies. You are a scholar of this college. This is a matter of honour. Whilst wearing the King's uniform, you have behaved disgracefully. You are not alone in this and I will deal with your brother and the others later but you were the senior boy. You will apologise in writing to Centenier Phillips. We will discuss the most appropriate way of dealing with the other matter.'

A small concession. My hands steadied, though the bright spots still burned my cheeks. 'As you say, sir, this is a matter of honour and for that reason I cannot apologise to Centenier Phillips. He provoked me. He wouldn't listen. He's a –'

'Renouf, how far do you think you can swim against the tide?'

'Well, sir, I can swim a hundred yards in about sixty seconds so, if I could maintain that speed, that would equate to about three and a half miles per hour. A spring tide will rise eighteen feet in the middle of its flood.' I paused, trying to give the impression I was calculating, though I was trying to work out what was behind the question. I gave up. 'Not very far, sir.'

'If there was a higher certificate in flippancy, Renouf, you would doubtless achieve the top grade.' He leant back in his chair and surveyed me as forensically as the biology master would a dissected frog. 'I do fear for you, boy. Your stubbornness will "*ensure that your voyage is bound in shallows.*"'

The quotation game was something I had learned so well from this master. 'Brutus might have been correct, sir but, however much the "tide is flooding", it's going to change and so is the "fortune". Caesar was a sailor, though it was the "ides" rather than the "tides" that got him.' I winced as the forced pun slipped out.

'Pearls before swine, boy, pearls before swine. I had such high hopes. You had an understanding. I remember we were reading

Julius Caesar around the room and some of your colleagues ceased their struggle to comprehend and started to giggle. You rounded on them and called them *"blocks, stones, worse than useless things"*. I reprimanded you at the time, couldn't have you doing my job, wouldn't have been right though I couldn't have put it better myself.'

His pipe was in his hand again and he started the automatic routine of lighting it. 'I shouldn't have given in to you over Antonio when casting the *Merchant of Venice* though. I should have insisted you play him. You would have made the perfect victim and you might have learnt the humility that was hard earned for Antonio by acting that part but no, you had to swap it for Shylock with your friend Marcks.'

'You know why I did that, sir –'

'Yes, yes, all very noble. The Christian plays the Jew whilst the Jew performs as the Christian, but what humility did you learn from playing Shylock? You just managed to swim a few more yards against that tide which will always drive you back – on your own admission. Wake up, Renouf. You will always encounter people like Phillips. Don't you understand, it is sometimes politic to lose and make a friend rather than win and confirm an enemy? Has my work with you been completely in vain?'

I stifled the obvious retort for I sensed that Mr Grumbridge was being sincere, had stepped aside from his role as headmaster and was now acting as mentor, even friend. Perhaps he was right. Why pick fights?

The pipe was now well alight and his silhouette wreathed in smoke. He sucked on the stem, leaving the question hanging in the air.

'No, sir, I do understand your concerns but I have to make my own way.'

'But why isn't that way to Oxford? Why this stubborn refusal to stretch your mind, to achieve academic enrichment?'

'You know the answer, sir. I love Shakespeare, love performing, love poetry, writing, reading, but those are hobbies.'

My father's voice seemed to take over. 'But I'm practical, I need real skills I can use to make a life for myself, my family. I want to learn about agriculture, about the science of the land. I want to get away from the island for a while. But you've heard all this before.'

'Yes, your father and I did have a brief discussion.'

I imagined there was more brevity than wit during that encounter. Arguing with my father wasn't like swimming against the tide; it was more like trying to plunge through ten-foot surf wearing wellington boots.

He grimaced. 'He wasn't overly impressed with the offer of the Raynor Award. Seemed to feel that £300 per year was insufficient recompense for the loss of your services, if I recall.'

In truth, it would have been enough but I couldn't do it without my father's full support. Caroline thought I was ducking out and playing safe with what I knew, that I had no sense of adventure, no courage. What I actually had was a sense of duty and no bloody choice.

I knew Grumpy had been disappointed for me, now he was disappointed in me.

'I'm sorry, sir. I will apologise to the centenier if you think it will help the college. I will also apologise to Mr Brewster and, if you insist, I will speak to Mr Hayden-Brown, and to Mr and Mrs Vibert.

He turned back towards me, a slight smile on his face. 'Of course you will, Renouf, of course you will. Whatever else, you have a strong sense of what is right, even though you perpetually seem to derive greater enjoyment from being wrong. I will write on your behalf to the centenier though I doubt he will appreciate the dramatic irony I intend to introduce in that particular missive. He is, in truth, an appalling man but one must respect the office, even if the badge is too big for its holder.'

I smiled at last, the tension ebbing away. 'Thank you, sir, if you're sure.'

'No need to trouble Mr Brewster. He and I had an amiable enough telephone conversation. He informed me just in case the police wished to make an issue of it and he would be able to report that he had dealt with the matter appropriately.'

'What about –'

'The girls and their parents? I leave that to your conscience.' He wandered over to the polished sideboard and picked up the crystal decanter. 'A small sherry, perhaps?'

'No thanks. Sorry, sir, I don't. Nothing religious, or anything like that. It's just that I've watched the older lads at the club trying to play water polo after a couple of drinks. It doesn't seem to do much for their performance. Didn't do too much for Falstaff either as I recall. I'm sure the time will come when I might be grateful for a drink, but it's not yet. *"Drink, Sir, is a great provoker of three things: nose-painting, sleep and urine."'*

Grumbridge chortled. '*Macbeth,* the Porter. You never cease to surprise me. There you are teetering on the brink of moral damnation and you can't manage a small sherry. Anyway, there are a couple of things I want to discuss with you. Shame you couldn't make the Bisley team this year. I saw you there this morning seeing off your brother. That's before I got this.' He waved at the letter again. 'Hand delivered no less. How do you think your brother will do in the Shield?'

Bisley, the Ashburton Shield for rifle shooting, Victoria's yearly chance to compete against the UK's best public schools. 'I'm sure we'll do well, sir. Some good cadets in the team. I'm sure my brother will keep up the family tradition.'

'Quite, though one rather hopes that he remembers which eye to close as he squeezes the trigger.'

Alan wouldn't waste time swimming against the tide. He preferred jumping off cliffs, go-karting down the steepest hills or teasing Victor.

'I shouldn't worry about that, sir, his favourite trick is to shoot with both closed.'

'I rather hope that is a feeble attempt at humour and not a serious recollection.'

'Humour, I'm afraid – not my strong point, sorry.'

'Well, let's draw a veil over that.' He waved it away. 'One more thing, Renouf, the end of term celebrations. I assume you will be helping with the swimming at the Palace Hotel. I know you prefects have got some plans; though I hope they don't involve placing my car on the roof again.'

'Of course not, sir. Perish the thought.'

'I understand you're also helping out with some redecoration in the library and taking some of the juniors for life-saving lessons before we break up.'

'Is that alright, sir?'

'Of course, it's most helpful now that you've finished your examinations. On that last day, the parents of our younger swimmers will have paid two shillings for a decent lunch before the swimming. Don't ruin it for them by trying to win everything. Losing, when everyone knows you could have won, shows true humility.'

I'd try that suggestion on Miko but doubted if Grumpy would approve of his answer.

I nodded politely.

'Well, thank you, Renouf, I think that's all. Unless you have any questions for me?'

I shook my head and turned to leave, then stopped. Dare I? 'Sir, there's just one thing. Part of my moral dilemma.'

'Go on.' His tone wasn't encouraging.

'I'm having difficulty with relationships, struggling to distinguish between love and –'

'Quite, quite, always a problem that.' He thought for a moment. 'I'm hardly the one to help. The best advice I can offer is think of Bassanio and the caskets eh? you remember? "*So may the outward shows –*"'

'"*be least themselves. The world is still deceived with ornament.*"'

'That's right. Don't be fooled by the surface emotions. Look deeper.' He paused. 'One shouldn't base one's life round Shakespeare, but he does deal with the matter rather well. Just be careful of the false emotions, especially that most dangerous of all.'

I looked puzzled.

'Think of the Moor.'

'Sir?'

'"*The green-eyed god*".'

'Jealousy?'

'That's right. Don't ever be trapped like Othello and don't be fooled by false counsel. Find the truth for yourself; even trusted friends can lie. Goodness, this serious stuff is making me thirsty. You sure you won't join me?'

I shook my head again as the headmaster drained his sherry and licked his lips in satisfaction. I started to leave.

'One moment, Jack.' I stopped in surprise at his use of my Christian name for the first time ever.

He placed his empty glass on his desk. 'How old are you?'

'Why, almost nineteen, sir.'

'Yes, yes. I know that, birthday in October, right? But that's not what I meant. How old do you think you are?'

'Sir?'

'Even though you are flippant, even facetious at times, you are essentially very serious-minded. Now that's a trait of someone closer to their thirties than twenties and it strikes me that you think too far beyond your age.'

I started to speak but he waved me into silence.

'This, uh, fascination with the opposite sex; your obvious confusion over relationships. You attempt to rationalise it all but it seems to me that you are not meeting with much success.'

I nodded in agreement. That was for certain.

'I can't advise you other than to suggest that you shouldn't be getting so involved yet. It is more sensible to wait.' He gnawed his lower lip. 'How old do you think I am?'

Now that was a devilish question. How could I avoid giving offence? He looked well into his sixties and, with his almost translucent skin and watery eyes, could be even older. 'Excuse me if I'm wrong, sir, but I would think you are about fifty.'

He laughed. 'That's very generous of you as I'm sure you think I look at least ten years older. You're pretty close though. I'm forty-four next month.' He looked at me as though there was a specific meaning in that number. I must have looked puzzled because he continued. 'Think, Jack. What would the date have been when I was your age?'

The penny dropped. '1914, sir.'

'That's right. I, too, faced your dilemma, though it was somewhat easier at my school. There were portraits of the old boys in their army uniforms stretching back generations on every wall. They were venerated.

I had a place at Oxford, due to start in that September, but in the patriotic fervour, I joined the colours. I was one of the fortunate ones, though, and apart from a small piece of shrapnel in my leg, I returned in one piece. But the things I saw, Jack, the things I saw...' he stopped.

I waited. He couldn't know that I had already had that horrific landscape painted for me by my uncle or that Miko had lacerated me further with his terrible story.

He coughed, cleared his throat. 'I'm sorry, Jack. My generation has failed. The war to end all wars hasn't and you will be faced with the same choices I had in that last glorious summer. And I'm not just talking about university.' It seemed he was on the verge of crossing a barrier of confidence with a student. 'I hope you understand what I am saying.'

I nodded and waited.

'There is going to be a war, Jack. It's not just scaremongering. You should be prepared to make a most difficult decision, as the last thing you want to take to war with you is a serious relationship. Start your studies by all means, but save your passion for your books. At least you can take some of those with you.'

He moved round to me, his hand outstretched. We shook.

'Good, luck, my boy. It's been a pleasure teaching you despite the challenges. Remember, if all else fails, read the sonnets.'

I coughed to hide my emotion. 'Thank you, sir, for everything.'

Grumpy turned back to his desk. 'Not at all, my boy, not at all.' He paused and looked out of the window, 'if I think of anything which might help, I'll let you know. Just close the door after you, there's a good chap.'

14

I'd closed the door on the rest of the school as well and spent the morning in the library tracing Miko's journey in an atlas. I'd also read some of the sonnets but couldn't absorb them, couldn't shake off the sadness of Miko's story. Surcouf, and those who thought like him, should be made to listen to such stories. But what would they hear?

I rode down to the pool at lunchtime. The tide was out so I pushed myself for thirty-two lengths of the 110 yard course. My body froze but even an hour in the cold water couldn't anesthetise my feelings.

I couldn't face school again so I took *Boadicea* for a long trip round the island. She did her best to lift my mood but even the exhilarating acceleration and the beautiful scenery failed.

I turned into Union Street at five-thirty and pulled up outside Fred's house. Rachel was waiting. She looked worried.

'What's the matter?'

'There's no one in.'

'What about Malita? Didn't she walk home with you?'

'She's not been in work. No message, nothing. I came here at lunchtime but it was all locked up. She's in trouble at work because of it. I don't know what to do.'

It wasn't unusual for Fred to disappear for a few days though I was surprised that Malita hadn't sent a message. The blinds were drawn but that was usual in this baking heat. I pulled *Boadicea* up on to her stand and eased myself off. An hour of swimming followed by several hours in the saddle had left me with concrete legs. Rachel should have laughed at my contortions but Malita's absence had spooked her. As I stumbled towards her, the Jaguar, which had been parked in the road the previous evening, crawled past. They were still wearing their hats. The driver stared at the road but the passenger examined us. His eyes were shaded by dark glasses so I couldn't read his expression. The car didn't stop.

'Who was that?'

'I don't know. They were here yesterday, parked up the road. They look a bit odd to me. Uncle Fred seemed concerned and spoke to Malita about them. I didn't hear what they said. You don't think there's a connection, do you?'

She looked puzzled. 'What do you mean? Connection? To what?'

Big mouth again. Of course, she wouldn't know much about Fred and his politics. It wasn't my place to tell her that my uncle was viewed with great suspicion by the local establishment. He claimed that his mail was steamed open and copied before it was delivered. He also claimed that all calls to and from his telephone were monitored at the exchange. Just how much was his own paranoia and how much was real, I had no idea. I knew I couldn't tell her any of that. 'Well, there's not much we can do. I can't return the bike then, shame.'

'Oh, Jack, you're not taking this seriously. I'm worried about them, but I don't know...' she tailed off as the Jaguar approached us again.

This time it slowed and pulled up behind *Boadicea.* The passenger door opened and a tall man eased himself onto the pavement. He left the door open and the driver kept the engine running. The stranger wore a grey three-piece suit with a white shirt and a red and blue striped tie. He doffed his hat towards Rachel and looked at the bike.

His voice was well modulated with no trace of an accent. 'Nice, very nice. SS 100, isn't it?'

I placed myself between him and Rachel. 'Yes, it's my uncle's. He's lent it to me.'

'You're Jack Renouf, aren't you?'

'How do you know that?'

93

'I believe you locals have a saying: "It is a small island."' He tapped the handlebar. I noticed some beads of sweat on his forehead. He must find it very hot in that suit. 'Do you know where your uncle is?' It sounded casual enough but there was an undertone in the query.

'I'm afraid I don't. He wasn't expecting me. He could be anywhere. Is he expecting you?'

'Oh, yes. He's always expecting us.'

I think he wanted to sound ironic but it came out as a sneer.

'Always on the lookout for us.'

'What do you mean? Who are you?'

'None of your concern, sonny. Sorry to have troubled you.' He doffed his hat again and retreated to the car. The driver muttered something to him. He turned back to me. 'Do you like puzzles, Jack?'

I found his use of my first name objectionable when he wouldn't tell me his so didn't answer.

'Well, here's one for you. That bike, *George VII*, you want to find out more about it? Bovington, May 13ᵗʰ 1935. Go look that up and then ask your uncle. See if his story matches the real one.' With that, he lowered himself back into the car and sat watching, waiting for us to move, as though they planned to follow, hoping perhaps that I might lead them to my uncle.

Earlier, Beresford had invited me to join him and some of the other prefects for a tour of HMS *Jersey* at six o'clock. His brother was her engineering officer and he'd arranged a private viewing. I hadn't intended on going but now, with these two watchers turning into followers, I thought it might be safer to be in company. They wouldn't think of looking for Red Fred on one of His Majesty's ships.

Ignoring them, I spoke to Rachel. 'I've been invited to look around our destroyer. Would you like to join me?'

'That sounds like fun but what's the time? I've got to get Mum and Dad's tea. No, Malita's right. Why should I have to do it all the time? They're quite capable. There'll be a row but I don't care.' She carried out this debate with herself while looking at the car.

Decision made, she walked towards *Boadicea*, swung her leg over the pillion and shuffled her bottom onto the seat. She glanced behind at the Jaguar. 'Why did he call the bike *George VII*? Didn't you tell me that was her previous name?' She giggled. 'Did your uncle steal it?'

'I doubt it but I'll be sure to ask him.' Though that was not top of my list of questions. I told Rachel to hang on then boosted the big bike off the line under full acceleration. We were around the corner before the Jaguar could react.

They caught up with us near the Weighbridge and followed all the way to the end of the Victoria Quay, where I parked up.

I had second thoughts when I saw that Beresford had invited most of the sixth form, including Saul.

'Are you prepared to meet the animals?'

She swung off the saddle, inspected her face in a wing mirror and rearranged her hair. 'Do they bite?'

'Occasionally, but only each other. They'll keep their distance from you – give them something to dream about tonight.'

She smacked my head then had another look in the mirror while I shrugged into my blazer and re-tied my tie.

Saul detached himself and walked towards us. He hugged Rachel and gave me a brief nod. He took her hand and escorted her to Beresford for introductions.

She was soon surrounded by admiring boys and quickly adopted by Beresford's brother.

Most of the crew were ashore so we were able to explore the confined spaces without any wolf whistles from sailors, though Rachel must have been aware of the probing eyes as she climbed up and down the endless companionways.

When we emerged on the open bridge, Beresford senior regaled us with a stream of facts and figures but I was distracted by Saul whispering to Rachel. I also spotted the Jaguar parked near *Boadicea* and looked, but in vain, for the two men.

As we were leaving, Saul sidled up to me. 'I want to speak to you.'

I wanted to talk with Rachel not him but there was an intensity in his voice I couldn't avoid. 'Can't it wait?'

'No, you bastard, it can't.' His raised voice provoked some curious looks amongst the group and Rachel gave a little shudder.

I was about to tell him where to go when she touched my arm. 'It's alright, Jack, I'll wait for you up there.' She pointed to the pier heads and walked off.

'Right, Mr Impatient, what's the problem?'

He pulled me aside out of earshot as the group dispersed. 'You're the problem. What have you done to Rachel?'

'What do you mean, "done"?'

'She's not the same. Look at her, she's upset. You've seen her eyes, she's been crying. And don't tell me you don't know why.' He prodded me with a nicotine stained finger, hot breath scalding my face. I stepped back, defensively.

'It's not what you think –'

'You don't know what I think. If you've taken advantage of her then I'll –'

'What? Hit me? Hurt me? You've no idea, Saul. Turf me in the harbour if you wish but there is nothing to be angry about.' I was tempted to tell him about Miko but I wouldn't say anything about Rachel's discovery about her parentage, or our new relationship.

He clenched his fists and, for one moment, I thought he was going to strike me. If he did, I knew I couldn't hit him back. I felt guilty about last night and knew I should have stopped it before we went for that swim but I couldn't change that now. I didn't know what I felt. Even Miko had recognised that.

I stared him down. He wasn't normally aggressive though he could give my father lessons in stubbornness.

Oh shit. I realised that he was the one who was hurting. His two best friends had developed a new intimacy and he was excluded. He must feel awful but what could I do or say to change that? His golden eyes were tinged with red, or was that a trick of the light?

I dropped my head and backed away. 'I'm sorry. There's nothing more I can say at the moment. Rachel wants to talk to me, now. Please excuse me.'

'You turd. You spend the entire winter raving about Caroline, bragging about her letters. Every bloody conversation we had was about her even when Rachel was there.' He lowered his voice. 'You were oblivious to Rachel, showed no feelings, treated her like another boy. Now you jump from Caroline to her like a fucking tom cat.' He walked away.

I watched his retreating back. Had I been that blind? Why did everyone expect so bloody much of me? I was yards from where I'd literally ditched Caroline twenty-four hours before. Apart from the stupidity with the towrope, we hadn't spoken since. If I didn't know what to say to Rachel, I certainly had no idea what to say to Caroline. "Sorry" would sound as pathetic as it had to Miko that morning.

I remembered Rachel was waiting for me. At least someone was.

She was gazing out over Elizabeth Castle. Several yachts were taking advantage of the tide and manoeuvring out of the harbour, calling out their destinations to pier head control as they passed. A few anglers were casting from the edge to the water, twenty feet below. Their silver spinners glittered in the evening sun. It was so peaceful, even the gulls were silent. Her arm was cold to my touch so I took my blazer off and draped it round her shoulders.

'Did you like the guided tour?'

She mumbled something but kept staring out to sea.

As a boy, I had stood there and imagined Nelson's wooden ships of the line, with their massive cannons slipping through the bay, white sails blossoming in the breeze. Over my shoulder was a metal monster, which could have sunk the entire British, French and Spanish navies in one afternoon without sustaining any damage herself. The world had moved on, science had taken over but, clever though we might be, we were still trapped by the most basic of human emotions.

Apart from the one banal question, I didn't know what to say to her, where to start. I waited, hoping that her brain was better developed in this respect than mine.

'It's very beautiful. We are so lucky, Jack. We could be in Hungary or Romania or Germany.' She stopped and contemplated the ocean again. 'I wonder how much longer we have...' she waved her right arm over the bay, 'before all this is gone.'

'Don't be silly, this isn't going. This isn't France, the continent. This stretch of water will save us.'

'I'm not being silly, Jack. I'm just worried, about me, my parents, you, Fred, Malita, and... Saul. I worry about him as well, you know.'

'And he worries about you. He thinks I've taken advantage of you.'

She looked straight through me. 'And have you, Jack? Have you?'

Perhaps my hesitation, my desire to find the right words, was answer in itself for she removed my blazer and handed it to me.

'I have to go now. I'm so tired. I don't want an argument with my... I don't even know the word, Jack. What do I call the people who adopted me?' Her eyes welled up and she brushed past.

'Rachel, let me take you home.'

'Thanks, Jack, you've done enough. I can walk. It'll give me time to think.' The fading sun was in her face, casting a long shadow behind her. The butterflies were crashing inside me again.

I gave her five minutes then trudged towards the bike. The Jaguar was gone. I could see Rachel's head as she walked over the hill. I followed, shadowing her, until she turned into Roseville Street. I waited at the junction until she reached her front door. On the way home, I rode past Fred's house. It was still empty. What a miserable day.

15

Wednesday

'Excuse me, where would I find out about something that happened on 13th May 1935, please?' I'd waited until the woman had finished stamping the cards before asking.

She looked up, disapproval behind her ornate spectacles. 'Issues this side. Returns that side. Questions at the information desk upstairs.' She reached for another batch of cards and raised her stamp. I was dismissed.

It was the first time I had used the Bibliotheque Publique in the States Building. Compared to the college library, it was massive, even intimidating.

The elderly gentleman upstairs was more helpful, almost friendly. Once he'd discovered that I was looking for something which might have happened in the UK, he directed me to the racks where back issues of the *Evening Post* were stored. 'Start there and see if there's anything in the national news. Once you've got a lead then you can try the *Telegraph* and *The Times* for the same date. We don't keep any of the others, I'm afraid.'

There was nothing about motorcycles for the 13th May so I tried the next few editions. I was about to give it up as a leg-pull, when I spotted a headline in *The Times* on 20th May. "Lawrence Dead. Fatal End to Cycle Crash."

With the help of my new friend, I found another headline from the *Daily Telegraph* of the 22nd May. "Lawrence's Death Crash at 50 to 60 M.P.H. Mystery of a Black Car. Boy Asked to Mount Cycle in Court." There followed a full report of the inquest.

I found it rather confusing as the rider was named Shaw, as well as Lawrence. I began to piece it together. Shaw or Lawrence had owned a Brough Superior SS 100, similar to Fred's, and had crashed in mysterious circumstances on 13th May. The rider was found unconscious at the scene and taken to hospital. He survived for another six days but died on the 19th. Shaw was the name he used while serving in the RAF but, in reality, he was Thomas Edward Lawrence. If the men in the car were correct, I had been riding the bike that had killed Lawrence of Arabia.

I had so many questions but the answers weren't in the news reports. Indeed, those raised questions of their own, especially about the mysterious black car and the odd facts surrounding the accident. Here was a skilled and very experienced rider who covered thousands of miles a year yet, inexplicably, lost control of his bike on the way home from the post office in Bovington. The reports hinted at some sort of conspiracy and, once I'd read his history, I could see why. This was a man who specialised in swimming against the tide and often succeeded.

According to the reports, he had been hiding from his fame for many years, though on the list of people who attended his funeral were generals, earls and well-known politicians, including Winston Churchill. While this was fascinating, I wanted to know if *Boadicea*, or *George VII*, had been his bike and how Fred had acquired it. Unfortunately, my uncle had disappeared along with the answers.

I needed to speak to Rachel but didn't want to go to her workroom. She'd told me how difficult the head seamstress was and I didn't want to get her into trouble. I would have to wait until lunchtime and try to catch her as she left. At least it was cool in the library, with its high-vaulted ceiling.

I decided to find out some more about my ghost rider and soon had a pile of books on my table. I knew I could be in the sea, but there was something comforting about digging into books in this quiet atmosphere. After all, if I wanted to study literature at Oxford, I'd be spending a lot of my time worming away out of the sun. If? What did I want to do and with whom did I want to do it? Miko was right, I still had a lot of learning to do about myself. The more I read about Lawrence though, the more I realised he had faced a similar problem until, at the age of forty-seven, it was resolved for him.

At one o'clock, I wandered out into the heat of the Royal Square, past the comatose pigeons and across King Street into the relative cool of the arcade in de Gruchys department store and waited.

Fifteen minutes later, I gave up. I'd missed her. Keeping to the shade, I walked to Fred's house.

It looked very different. The curtains had been opened. I sighed in relief. Now perhaps I could get some questions answered. I knocked on the front door and waited. There was a scuffling sound from inside then Rachel's voice. 'Who is it?'

'Me, Jack. What are you doing in there?'

The door eased open and she dragged me in. I was appalled. It looked like a Guernsey guesthouse after our water polo team had visited. Drawers were lying on the floor – paper was everywhere. Even the chess pieces were scattered about the room. Utter chaos.

Rachel looked very upset. 'Malita wasn't at work again so I came straight here at lunchtime. I knocked on the door and tried the handle. It was open so I came in. The lock's been forced. I've never seen anything like it. We must tell the police.'

'Wait. Let's just check first.' I wasn't sure Fred would want the police poking around his house but couldn't tell Rachel that. I wanted to see if this was a burglary, or whether someone had been searching the place. Fred and Malita didn't have many treasures and, from a quick inspection, there didn't seem to be anything missing. My uncle, well aware of the official interest in his affairs, would have hidden anything of importance.

Even his workshop had been vandalised, though the sight in the sitting room that met me was more upsetting. They'd systematically worked their way through his record collection and taken a hammer to Caruso, Gigli, and Bjorling. They were clearly not opera lovers and this savage behaviour made my stomach lurch. I picked up the pieces and resolved to replace as many of his precious records as I could, whatever the cost. I wondered if the men in the car had been involved. I looked out of the window but there was no sign of them.

Fred had converted one of the bedrooms into a workroom for Malita as she did some private dressmaking. They'd smashed her sewing machine and torn up her pattern books. Rachel started to cry when she found the mess. I knew they were planning to start their own business together and Rachel hoped to persuade her father to let them rent one of his shops for a reduced rate. They both wanted their independence so this was very important to her. The wrecked machine and ruined pattern books would be difficult to replace. This wasn't mindless and it wasn't a robbery. It was a cold, calculated and vicious warning. It might even have come from the police themselves.

'I think we should wait until they return before we go to the police,' I suggested.

'But what about the house? We can't leave it unlocked. We can't leave it like this. We don't know where they are, when they are coming back or even if ...' She stopped; the next thought was too horrible. She was right. We had to inform the police, officially. At least they would then have to do something.

I still felt dubious though. 'Let's just give it until this evening. They might be back then.'

'No, Jack, I'm going to report this now. You can come if you want or... please yourself, but I'm going.'

She picked her way over the littered floor and out into the dusty street.

I checked the door but could see no sign of forced entry. I closed it and followed a hundred yards behind as she marched towards the town hall.

She was standing at the counter as I entered the paid police area. Fortunately, Rachel had gone to the Bluebottles rather than the on-duty centenier, who might have been my dear friend Phillips. A uniformed constable was talking to her but stopped when I arrived.

He scrutinised me. 'That's it. I knew I'd seen you before.' He looked back at Rachel with a smirk. 'But now he's arrived, I remember where. Of course you're wearing more clothes now.'

I watched her face turn crimson and felt a growing nausea in my own belly.

She recovered first. 'Stop leering. That's all over.'

'Not if you've got a memory and a bright torch, young lady.' He looked her up and down. If anything, the smirk was larger now.

I pushed in front of her. 'We've come to report a break-in, not to be humiliated. Can you deal with it, or is there someone else more sensible you can call?' Big mouth, still out of control.

He pulled the leather bound incident ledger across the counter. 'Right, sonny. Escaped from school, have we? Name?'

'Renouf, Jack. You probably know my uncle, Jurat Poingdestre.'

He lifted the pen and pointed it at me. 'Listen, Master Renouf. I don't care if your uncle is Neville Chamberlain. You have a complaint. We do this by the book.'

That would soon change when he found out my other uncle's name, I guessed.

'I've told you already. We want to report a break-in,' Rachel said.

'Name?'

'Oh for God's sake. Vibert, Rachel Vibert.'

'You don't have an uncle to impress me with?'

'Excuse me, but are you local?' I asked.

'No, but what is with you people? Does it matter? I'm from Southampton and we do things properly there. We don't care about people's uncles.'

'That's a shame because this break-in has occurred at my uncle's house.'

'What, Jurat Poingdestre's?'

'No, Frederick Le Brun, 18a Union Street. Just around the bloody corner.'

'That's enough of that.' He scratched his head. 'Le Brun, you say. That rings a bell.'

A bloody big one, I said to myself. 'Yes, his house has been broken into and smashed up.'

'Where is he, this Frederick Le Brun?'

'We don't know. We haven't seen him or his...' how could I describe Malita? 'companion since yesterday. They've... disappeared.'

'Did I hear someone say Frederick Le Brun?' Another policeman, this time a sergeant, poked his head around the partition.

'Yes, my uncle.' Time for big mouth again. 'You might know him as Red Fred.'

The sergeant grimaced. 'I'll deal with this, Stokes. You two, wait there.'

He disappeared and we waited.

After a few minutes, another man, wearing a crumpled suit, entered from the office door, clutching a panama hat.

'I'm Inspector Le Feuvre. Yes, we know your uncle. I suggest we walk there and have a look at this break-in. As you say, it's just around the corner.' His smile was predatory. Fred was going to kill me for this.

He seemed to know the way so we followed him. When we reached the front door, I realised how foolish I'd been. If the police were intercepting his mail and monitoring his phone, wouldn't they just love an opportunity to be invited into his house when he wasn't there to watch them?

Rachel must have read my mind as she stepped in front of the inspector. 'Perhaps we should wait until he gets back.'

'What, and leave the place unlocked? Do you have a key?'

'No.'

'In that case, I think we should look inside and I'll get a photographer to record the damage.'

'No, wait. I can get the place locked up. My father's a builder. He'll put a new lock on the door,' Rachel volunteered.

'Just one moment, young lady. You've reported a crime and now you seem to be trying to stop the police investigating it. That's a crime in itself.'

I stepped in. 'Perhaps not, Inspector. The issue is security. If we can lock the place up, you can keep an eye on it until my uncle returns. It is private property, after all.' I looked at Rachel for help before I started digging myself in any deeper.

She mouthed, 'Jurat'. Of course, he was local and would understand.

I lowered my voice. 'I tell you what. I'll pop down to my Uncle Ralph's office, Jurat Poingdestre, and see if he agrees.' Fat chance of that. Ralph despised Fred even more than my father did but would the inspector know that?

He was debating my suggestion when I had another inspiration. 'Two men in a black Jaguar have been observing the house. They might know what happened. Why don't you ask them?'

'Ask whom? Where are these men? Can you describe them? Do you have the registration number of their car?'

Good questions, to which I had no good answers.

'Yes, the car number was J 478.' Rachel replied. 'Perhaps you know them?'

He glared at us. 'I'll check. We have your names.' He turned away. 'You'll be hearing from us. I will note that you are taking responsibility for this house. I suggest you contact the insurers and let them know what has happened. You, Renouf, seem very much like Mr Le Brun. I'm not sure if that's a good thing for you.' He marched off.

'Cripes. I don't believe what we've just done or why. What's going on, Jack? Why don't you want them in there?'

'You know that Fred is a Communist?'

'Of course, everyone does. It's hardly a secret though I'm not sure what it means.'

'I can't really help you there but he believes the authorities are out to get him.'

She looked puzzled. 'But he's harmless, isn't he?'

'Obviously not. Look at this mess. The police seemed very interested. My father thinks he's dangerous, Uncle Ralph hates the sight of him. He's also got some connections to other Communists in England and France, I think – has Malita ever said anything to you about his politics?'

'No, the sort of things we talk about would bore you men senseless in minutes. The price of lining, how to get five skirts out of a bolt of cloth instead of four –'

'I see what you mean. You probably don't have any time left for gossip, do you?'

She laughed.

I looked at my watch. 'Can you get your father to put a new lock on the door?'

'Of course not. He wouldn't do that without the owner's instructions and guarantee of payment. It bought us some time though. Why didn't you tell me before?'

I shrugged. 'Sorry, I didn't think you needed to know.'

'You've got to start trusting me, Jack.' She sighed. 'Well, what are we going to do? We can't stand guard here forever.'

'Leave it to me. I'll get a hasp and padlock and fit them to the back door. I'll fit a sliding bolt to the front door from the inside. I noticed there are some in Fred's workshop. I'm sure I can find enough undamaged tools.' It was a simple enough job. If I could strip a tractor, I could secure a door. I should have thought of that before we went to the police station.

I took her hands in mine. Despite the heat, they were cool. 'I'm sorry... for everything. I'll deal with this now. You go back to work.' She smiled at me; she looked so vulnerable, my heart lurched.

'Shall we meet later? Here, this evening, say seven-thirty?' She hadn't let go my hands. Hers felt soft and vital.

'That's fine. I've got to go home and tell my father about this before the police get to him. There are some other things I have to tell you as well, about the bike and,' I paused, then squeezed her fingers, 'other, more important things, about us –'

She removed her hands and placed one finger on my lips. 'Shush. That can wait. We mustn't be late tonight. I need some sleep. Remember, we've both got a big day tomorrow. You've got to get that qualifying time.'

'And you're trying to relieve Caroline of the springboard-diving cup.'

In all the chasing about, I'd almost forgotten. How could I? I would be up against Fletcher and Rachel had a fight on her hands to win the trophy, which had been donated by Caroline's father.

Miko had been training us for those competitions, had made them our main focus. Like most of the club, I would be rooting for Rachel, though I had a very different reason now.

16

Father claimed there was always work to do on a farm, though it seemed Mum was the one who did most of it. She wanted to know why I was home so early and I gave her an excuse about having to come back to collect some kit. In truth, I was meant to be weeding some old widow's garden as part of the college's community service programme. Mrs Buezval was a dear and I was sure she wouldn't report me. She'd be disappointed but I'd try to get there before the end of the week to save her from the rampaging chickweed and dandelion.

Mum swallowed my story then insisted I swallow some lunch. I hadn't felt hungry for a couple of days but I didn't want an argument and didn't want to explain that I was so confused that hunger had switched itself off.

'Where's Father?'

'You haven't eaten much. Are you feeling alright, love?' She pointed at my plate.

'I'm fine. It's all this training. I think my stomach has shrunk. Is he coming in for lunch?'

'You know your father, busy, busy, busy.' Her tone was ironic. 'He took his rifle. I think he's gone to the top field. Trying to relive his youth – imagine he's with Alan at Bisley.'

That was a frightening thought. According to Fred, my father had been a sniper in the trenches and hadn't wasted any bullets. He'd been the JRA champion many times since and was still fascinated enough with paper targets to compete most weekends. I sometimes wondered if Alan had chosen shooting over swimming so that he could be closer to our father. It was clear to everyone that he worshipped him. I often felt left out but then Alan would argue that I couldn't do anything wrong in Mum's eyes. Apart from not eat, that is.

I debated whether I should tell her about Fred and Malita's disappearance but she was such a worrier and I didn't want to see her upset. Alan was right – we were very close. I watched her fussing around in the kitchen. She might be forty-eight but she was still very attractive, beautiful in certain lights. I wondered what she must have looked like at eighteen. There were some posed photographs but I couldn't visualise her. I'd never seen her in a bathing costume and I tried to imagine the scene where Father and Phillips were fighting over her.

Sometimes I found it difficult to understand why she put up with my father, even more difficult to accept that they had a close relationship. He ranted about everything but she never rose to his bait. If he wanted an argument, he turned on me, knowing how easy it was to get a response.

She stopped, aware of my scrutiny, and smiled at me the way only a mother can. A smile which asked if there was something I needed to tell her.

There was, but I couldn't. Instead, I felt guilty because I had so many secrets I couldn't share with her. If I started talking about Rachel and Caroline, I knew she'd pry everything out of me and I couldn't face that.

I tried harder with the beef stew and made a little progress, by dropping a few scraps for Alan's cat, Tonto, while she wasn't looking – sufficient to clear space on my plate so that she let me scoot off to find my father.

I heard the sharp crack of the Lee-Enfield as I approached the field. We'd set up a 200 yard range in the top field and built some earthen butts to protect our neighbours from flying bullets. I practised occasionally and it was useful to have such an exposed field with varying wind conditions.

Given his volatile nature, I was surprised that Alan had mastered the art of quiet calculation, controlled breathing and the iron patience that was necessary to hit targets consistently at long range.

I approached him and picked up the spotting scope. His grouping was immaculate. I imagined a soldier's helmet and what would happen to it, and the head it contained, when struck by a bullet travelling faster than the speed of sound. I shuddered.

He rose from the prone position, removed his ear protectors then noticed me. He looked startled. 'What the hell are you doing, sneaking up on me like that, you blithering idiot?'

A good start. 'Sorry, Mum told me you were here –'

'She didn't tell you to go out and get yourself shot, did she?'

I hadn't taken any risks, but he was angry because he hadn't spotted me. I didn't tell him any of this. I needed him calm. 'Sorry.' I suppressed the rest just in case it might be construed as sarcastic.

'What do you want? Why aren't you in school, drooling over Shakespeare?'

In his anger, he'd given me a clue. I knew he didn't have much time for acting, had come to watch me play Shylock under sufferance and dire threats from my mother, but he'd never been this blunt before. I wondered if he thought I was turning into some sort of "nancy boy". That would be the end. Perhaps he'd been teased by some of his friends about his "actor" son. He was a man almost throttled by pride. With a Communist for a brother-in-law and now an "artiste" for an elder son, he would make a cheap target for his Masonic brethren.

I was tempted to walk away to avoid another argument but I realised that the police would call soon about Fred and it would be a lot better if I told him before that happened.

'No. It's more serious. Uncle Fred has disappeared and his house has been broken into.'

He stared at me then started to laugh. 'That's not serious. It's no more than the commie bugger deserves. I hope they burned his bloody books.'

'That's bloody unfair. Malita is missing as well. You haven't seen what they've done. His house is wrecked.'

'Don't you bloody swear at me, young man! Why are you sticking your nose into that bugger's affairs, anyway? It's got nothing to do with you. And why aren't you in school? I'm not paying bloody fees for you to swan around the bloody island.'

109

'You don't pay bl... fees for me. I got the scholarship – remember? It's Alan you pay the fees for.'

'Don't you raise your voice to me. You're not too old for a thrashing, you know.'

He meant that. He was right, I wasn't too old and he certainly could give me a thrashing. Perhaps he needed to slap me around a bit. Get rid of some of his anger. But could I take it without fighting back?

'Why do you hate me so much?' I'd said what I'd been thinking for months. Now for the consequences.

He snorted. 'Grow up. You sound like a bloody girl.' He pressed closer to me. 'Here, this came for you this morning. I opened it.' He shoved a folded envelope towards me.

I could see it was a telegram. I unfolded it and extracted the single sheet. It was addressed to me. "IN FRANCE STOP RETURN WED EVE STOP FM ENDS". I exhaled with relief.

'Not serious at all, was it?'

Grumpy had explained that the word sarcasm had its roots in Greek and meant to "tear the flesh". Mine felt suitably shredded but I didn't mind. Fred and Malita were safe and I needed to tell Rachel. I didn't need to fight with my father, didn't care anymore if he hated me or not. I turned away and started to walk back.

'Where do you think you're going? I haven't finished with you yet.' He reached out and grabbed my arm.

His fingers were like a vice. He wanted to hurt me. I felt the control slipping from me. I couldn't let him do this. I had to fight back. I would have the chance for one punch before he flattened me. I would have to make it count. I clenched my fist and prepared to swing.

'Monsieur Renouf, Monsieur, *aidez nous*.' It was Loïc, one of our Breton workers. He was running towards us as though his shirt tails were on fire.

The vice was unclamped from my arm as Father turned to Louis. 'What is it?'

The Breton skidded to a halt and screeched at us in rapid French that Victor had escaped and was loose in the yard looking for some cows to hump.

110

'That's it. I've had enough of that bloody animal.' Father shoved me aside, grabbed his rifle and strode off towards the farmhouse.

I followed. Loïc traipsed along behind, happy to keep us between him and the rampaging bull.

According to Loïc, Victor had charged the gate and burst through it. I don't think Father believed that any more than I did. Victor might be vicious but he wasn't stupid and had worked out from previous experience that his nose was soft and the metal bars were hard. Someone must have forgotten to secure it. The only one who went into that field was Mum. I didn't want her shot as well, so I thought I had better keep close to Father.

If Victor hadn't been so dangerous, I would have found the scene in the yard quite amusing. Corentin and Katell were on the roof of the cowshed hurling Breton insults at Victor, who was testing the door with his snout.

There were two pregnant cows in the shed. The rest were in the lower field, which was fenced off. Victor would soon realise he couldn't get to any of them and start on anything soft he could find to batter. That included Fred's bike, which I had left outside the house.

Father stopped, ejected the magazine and started loading .303 cartridges. One of those would go straight through the bull at this range. I wasn't surprised he wanted to shoot him. We'd barely recovered the cost of his purchase in servicing fees before he revealed a truculence as dark as his chocolate coat.

Word had spread that he'd broken the back of an expensive young cow during a violent mating and now no farmer would risk his services, however much Father offered to cut the price. Just standing still, he was costing a fortune in feed. It was Mum's misplaced affection that kept him from the abattoir. Father couldn't stand disobedience and Victor had crossed him once too often.

He clicked the magazine into place. For once, I didn't disagree with him. I just hoped it would be a clean shot. I didn't think Father would miss but he might want him to suffer a bit first. I chided myself for the uncharitable thought but I believed him capable of it. He raised the rifle and took aim just as the kitchen door opened and Mum walked out holding something in her hand. She hadn't seen us.

'Stop. Don't shoot!' I grabbed for his arm.

She heard that and so did Victor. He raised his great head and searched for the source of the shout.

Mum looked up and spotted us. 'Put your gun down, Aubin. I'll deal with this. Don't you dare shoot Victor.'

'Stand back, Mary. He's dangerous. Get back in the house.'

She ignored him and called to Victor. He recognised her voice and lowered his head as though ready to charge. Father kept the rifle aimed as Mum approached the bull. She reached out her hand. He snorted and pawed the ground.

I could see his flanks heaving and realised that he was confused. We'd trained him to hump cows. Why were we stopping him? Perhaps he was in as much emotional turmoil as me. I felt sympathy for him. Poor, dumb animal. Mum got closer, blocking a shot to Victor's head. She patted his neck with her left hand and pressed her right to his mouth. He nuzzled it while she slipped her left along his head to the nose ring. She pulled his head up until we could see that she was feeding him sugar cubes. Docile now, he allowed her to lead him back to his field. As she passed us, she winked.

Later, having polished off the equivalent of two lunches to my half of one, Father cleared the table and started stripping his rifle. Mum flicked at his head with her apron but didn't make any other comment as she placed mugs of tea in front of us. I didn't know what the female equivalent of *cojones* was but she had them.

'Are you going to tell him, Aubin?' She prodded him with her finger.

'No.'

'Why not?'

'I was going to wait until Alan got back, tell them together.'

She looked at me but spoke to him. 'That's silly. I'll tell him then.'

'As you wish.' From his tone he certainly didn't. He continued to clatter the rifle bits around the table to make his point.

'What is it I am to be or not to be told?'

'Huh, more bloody Shakespeare.'

'Aubin, please no swearing in the house. You promised,

remember.' Her voice was soft and he muttered something as he pulled the cleaning cloth through the barrel of the disassembled rifle.

'Ignore him, love. We've got some good news. We got the cheque from the merchant this morning for the spuds. It's much larger than we thought so Dad is going to install a telephone.'

I looked up in disbelief. He had railed about the expense so often even though it must have been very inconvenient for his business and for running the Masonic Lodge.

'And that's not all. We're going to have a bathroom.'

Now I was surprised. How often had he declared that toilets were for namby-pambies? Real men pissed in the cow shed, shivered in the thunder box and washed under the pump in the yard. Only women were allowed to use the honey bucket.

At least we had showers at school and Saul's apartment had everything the modern family needed, including central heating. So he'd given into Mum at last. Good for her. Two little bits of civilisation were about to invade the wilds of St Martin.

'He's taking me into Romerils to choose the suite, aren't you, dear?'

I'd like to be a fly on the wall when they were choosing. I pitied the salesman who would have to deal with them.

'That's enough. Don't get too excited. We're just getting the basics. No fancy colours and you're not going to be prettying yourself up in there every day. The soakaway won't cope with it.' He sounded gruff enough but I suspected he was pleased to be able to afford to provide her dream at last. He'd die rather than show that though. One day I would understand him, perhaps.

I looked at my watch and lied. 'I have to get back to school for the match.' I wanted to get the news about Fred and Malita to Rachel. I couldn't wait until seven-thirty to see her again.

'Take it easy, love, on that big bike.'

Father slotted the bolt back into the rifle with a loud slap. His tone was harsh. 'I don't want to see that thing here again. Take it back to your uncle and leave it there. Use your own. You were quick enough to ask for the money to buy it.'

Another example of his selective memory. I'd worked for every penny, but there was no point in arguing. I wanted to get away from him before we started fighting again.

'I'll get the bus home. See you later.' I pecked Mum on the cheek, grabbed my cricket kit, to maintain the charade, and eased out of the door before he could complete the rifle's assembly and start practising on me.

17

I checked the padlock on the back door. As far as I could see, no one had tampered with it. I didn't want Malita to see the devastation in her home but felt that it would be unwise to clear it up. Fred might find some clues. I'd have to make sure I met him before he got home.

I rode to the harbour to check the boat schedule. Because of the low tides, the *Brittany* was due in much earlier than I expected, at six-thirty. I'd have to meet Rachel from work at five, or she'd miss them. I couldn't imagine he would come back from France by any other means.

I didn't want to spend any more time indoors and I didn't feel like training. I could go and see Miko but he would be working. Of course, I could go and do some weeding for the widow, but I decided to head out west and have a bit of fun in the surf.

No wind plus slack tide equalled no surf so I bought some suntan cream from the kiosk at Le Braye, changed into my costume and tried to toast myself to Nutty's colour.

Stretched out on the hot sand, I thought about Caroline and Rachel and engaged in the fruitless pursuit of comparing and scoring their attributes. I fell asleep before I got below their necks and was dreaming about tulips when some kindly soul prodded me awake, claiming she could smell burning flesh.

I missed Rachel again. She'd be upset if she thought I hadn't bothered to tell her and I didn't want her wandering in just as Fred and Malita arrived at their devastated house. I knew her father wouldn't have a telephone so I would have to go to her house. Perhaps I was being stupid again but I needed to see her, talk with her, touch her.

Her father opened the door. I'd never been this close to him before. He was tall, broad, well-dressed and very grey. He filled the doorway. He didn't look happy.

'Sorry to trouble you, Mr Vibert, but is Rachel in?'

He inspected me as he would a piece of timber infested with woodworm. He weighed his response. 'Not for you.' And shut the door.

I stood there quivering with frustration and a growing rage. How bloody rude. He might bully his daughter but he wasn't going to bully me. I banged on the door. I waited. I could hear raised voices. The door swung open and he stood there holding a walking stick. The greyness had gone. His face was now a vivid red.

His voice held an anger far greater than mine. 'The police have been. I do not want you to see my daughter again, ever!' He punctuated his words by banging the stick on the tiled floor. 'Leave. You are not welcome.'

'But, Mr Vibert –'

'Go!' he roared.

I went.

His vehemence was still ringing in my head an hour later as I watched the British Rail steamer slip through the pier heads. I spotted Fred and Malita on the upper deck and waved. They spoke to each other and Malita gave a puzzled wave back. Of course, they weren't expecting me.

Once they were through immigration, I rushed up, still bristling with anger and injustice.

'Yak, this is nice surprise.' Malita hugged me.

Fred looked concerned. 'What's happened?'

I start to blurt it out in a frenzy of words. He dropped his case and pulled me aside, away from the other passengers.

'Not here. Let's walk back. Tell us on the way.'

We left *Boadicea* and, by the time we reached his house, they had the full story, including my confrontation with Mr Vibert. I did leave

116

out the bit about the nude swimming but realised that I would have to explain the police interest in us soon. I unlocked the back door and gave him the key.

They picked their way over the mess. Fred scratched his head. 'Shameful, brutish, but not unexpected.' He picked up the kettle and started to fill it. 'Jack, clear some space at the table, we need to have a chat.'

'I think you need to see the rest of the house, Uncle. They've been very thorough.'

'I expect they have but there was nothing important here. That's why they smashed it up. They didn't find what they wanted.'

Malita collected the teapot and some cups. 'You right. We go to France in time.'

She sounded so calm. I had expected her to explode, cry, rage, but she seemed to accept this violation of her home as unexceptional. Of course, they had experienced far worse in Spain. She shrugged out of her coat, picked up their two small cases and placed them in the hallway. I heard her footsteps on the stairs and waited for some response to the wreckage upstairs, but there was none – just the sounds of clearing up.

Fred clapped a hand on my shoulder. 'Don't be upset, Jack. It's just objects. No one has been hurt. You did well, keeping that fascist Le Feuvre out. He may have swapped his black shirt for a blue uniform but he's still a bastard. I'll tell you about him one day.' A wicked grin creased his face. 'You must realise that you're in the black book as well now.'

'Will you ask the police to investigate?'

He laughed. 'They haven't seen inside, have they?'

'Not while we were looking.'

'If they turn up, I'll tell them a couple of cats must have got in somehow and gone berserk. I'll say I forgot to lock the door. They know who did this. They won't bother me anymore. They'll have a good laugh at the station.'

'Why, Uncle? Why do they hate you so much?'

He brushed some broken china off a chair, sat down and poured the tea. 'No milk I'm afraid, they smashed the bottles as well.' He wrinkled his nose at the black liquid then blew on it before he answered. 'The police don't hate me as such. It's business, purely business. I dare to be different, challenge the oligarchy that runs this island. A few years ago I helped set up a union for the dockers. The masters were spitting feathers. We demanded a decent wage, threatened to strike if we didn't get it. You know what they did?'

'No.'

'The biggest shipping company hired casual non-union labour at a much lower rate. We persuaded them to join the union as well. The masters sacked them. Then, and this is the struggle we face, Jack, the bastards got the parish to send those unemployed who were claiming relief to unload the boats for nothing. Bloody difficult to fight that.' He grinned. 'But we beat them in the end. Jersey's now a closed port. They have to use union labour. We have to watch the masters all the time though. They'll use any little trick to increase their profit at our expense.'

My father had said something about the union menace but I hadn't made the connection at the time. 'Are you still organising the union then?'

He laughed. 'No. The Transport and General Workers Union sent someone from the UK to do that. Let's say we didn't see eye to eye. He's an appeaser. Wants to work with the masters. I want to rub their noses in it and use the power of massed labour to level things out. I got my marching orders but the fight isn't over yet. Anyway, don't worry about the police, most of them are union members. They're paid to protect the law. They just follow orders.'

Like the border guards in Romania. I wondered if my uncle wasn't being a little naïve.

'I know what you're thinking, Jack. Perhaps you're right. It starts with property, broken windows, wrecked businesses, then they move on to breaking people. Don't worry, that's not going to happen here. In a few months, they'll have bigger fish to fry. The world is about to be turned upside down, Jack.' He got up and walked to the window. 'They're back, I see.'

I peered over his shoulder. The Jaguar was parked up the road. Perhaps I should tell him about the search they had sent me on. He moved into the hall and came back with his suitcase. He placed it

118

on the table and opened it. 'The real irony is that I seem to have united two opposing factions.'

'Uncle, the men in the car told me to check –'

He ignored me. 'I'm prepared for them, they won't break in again.' He lifted a bundle from the case and unwrapped it. I watched, fascinated, as the protective cloth dropped onto the table and he was left holding a black revolver.

18

Thursday

He pointed the black Webley revolver at me with a malevolent grin. A sudden gust of wind rippled across the water. I looked away from Phillips and forced my eyes to focus on the glittering stars sparkling off my lane.

'Your Excellency, Lieutenant Commander McKillop, Mr Hayden-Brown, ladies, gentlemen and members of His Majesty's Ship *Jersey*, welcome. We hope you will enjoy our short gala. I say short because, as you can see, the tide will be upon us very soon. No need to panic in the stalls, it's a small twenty-six footer and will just creep over the walls. Nevertheless, we have to finish by three o'clock, as our guests have to be at Springfield for the official presentations to the ship. We hope that, once we have finished here, you will be able to join them. Please come back this evening though as we have Tommy Arnold and his band playing on the Blue Terrace. Refreshments will be available and admission is only one shilling and sixpence.'

Brewster paused, looked around and, catching the steely glint in the lieutenant governor's eye, as well as his hissed "get on with it man", brought a halt to his commercial and picked the programme up from the table. 'We will start with the swimming, then a springboard diving competition. Following that, tide permitting, there will be a water polo match: Jersey Swimming Club versus HMS *Jersey* and guests.'

The governor hooked out his fob watch and held it up. There were titters of amusement in the crowd. Hearing the laughter, the manager bowed towards the governor, picked up his programme and announced, 'The first race today, in our match with the Royal Navy, is the men's one hundred yards freestyle.'

The governor nudged the captain of the destroyer, who was sitting alongside him and showed him the watch. Brewster caught the movement and hurried on.

'Representing the Royal Navy and HMS *Jersey*, in lane one, is Petty Officer Sims.' An enthusiastic cheer rang out from the spectators clustered around the pool. The lookout was full and younger members dangled their legs from the four diving platforms. Further along, the paying public and members of the ship's company sat in the lunchtime sun on the benches and small grandstand. I spotted Caroline's father, who had donated a trophy, sitting with the official party. He looked less than comfortable in the heat. I couldn't remember the last time my parents had made the effort to watch me compete. Rachel's had never been.

The fifty-yard course was enclosed in this bowl of expectation as Brewster's amplified voice cut through the shouts.

'In lane two, representing the Jersey Swimming Club, please welcome Gerry Fletcher.' The volume doubled as the locals welcomed the senior champion. I continued to stare at the water, trying to see it as a tunnel through which I had to swim. Miko had tapped my head before I had changed. *You win or lose in here!*

'Please welcome, swimming in lane three as a guest of the Royal Navy, the Universities Champion of the Netherlands over one hundred metres, Mr Rudi Kohler.' The cheers were generous though not overwhelming.

I tried to see beneath the sparkling surface to the sand and weed ten feet below.

'Finally, in lane four, representing the Jersey Swimming Club, holder of the junior one hundred yards record, please welcome, Jack Renouf.' A partisan roar echoed around the small amphitheatre and I bit my lip to hide any smile. Brewster always overdid it on these occasions.

'Timekeepers, judges?' The officials raised their hands. 'Mr Starter?'

Phillips cleared his throat. 'Competitors!'

The four of us stepped down onto the concrete blocks and

shuffled our feet. I tried to ignore Kohler on my right. He'd already dived in and swum half a length and back, as a warm up. To show off his muscles, he'd grasped the concrete wall and hoisted himself the three feet up to the starting blocks.

Fletcher had bent down, splashed his face with a handful of seawater, rinsed his mouth with it then sprayed the residue into the Dutchman's lane.

The petty officer had kept his tracksuit on until the last possible moment, no doubt hoping the retained body warmth would protect him for the length of the race.

I'd followed Miko's advice and gone through a stretching routine to warm my muscles rather than cool them down with a quick plunge like the Dutchman. At least I wouldn't see him on the first fifty yards as, despite Miko's best efforts, I hadn't mastered bi-lateral breathing. I wouldn't be able to see Fletcher either. I would have a face full of both of them on the way back though.

'Competitors!' Phillips' voice boomed out across the water. 'Take your marks.'

The four of us crouched down. I touched my fingers to the concrete either side of my toes. Phillips raised his starting pistol and held us for what seemed like minutes before pulling the trigger and shattering the air with the booming report of the blank cartridge. Seagulls screeched in fright as I launched myself into space.

I sliced into the water at a flat angle, stinging my chest and thighs, submerging, torpedo-like, for several yards before my momentum propelled me to the surface in a cascade of spray. I stretched my right arm to its full length and caught the green surface with my cupped hand. My neck turned with the roll and my mouth sucked in air as I pulled through, letting my left arm swing over to complete the stroke. My feet kicked hard from the hips, stabilising my body as I crawled over the water. I completed two full strokes before my next breath, blowing the air and salt water out through my mouth and nostrils when my face submerged. I could see the rope, lined with cork floats, inches from my face and corrected on the next pull cycle to centre myself in the lane.

Most of the spectators and all of the swimmers were on my blind side. I could see the distant wall and the raft, under which Rachel...

122

I stifled that thought and ploughed on. I could sense Kohler in the next lane but couldn't tell whether he was ahead or behind.

The Dutchman's feet were pounding away much faster than mine. That could be a mistake as the large leg muscles use up far more oxygen than the arms with little added benefit. I feathered my kick, saving the energy I would need for the final sprint. I surged on, trying to capture that elusive feeling of floating over the water, to slip into that rhythm which made best use of my muscle efficiency. I had to stay calm, not thrash at the water, and try to fight my way ahead. *'Don't think. Swim. You think, you sink!'* Miko's final words.

On the next cycle, I raised my head to sneak a glance at the wall. It was a couple of complete strokes away as I focused on preparing my body for the flip. I had to drop my right shoulder, roll onto my back, wait for my hand to touch the wall then rotate quickly into a somersault. I would then be in position for my feet ready to push off and aim for the surface or I could play safe and spin-turn with one arm on the wall. Bugger that, I'd practised this flip so many times now, I could do it. If I failed, I would be smelling Kohler's feet.

Now or never. I sucked in a deeper breath, reached with my right arm, rolled, felt for the wall then tucked my chin into my chest, pulled my knees up and rotated backwards. The sky disappeared into a blur of dark green as I somersaulted. Miraculously, my feet were in position, knees still bent to allow me to use the full spring effect as I thrust forwards, aiming for the light.

I held the glide until I broke surface and reached out for my next stroke. Success – I'd carried my speed and must have gained at least a yard on Kohler. I rotated my head to breathe and now I could see the others. *Blast his eyes*, Kohler had flipped as well and had edged ahead of me. I was level with his waist. I needed to catch him, whirl my arms, sprint after him but Miko's voice whispered in my head. *Patience, he use too much energy. Wait, he tire. Keep rhythm. Wait.* The voice was right, I had to keep it smooth, keep the sense of gliding over the water.

On the next breath, I could see Kohler's elbows. The others were just a fountain of spray behind the two of us. I concentrated on pulling with my left arm and held my breath for a double stroke. On the next left rotation, I could see Kohler's shoulders alongside mine. I felt calm, in control. I increased the pace and my leg-beat. The air exploded from my nostrils and mouth as I extended my whole body down the imaginary centre line of the lane. I could hear muffled shouts as we reached the halfway point of the length. On my next breath, I was aware of the crowd standing and I pulled harder still as my face rotated back. I could see the sandy bottom ten feet down; too deep to see our shadows as we sped across the surface.

Fifteen yards to go and the high wall loomed in front of us. Now! I kicked hard, took a deep breath and signalled full speed to my arms. I felt my body rise and I stretched as far as I could before catching and powering my forearms back to my sides. The wall filled my horizon and, with lungs bursting, pulse pounding in my ears, I reached for the smooth surface. I sensed a shadow sweep past on my left before my hand slammed into the unyielding concrete and I stopped dead. I'd left it too late.

Gasping and wheezing, I clung onto the wall, aware of the timekeepers crouching above me. I pushed off and paddled back a few yards, conscious now of the tumult in the crowd. I knew I'd lost. I turned to look at Kohler, who was hanging on his lane rope. The Dutchman reached out his hand to shake mine. Our fingers touched. Fletcher and the petty officer were also shaking hands.

I looked up at the recorder's desk. There was a heated conversation taking place. Three timekeepers and my lane judge were arguing with Mr Brewster. I looked back at the turn. There was no red flag so I hadn't been disqualified.

I trod water, trying to get my breathing back to normal. Miko had been right again – too much thinking. I didn't want to leave the water – wanted to swim away to the far wall and slip over into the rising tide. I'd let him down. I didn't know what I feared most – the sorrowful shake of Miko's head or the arrogant smirk on Kohler's face. I was trapped. I would have to hide my disappointment from the crowd with a brave smile. I practised beaming at the wall while we waited for the starter to release us. It seemed to be taking a long time.

Phillips got a signal from the table and waddled towards us. I was sure he was scowling at me.

'Competitors, please leave by the steps.'

I was closest so ducked under the rope and swam underwater, grateful for the coolness on my overheated face. I emerged and climbed the short flight to stand behind the officials.

The loudspeakers burst into life. 'Your Excellency, Lieutenant Commander McKillop, Mr Hayden-Brown, ladies and gentlemen, the result of the one hundred yards freestyle race. First, in a new "All Comers" record time of fifty-three and one tenth of a second – Mr Kohler.' The crowd gasped at the time, which was seconds faster than anyone had ever swum before in this pool. I held my breath – I hadn't been that far behind. I must have broken my personal best at least. Brewster waited for the applause to subside. 'Second, in a Jersey Swimming Club, Island, Channel Islands, and Southern Counties record time of fifty-three and seven tenths seconds, Jack Renouf.'

The roar from the crowd drowned the rest of the results. I was stunned. I had broken the minute by over six seconds. My eyes stung from more than the salt. Hands slapped my shoulders and Brewster left his table to congratulate me. I felt dazed.

Saul stepped through the crowd and hugged me, careless of the salt water on his linen suit. He took his hat off and placed it on my head, grabbed my wrist and waved my arm aloft. I followed the line of his arm and saw Grumpy standing in the front row of the lookout. Our eyes met and he smiled – gave me the thumbs up sign. I guessed he believed I had heeded his advice and thrown the race. I looked around. How many more believed that I had put discretion before valour? If only they knew that I had given everything I had to beat him. Kohler would know and that was punishment enough.

I'd broken all the records and had now qualified for the Southern Counties Olympic training programme. I should be overjoyed but instead I felt angry with myself. In all the tumult, I had missed the rest of the results. I lowered our arms and looked at Saul.

'How far behind was I?'

'A touch.' Saul retrieved his hat and poked it in my face as a

125

reminder. 'You were pulling ahead though – another few feet and there would have been clear water between you. You thrashed that sod Fletcher, that's the main thing. Come on, I'll buy you a Coke.'

He steered me up the steep steps to the terrace, basking in the reflected praise being heaped on me by the spectators. Coming second wasn't so bad after all.

I couldn't see Caroline but supposed she was by the diving boards congratulating her Dutchman. I didn't care.

I hadn't seen Rachel, though, and worried that she might not turn up. She should have been at work that morning. Malita had promised to explain everything to her. Before I'd left, I'd begged both of them not to frighten her and not to mention the gun. I was worried that Fred might do something irrational and began to understand my father's concern.

I'd missed the bus again and Fred walked me back to retrieve *Boadicea* before taking me home. After that manic ride, I didn't want to sit on that pillion for some time. In fact, I wasn't sure I wanted to see too much of Fred in the near future. I had enough problems of my own to deal with. At least the race was out of the way. I should have felt elated but I was empty inside, drained after the last few days.

I was pleased that Saul was talking to me again. If only Rachel would arrive soon, I would feel a lot happier. Thursday was half-day closing so she should have been here by now. I looked along the bridge but it was empty. Miko would also be waiting for her. I suspected that most of the club members were looking forward to her confrontation with Caroline, even more than they had wanted to see me beat Fletcher.

19

I was still in a daze. My body, striving to recover the energy debt, reduced the flow of blood to my head, making me feel faint and weak. Saul was also concerned about Rachel and tried to quiz me about her absence. My explanation that she might have had a row with her father didn't convince him. The cola was a mistake and I had to hurry off. My stomach, which had suffered such torment, finally conceded defeat and I retched in the toilet.

Cookie found me there, picked me up, threw me under the shower, dried me off then led me down to watch the rest of the swimming.

Saul had disappeared.

Cookie wrapped a towel round my head and forced me to struggle into my tracksuit for, despite the heat, I was still shivering.

Miko stopped me and tapped my temple. Then he hugged me and slapped my back. If his smile had been any wider, his face would have split apart. He tapped his watch and asked if I had seen Rachel. I shrugged and he gave me one of his Romanian looks.

Cookie dragged me away, dumped me next to Joan Le Marquand and asked her to keep an eye on me. Joan was a good friend. Competing for Great Britain, she'd come tenth, three years before, in the Olympic high board championship in Berlin. Joan hugged me, excited by my record.

We watched the rest of the races together. I was in no condition to take part in the relay and Nelson didn't call for me. Even though we had loaned them some of our better swimmers, the navy team were no match for us and that part of the contest ended in a decisive win.

The diving was next and still there was no sign of Rachel. Caroline, who had ignored me so far and spent the afternoon with the Dutchman, would be defending her cup, donated by her father, in the three-metre springboard section.

As the foreman and his assistant were hauling in the lane ropes, I spotted Saul hurrying down the steps. He trotted towards Miko and they had an animated conversation. Miko rushed off towards the changing rooms and Saul walked towards us. I could see Caroline watching him but she must have sensed my eyes on her as she flicked her head and turned back to Kohler. I wondered what she was thinking. If Rachel failed to show, there wouldn't be a competition as two of the club's best divers were away training in France and Joan preferred high board.

Caroline would want to demonstrate her superiority. They weren't just competing for a cup anymore and everyone in the arena would know that. I felt certain that Rachel wouldn't decline the challenge. She'd run away, been kidnapped, her father had locked her in a cupboard. My imagination ran riot but there was nothing I could do.

Saul sat down, a knowing grin on his puffy face. He tapped his nose. 'Caroline's in for a surprise.' He pointed towards the lookout.

Miko walked down the steps a few paces in front of Rachel. A murmur rose from the crowd as they spotted her and there was a swell of applause as she reached her place under the boards. She didn't acknowledge it but started stretching under Miko's direction. My pulse was racing again.

'Gadzooks, but her father is a right royal pain in the arse. I thought I'd have to pay him to release her. Quite a scene, I can tell you.'

I looked at him in amazement. He'd been into the lion's den and rescued her? I was speechless.

Brewster's voice echoed over the loudspeakers. He was soon in full flow, stretching our patience with a detailed explanation of the rules and procedures, before he announced the first diver.

'Miss Hayden-Brown will perform a forward dive, straight, standing; degree of difficulty is one point six.'

128

He kept her waiting as he launched into another explanation of the scoring formula that would tax the average maths teacher though, if Saul didn't get too bored, I knew he could work out the result in his head.

Joan hissed. 'Get on with, you windbag.'

Caroline made good use of his ramblings by rearranging her hair and twisting from side to side to show off her sleek figure as she stripped off her tracksuit to reveal a new ultra tight purple costume. She raised her arms to reach her head and tie off a matching ribbon on her ponytail. The effect was very seductive but, as three of the judges were female, it was a wasted effort. Not on me though. That hollow feeling of loss was there again, or was it just hunger?

Having climbed the ladder, she paused, waiting for silence from the spectators then took four long steps forward into the hurdle, planted both feet on the edge of the long wooden board and launched herself high into the air.

'Excellent elevation,' commented Joan.

She plunged past the end of the board and knifed into the water three metres below. She emerged with a smug smile and acknowledged the loud applause.

Brewster blew his whistle and the scorecards were held aloft. The highest was eight point five from old Arthur, who brought to diving the same degree of impartiality that Phillips brought to water polo. He must like purple ribbons. The lowest was six point five. Those two scores would be discarded and the other three added up and multiplied by the tariff.

'Thirty-two point eight and average ten point nine.' Saul was still awake and had completed his calculations before Brewster had finished calling out the scores.

'That's a bit generous. If you're right and they carry on like that we're going to see some ridiculous totals.' Joan sounded rather annoyed.

There was a slight pause as the officials worked out the score, which was as Saul had predicted.

'Next, with the same dive, is Miss Vibert.'

I had been watching Miko prepare Rachel by helping her stretch and rotate. I had to confess to a pang of jealousy as he manipulated her body. He helped her shrug out of her tracksuit. Instead of her usual staid black, she was wearing a crimson costume as figure hugging as Caroline's. She tucked her hair into a white cap and seemed surprised at the applause and wolf-whistles from the gallery. She looked gorgeous but I sensed her nervousness and caught a quick flick of her eye in Miko's direction before she climbed the ladder up to the board.

She started her move forward. Like Caroline, she took four steps though they seemed more deliberate, mechanical even. Her elevation wasn't as good and her entry sounded like a large rock being dropped into the water. Her highest score was six and the lowest from Caroline's admirer, a four.

Joan patted my arm. 'Don't worry, she'll get better. Do you know if she made that costume herself?'

'How would I know that?'

She grinned. 'Sorry, I don't suppose you two waste time discussing such trifles as Lastex fibres.'

Did she know something? Had Rachel been confiding in her? I grinned back. 'I hope she improves. After all the training she's put in at the gym she deserves to do well.'

Joan grunted. 'Humph. Best not to talk about that.'

As the water polo players were suspicious of Miko, so were most of the divers. His contention that, to be successful, they had to be good gymnasts and spend more time on the mats in South Hill Gym than they did on the boards didn't impress many of them. Diving, for most, was about graceful movement through the air, not sweating on apparatus indoors.

In the second compulsory round, Rachel pulled back a small amount of the deficit with her standing back dive, scoring thirteen to Caroline's twelve point seven. She seemed more confident and her layout, according to Joan, had been technically perfect. I found it stunning. My pulse was now steady at 120.

Caroline responded with an imperious reverse dive. For the moment I was the invisible part of an emotional triangle, though I'd caught the odd glance from those who knew. The tension was beginning to make me light-headed. She gained a nine from her male admirer who managed to keep a straight face, as there were some obvious giggles from the crowd when he held up his card.

Overall, she scored twelve point seven, which Joan thought was a fair result.

Rachel followed though she took some time to settle the board as she gripped it with her toes. Her execution was flawless and she hit the water like a spear with that rare ripping sound which signifies the perfect entry. She received an eight and two seven point fives, which gave a total of fifteen point three – by far the best dive so far. She was now point eight behind Caroline. I felt sure Joan could hear my heart hammering in my chest.

The compulsory section over, the divers had to hand in their three voluntary dives, which they were then not allowed to change. Rachel seemed to be arguing with Miko and I sensed that she was unhappy with at least one of the choices.

Brewster halted their argument by calling the divers to the table to submit their planned dives. Rachel still looked agitated, much to Caroline's amusement, but she deposited her hand written sheet, shrugged her shoulders and stalked back to Miko who rolled his eyes in exasperation.

Caroline was first to dive again and Brewster announced that she would attempt a forward running dive with two and a half somersaults in the pike position. This had a degree of difficulty of two point four and drew a small gasp from the crowd when he described it.

Joan nudged me. 'That's a bit of a risk. The spring's not right.'

Caroline bounded forward but her take-off seemed hesitant and she didn't achieve enough initial height to complete the two and a half rotations. She spun out with her body still bent and her legs went over on entry. Her favourite judge gave her a seven point five but the rest of the marks were lower.

Saul had her total within seconds. 'Fourteen point eight. She could –'

'That's because of the tariff,' Joan interrupted. 'It wasn't a good dive. I'm surprised she got that much.'

'Next, Miss Vibert who will attempt the same dive.'

Joan gasped. Perhaps that was the source of the argument. Miko was pushing her into something she didn't feel confident about. I knew that feeling. I held my breath. Rachel's execution was almost

131

identical as she failed to get the necessary height from her spring. Saul had the calculation: fourteen point four. Caroline was still ahead on points even though they had won two dives each.

Joan was as detached as ever. 'That's daft, trying high tariffs when the board isn't right.'

Caroline attempted a forward somersault with two twists and another high tariff for her next dive and again failed to meet Joan's approval. She scored fifteen point two though, while Rachel managed twelve point three for a forward one and half-running tuck, which she executed well.

After five dives, Saul calculated that Caroline led Rachel by four points.

For her final dive, Caroline chose a reverse one and a half somersaults with tuck and a tariff of two point zero. She got nine from her friend but six point five from everyone else for an average of thirteen.

'Rachel will have to score at least seventeen to equal her.'

We didn't doubt Saul's calculation but Joan laughed. 'There's little chance of that. The best that Marjorie Gestring scored was just over sixteen in the Olympic final. Sorry, Jack, but, even with this crazy marking, I can't see that happening.'

I tried to speak but it came out in a rush. 'Just be patient, Joan. There's the Miko factor to consider.' It was wishful thinking, but Rachel seemed more settled and Miko was smiling. Had he given her the confidence?

'Miss Vibert's final dive...' Brewster turned to the scorer and, even though the microphone didn't pick it up, his voice was incredulous enough for us to hear the query. 'Are you sure?'

The scorer nodded.

'Her final dive will be an inward dive with two and a half somersaults in the pike position. This has a degree of difficulty of three point zero.'

This time the gasp from the spectators could be heard as far as the Dicq Rock.

Joan's mouth hung open in disbelief. 'She's mad; he's mad; they're both mad. She can't pull that off. Even Pete Desjardins couldn't manage it and he designed that board.'

Saul raised his eyebrows and expelled a long breath. Miko looked confident and Rachel seemed calm as she climbed the ladder and assumed her position.

Miko called out to her. I thought it was a word of encouragement but it was an instruction. She grabbed the handrail and reached out with her foot to the ratchet mechanism, which moved the roller fulcrum under the board. She nudged it back several notches to increase the spring of the board. This was an even greater gamble as she obviously hadn't had a chance to test it. I couldn't watch.

We guessed that the board had been set up by the heavier male divers who had been practising earlier. They must have pushed the fulcrum forward, which was why the lighter girls weren't getting the height. This could catapult her into the heavens if she got it wrong.

She waited until the crowd was quiet. Even the seagulls stopped to watch this one. I sucked in a deep breath and steeled myself to watch the tragedy unfolding in front of me. As soon as she moved forward, the scoring would start. She stretched her body to its full height, looked towards Green Island in the distance and strode to the end of the board, absorbing its deep dip as her weight pulled it down. Without hesitation, she pivoted on the very edge to face inwards.

I focused all my energy, hoping to project a wave to support her but she was well beyond my reach now – a lonely, vulnerable figure. Yet I was close enough to see her rib cage expand as she drew in her final breath.

She started to bounce the board into vertical momentum. She waited for the up thrust then allowed the elasticity of the movement to launch her skywards. She must have gained two metres before she bent from her hips, straightened her legs, pointed her toes and started to rotate. She had finished the first somersault before she passed the end of the board again. My heart stopped as she missed it by an inch before completing the final rotation a fraction too late to get full extension. Her entry produced the sort of white water that Miko wanted from polo players not divers.

The crowd held its breath as she surfaced – all eyes on the judges. Seven, five point five, five point five, five point five, five

133

point five and six. Not the highest scores of the afternoon by a long way. Saul shrugged. He hadn't been able to make the calculation. Like us, he had been too focused on Rachel, who now floated on the surface, looking anxiously at Miko.

After an age, the PA system hissed into life. 'Miss Vibert's high tariff dive has scored a total of fifty-one points – an average of seventeen exactly.'

'They're level. Seventy-nine point three each.' Half a dozen seagulls took flight at Saul's shout. Several spectators turned towards him.

'They're level on ordinals as well,' Joan added.

'What?'

'Positions, Jack. They each won three dives. 'They would have come equal fourth in the last Olympics with those scores. That shows how accurate the judging is.'

After a long pause, during which the scorer's pencil seemed to be doing some high tariff dives of its own, Brewster made the announcement. Saul had been correct – they had the same score. How ironic.

From the volume of the cheers, it was clear that the audience had made its own decision about the winner though and Rachel left the water and rushed to hug Miko. She turned towards us and waved. I wanted to hug her as well but I wasn't sure that would be welcomed.

There was more discussion at the table before Brewster picked up the microphone again. 'Under the rules of this competition, the trophy, if defended, will be retained by the current holder in the event of a tie. I therefore ask Miss Hayden-Brown to step forward to receive it from His Excellency.'

The silence was embarrassing, even the governor seemed hesitant but Caroline strode forward and relieved him of it. She had enough sense not to hold it aloft in triumph and hurried over to Kohler, who wrapped his arm around her. I felt no sense of jealousy – perhaps the green-eyed monster was dead, had sunk without trace to the bottom of the diving pit.

After the diving was over it was the turn of the water polo teams.

The navy only had five players so Brewster invited Kohler and Cookie to play for them. I was still suspended so wouldn't have a chance for another confrontation with my Dutch friend. I felt relieved so stayed in my seat and tried to relax.

The Jersey team was far too strong and, even though Kohler played very well up front, he didn't get any real scoring chances. Nelson seemed to enjoy marking him though no blows were exchanged. Kohler looked far more comfortable as a forward. I wondered why he had chosen to play as a full back and mark me in the previous game.

After my swim and the diving, the rest of the afternoon was an anticlimax. There was some light relief when the tide, hurried by an increasing swell, started to slip over the pool walls earlier than expected. It tugged the pitch and goals backwards and sideways as it surged in and sucked out.

The two teams shook hands to the applause of the handful of spectators. Even Saul had slipped away and there was no sign of Miko.

Brewster was struggling with the trestle table and beckoned me over to help him. It was a bit like folding a deck chair and, unless you had the knack, it could frustrate you. He hadn't but I had and was pleased to assist. We carried it back to his office. I felt he was going to say something but he just nodded his thanks and sat down at his typewriter.

On the way back to the pool side, I came face to face with Caroline. She was walking under the diving board, holding Kohler's arm. She glared at me and hissed "bastard" as we passed. Kohler said something which made her laugh.

Devoid of a suitable response, I could only smoulder and move on to collect my kit. I needed to rehearse some "spontaneous" retorts in case we bumped into each other again.

Rachel and Joan were sitting on the wooden bench overlooking the diving area talking quietly. They stopped as I approached. Rachel smiled. I smiled back, very unsure of myself.

Rachel spoke first. 'Well done, Jack. That was a fantastic race. We're so proud of you –'

'But I didn't win.'

They both laughed.

Rachel patted the seat beside her. 'Seven seconds faster than you've ever swum before, Jack. You can bet Miko's already worked out a new training programme for you. Besides, the Dutchman is older and more experienced. You did so well.'

'I thought you'd missed it.'

'I almost did. There was a problem at home. But no, I saw everything. I managed to squeeze in next to your headmaster.'

'It's just that I didn't see you,' I said.

'I went straight to the changing room after the result. Wow, that was so fast.'

I must have looked puzzled. 'What's wrong?' she asked.

'It's just that Saul said you weren't here. He went to rescue you from your father and he had to bribe –'

'How silly.' She laughed. 'Saul is such a liar. He knew I was here. He was playing games with you.' She was giggling now.

'What's so funny?'

'I'm just trying to imagine him arguing with my father. You've met him now. He allowed you a few seconds. How long do you think he'd give Saul?'

Yes, it was a funny picture. I picked up the rhythm of her laugh and, as it subsided, we locked eyes. She moved closer.

I wrapped her in my arms and whispered. 'You looked so beautiful this afternoon, you made my heart sing. I just wanted to get on that board and hug you in front of everyone.'

She stayed close but stiff in my arms and whispered back, 'Really. That's interesting. Shame you didn't.'

Joan stood and chuckled. 'I'll leave you two to mate in private.'

Rachel reached out and grabbed her arm. 'No, stay. Jack and I aren't going to embarrass you. Gosh, I feel exhausted. I don't know about you but I'm still trembling.' She did know. We both did. I was and she wasn't. Instead, she seemed cool and in control. I felt that hollow feeling of loss again. 'Miko thought the judges were too generous but I suppose it was entertaining. But enough about that. Let's talk about Jack's race.'

I started to protest but she spoke over me. 'It was amazing to watch, Jack. I don't suppose you could hear the crowd – they were in a frenzy. Miko almost exploded after your turn. What was exciting, though, was watching the judges. Brewster must have realised how fast you were going because he called all the backup timekeepers to him and told them to put their watches on you. I was watching you with one eye and the frantic activity around the finish with the other. Centenier Phillips was brandishing his gun as though he wanted to shoot someone.'

'That would have been me, then.' I felt like he had.

Joan touched my wrist. 'I've got to go, Jack, but there's something I want to ask you. Rachel has been telling me about your little water polo episode with the Dutchman on Sunday. Do you know any more about him?'

'Why?' Rachel and I spoke at the same time.

'It's odd, but I'm sure I've seen him before.'

'He's only been here since Friday. He's a student on holiday with his uncle.'

Joan snorted. 'Or so he says. There is something very familiar about him. I've been studying him, especially his swimming action. I couldn't swear to it but I think I saw him at the Schwimm Stadion – in Berlin, during the Olympics'

'No wonder he beat me if he was good enough to be in the Dutch team.'

Joan hesitated. 'No, if I'm right, he wasn't in the Dutch team. He was a member of the 200 metre relay team. The German relay team.'

20

'You klutz, Jack. For someone so bright, you act like a complete schmuck over girls. For fuck's sake, can't you see what's happening?'

'Stop swearing, Saul. Dress like a stupid gangster, if you must, but stop trying to act like one.' I tapped his black homburg. 'It's not as if your *"head is worth a hat."*'

With a flick of my wrist, I sent it sailing out over the terrace. It wobbled in the evening air, its flight disturbing the moths around the spotlight above Nelson's table before plopping into his wife's lap. She looked up in bewilderment before Nelson grabbed it from her, spun round to see where she was looking and prepared to launch it over the rails into the water.

'No! Please Nelson!' Saul screeched.

Nelson smiled and put it on his head. The crowd around his table cheered then took up the cue and started to plead with him, mimicking Saul's South African accent.

'Bastard.' Saul turned on me. 'What did you do that for?'

'To shut you up. Keep your nose out. You know as much about girls as I do and don't pretend otherwise and speak properly. You're meant to be educated. So what was my reference?'

'Head not worth a hat? *As You Like It*, you arse; Rosalind, and wouldn't you just love to play Orlando?' He leant closer to me and wrinkled his nose. '*"This is the rankest compound of villainous smell that ever offended nostril."* What is that? Disinfectant?'

'It's Zizanie by Fragonard. Something Caroline gave me. It's supposed to go well with evening wear.'

'*Stront vir breins.* You let her choose your cologne as well. And you're still wearing it. *Poephol* – you deserve each other.'

'Well it's better than smelling of old tobacco and rancid hair oil, like you.'

'You don't know my reference, do you?'

'Fortunately, I didn't have to swallow the complete works of the Bard as a punishment for my foul-mouthed behaviour in class. But, as you did, I'm sure you're going to tell me.'

'"*A pox on you.*" Any scholar would tell you its Falstaff from the *Merry Wives of Windsor*. Anyway, what's wrong with my hair preparation? I'll have you know that this is the best Brylcream you can get – straight from the vending machine outside the shop.'

'I've heard that the machine is down to its last few pints and those have been there since last season.' I couldn't be angry with him for long but I had to try. 'Anyway, I've got a bone to pick with you.'

'Hah, I will eat with you, drink with you... but I'm not going to pick bones with you.'

I ignored his attempt to get the game going again. 'Why did you lie to me about Rachel?'

'Which particular lie was that?'

'Rescuing her from her father and all that nonsense.'

'That was a joke, you dummy. I wanted to see if you really cared.'

'And?'

'So, I was wrong. You do. But what about madam?'

'You tell me. We're not speaking.'

'You chuck her in the harbour, she sees you cavorting with her rival. So, what did you expect?'

'Well you're not much bloody help.'

'Tut, tut.' Saul reached into the inside pocket of his white tuxedo to extract a silver cigarette case. He'd been flaunting his eccentricity for years, careless of what others thought. For all that, he was still my closest male friend but I was beginning to regret giving him the edited version of the episode with Rachel at the pool and my suspicion that Caroline had called the police. Yet who else could I confide in? I hadn't mentioned Joan's belief that Kohler was German, nor that Rachel had discovered she was part Jewish. He, of all people, would understand what that meant to her but I was sworn to secrecy. It was up to her to tell him, not me.

Tommy Arnold's band started to play again and Saul watched in horror as Nelson took his hat for a dance. Soon it was being passed from couple to couple and I had to pull him back from running down the stairs to make an even bigger fool of himself by trying to retrieve it.

It was another spectacular summer's evening, the merest breath of wind. As the warm glow from the west faded, the rich blue of the sky seemed to drain into the sea, sharpening the horizon to a knife-edge. Spotlights, which had sparkled in the pre-dusk light, now dazzled on the terraces. The party of officers and ratings from the destroyer, in their best uniforms, were mingling with the club members. Some of the younger females were flirting. Saul shared his thought that it wouldn't be long before Wendy, the club "bicycle", ushered one of the matelots up to the cabins to test her tyres.

We rested our arms on the railings, observing, but apart from, the ball below. Saul smoked in what he believed to be a sophisticated way while I coughed in his ear. How long before he brandished an ivory holder for his du Maurier fags I wondered. There was no sign of Caroline or Rachel.

I poked him in the ribs. 'What's the time?'

He clamped his half-smoked cigarette between his teeth and extracted a gold hunter watch from another inside pocket. He held it at chain's length and angled it so that the floodlights above us illuminated the face.

'Nearly ten o'clock'. He started to cough. His fag dropped from his mouth, bounced on his chest and deposited a column of grey ash, then landed on his shiny leather shoe.

I bit my lip.

He dusted himself down and nudged me. 'Well, my prince, I think Cinderella's just arrived.'

I looked towards the end of the bridge and spotted Rachel swishing through the gate in a long black evening dress with a full skirt. Her hair was coiled up and she was wearing short white gloves, which covered her wrists. She had a white shawl draped round her

140

bare shoulders. What looked like my Saint Christopher on its silver chain nestled above her cleavage.

'You'll catch a few moths if you let your mouth hang open like that.' Saul clapped me on the shoulder of my borrowed dinner jacket. 'She does look stunning though. You wait here and catch the insects, I'm going to ask her to dance.'

Before I could react, he was racing down the steps. He rushed across the floor, recaptured his homburg from Nelson's head and dashed towards Rachel. He skidded to a halt in front of her, his hat back on his head, and bowed, removing the homburg with a flourish.

I couldn't hear their conversation but I could see her laughing and soon they were dancing. While I had focused my physical efforts on sports training, Saul had spent his time in the Plaza de Danse and now had all the moves. They looked good together and those miserable butterflies of jealousy were trapped in my stomach again. Rachel followed him with ease as the music changed into a quickstep and he spun her round the floor.

As Saul had predicted, Wendy clattered up the steps in her white high heels, a young seaman in tow, heading for the darkness of the upper crescent of cabins. I ignored her girlish giggles as her partner patted her ample buttocks but I was left with the image of the poor matelot riding downhill without brakes.

I waited until they'd found their berth then descended the steps quietly and stood in the shadows by the manager's office, where I could watch the gyrations on the dance floor.

I looked around for Joan but couldn't see her. She had told me that she thought she had some photographs of various swimmers from Berlin and would look through them to find Kohler. Perhaps she was mistaken.

The band changed the tempo into a waltz and couples started leaving the floor, including Saul and Rachel. They spotted me, manoeuvred their way through the tables and chairs, stopped at an empty one and called me over. I could no longer sulk in the shadows so I joined them.

'You look stunning, Rachel, that's a lovely dress.' I wanted to say much more, but not in front of Saul.

'She made it herself, Jack. She's very clever, and such a willing partner as well.' He winked at me. 'Come on, sit down and let's have a drink.' He signalled the nearest waiter, who ignored him. 'Sod it. I'll go and get them. What would you like, Rachel?'

She looked unsure. 'Just a small glass of wine, please. Perhaps with some lemonade in it.'

'Well, we all know what you want, Captain Virtuous.' Saul marched off to fight for attention at the bar.

I looked at Rachel, soaking in her freshness, the warmth in her eyes. My stomach still churned. I knew Saul found her attractive but couldn't believe that she could fall for his louche persona, cultivated from watching too many Hollywood films. However, if she saw beneath the contrived act, she might find him a fascinating and attractive young man. I realised that I didn't want her to make that effort, so perhaps that was jealousy nibbling away inside.

'You really do look fabulous tonight.'

'Why thank you, sir, you don't look so bad yourself – my compliments to your father's tailor.' She looked around to see if Saul was returning then leant across the table. 'How much have you told him?'

'Too much. He knows about our... swim but nothing else.' I reached across to hold her hand.

She avoided my touch until she'd discarded her shawl and peeled off her glove. 'No wonder he's been cool.' She sighed. 'There's so much to talk about, but not here.'

I felt the warmth through her fingertips and teased them with mine. 'Shall we go for a walk?'

'We can't leave now. Saul will be back any moment.'

'Okay, after the dance. I'll tell him I'm walking you home.'

'But he's planning to invite people back to his place.'

'Well tell him you have to get something before or –'

'That's enough of that. Find your own date.' Saul presented Rachel with a glass of champagne, placed a similar glass down for himself then extracted a Coke bottle from one pocket and a tumbler from the other for me.

He sat down between us, pulled our hands apart and offered Rachel her discarded glove. 'Don't make me feel like a gooseberry.

Here, Jack, do you want to liven that up?' He reached into his jacket and pulled out a slim silver flask. 'Best cognac.'

I shook my head then turned to Rachel, who surprised both of us by nodding. He dribbled some into her glass then poured a good measure into his. 'Bottoms up.'

Rachel giggled as the bubbles went up her nose. 'This is fun. I do hope you are going to let Jack dance with me, Saul.'

'Hey, talking of dancing, here's one for you. There's this couple preparing for conversion to the Jewish faith.'

I groaned. Of course, he didn't know. I glanced at Rachel but she was wearing the expression she usually reserved for Saul when he attempted to amuse us with one of his stories.

She considered him over her glass. 'I hope this isn't going to be too rude.'

'Relax, it's pretty clean. Anyway, they meet the rabbi for their final session and he asks if they have any last questions.

'The man asks, "Is it true that men and women don't dance together?"

"Yes," says the rabbi, "for modesty reasons, men and women dance separately."

"So I can't dance with my own wife?"

"No."

"Well, okay," says the man, "but what about sex?"

"That's fine," says the rabbi, "it's a *mitzvah* within the marriage!"

"What about different positions?" the man asks.

"No problem," says the rabbi.

"Woman on top?" the man asks.

"Why not?" replies the rabbi.

"Well, what about standing up?"

"No, *certainly not!*" says the rabbi. "That could lead to dancing."'

We both laughed though Rachel's turned into hiccups caused by the bubbles rather than the humour.

'You see. You don't have to be rude to be funny.'

'Where did you get that one?' I asked. 'Your cousin Ruben again?'

'Sure, Jack, he keeps them coming. He's writing them all down and is going to publish them.'

'Who's Ruben?' Rachel spoke through her hiccups.

'My second cousin. Works as a manager at the Hillcrest Country Club in Los Angeles. Most of the members are a bit special.'

'In what way?' she asked.

'They're Jewish.'

She shrugged. I wondered if she was trying to forget her own secret. She was certainly giving no indication to Saul. 'And?'

'Well, here are a few of the names. You work out the rest. Jack Benny, George Burns, Milton Berle, Groucho Marx... you want me to go on?'

'Surely they wouldn't tell jokes like that in public,' she said.

Saul sighed. 'Of course not, but that's the joke. They don't know that Ruben is writing them down.'

She still didn't look too impressed and Saul rolled his eyes at me.

The band changed tempo again to a quickstep and couples started to return to the floor.

I stood and bowed. 'May I have the honour?'

'When you feel my tap on your shoulder that means it's an "excuse me", so go and tap someone else or sit down, otherwise I'll pour your Coke into your pocket,' Saul cautioned.

Rachel allowed me to lead her onto the floor. We soon got into a comfortable rhythm and I pulled off some good reverse turns, surprising myself with some nimble footwork as I held her tight and swirled her round. We were concentrating so much on our movements that it was impossible to talk.

As we pivoted in the corner nearest the gate, I saw Kohler and Caroline arrive arm in arm. I stumbled and we almost fell. Rachel had her back to the gate and didn't spot them sweep in. Everyone else did and the whole clockwise gyration seemed to pause as all eyes focused on them.

Caroline was wearing a long clinging gown cut low at the back; her neck shimmered with diamonds. She held Kohler's arm with casual ease, the pair of them smiling like Hollywood stars. The moment passed and the dance continued.

Rachel, aware now, stopped and manoeuvred me off the floor. 'I think I've twisted my ankle.'

'I'm sorry. I stumbled.'

'I can see why. Come on, let's sit down and keep Saul company.' Caroline and Kohler swept past us.

'Schiaparelli, if I'm not mistaken. Quite good work.' Rachel cast her professional eye over Caroline's dress. 'Perhaps a little tight round the hips, a trifle loose under the bust; could do with a little alteration.'

Saul laughed. 'I don't think she'll let you get close enough with your pin cushion, my dear. That'll have been a few hundred guineas, I'll bet. He looks a bit like a stuffed turkey though.'

But Kohler looked completely self-assured. He nodded in our direction. Caroline ignored us and they joined Brewster's table.

Now, my stomach was confused. There was no contest really. Caroline was the most beautiful woman there, and she knew it. I had been as intimate with her as it was possible to be and she swore I was her first. I had never been completely sure, had always suspected that there had been others when she was away from the island. Yet, here we were separated by a few feet and ignoring each other's existence. Who could I ask for advice? Saul? Rachel? I turned to look at her now and saw a face which was a mask of disappointment. She couldn't have read my thoughts, could she? Was my expression that obvious? I felt helpless.

Saul kicked me hard under the table and turned to Rachel. 'May I?'

She let him lead her to the floor.

I sipped my Coke and tried to avoid looking at either Rachel or Caroline.

Saul spun her round as the band struck up the "Blue Danube". Soon Kohler and Caroline joined them. All eyes, including mine, seemed to be on the two couples and others slid out of their way as they began to compete. Saul was a better lead than Kohler but Caroline, with her flashing diamonds and blonde hair, drew the light and the attention more than Rachel.

The music changed to another quickstep. Saul shifted gear and took off, leading Rachel in a dazzling display, which Kohler didn't have the skill to follow.

He began to look awkward and Caroline found it difficult to

anticipate his moves. He faltered and she almost tripped. I knew she wouldn't stay around to be beaten by Rachel. Sure enough, she pulled Kohler off the floor and sat him down.

Eyes glittering with the hardness of her diamonds, she strode towards me.

'Get up, darling, and look as though you want to dance with me.'

Perhaps if Saul and Rachel hadn't been so dazzling, and my stomach hadn't been trying to digest the *"green-eyed monster"*, I would have told her to bugger off, but she'd caught me by surprise again and I didn't have a rehearsed response.

She grabbed my arm and tugged. This was insane but I rose and tried to look as though I was in charge and not being dragged onto the floor. I caught Kohler's eye and was sure it was amusement rather than anger I saw.

'Now dance, darling, show Rudi how it should be done.'

She pressed hard into me, enveloping me in Vent Vert, Greta Garbo's favourite. Her breasts jiggled against my chest as I launched us into a pursuit of Saul and Rachel. As we turned, she trapped my thigh between hers and squeezed. 'Get closer to them.'

Why couldn't I stop, dump her on the floor, stamp on her, make her look a fool? But I couldn't. The world spun as we twirled around. Her breath, the excitement in her eyes, the challenge in her face. The misery of the past few days evaporated like morning mist. All that despair, the sleepless worry, was wiped out. She still wanted me. She couldn't fake that. I ached for her, wanted to absorb her completely, wanted time to stop.

It did. She pulled out of a turn as we closed on Brewster's table, swung away from me and spun into Kohler's arms, triumph on her face. She'd won and I had been devoured and then dumped like the wrapper from a candy bar.

I stood amazed, ashamed, stupid. Others averted their eyes as I shuffled back to our table. Saul was sitting. Of Rachel, there was no sign.

'You clueless bastard. What have you done?'

'Where's Rachel? '

'Where do you bloody think? She's gone home.'

'I must go after her, apologise.'

Saul grabbed my arm, his fingers digging deep. 'Oh no you don't. You leave her alone. Don't you think you've hurt her enough?'

'I'm sorry, but what could I do?'

'You know very well what you could have done.'

'She used me, Saul.'

'Of course she did. She always has. She doesn't want you, but she doesn't want anyone else to have you either.' He stopped and pulled me round to face him. 'Do you really care for Rachel?'

'Very much, but Caroline has her claws in me. I can't shake her off.'

'Of course you can. You just have to be strong. You had the chance on the dance floor. You should have dropped her and walked away.'

I nodded in despair. 'I should have punched that arrogant Kohler on the nose as well.'

'*Kwas*, do that and you'll give Caroline a real victory – make you look like a pathetic, jealous lout. I know you're angry with her but don't take it out on him.'

I slumped in my chair. 'Have you still got your flask?'

Saul laughed. 'Now, that's the spirit – take it like a man and get sloshed.' He handed over the flask. 'Careful now, sip it, don't gulp.'

I unscrewed the cap and tilted the flask to my lips. The fiery liquid burned everything on its way to my stomach. I waited for some sensation, for whatever it was spirits did for you. An explosion of warmth shot up as the raw alcohol hit my bloodstream and surged into my brain. I sipped some more and waited for the rush.

Saul watched me. 'Look, I've invited a few of the gang back to my place. The parents are still away, so we can have a bit of fun. Where did you leave your dad's car?

'In Cleveland Road.'

'It'll be safe there. You can stay the night. I tell you what. I'll go and get Rachel and take her back. You come and join us in about half an hour and you can try to make your peace with her.'

I nodded again and raised the flask.

'Steady. I think you'd better give that back.'

'No, it's fine. I'll be okay. I'll join you later.' I clung on tightly to the flask and Saul shrugged.

'If that's what you want, but don't slug it back and don't lose it.' He got up and wandered around the tables, inviting our friends to his party.

I watched him walk up the bridge then turned my attention to Caroline and Kohler. They were dancing again, ignoring my brooding presence. I tipped the flask back and gulped a mouthful of cognac, relishing the warmth as it flowed through me. I continued to watch them and noticed that Kohler took the occasional glance in my direction.

In between mouthfuls, I tried to summon some put-downs I could use for my next encounter with the golden pair. But my library of clever remarks was as jumbled as my head.

I'd never tried alcohol before, didn't know what it felt like to be drunk. Surely it would take more than half a flask of whatever this was? I could see perfectly well, my cheeks were burning but that was probably with embarrassment and guilt.

I should get up and go after Rachel but what would I say? If I couldn't think of anything clever to throw at Caroline, how could I find the right words to apologise to Rachel?

I swallowed another slug and rattled the flask. Empty.

I placed it in my inside pocket and pulled myself up. The table was unsteady. This was silly but it made me smile. I blinked away the fuzziness, stood up straight and surveyed the dance floor. Something Saul had said twirled in my head. It would make a good rehearsed response only I would have to get it in first so it wouldn't be a response. That would make it a provocation.

I smiled. That was it, to avoid the embarrassment of not knowing what to say, I should get my response in first. I felt a warm glow of confidence. I'd found the solution. Now I had to share it.

Everyone was waltzing, spinning round. I aimed for a gap between two other couples but it closed before I could reach it. There was some bumping and apologising then I was through and waltzing behind Kohler. Caroline glared at me but didn't speak.

I tapped him on the shoulder. 'Excuse me.'

Kohler stopped then shrugged me off but I grabbed his jacket. 'Excuse me!'

Caroline responded. 'It's not an "excuse me", Jack, please sit down.'

She peered at me. 'Have you been drinking?' She laughed. 'He has; Jack has broken his vows. He's taken some Dutch courage. Excuse the pun, Rudi.' She giggled. 'Leave us alone, Jack. Playtime is over for tonight.'

I prodded Kohler's shoulder again. 'Excuse me, I wish to dance with the lady.'

Caroline hooted. 'Oh, please. Go away, there's a good boy.'

'You bitch. You used me.' I said it without anger.

'How dare you speak to a lady like that!' Kohler turned to face me. 'Apologise at once, you stupid boy.'

I felt as calm as I had ever felt, I glowed with calmness. Calmly, I pulled my arm back and punched Kohler on the nose. He stumbled backwards. Blood spurted over his white shirt and sprayed Caroline's shoulders. He tripped and landed on his backside. Caroline stood speechless, mouth agape.

'Now that I've excused him, I don't wish to dance with you anymore. Good night.'

Response delivered and, before anyone could react, I walked, in an almost straight line, off the floor, through the gate and up the bridge. I managed the whole length without falling once. See, Kohler, that's how its done.

21

'Where the hell have you been? *Gotteniu*, look at the state of you. Oh no you don't. Take those sodden shoes off before you ruin the carpets – and those bloody trousers.'

Saul forced me to remove the offending articles before he ushered me into the apartment. A gramophone was playing in the lounge and I could hear occasional bursts of drunken laughter through the closed door.

'Welcome to the asylum, Jack. Come and have a coffee, you look as though you need one.'

In the kitchen, Saul reached for the percolator and poured a mug of thick aromatic coffee for me. I'd removed my jacket and now sat in my underpants and shirt on a stool at the breakfast bar. Saul's parents prided themselves on keeping up with the latest American furnishings and spared little expense on their exclusive apartment. He reached for a bottle of brandy and prepared to drop some into the hot liquid.

I stopped him. 'Enough. It's taken me an hour to get rid of the last lot.'

'That's what you think. It'll take your kidneys a lot longer than that to recover, from what I hear.' Saul grabbed my right hand and examined the bruised knuckles. 'You really are a prize idiot. I suppose you'll claim it was the demon drink. Did you bring my flask back?'

I reached back into my jacket pocket and placed the silver flask on the table.

Saul picked it up and shook it. 'Empty; well I hope you didn't spill any.'

'Certainly not. Is Rachel still here?'

'You have to be joking. She left ages ago. You didn't expect her to wait while you swam round the island, did you? Just where have you been, as a matter of interest?'

'I went down to the rock pool at la Collette'

'What, in the dark? You're even madder than you look.'

'I needed to cool off so I stripped and jumped in.'

'You could have drowned, in your state.'

'No I was fine. It was very relaxing, lying back trying to make some sense of the stars. I had to submerge a few times to stop them spinning though. I even managed to get dressed after, though drying myself on my shirt tails was a bit difficult.'

'So why are you –'

'I slipped as I was leaving and slid back in up to my knees. It was so funny I just couldn't stop laughing. It's not easy walking in wet shoes but I thought I had better get here rather than drive home.'

'Too bloody right.'

'What are the others doing?'

'Oh, the usual. The boys turn out the lights, their hands wander around. The girls slap them back, get up and turn on the lights. And so it goes on. None of that lot are going to make it to the bedrooms.

'What did Rachel say?'

'You don't want to know.'

'Did she find out what happened after she left?'

'Oh, yes. The whole bloody island knows by now. I dare say you will be up before the constable this time. Your best defence is to plead insanity complicated by excessive alcohol consumption.'

'Does anyone know what happened to Caroline?'

'Sure, she, and her bloodied consort, left soon after you and were last seen getting into her car.'

'Christ, what a mess. What am I going to do, Saul?'

'Join the Foreign Legion, seek refuge in a church. How the hell do I know? Just drink your coffee and try to sober up in case the police come looking for you.'

'I'm famished. You got any toast or biscuits?'

He grabbed a large tin of Huntley's best and shoved it at me. 'We need a plan, a bloody good plan –'

151

The doorbell rang before he could continue.

'Who the devil's that? Not the bloody neighbours again, I hope. Sit tight. If it's the cops, I'll tell them you drowned and show them your shoes as evidence.'

He opened the kitchen door and went out into the corridor.

Perhaps it was Rachel. Oh God, I hoped it was Rachel.

'Out of my bloody way, you moron. Go on, push off.'

Caroline burst into the room, reached around the table and grabbed my arm. 'I need to talk to you. Now. Come on, up, out of here.'

She turned back on Saul. 'Is there a bedroom here we can lock from the inside? Come on, show me.'

He backed away as she dragged me into the corridor. The door to the lounge opened and several faces peered out at the commotion.

'Get back in there, you cretins. Mind your own business and stay away from me!' she screamed at them, still dragging me like a stubborn dog.

The faces disappeared and the door closed quickly.

'Saul, your parties are getting worse. Which door, damn it?'

He pointed to the one opposite.

She barged in and spun me around her so that she was between me and the door. She slammed it and turned the key. The room was empty with only a soft glow from a bedside lamp. It was clearly Saul's parents' room as it was dominated by a large double bed. She rushed at me and flung her arms around me.

'You bastard. What have you done to me?' She pushed me away and pummelled my chest with her fists. The attack reached a crescendo of anger then slowed to a steady beat until her shoulders slumped and she started to sob. Great, breathless, heaving sobs.

She blinked at me, used the backs of her hands to stem the tears and tried to get her breathing under control. She stared, took in my bare feet and legs and sodden shirt tails and her wracking cries started to transform, like a change of musical key, to hysterical laughter. She pointed at my legs and tried to speak but couldn't control her tongue. She turned back to the door, pulled the key out and flung it into the far corner of the room.

She took a deep breath. 'We don't leave here until we've sorted this out. Understand?'

I nodded, though I still shivered. From shock, cold, exhaustion, relief? I had no idea.

She advanced towards me again and pushed me, gently this time, onto the bed. 'You're wet. You must be cold. Get in the bed, you need to get warm.'

I wanted to resist. I really did, but I couldn't find the strength. I started to slide under the covers.

'Take your shirt off first – you don't want to dirty the sheets, stupid.' Her voice was much warmer now.

I undid the studs, which had almost defeated me after my swim, shrugged out of the shirt and turned to the bed.

'And those as well.' She pointed to my underpants.

I stepped out of them, tingling all over, with the goosebumps of anticipation softening my resistance. I slid under the cool silk sheets and pulled the blankets and counterpane up to my chin – my own pathetic Maginot Line.

She waited for me to settle then reached behind and undid the clip holding the top of her zip. She eased the long dress off her shoulders and shook herself out of it. She was naked underneath. She unclipped her diamond necklace and earrings, dropped them to the floor then moved her scented beauty to the bed.

I shuffled along and made room for her. Her body was cool against my rapidly heating skin. She rolled onto her side and caressed my face with her fingers.

'Kiss me, Jack.'

There was a hammering on the door. Saul's stage whisper. 'Beware the siren voice.'

'Ignore him. He's drunk,' she said

That didn't make him wrong. He was too late though, I'd already been lured onto the rocks. She pressed her mouth to mine and forced my lips open. Adrenaline surged through me and I kissed her back, gently at first, then with mounting urgency.

She rolled over, pulled me onto her and ran her hand along my back. She teased her tongue over my lips then eased her legs apart. 'Jack, please love me, now. Don't stop.'

Shifting her position, she pulled me deep and moved with me, slowly at first then, catching my rhythm, she started to dictate the motion, rising up and plunging down.

I was lost, captivated by the primal movement yet I paused. 'What about –'

'Shush, it doesn't matter. I'm safe. Just relax. Let's move together, gently this time, slowly, there, feel me through your body. Love me, Jack.'

I tried to ride the wave as it built under me, tried to stay on the crest and control it, prolong it, but it swept me up and rushed me forwards until I shuddered into the shallows and lay panting gently on her, my chest pressed into hers.

She wrapped her legs around me, trapping me inside, and kissed me passionately. 'Thank you, Jack. You'll never know how important that was.'

'I'm sorry if I was too quick. I'll be better next time.'

'Don't be silly. You were fantastic, Jack. Now rest for a while, be still.'

She wrapped her arms around me, pulled my head into her neck and caressed the small of my back.

My body flooded with relief. She loved me after all, had come back to me, despite my stupidity. I was dazed but glowed with happiness. I tried to put my feelings into words, muttered clumsy phrases.

She listened while she kissed my eyes, her breath sweet and warm on my cheek. 'Shush, relax and sleep.'

I surfaced through multiple layers of cool water, my eyes blinking awake, aware of a scrabbling sound in the room. Caroline wasn't in the bed. I lifted myself up on my elbows. My head throbbed, heavy anvil blows clanging inside. She was in the corner of the room, on her knees, searching for something.

'What are you doing?'

'I'm looking for the bloody key.'

'Why? Come back to bed.'

'I've got to find it. I need to go.' Her voice was becoming strident. She had changed yet again.

I crawled out of the bed and along the carpet and made a lunge for her naked back. She slapped me off.

'Stop it. We've got to find the key.'

'Okay, if you insist.' I wriggled around, half searching, rather enjoying the sight of her bottom as she crawled around. I was growing hard again and made another attempt to wrap my arms around her.

She turned fiercely on me. 'The key first!'

My probing fingers found the little piece of metal. I clasped it in my hand and retreated to the bed. She darted after me and tried to prise it from my grasp.

'The key after,' I said.

Furious, she slapped at me and caught the top of my head with her fingers.

'Hey, that's enough. What's wrong?'

She grabbed my wrist in one hand and bit my fingers to force me to release the key.

I pulled away, angry now. 'What's changed? Why are you so anxious to go?'

'Bastards. Men, you're all bastards.

'You've been with him, haven't you? Haven't you?'

'No. I haven't –'

'That's what all this is about. You've been with him and you want me as your...' I struggled for the word, 'insurance.' The thought was too horrible.

'No, Jack, you're wrong. Nothing happened. I was angry with you and turned it onto him. We argued. I took him back to his hotel then drove around trying to find you.'

I closed my eyes. 'And how did you do that?' I already knew the answer.

'Well, there was no one else around so I went to Rachel's.'

'For Christ's sake, you stupid woman. Why the hell did you do that?'

'I had to find you, Jack. I thought she would know where you were.'

'What did she say?'

'She was very polite. Suggested I try here.'

'I don't believe you.'

'She was calm, almost disinterested.'

'You had sex with him, didn't you?'

'No. I swear we didn't. I wouldn't. How can you say that after what we just did?'

'It's because of what we just did that I can say that.' My head was pounding but it wasn't the alcohol.

'You don't know what you're saying. That's so cruel, Jack.'

'Save the crocodile tears. You're not fooling me again.'

I spoke quietly now. Resigned to the fact that she had used me once again and this time had gone too far. She obviously hadn't been able to control Kohler and he had left his seed inside her.

He would disappear and she would be left to carry the burden. But there was always the fall guy, Jack. Let him think that any unfortunate result would be his and he would have to look after her, marry her.'

I held out the key. 'Here, take it, go on.'

She stared at me. 'Do you really believe that if I got pregnant I would have the baby?' She gathered up her dress and struggled into it.

I watched her in silence, the key cold in my hand. I didn't know what to think. I was immobilised again.

She finished her adjustments and held out her hand. I dropped the key into it and watched her turn away. She opened the door and paused on the threshold.

'You silly, silly fool. You have no idea what you have thrown away.' Then she was gone.

The front door thudded behind her.

22

'"*Put out the light, and then put out the light:*"'
I banged my fist on the rusting bonnet of the old Renault.
'"*If I quench thee, thou flaming minister,*
I can again thy former light restore,
Should I repent me –"'
'Why are you talking to the tractor in Old English? It's French, for God's sake.' Alan had crept up on me.

Startled, I turned, book in hand, and waved it at him. 'Do you think, Saul is Iago?'

'What are you talking about? Does "Yago" mean a Jewish pain in the arse?'

'Alan, you are a *"foolish gnat"*. Haven't you read *Othello* yet?'

'Oh, I get it. Another of your Shakespearian fantasies. We thought you'd had your fill playing that bloody Jew in that awful play. Don't you realise how embarrassing that was?'

He grabbed the book. '*Othello, the Moor of Venice*. Hang on, wasn't your play about Venice? But it wasn't about a Moor; it was about a Christian merchant, wasn't it – played by Marcks? Now that was a bloody joke for a start. Anyway, what's a Moor when he's at home?'

I pulled the book out of his hand and placed it on the groundsheet where I'd left the carburettor I was meant to be repairing. Alan had obviously slept through the casket scenes in the play. 'The Moor in *Othello* is a black man, a famous general.'

'Oh, now you want to play a nigger as well as a Jew? What's wrong with you, man?'

'I don't want to play Othello, I'm just trying to understand how his closest adviser, Iago, can poison his mind so easily.'

'Ah, ah. Now, I do know about poison and Shakespeare. Very fond of that, especially in *Romeo and Juliet*.'

'Not that sort of poison, you *"clay-brained peasant."* He persuades Othello that his wife has been unfaithful and he kills her – *"puts out the light."* Then he finds out Iago has been lying and has him tortured to death.'

'Not one of his comedies then?'

'No, Alan. It's about jealousy – *"the green-eyed monster."*

'Oh, I get it now. You and that bitch Caroline. So you think Saul might be poisoning you against her. Bloody good luck to him, I say. He probably wants her for schlong exercise. From what I hear, she won't need to be asked twice.'

I froze and glared at my brother. I felt the blood rushing to my face and clenched my fists. That bloody woman had destroyed my relationship with Rachel, had made me suspicious of Saul and now I was angry with Alan because he might have told the truth about her.

I gritted my teeth. 'What are you doing here, anyway?' I noticed the rifle slung over his shoulder and the spotting scope peeking out of the canvas shooting bag on his hip. 'I heard some shots earlier. Was that you trying to hit the barn with your eyes shut?'

'Ha, bloody ha. If you must know, I was sighting the new Aldis scope I picked up at Bisley. Good grouping at 400 yards now.'

'Pity you didn't have it for the competition. Remind me where Victoria came.'

'I've had enough teasing about that from Dad.'

'Fifty-third wasn't it – out of seventy-six, and you let those Guernsey "donkeys" beat you.'

'Alright, alright. At least I had the top score of our team.'

'Hah, did the rest forget their spectacles?'

'You're just jealous because I scored more than you did last time.'

'Hang on. Did you say you've been zeroing it at 400 yards? Where, for God's sake, Alan?

'Relax, I was only shooting along the cliff and into the hedge. There's enough earth there to stop the bullets.'

'So long as you don't get the elevation wrong, send some over and puncture any of Charlie Le Riche's cows. I hope you checked with Father first.'

'He won't mind,' he looked slyly at me, 'will he?'

'Not until he gets a complaint from the constable. He had enough problems getting permission for the range in the top field. Shooting across there's not legal, is it?'

'Suppose not. But I'll say I was firing blanks to scare off the crows.'

'And who's going to believe that? I suppose you'll be shooting out the light at the end of the breakwater next to check your long-range grouping.'

I wish I hadn't let that thought out because he strode towards the tractor and unslung his old Short Magazine Lee-Enfield Mark III, or *Smellie* as he called it. He rested it on the bonnet and pressed his right eye into the rubber cap of the telescopic sight. It only had a three times magnification but was a lot more effective than the basic iron sights. I picked up the spotting scope and tried to zero in on the navigation light on the end of the breakwater.

'How far do you reckon, Jack?'

I tried to focus on the problem – anything to take my mind off my misery.

'Too far – about 1,300 yards with at least a 100 foot drop. Too many variables. Height differential is only the first problem. With wind drift, slight differences in powder load, atmospheric pressure and uncertainty about yardage it could take you several clips before you got the range. By that time you'd be under arrest and Father would be waiting to shove the barrel somewhere you wouldn't like it.'

He grinned as he adjusted the sight. 'I bet Dad could do it, though.'

'He probably could but wouldn't. He's drummed safety into us enough times, though he seems to have failed with you.'

He shrugged. 'Strange thing he said to me when I showed him the scope. You know he refuses to talk about what he did during the war.' Alan had adopted a conspiratorial tone. 'Well, he said that these scopes were at their best at dawn and dusk.'

'So?'

'Well, do you think he might have been a sniper? I bet he killed loads of Germans.'

'Why don't you ask him?'

'Don't be daft.' He levelled the rifle and squinted through the scope. 'You know, anything up to 600 yards would be a simple shot with this. I could sink any of those boats with a couple of bullets from this angle. Straight through – they wouldn't know what had hit them. Blow out their bottoms – no problem.'

'No, you imbecile, the bullets would go straight through their planking and leave small exit holes. You'd need several magazines to turn their bottoms into colanders.'

'Scare their crews though, wouldn't it?'

'I think we'd all be a lot safer if you put the rifle back in the gun safe and played with your toy soldiers instead.'

'Don't patronise me.' He lowered the rifle. As usual, he'd gone from being silly to angry at the same speed as a bullet leaving his rifle. 'You're as blind as the rest of them, Jack. Laugh now, but we're going to need all the soldiers we can get soon – especially those who can shoot straight.' He grabbed the scope from me and put it back in his sack. 'Anyway, I came to find you because dinner is ready, which is more than can be said for *Alphonse* here. I thought you were fixing his breathing.'

'Ha, Ha. *Alphonse* is no more. He is a dead tractor, an expired vehicle, sans breath, sans heart, sans everything.' Most of the farms still used horses in preference to these new fangled contraptions. Hands full of oil, yet again, I could understand their reluctance to change.

'Never mind that. Come on, before they start shouting. There's another surprise waiting for you.'

I wrapped up the pieces of carburettor in an oiled cloth and followed my brother across the top field and down into the dip where the farmhouse had stood for several generations.

I touched one of *Boadicea's* cylinder heads with my fingers. 'Still warm, what's he doing here?'

'I don't know. But it's a nice surprise – should be a bit of fun if he and Dad start up.'

We skirted the bike and approached the kitchen door. Alan went in first while I gathered my thoughts. This could be about the photographs I'd collected from Joan's house on Friday – I hadn't had the nerve to go near the club since my performance at the dance.

I had examined the photos with a magnifying glass and there could be no doubt. Kohler's face was very clear. He was posing with three other Germans, all wearing the national badges of the Third Reich on their tracksuits. I'd asked Joan if she thought Kohler had recognised her but she doubted it as she had only been sixteen at the time and a member of the British team, which had avoided mixing with their hosts. Joan was leaving the following day for a training camp in France and she hadn't objected to my borrowing the prints. I'd agonised about whom to share them with but, in the absence of any other inspiration, I had gone to Uncle Fred.

He'd been pleased to see me and intrigued with my information. Now he was here risking my father's wrath. He must have discovered something of importance.

'Jack, come on, love. Uncle Fred is here.' Mum's voice was clear above the clatter of the saucepans as she reached the final stages of preparing dinner. I took Fred's outstretched hand. He didn't seem to mind the oil. Alan was struggling to open a bottle of our homemade cider.

My father clattered down the stairs and filled the room. His face was already flushed. He advanced on Fred. 'Why are you still here? I told you to bugger off five minutes ago.'

'Aubin, don't start that again. He's not here to see you. He wants to talk to Jack –'

'Well there he is. Bugger off and talk outside, the pair of you. And don't be long. We're about to eat.'

'I'm sure they'll only be a few minutes. I can delay serving that long. Why don't you sit down, dear, and drink some cider. Better still, see if you can help Alan open the bottle.'

Alan glowered and handed the bottle to Father, who spun the cork off with one twist of his massive hands.

23

Fred ushered me outside and pulled me down to inspect *Boadicea*'s spark plugs. 'Sorry, but it's urgent. Why the hell your father won't subscribe to a telephone I don't know. Look, those photographs you showed me. I took them to St Malo yesterday and showed them to a friend. She telephoned this afternoon.'

'I thought your phone was monitored?'

'We have a code. I rang her back on a different number from a public phone. Look, we must keep this just between ourselves. I don't want to give your father any more excuses for hating me.'

'What is it between you two anyway? Why this feud?'

Fred bit his lip. I was sure I saw some moisture in his eyes. 'Not today, Jack. One day perhaps, but you will need to get his side of the story as well. Forget that for now if you can. The important issue is this Kohler character. My source believes that he, or those he might be with, are seen as important. If you feel up to it, I want you to find out more about him. It might mean some deception on your part – you might even have to speak to Caroline.'

'Okay, but that last bit might be difficult. What am I looking for?'

'That's the problem, I don't know. Look, hop on the bike and let's take her for a run up the lane. There's something I need to give you.'

He kicked her into life and I slid onto the pillion. We chugged up the narrow lane, keeping the tyres in one of the ruts made by the tractor rather than on the slippery grass ridge in between. Once out of sight of the farmhouse, Fred stopped, switched off and propped

Boadicea onto her stand. He removed the canvas holdall from the rack behind the pillion seat and extracted a camera.

'Take this. You know how to use one?'

'I've used a Box Brownie but this looks very complicated.' I peered at the chrome and leatherette body with its dials and large lens.

'It's a Leica.'

'What's this FED mean then?' I had turned the camera over.

'It's a Russian copy made in the Ukraine. Don't worry, it works very well. Use it for the long-range shots.' He unwrapped a much smaller camera from the roll. 'This is a Riga Minox – Latvian. Use this for close work. Look, it's easy to hide in your pocket.'

I accepted the tiny camera. 'Where did you get this, Uncle?'

'That doesn't matter, Jack. Will you help?'

I looked at both cameras, weighing them in each hand. 'What's this really about? It's not about Rudi Kohler, is it?'

Fred shrugged his shoulders. 'We don't know, yet. You're right though, it's not your friend Kohler – it's his companions who are of interest.'

'But isn't this spying, Uncle?'

'Yes, Jack. I'm afraid it is. Strange though it may seem, this sleepy little island of ours is very attractive as a meeting place for all sorts of unusual people. The security services are very active in Switzerland, France and Belgium but here... well we don't like upsetting the tourists, do we?'

'But it's not as though we're at war with Germany.'

'Well, that's a matter of opinion. Some will say we have been since the time of Bismarck, though we haven't always been shooting at each other. The secret war, if you will, has always been happening and it's not just the English versus the Germans. Please, Jack let me explain another time. I need to know if you will do this.'

'What is it you want me to do?'

Fred took the FED camera from me and pointed it up the track. 'Use this to show locations. If the people you are following go into, let's say, a bank or a law office or even the States Building –'

'You think the States are involved?'

'I don't know, Jack. There's no doubt that in England some very senior members of the establishment are involved with the Nazis. Just keep your distance. If you're sure no one is watching you, take some snaps, or pretend to be a tourist. It would help if you had a girl with you to pose in front of buildings and make it look natural. What about Rachel? Lita tells –'

'No, Uncle. I am not getting her involved in this.' Though it was tempting, I dismissed it. 'And don't ask me to use Caroline either. The last time a camera got between us, she ended up in the harbour.' I held up the miniature camera. 'And what would I use this for?'

'Close-up work – again, make sure no one can see you and... if you happened to stumble across some documents that you could photograph without anyone noticing, that would be helpful. They're both loaded with film, though you'll have to bring them back to me to develop.'

Perhaps I had made the wrong choice. I should have known he'd try to get me involved in one of his crazy schemes but I wasn't in the mood to defeat the world conspiracy against the working man. I handed the little camera back.

'I'm sorry, Uncle. You are asking too much. I'm sorry I got you involved. I just wanted to know why Kohler was disguising himself; but he's only a student. I don't know anything about his associates – they're none of my concern. I let my curiosity get the better of me. Despite what you say, we are not at war with Germany and I don't think we will be; in fact, we have a direct air link with them now. I read in the *Evening Post* that it takes just six hours to fly direct to Berlin. No, I'm sorry. I just don't want to get involved to this extent. My God; if Father found out he'd... I just don't know what he'd do but –'

'I understand, Jack. I do.' He sounded as though he didn't, sounded disappointed, and I felt my cheeks warming with embarrassment. Was I turning him down because I was afraid? The casual way he had smuggled in a revolver and the talk of his mysterious associates had been worrying me.

I watched as he wrapped the cameras in the canvas bag. He placed the package on the pillion seat, limped away from the bike and struggled up the low bank and stood, surveying the bay below.

In the distance was the smudge of France, only twelve miles away, and half-way out, was the reef of the Écréhous, owned by Jersey but still a bone of contention with our Gallic neighbours. 200 feet below us was the sweep of St Catherine's Bay, enclosed by the long arm of its breakwater. We could see its whole, wasted length from here, thousands of tons of beautiful pink granite squandered by some foolish English civil servants a century before. I watched his shoulders slump and then heave. He walked towards me.

'I'm sorry, Jack. If the world was different and this...' he waved his arm over the channel separating the two cultures, 'was secure, forever... but it's not.

'Spain was beautiful, you know. Less green, perhaps, but as peaceful as this. People trying to live their lives, loving, creating. Then it all exploded in their faces. The Germans came to crush their revolution, brought their bombs, blasted villages and cities apart. Why? Because they hated socialism? Yes, of course. But the real reason was to practise, prepare their war machine so that they were ready to slice through our rotten democracies like your father's knife through that beef that's waiting for you now.'

He turned and held my wrists. 'It was very wrong of me. You're only eighteen, your whole life ahead of you. Unlike me at your age, you have a wise head. Mine was full of adventure and I've found it. It's shaped me in a way I hope no one else will ever be shaped. I have no choice now, but you do.

'There is going to be a war, Jack. The Germans will take France, perhaps in weeks. They'll take these islands because they are there. They might then offer a peace to Britain, an alliance even, before they turn their might on Russia and crush her to dust. That's the future, Jack. It may even be too late to change it but I'm not going to stop trying.'

I wanted to pull away but couldn't.

Fred released his hold, letting his hands fall to his side. 'Have you ever wondered about Malita and me? Why she is so sad? So much in pain?' His voice was almost a whisper now.

I knew they had fallen in love when Malita was assigned as his interpreter in Madrid, and he had told me about the horrors of civil war.

165

'Uncle, you don't –'

'We think we were betrayed because they came for us in the middle of the night. They weren't very skilled in interrogation, Franco's thugs, and the German advisers had been called in to help. It seemed that too much information was being lost with the dead bodies. They didn't wear uniforms, just smart suits.'

His voice had changed to a monotone, almost mechanical, clipped, distant. 'There were two, one spoke excellent English, the other passable Spanish. The leader was very polite, even courteous. Had me patched up after the local police had finished their introductions. He was quite rational, though that quickly disappeared when I wouldn't tell him what he wanted to hear.

'He turned me over to the local thugs and left with his colleague. It's an odd thing but, after a while, you slip below physical pain. That's when they start the mental torture.' He stopped.

I waited, horrified.

'Then they brought Lita to me, made her watch whilst they removed my teeth with a little hammer – one at a time. I gave them some false names and they sent for the Germans. They listened and went away again.

'Later their leader returned, never raised his voice, was always calm, face expressionless. He told me that I had lied to him, had given false names and wasted his time. It was inconvenient, he said, and it wouldn't happen again. He waved his hand, dismissing me.

'My heart leapt, I thought he had given up, had others to interrogate – then he smiled for the first time and turned to Lita. The younger, Spanish-speaking one, took over. He had her strapped to a chair, her clothes ripped off and her legs clamped apart. Two of them held my head, forced me to watch as he probed her personal places with a metal claw –'

'Please, Uncle, you shouldn't –'

'Jack, she was carrying our child.'

I watched him as he straightened himself and focused on the horizon – a thousand-mile stare all the way to Spain.

He started again in a rush of words. 'She screamed at me to tell them nothing. Then she just screamed and screamed until she passed out. They threw water over her and started again. Only his time they gagged her. They gagged me as well so, even if I broke, I wouldn't be able to speak. I thought then that they had lost interest in the information, that we had delayed them for too long for it to be of use. All they wanted was revenge.

'Someone banged on the door and they were called away. They left her bleeding in her stinking chair. Our guards smoked, indifferent to the torture. The Germans returned with grim expressions on their faces, followed by two men struggling with a brazier. They lowered it between us, almost symbolically. The leader removed my gag whilst his colleague spoke to Malita in her language. Then he put on a thick glove and heated the metal claw in the flames. That's when I told him what he wanted to know. They threw us into separate cells and left us to rot.' He dropped his head.

'We owe our life to a young Spaniard, Carlos Bayo. He bribed the guards and got us out and to the coast at Gijon. We had held out long enough for our comrades to escape to the hills. They treated us like heroes, patched us up and smuggled us by boat to France.'

He turned back. 'Lita would never have told them anything. She would have died first, but they knew my weakness, must have seen it in my eyes when they brought her to me. I don't think she will ever forgive that weakness, despite what she says. We only have each other now. We can't have a child, can't even make love and, every time she has a call of nature...' he stopped.

I listened to his breathing, ragged, tormented. I was dizzy with anger, my stomach churned with hate for the torturers and despair for Malita. I turned away from my uncle and walked back to the bike, picked up the canvas package and started back towards my home.

24

My neck was trapped as the left bicep and forearm squeezed together, compressed my windpipe and cut off the flow of air to my lungs. The spray splashed into my eyes as I clamped my mouth shut to prevent my remaining breath from escaping under water. I arched my back in an attempt to relieve the pressure then swept my right hand up and grabbed my assailant's left wrist. Locking my left hand onto his left elbow, I ducked under, sank to the bottom and pulled his weight down with me. I pushed his left arm away, wriggled my head underneath, tugged against the joint then twisted sideways behind him. Jerking his arm up, I subdued him in a wrist hold and elbow lock. We bobbed to the surface.

I kneed my brother in the buttocks and whispered, 'Not so tight next time, you stupid bugger.' I released the arm hold, slid my left hand under Alan's chin and started to pull him to the pool side using a sweeping side kick. I spun him round, placed both his hands together on the concrete six inches above the surface, pressed my left hand on top to prevent the "body" slipping in again and, using my right hand as a lever, hauled myself out. I crossed his arms, grabbed a wrist in each hand, bent down then heaved him out of the water, twisting his arms in the process, and deposited the grinning fool in a sitting position on the side.

I turned to the group of Alan's classmates. 'It's not as difficult as it looks. The key is not to panic and to act decisively. Remember, a drowning person will literally grasp at straws. Never turn your back because he'll drown you with him.' I felt such a fraud. I'd never saved anyone – it was just book-learned theory and simulations.

I fielded their questions just like a proper teacher though I stopped droning on when I spotted the first yawn. 'I've done enough talking. It's time for you lot to get wet. Last one in…'

I continued to teach life-saving techniques to the class, while Martlew, their teacher, sat in the shade sipping a lemonade.

After the class was over and the boys were towelling themselves dry, I watched Kohler's table as surreptitiously as I could. Still no companion. I wondered how much longer I could drag this out. The master seemed relaxed enough so I approached him.

'They've worked pretty hard, sir. Any chance of them having a little sunbathing time before we go back?'

Martlew pulled out his fob watch and winced at the time but nodded. 'I suppose so, Renouf. But, I say, this is all jolly violent stuff you're teaching them. Aren't you meant to be showing them how to save lives?'

'Of course, sir, but in life-saving situations there can be extreme danger. I have to teach them how to approach safely and how to escape if it all goes wrong. It's purely defence, sir. They need to know how to manage aggression, albeit unintended, in these situations. They need to be prepared.'

'Quite, thank you for the speech, Renouf. Perhaps you might share your sentiments with Mr Chamberlain.' He looked at his watch again. 'Another twenty minutes then we have to get back – there's some Latin to be learned.'

I gave them the good news and chatted to some of Alan's friends, all the while keeping an eye on Kohler.

Martlew looked at his watch again and started to get up just as Kohler stood to welcome three older men who had just approached his table.

My mouth hung open in surprise as I recognised one of them as Hayden-Brown, Caroline's father. I reached into my bag for the FED camera and turned towards the master. 'Excuse me, sir, would you mind if I took some photographs?'

He rolled his eyes and tapped his watch. 'If you must, Renouf, but do hurry up. Virgil has been waiting long enough.'

I mustered the boys, pushing them further around the pool so that I could get a good picture of Kohler's group. I fussed around the swimmers, getting behind them and taking some shots of the German without aiming the camera.

Alan watched me with a puzzled expression. 'What are you up to?'

'Can't say anything now but do me a favour and start a towel fight. Take it round the pool, I pointed in Kohler's direction, I'll tell you why later.'

He smiled mischievously. A prefect asking him to misbehave? He didn't need a second bidding. He grabbed a towel, dipped it in the pool and started flicking one of the boys. The others joined in, game for a wet towel fight – anything to delay Latin verbs.

Alan rushed off towards Kohler's party, giving me the perfect opportunity to aim at the group and shoot. Satisfied, I put the camera back in the bag and helped the master round up the reluctant Latin scholars.

Angry that he had been taken advantage of by his charges, Martlew clipped Alan round the ear. Alan didn't rat on me but the look he gave me left me in no doubt that he would be presenting his bill later.

I looked up. Kohler and company had left but their images remained.

The sounds cascaded through the glass of the French windows, as Caroline pounded out some crashing chords – Beethoven probably. I peered through the vibrating glass and watched as she attacked the keyboard. Her body hunched over for the intricate trilling passages then arched like an eagle as she drummed the deep base chords. She was immersed, drowning, in the passionate sounds, oblivious to me as she swayed with the rolling rhythms. I watched as her bottom shifted on the cushioned stool, sweat pouring down her back as she built to a frenzied crescendo.

She slumped, then reached for the sheets of music and started again. She stopped, mid-phrase, and spun round, squinting into the evening sun. She dropped her hands, leapt up then strode across the parquet floor, kicked aside the curtains, which had been dumped on the floor, and pushed the French windows open.

I flinched – struck again by her vitality and beauty. She confronted me, hands on hips; the moisture from her neck and chest collecting between her breasts, staining her frock. Her face was flushed, eyes shining with something I hadn't seen before. Not anger, something more like frustration and confusion.

'Come in then, close the doors.' She strode back to the piano and banged her fists on the lid. 'Help me get this off.'

I struggled with her to unhinge it and place it against the wall. It took some time before she was happy with its placement.

'What difference does it make where you put it?' I asked gently.

'Of course it damn well matters. I've got to get the acoustic bounce right. I hate this bloody room. I need more reverberation. It's dead, soaks up all the energy. Even with those blasted curtains down it's hopeless. At least that polished lid will give some reflection.'

She flounced back to the stool. 'Now, stand over there.' She indicated the corner. 'Out of the way.' She glowered at me. 'Whatever you have to say can wait until I've gone a couple more rounds with Ludwig.'

I shuffled over to the corner and stood like a naughty school boy. At least I could see her face from there.

She started to play again. The sounds were thrilling, her dexterity amazing. I was absorbed, but sensed that she wasn't happy. She stopped her flying fingers again in the middle of a complex passage. '"La relativa scopata inutile,"' she shouted and thumped the keys.

I didn't understand the words but her tone was clear and I was sure she wasn't reciting a musical direction. Saul swore in Afrikaans. Her preference was Italian.

She saw my puzzled look. 'I hate this shitty piano. I asked him to get me a concert grand and what does he bring back? A bloody Bechstein D, older than him. Do I bloody well care that it's been played by Cortot in some crappy concert in Paris? Schnabel would spit on it. I wanted a Steinway – a decent-sized one as well, not this piece of rubbish.'

She stopped her tirade and called me over. 'Come here. Tell me something.'

I walked towards her, skirting the discarded chairs and rugs.

She reached out and grabbed my wrist. 'How can I get the passion into this? Do I have to be a man?'

171

Her intensity was frightening. What could I say? I didn't know much about music. I glanced at the sheets on the piano's deck. Beethoven. So I had been right about that. Piano Sonata No. 23 in F Minor, op 57 and, in brackets, "Appassionata". Bit of a clue that, but what was she asking? Was it about strength or feeling?

'I asked Schnabel the same question, you know,' she continued before I could respond. 'We were in his piano room at Tremezzo, overlooking Lake Como. Do you know what he said?'

I shook my head. I remember her writing about Schnabel and his extraordinary abilities. She confessed that he'd frightened the pants off her. I hoped she hadn't meant that literally, as he was old enough to be her grandfather.

'He laughed and told me to stop trying so hard. What use was that? How can I get the passion, Beethoven's manic intensity, those roaring fortissimos without bloody trying hard?'

'Perhaps –'

But she cut me off, pulled me towards her and pointed into the piano. 'Look, that soundboard, it's beginning to split; the plate's fine and, yes, there's Cortot's signature. My bastard father must have paid a fortune for this pile of junk. Oh, Christ. I know it's not the piano. It's me.

'Look, Jack, I've watched you play water polo, the way you and the others throw the ball. It seems so effortless, yet so powerful. I've tried and it's just pathetic. I can't get the momentum. I'm not weak, so why can even the youngest boy throw a ball better than me?'

I was incredulous. It was as though none of the unpleasantness between us had happened – as though we were still a close couple. I would never understand women. She had a temporary use for me as Mr Practical. But that wasn't why I was there. Fred had overridden my objections, begged me to be pleasant. The information was important.

I swallowed my immediate response and decided to be helpful. 'I think it's about levers and timing.'

'That's what Schnabel said, "Levers; don't try to force it through the arms. Use your fingers as levers, control the volume through the speed of descent. Don't use arm force as it is too slow. Playing is fundamentally movement." Does that make sense to you?'

'It makes sense for water polo – I don't know about piano playing though.'

She was excited. She pushed me away and sat down again. 'Listen.'

She picked the opening passage from the third movement. "Allegro ma no troppo; presto" it said on the sheet, though I had no idea what that meant. She accelerated into it, keeping her arms just above the keyboard and focusing on her finger movement. A blur of perpetual motion mesmerised me as the notes reverberated around the hard surfaces of the room. I felt my eyes pricking with tears of delight.

The notes hung in the air long after the crashing finale. She turned to me, her face empty again. 'Jack, I still can't feel the passion.'

Her expensive lessons with Schnabel had given her the answers. She just needed to be told them again.

'What's so special about Schnabel?'

She rolled her eyes. 'Artur Schnabel? Only the greatest concert pianist of our time, stupid. He's also a brilliant teacher. There's nothing he doesn't know about Beethoven.'

'Is he German?' I was looking for some way of starting the conversation about Kohler and her father.

'Of course, but he doesn't live there anymore.'

'Why not?'

'Jack, don't you know anything? He's a Jew, stupid. He left when Hitler came to power, silly really, but he was frightened, moved to Italy and now he's gone to America, so no more lessons for me – until Daddy...' She stopped and I thought I saw a new colour rise in her cheeks.

'So what did Schnabel tell you about passion, Caroline?'

'He told me I'd need one of these.' She reached for my crotch and I let her squeeze, absorbing the pain. She released her grip and moved her body into me. 'He told me not to try to inject the emotion into the music.' She put her arms around my neck and nibbled my ear. 'He told me to listen to the sounds, let them create the emotion in their own right.' She kissed my cheek. 'I truly hate you, Jack, but the feel of you is creating a different emotion in me.'

173

She spun away, sat down again and looked at me. 'It's simple, according to Schnabel – the emotion should flow from the music into me and not the other way round. So why doesn't the music sound right, Jack? Why doesn't it flow into me like you do?'

I swallowed, trying to keep myself under control. She had broken through again. I'd tried to explain to my uncle that he would be sending me into a minefield but he didn't seem to understand. He'd taken the film from the camera and replaced it with a fresh one. After I told him about Hayden-Brown, he had been insistent that I talk to Caroline about Kohler. My heart had been in my mouth most of the way and now I was once again trapped in her web, with little hope of gaining the control I needed to get the answers; but I had to try, for Malita, if not for myself.

I tried to think of a reply but she had turned back to the keyboard. She started to play a slow passage with heavy bass chords. She looked at me, a ghost of a smile on her lips while her hands caressed the keys. Now she was listening to the music and not the sounds she was producing. She played on, her fingers dancing over the keyboard. Her smile spread as though she had found Beethoven at last. I waited, once more captivated by her. Could I ever escape? Did I want to?

She ran straight into the last movement as the sun slanted off the upturned Chippendale chairs and the curled up Ghiordes rugs, its beams radiating like stage lights as Beethoven, through Caroline, struggled to his manic conclusion.

She clapped her hands in excitement, leapt off the stool and wrapped herself round me kissing me passionately on the mouth. I pressed back, Beethoven still ringing in my ears, wanting to become one with her again but she pulled back, released herself, pushed me away and picked up one of the upturned chairs. She motioned me to pick up another and we sat side by side looking out on the sloping lawn.

'Now, why did you come to see me, Jack?'

I sensed that to tell her the real truth – that I hadn't stopped thinking about her for days, that I blamed myself for the stupidity of our last meeting – would be fruitless. It would lead to recrimination. Despite the kiss, the fondness, she had said she hated me and I believed her. She wasn't ready to forgive me yet. I decided to be business like, to tell the other truth, though not all of it. 'I wanted to talk to you about Rudi.'

'Why?'

'I'm curious. I saw him again today with some friends at the hotel. He seemed friendly enough, didn't want to get his revenge.'

'He's bigger than that, Jack.'

'Have you been seeing much of him?' I managed to keep my voice neutral but didn't fool her.

'Really, Jack, what a question? After what you said, does it matter if I see him or not?'

'I deserve that but I'd just like to know, that's all.'

'Know what?'

'Is he German?'

She exhaled slowly. 'Is that all? I thought... no, never mind what I thought. Yes, I think he is. I think he and his uncle are pretending to be Dutch because of their business dealings with my father. They don't want to cause any embarrassment. You know, with all the talk about war in the papers.'

'Did you ask him?'

'Of course not, that would be very rude.'

'But you were very angry with him last week... you told –'

She interrupted, irritated now. 'Yes, I was but it wasn't because he was German. It doesn't matter anyway.'

'Have you seen him though?'

'Yes, in fact he was here yesterday evening. Don't get agitated... it's not what you're thinking. He wasn't alone. Father invited him and his friends to dinner and I had to play the hostess. Bloody boring it was as well.'

'What do you mean?'

'It was all business talk... I tried to introduce some culture. They were polite, discussed music for a while but soon got back to their bloody economics and diamond nonsense. Normally, the bastard shows off and tells guests about my playing, even gets me to demonstrate his investment, but he didn't seem aware of me, he was so wrapped up in their discussions. I excused myself with a headache but only Rudi showed any concern. I think he wanted to talk to me but his uncle wouldn't let him leave the table. Anyway, why are you interested?'

'Just curious.'

'Jack, you're fibbing. What's going on? Are you spying?'

I felt a hot rush of blood to my face and was sure she could see the change of colour.

'Come on, you can tell me.'

'I think I've outstayed my welcome. Let me help you put the room back together before I go.' I walked towards the upturned piano lid and waited for her.

Instead, she moved towards the window and went outside. She returned moments later. 'Ah ha. That's your uncle's bike, isn't it? Red Fred. So that's what it's all about. He's the one who's curious, not you.' She laughed. 'How intriguing. Do you suppose he is a Communist spy? That would be fantastic. Are the "Reds" checking up on my father's dodgy businesses?' She clapped her hands. 'Wouldn't that be so delicious. Give the bastard a fright.'

She waltzed over to me. 'Come on then, tell me what you know and I'll tell you what I know. Deal?'

'Only if you promise not to tell your father.'

'He wouldn't listen to me if I told him there were burglars breaking into his safe. He never takes me seriously, I'm just a decorative inconvenience... enough about him. What's this really about?'

We both seemed cursed with distant, dismissive fathers, perhaps that had drawn us together but now wasn't the time for analysis. 'I don't honestly know but I've been asked to find out about his guests. Do you know their names?'

'I might but you need to do better than that. Who wants to know and why?'

'Okay, my uncle thinks he might be part of a fascist plot –'

She hooted. 'Really. What nonsense. He's only interested in one thing.' She rubbed her fingers together. 'Sometimes, I think he's more Jewish than Saul. They certainly share an interest.'

'In what?'

'Diamonds, silly. Don't you remember last month when Saul showed us that roll of – what did he call them?'

'Industrials I think. He got them from his father's safe. But he was just showing off.'

'Maybe, but they were real enough.'

'Could have been fakes for all we know.'

She shrugged. 'I think that was what they were worried about last night.'

'Who was worried?'

'Rudi's uncle and that English creep, Sir something or the other.'

'What about Rudi, was he worried?'

'Not so you'd notice. He looked more bored than me. The other two, some sweaty chap and another German, seemed fascinated.'

'You can't remember their names?'

'No, silly, I was thinking about other things.'

'Such as?'

She snorted. 'Good try. But it wasn't you – not unless you write piano sonatas in your spare time.'

'So they thought these diamonds might be fake?'

'Not for long. Father brought in some samples and flashed them around. The sweaty one seemed to know all about them, where they came from, all that nonsense. It was the other German, Shitz, or some name like that, who was all over them. Stuffed one of those funny magnifying glasses into his eye socket and squinted over them. He looked ridiculous.'

'But what does it mean? Are the Germans buying them? What do they want with jewellery?'

'Beats me. Perhaps the Fuhrer likes dressing up – I don't know. There's a lot of them though.'

'How many?'

'The bastard won't be back for a while so I'll show you. Come on.'

She grabbed my hand and dragged me through the conservatory, along the corridor and into the kitchen. She lifted a set of keys off a wall rack and unlocked the door to the cellar. I'd been down there with her before when she'd tried to ply me with some of her father's best wine. I'd refused then but this information about diamonds was something Uncle Fred would relish.

We clattered down the stairs, past the tiered racks of bottles to a cage at the end of the cool room. Inside, on the walls, were his precious vintage wines and ancient brandies but on the floor were four crates.

She unlocked the cage and ushered me in. 'There, have a look for yourself.' She pointed to the first one. 'That's been opened. Just lift the lid. Don't pinch any.'

The crate was solidly made from some sort of tropical hardwood, about two feet long, eighteen inches high and about the same in depth. Something was stencilled on the top: "Forminiére" and the initials "SGB". There were metal handles on each long end and a locking clasp on the front though the padlock was open.

I lifted the lid. No velvet rolls, just layers of small diamonds separated by black cloth. Thousands of the little buggers. They looked different from the ones Saul had shown us. His were clear though he told us they were roughs, or industrials. These were of a similar size but ranged in colour from yellow through gold to a warm brown.

'See, I wasn't making it up. I must say they look a bit grubby, dirty even – not much sparkle. Go on – grab some.'

I must have looked startled.

'Don't worry. We're not stealing them. I've got an idea. Go on, bring them here.'

I dug out a fistful and handed them to her.

She shoved them into one of her dress pockets. 'Put everything back the way it was. Don't worry about fingerprints.'

I closed the case then, on an impulse, lifted it up. I was used to hefting hundredweight barrels of spuds and reckoned this weighed more than half that. I lowered it carefully, replaced the padlock but didn't close it.

'How long have they been here?'

'Don't know for certain. A few days. I think he brought them in from St Malo when he took *Lorelei* there last week.'

'So he's still got that floating gin palace?'

She sniggered. 'He still can't drive it though. Needs to hire someone to get it out of the harbour. He uses it for...' she stopped. 'Well, less said about that the better.'

I suspected she'd been about to say he used it for the same

purpose as we had. Only his wife hadn't been on the island for well over a year.

She poked me in the chest. 'I know what you're thinking so stop that now. We've got work to do. Come on.'

'What work, where are we going?'

'You're giving me a lift on that big throbbing machine of yours and we're going to see Saul to ask him some questions.'

25

'*Wat die hel doen jy?*'

'Diamonds, Saul, tell us about those diamonds.' Caroline barged past the startled boy, dragging me in to the apartment with her.

'*Kak!* Look at the state of you. What have you two been up to? No, don't answer that. I don't want to know.' He trailed behind us until we were all in the lounge.

Caroline hadn't bothered to change out of her sweat-stained dress and her hair was a mess after the ride on *Boadicea*.

'What about a drink? Have you still got that Rarete Calvados?' She was already poking about in the cocktail cabinet.

Saul looked at me, a mixture of bemusement and irritation on his face.

'Ah, here it is. Come on, you two, this will wake us up.'

'Steady, girl. That's sixty years old, my father would rather shag a goat than see you wasting that.'

'Too bad he's not here then. We'd love to see that, wouldn't we, Jack? A Jew shagging a goat. Shouldn't it be the other way round?' She tossed each of us a cut-glass tumbler and pulled the cork.

'Not for me, thanks – I had enough the other night.'

'Don't be pathetic, Jack. It didn't hurt your performance.' She giggled as she splashed a large measure into Saul's glass, filled her own then advanced on me. I rolled my eyes but let her pour the amber liquid into the tumbler. 'Right, let's sit while Saul tells us all about diamonds.'

'What is going on? You two aren't getting engaged, are you?'

Caroline spluttered a mouthful over her dress. '*Jou klein kakfokker*

– you see, I remembered some of your God-awful language from that little lesson you gave me.'

'What lesson?' I challenged.

'Never mind, Jack, you don't need to know'

But Saul's face was bright red and I knew. 'You bitch and you, you –'

'Stop it, Jack. It was just a bit of fun, wasn't it, Saul? I showed him something of mine for a dare and he showed me something small belonging to him. I laughed. He swore. Then we had another drink. That's all. Anyway, boys, minds off sex now, and let's talk about diamonds.'

'Why?'

'Because you're the one who was showing them off last month. Remember, when your father was in South Africa you went to the safe and brought out that velvet package and let us see the little sparklers?'

'Yes, and you got mighty excited because you thought they were high-grade diamonds.'

'And how many did she want to accommodate your "little something"?'

Saul's colour had subsided but his voice was still embarrassed. 'Too many.'

'You... I was going to say Judas but I think Iago might be better.'

'Cut the Shakespeare, you two. It didn't happen. I would always have asked for too much. Happy now?'

I continued to glare at Saul then took a sip of the Calvados. It seemed a lot smoother than the cognac; perhaps I was acquiring a tolerance to the evil stuff.

'Have you still got them?' she asked.

'Not those but I've got a different batch.'

'Go get them... go on, shoo.'

I marvelled at the control she had over us, as Saul disappeared into the corridor.

'Now, don't mention the Germans,' she hissed at me. 'Just say I'm checking up on one of my bastard father's deals.'

'What about those diamonds in your pocket?'

'Keep quiet about those as well. I'll show them when I'm ready.'

Saul returned with a roll of black velvet, much like the one he'd shown us before. He'd boasted then about his family's involvement in the trade as South Africa was the world's leading supplier of diamonds. However, he'd told us that the little sparklers, as Caroline had dubbed them, were just industrials and not worth cutting and polishing.

'Well, let's see them.' She cleared a space on the walnut coffee table by sweeping everything onto the floor.

Saul knelt down and unwrapped the velvet until the hundreds of little diamonds were revealed. 'These are small roughs. We trade them for cut stones – quite profitable.'

'Is that all they're good for – trade?' I was confused.

'*Kwas*. Without these little buggers you would have no manufactured goods, no aircraft engines, no gyroscopes, electronic parts, torpedoes, tanks, artillery –'

'Why?'

'Hardness, Jack. As simple as that. Little test for Caroline. Which is the hardest? An opal, an emerald or a ruby?'

'How the fuck do I know? That's why we're here.'

'You'd think a woman would know that, wouldn't you, Jack?'

'Don't draw me into your fight. Just tell us and explain what it's got to do with manufacturing.'

'Simple test, if you can scratch gemstone A with gemstone B, then B is harder. The answer is an emerald can scratch an opal but a ruby can scratch both. There's something invented by a Frenchman called the Mohs Hardness Scale. Talcum powder is the lowest mineral with a score of one, opal is five point five, emerald is seven point five and ruby is nine.'

'Sounds a bit like diving scores to me. Miss Hayden-Brown, four emeralds and one opal.' I could have added Miss Vibert, four rubies and an emerald but Caroline slapped my wrist before I could form the words.

'I still don't understand what you're talking about. Make it simple for me, please, Saul. I'm only a confused woman.'

'Sorry. A diamond is ten on the scale. There is nothing harder but there are hard tens and soft tens –'

I interrupted. 'Enough, we get the picture. But where do your little buggers come from?'

'Is there no end to your ignorance, Jack? Caroline will appreciate this. It's quite sexy.'

'Go on, seduce me then.'

Saul smirked. 'I do have a gem in the safe which would do just that but my father would kill me.'

'Interesting choice, Saul. What did Shylock say when Jessica ran off with his diamonds. *"I would my daughter were dead at my foot and the jewels in her ear!"* These little baubles generate some unhealthy passion, don't they?'

'I said cut the Shakespeare. How are they made, Saul?'

'As I said, it's quite sensual. About one hundred miles down, into the mantel of the Earth are these carbon atoms. They're pressed together in layers under pressure until a diamond is born. With me so far?'

We nodded, Caroline smiling more than me.

'Then comes the eruption, plasma drills its way upward, searching out weaknesses in the rock above. It moves at about ten miles per hour – twice as fast as you can swim, Jack – grabbing diamonds as it accelerates. It's called kimberlite.'

'Is that what Kimberley in South Africa is named after?'

'And these apartments, that's right, Jack, perhaps you're not as dumb as you look. As it nears the surface, the pressure containing it decreases and gases in the kimberlite expand, just like they do in a bottle of champagne when you pull the cork.'

Caroline clapped her hands.

'She's got the picture. As the mass of blue ground containing these little beauties and their bigger brothers nears the surface, it reaches speeds of one hundred miles an hour, or as fast as that motor-bike you keep boasting about. It explodes through the surface and scatters the harvest far and wide. Exciting, eh?'

'Have you seen one of these explosions, Saul? What's it like?'

Saul was taking a sip of his Calvados as Caroline asked her question and he almost choked in a spasm of laughter.

'What's so funny?'

He wiped the liquid from his shirt. 'Caroline, the last time this happened was fifty million years ago, but I'll sell you a ticket for the next event if you wish.'

Even Caroline saw the funny side, though it wasn't often that she laughed at herself.

'So who owns these diamonds?'

Saul tapped his nose. 'Have I told you the one about the vicar, the priest and the rabbi?'

'Not one of you feeble jokes, Saul. Not now. We don't have the time.' Caroline sighed in exasperation. 'What on earth could that have to do with diamonds?'

'Patience, my dear, and I'll tell you.' He winked at me. 'The three of them are sharing a drink and the discussion turns to collections.

'The vicar says, "We in the Church of England are very democratic so everything is shared equally. Half goes to God, the other half to supplement my living."' Saul's plummy voice was spot on.

'The priest shakes his head in disbelief. "Our church is for the glory of God so I only get to keep ten percent."' The Irish accent wasn't too convincing but he hurried on.

'The rabbi laughs and rubs his hands together. "We are more realistic. I take the collection plate and toss the contents into the air. What stays up goes to God. I get the rest."'

He looked at us in expectation so I yawned.

Caroline smacked her glass down on the table. 'So, what's the answer to my question?'

'Humourless peasants. If you must know, my tribe seems to own most of them. Well, Sir Ernest Oppenheimer at least, and his De Beers cartel.'

'He's Jewish?' Caroline asked.

'He joined the Church of England about ten years ago,' Saul replied.

'So he's not Jewish?'

'Would it were that simple. You've heard of the Nuremburg Laws?'

'The *Evening Post* ran a series about this earlier this year. I remember listening to my father rant on about it.'

'About the laws or we humble Jews?'

'Surprisingly, he found the German attitude disgusting.'

'Oh, that's fine then. Perhaps he should have written the deformed house painter a stiff letter.'

Caroline and I studied our feet.

'Ignorance is bliss, I suppose. Hitler's got this thing about Jews. Blames us for Germany's defeat in the last war, amongst other things.' He sighed. 'It's bad and only going to get worse. Four years ago at the Nazi party conference in Nuremberg they tried to define a Jew. God knows, we've been trying for millennia but we're not as clever as Hitler –'

'Before you tell us what the Nazi's came up with, how do *you* define a Jew?' I was sure Rachel would be interested.

'As I've said, it's debatable but generally you need to have a Jewish mother. A Jewish father and gentile mother isn't enough.'

'So how different was Hitler's definition?' I asked.

Saul looked uncomfortable. 'Remember this isn't just a paper exercise. People have lost their jobs, their houses and their lives because of this.'

I remembered Miko's story and cursed myself for being so insensitive. 'Sorry.'

'Some of it is plain stupid, like forbidding Jews to fly the swastika. Jews can no longer marry German citizens and all such marriages were voided. Jews can't shag Germans anymore. They can't hire German females. Jews were denied German citizenship. So to be a Jew in this Third Reich you needed to be cursed with three full Jewish grandparents. That didn't net enough so its been made easier – two grandparents is sufficient now and next year, who knows, perhaps shaking hands with one could qualify you. But do you know what was really sickening?'

We shook our heads again.

'There was no public outcry. Jewish doctors, lawyers, musicians, teachers, scientists; people who had done so much for their country were suddenly outcasts. And yet there were no protests.'

'Would protesting have made them Jewish as well?' Caroline's skin was thicker than mine.

'Probably.' Saul glared at her. 'But you wanted to know about Oppenheimer. He was German, became British, renounced his Jewish faith and became a Christian.'

'The fate that Shylock dreaded most of all – even more than the loss of his diamonds.'

'That's right, Jack. Only renouncing your religion cuts no ice with the Nazis. They are obsessed with blood. You could become a Hindu, a Buddhist or even the bloody Pope but, to them, you will always be a filthy Jew.'

'But Oppenheimer is British now?' Caroline sounded confused.

'Only in his eyes. There are enough fascists in England who would still see him as a Jew. But enough about my tribe. You wanted to know about diamonds. Well let me tell you this. Sir Ernest, the reluctant Jew, has organised it so he and his company, De Beers, own most of the world's diamonds. He has dedicated all of his career to protecting the price of diamonds by any means available. If he doesn't want a country to have diamonds then, short of declaring war on him, they don't get them. He is loyal only to himself – even the Americans can't push him around.'

'But surely he sells at the right price?'

'Not necessarily, Jack. The diamond trade is very… complicated. Forget all the jewellery for the moment. The industrials are absolutely essential, so he who controls them controls the world's manufacturing process, yes?'

'Yes, but –'

'There are leakages and other sources. So there are many trying to bypass De Beers. It's all about quantity. The world's largest diamond was the *Cullinan*. It weighed over 3,000 carats, or about one and half pounds. Three polishers worked their bollocks off cutting it into nine jewels. The biggest of those was the *Great Star of Africa* which weighs over 500 carats.'

'That's in the Crown Jewels, isn't it?'

'That's right, Caroline, safe from your little paws in the Tower of London.'

'What about your diamond, Saul? *Jacob*, the one your father named his boat after?' I asked.

'Don't rub it in. I told you that in confidence.'

'What's this, keeping secrets from me?' Caroline swivelled to look at Saul.

'No, it's a family legend. My great grandfather, Jacob, is

supposed to have discovered a large white, which weighed in at 200 carats. He found a buyer and had it polished into an oval but this Indian shyster cheated him and he was forced to sell for a fraction of its worth. My father named the boat after him as an ironic reminder. Allegedly, the Indian sold it on to the Agha Khan for over a million rand.'

'My, Saul, you could have been rich. I do find that *so* attractive in a man.' She reached over to stroke his face.

'Stop teasing him, Caroline. Remember why we're here.' I pulled her back. 'So where else can someone get industrial diamonds?'

'Who would this someone be, Jack. Are you talking about Germany?'

I tried to keep a straight face. 'Britain, Italy, Germany, Japan, any of those.'

'Well, let's pick America as you didn't mention it. From what I've heard, it would need about six million carats of industrial diamonds per year to feed its factories, so the only place is South Africa.'

'What about the Belgian Congo?'

Saul looked suspiciously at Caroline. 'What do you know about the Congo?'

'Nothing, I just heard someone mention it.'

Saul grinned. 'I don't suppose that would have been your father by any chance?'

'It might have been.'

'The Belgian Congo has mines but De Beers controls them. Look, if you know something, I think you should tell me. I can find out more from my father when he comes back. Hey, I could telephone my uncle in London now. He can tell –'

'No! This must remain our secret. Promise me, Saul.' Caroline fixed him with one of her looks.

He lowered his head. 'If you insist.'

'I do, but you know more than you're letting on. Don't you?'

'No. Honestly, I don't. Father has spoken about what might be happening, how De Beers has stifled production everywhere else in the world to protect its position.' He slid his hand into the pile of

187

diamonds and held them up before letting them trickle through his fingers. 'Perhaps Oppenheimer secretly trades with all the nations, smuggles his own diamonds. He has a massive stockpile of industrials in London over twenty-five million carats, but rumour is that they're of very poor quality. Much of it is boart and only useful for crushing into abrasive grit. He can't unload them until all other production has dried up.'

'How do you know so much about this business, Saul?' Caroline challenged.

'Only what I've picked up round the dinner table. I suppose Jack's dinner table talk is about bulls screwing cows and planting potatoes –'

'Fat chance. For one, we have dinner at midday and there's precious little conversation. We have tea in the evening and then we poor toilers of the soil are so bone weary, we go straight to bed.'

'Ha, bloody ha.'

'I understand what you mean though. Uncle Fred and Malita have more interesting conversations about the world revolution.'

This amused Caroline. 'On the rare occasions we eat together, we hardly speak as it only leads to arguments. Last night was an exception.'

'What happened?' Saul asked.

'I'll tell you later. You finish your story first.'

'Anyway, my parents are obsessed with diamonds. They want me to join one of my uncles in London when I've finished school, learn the trade properly.'

'Will you? I thought you were like Jack, obsessed with stuffy old Shakespeare.'

'And so I am but that subject is *verboten* in front of you.'

'Saul, *du gehst mir auf den Sack.*'

'*Ich fresse einen Bessen –*'

'Hey! Stop it, you two.'

She poked her tongue out. 'He started it.'

'Did I fuck. She called me something rude.'

'Calm down. I didn't realise you both spoke German.' That explained a lot about Rudi.

'You speak French, we don't, so have a conversation with yourself

188

if you want.' Saul spun a diamond on the table. 'Do you want to hear the rest?'

We nodded.

'All I do know is that our family has been in gems and diamonds for a couple of generations and we can't afford to upset De Beers.'

'Why? It's just business, isn't it?' I asked.

'With that much money involved it goes way beyond business. De Beers are very defensive.' He paused. 'Even with your limited cadet force training, you can tell us the best method of defence is...'

'Attack.'

'Exactly. And that's what they do. They don't just guard their assets, they seek out their enemies and... deal with them.'

'How?'

'They don't usually leave evidence. Let's just say they neutralise them.'

'As in murder them?'

'Impossible to prove but no one in the diamond trade would be foolish enough to enquire. Now, are you going to tell me about your dinner party and what all this is about?'

Before she could start, I had some questions for him. 'Do the initials SGB and the name Forminiére mean anything to you?'

'Ah, the Belgian connection you mentioned. SGB is the Société Générale Belgique and I believe Forminiére is one of their larger mines. De Beers has a majority stake and controls production through the Diamond Trading Company. It's even got a registered office in Jersey. Next time you're in Hill Street, check those brass plates outside the lawyers' offices.'

'What about these, Saul?' Caroline didn't like being upstaged. She dug into her pocket and scattered the diamonds onto the table.

Saul gasped, picked up a couple then hurried out of the room.

'What are we going to do about this?' I whispered.

'I don't know. Let's see what he says about them.'

He returned with an eyepiece. 'This is a jeweller's loupe, twenty times magnification. I'm no expert but I think I can tell the quality of these. My uncle could tell you the origin as well.' He examined a few at random.

'Excellent. These are the best. Top of the hardness scale. You can tell by how the crystals are aligned. How many did you say there were?'

I answered. 'We didn't but I reckoned each crate weighed over half a hundred-weight. Deduct the weight of the crate and packing, that leaves about fifty pounds of diamonds.'

He whistled. 'If they are all of this quality then it's quite a horde. Four crates you say, that's 200 pounds. Must be over 400,000 carats. Enough to keep the Nazi's in production for a few –'

Caroline interrupted. 'No one mentioned Germans.'

'I may be Jewish but I'm not stupid. Germany is desperate for industrials. That's where the money is. No one dares sell directly to the Nazis so the market is open for chancers like your father and his friends.'

She considered for a moment. 'Okay, so he's dealing with Germans. These are only a sample though. If I'm right, they were discussing shipping a whole lot more.'

'It's a long way from the Congo. It's on the west coast of Africa, only a small frontage onto the Atlantic. Probably steamer to Lisbon, they're leaning towards the Nazis so no questions asked there. Onward to Belgium or straight to Germany.' He paused in his musing. 'That's the catch. Can't use the direct route. Too obvious and not enough profit. Some middlemen needed. A trading company registered here with proxy shareholders would be ideal. No tax or awkward questions. Not a De Beers subsidiary like DTC though. It would have to be something more opaque, probably a holding company. Perhaps not the one you mentioned, SGB, they're legit. That's your father's role I suppose, putting together some sort of deal –'

'So what are they worth?' She sounded impatient.

'Keep your wig on and I'll try to work it out. Let's see. This sort of quality purchased at source with cheap labour, probably less than two shillings a carat. Times 400,000 works out at about 40,000 pounds sterling. Germans would pay a minimum of three pounds per carat that's £1.2 million and a profit of £1,196,000 on this sample alone. Take away your shipping and handling costs, bribes, wastage, hired help, etc, and, whoever has stumped up the cash, is looking at a net profit of well over a million. Enough to kill for.'

We considered that in silence.

Suddenly the enormity of the transaction hit me.

'Never mind the bloody profit, we can't let these get to Germany!' I shouted.

'Don't be daft, Jack. My father's a bastard but we can't steal his diamonds.'

Was she dreaming of a better piano, a faster car, or had she just realised how big this was as well?

'I don't mean steal them. We have to inform the authorities.'

Saul chortled. 'Perhaps the authorities already know, perhaps there's a slice for them?'

'You're right. It's none of our business though I would have thought, you in particular, would have wanted to stop Hitler getting hold of them,' I said.

'Don't be naïve. If this deal fails, there are plenty of others willing to take the risk. Look at the rewards. Short of bombing the mines and blowing up the stockpiles, you're not going to stop Germany getting diamonds.'

'Perhaps not, but I might be able to stop them getting *these* diamonds. Uncle Fred will know what to do. Even if he won't, I will –'

'Stop. That's enough. This is our secret, remember. No one else must know.' Caroline grabbed my face, forced me to look at her. 'Promise me, Jack.'

Her voice was calm but her eyes were full of worry.

'I'm sorry but we have to stop this. We can't just let them get away with it.'

Her eyes moistened. She blinked furiously. 'I trusted you. You can't betray me.'

Even though I'd had plenty of practise in the last few days, she was right. I couldn't. Then I thought of someone else who'd been betrayed and what had been done to her by the merciless bastards who would benefit from these diamonds. Caroline was right. It had to remain a secret, but only from her. Whatever I did, whoever I told, I must ensure she was protected from the truth.

I tried to look reassuring. 'Don't worry. It will remain between us.'

She pulled me to her, clasped her arms around my neck and

pressed her body tightly into mine. She stood on tiptoe, pressed her mouth to my ear. Her breath was cool.

'Thank you.'

That familiar body promised so much again, shaped itself to mine. I couldn't stop my reaction but, as soon as she sensed it, she shifted her hips away and removed her arms.

'I need time to think this through. Saul, be a dear and order me a taxi.' She bent down, scooped up her diamonds and thrust them back into her pocket.

'Ask the driver to meet me at the Dicq. I need a walk.'

'But, I can run you home. It's no –'

'Thank you for the offer, Jack, but I can't think straight while I'm clinging on to you,' she said, 'and you can't either.'

She followed Saul into the corridor where the phone was kept. She paused at the door. 'I know this is difficult but you have to think it through as well.' She looked down as though she was engaged in an internal argument.

Apart from Saul's distant voice on the telephone, the apartment was silent. She was only feet away yet that enormous gulf was between us again.

Finally she looked up and directed her gaze at a point above my head. 'Please don't read too much into what's happened between us today. Remember how easily you betrayed Rachel. Think about that before you break any more promises.'

Message so clearly delivered, it pinned me to the floor. She twisted away and hurried into the hall.

When Saul returned, I was still rooted to the spot.

He refilled his glass and offered me the bottle.

'No thanks.'

'"Well, here's another nice kettle of fish you've pickled me in!"' He raised his glass. 'How are you going to get us out of this one?'

Like Caroline, I needed time to think. 'I don't know but this isn't a film, we're not Laurel and Hardy, and I can't see a happy ending.'

'You're going to tell your uncle, aren't you?'

'I might. Don't worry, I'll keep you out of it.'

He tilted his head and emptied the glass. 'Oh no you won't. Whatever you're plotting, count me in. It's as much my fight as yours.' He refilled my glass and thrust it at me.

This time, I accepted and waited until his was full.

'*Le'chaim!*' I said.

'Very good. *Prost!* Coupled with *Bumsen Sie Hitler*.' He sat down. 'Now what are you thinking?'

'What's the safest way to sabotage a boat's engines without leaving any trace?'

26

Tuesday

'On the balcony – there.' I indicated behind me while trying to remain camouflaged in the dappled shade under a chestnut tree.

Malita glanced over my shoulder. 'Yes, I see many men, standing. Who are they?'

'The tall one on the far left, that's Kohler's uncle,' I whispered. I didn't want our interest noticed.

'Who are the others?' Rachel hissed.

I'd arranged to meet Malita in the Royal Square during her lunch break from de Gruchys to report progress. To my surprise and discomfort, Rachel had appeared with her. My heart had almost stopped with embarrassment. I hadn't had the courage to face her since the evening of the dance. She looked tired and a trifle sad but didn't seem to be angry with me. I wondered why Malita had brought her. What had Rachel told her? Was she hoping to get us together again?

Rachel avoided more than the briefest eye contact but declared how pleased she was to escape from the steaming sweatshop of their workroom.

The group I had been following most of the morning had now been joined by some members of the States Assembly during their lunch break and were drinking outside on the shaded balcony of the United Club.

I didn't turn round. 'The elderly one, in the navy pinstriped suit, is Jurat Hurel, vice president of the Finance Committee.'

'Didn't you tell me that one of your relations was president of finance?' Rachel asked.

194

'That's right, Mum's cousin, Ralph, though I've always called him Uncle. But he's not there. I wonder if he knows about Hurel.'

'I recognise Hayden-Brown.' Rachel's tone implied she would rather spit on Caroline's father than merely spot him.

'I've been following them since ten o'clock. I'm going to have some explaining to do tomorrow. I was supposed to be taking a swimming lesson for Martlew at the Palace.'

Earlier, I'd been called to the bursar's office and handed an envelope. The handwriting was Caroline's and my heart had jumped. I'd hurried into the corridor and ripped it open. Inside was a single sheet. "States Chamber. 10:00 today. That's all the help you get. Do not contact me again". What had I expected?

I'd sent a message to the Latin master offering my apologies, changed into cream slacks and a plain white cotton shirt then borrowed a panama hat from Saul's locker. Slipping into town, I'd tried my best to look like a tourist as I headed for the square.

'They're moving,' Rachel murmured. 'It looks as though a waiter is calling them to their seats.' She ducked her head. 'Don't turn around. One of them is standing at the balcony looking our way.' She dropped down, tugging Malita with her, and pretended to be looking for something on the granite flagstones.

'Is all right. He has gone.' Malita stood and smiled at me. 'You have done well. Fred will be pleased.'

'Yes, but how do I get the photographs of the two new ones from the bank? I can't waltz in and start taking snaps while they're eating, now can I?'

'Malita and I could go up there and have a drink, admire the view and take some shots with them in the background.'

'Unfortunately, Rachel, the United Club is men only and wouldn't let you in even if you were someone's guest.'

Malita snorted. 'How very British.' Then her face split with a broad smile. 'That is the weakness.'

'What do you mean, weakness?' Rachel asked.

'The British don't see the servants, no?'

'No, I mean yes. You're right, Malita. But how does that help.'

She tapped her nose. 'Give me small camera.' She reached out as

I removed it from my trouser pocket. She stood up, patted down her dress and walked towards the side entrance of the United Club.

Rachel and I watched as she rang the bell and waited outside. A short man in brown overalls answered and listened to her. He seemed to be shaking his head but then shrugged and disappeared inside.

Minutes later a man wearing a short white coat appeared and greeted Malita with a hug and kisses on both cheeks. There was much gesticulating and more kisses before he went back into the club. Malita returned with an even broader smile on her face.

'Well, what was all that about? Who's that waiter?' I asked.

'Emilio. He work there much time. Also, he friend. He think like Fred and me. He work, you know, how you say? For the party.'

'So you gave him the little camera and asked him to photograph our friends?'

She nodded.

'What if he's caught?' Rachel sounded anxious.

Malita shrugged her shoulders. 'Is no matter. He hate job. But no worry. He no make mistake. He bring to me camera later.'

She reached out. 'You give big camera. I take and Fred make printings. You come at *seis,* six o'clock. I make for you tea.' She looked at Rachel, including her in the invitation.

I didn't know whether I should press her to join us as well as I was still reeling from my encounter with Caroline the previous evening.

I'd replayed the whole scene over and over while I tried to get to sleep but I still couldn't work out what, apart from hate, she felt for me. I even examined the individual words she had used, trying to pick hidden meanings out of them.

I'd finally dozed off replaying a very different scene: Rachel, the sun sparkling off her enticing grin as she dangled a spare swimming costume in front of me and made me beg for it.

Rachel looked at me before she answered Malita. My mind cleared and I realised that I really wanted her to accept the invitation but, before I could speak, she replied.

'Thank you but that was enough excitement for one day. It was good to get out of the hothouse for a while though. Come on, Malita, we had better get back before they send out a search party.'

'Rachel, please...' I spoke, but it was to her retreating back.

Malita rolled her eyes at me. 'I try but...' she shrugged and followed Rachel back to work.

I stood there feeling foolish and helpless until the drips from the tree reminded me I should be in the pool. I hurried off, trying to think of a convincing excuse for Martlew – preferably in Latin.

I'd left *Boadicea* parked in Museum Street so I made my way there, through the town centre. I cut through the market and, to stop my stomach grumbling, I bought an apple.

As I was paying, I had the feeling that I was being watched. In the mirror behind the fruiterer, I spotted the man who had given me the date of Lawrence's accident hovering by one of the butchers' counters. He didn't look as though he was purchasing a joint of beef.

I left via a side entrance and stopped outside Donaldson's music shop to check for reflections in the large window. My eye was drawn to a display of gramophone records, including an HMV Red Label double-sided copy of Jussi Bjoerling singing extracts from "La Bohème". The sad image of the pieces of broken shellac lying in my uncle's front room reached out from the brightly-coloured record sleeves to taunt me.

I refocused and checked the reflection. My follower was still there, back turned, pretending to study the contents of the newsagent's window on the other side of the street. Had he been trailing me all morning? Was he just curious or did he intend to stop me? My heart was racing as I turned into Museum Street and hurried towards the bike.

I was nearly there when the Jaguar turned off Belmont Road and ghosted to a halt in front of *Boadicea*. I slowed and peeked over my shoulder. He was less than fifty feet from me and closing in.

The street was empty apart from a grey Morris van parked outside one of the terraced houses. The rear doors of the van were gaping and the front door to the house was open. I edged towards it. I didn't know who lived there but I felt the need for company. I was about to cross its threshold, when the tall man, who had spoken to me about Lawrence, blocked my way.

He smiled without humour. His voice was deep, throaty. 'Good of you to stop. Mind if we have a chat?' He gestured in the direction of his car. I could hear its engine running.

I started to back away but felt the hot breath of the other man on my neck. 'Keep calm. We just want a quiet word. Won't take long. Be a good lad and co-operate.'

I swivelled to face him. The brim of his black hat shaded his eyes but his expression was menacing. Shorter than me, he was built like a rugby forward. His suit was crumpled. I could smell fried breakfast on his clothes and stale tobacco on his breath. The other man was pressing into me, his hand gripped my elbow. My throat was dry and I couldn't speak. I didn't want to go with them but my escape route was now blocked.

Flight, fight or surrender? What would they expect least? I measured the gap between myself and the doors of the van. If I jumped in, I could get to the driver's seat and pound on the horn. That might frighten them off.

As his grip tightened, I jerked my arm forward and twisted backwards towards the van. His hand slipped free and I threw myself into the back and scrambled for the steering wheel. The van smelled of gas and there were tools scattered on the floor. I yelped as my knee scraped over something sharp and my hat flew off. The steering wheel was almost in reach.

I stretched out for the horn but strong hands grabbed my leg and I was hauled backwards and dumped in the road. I'd never felt so frightened. I curled up, waiting for the blows. Instead, there was a raucous laugh.

'What the hell are you doing, Jack?'

I peeped out from under my arms. Cookie was standing over me. 'You trying to steal the gas company's van?'

I exhaled in relief. I couldn't disguise my trembling as I scrambled up and fell against him. 'Joe, thank God it's you.'

'What's going on? Who were those two?' He pointed down the street as the Jaguar turned right and slid around the corner.

'I don't know. They grabbed me so I jumped in the back. I was going to bang the horn to get help.'

'Just as well I came out when I did, the bloody thing doesn't work. I've just delivered a cooker for my aunt.'

He turned back, closed the front door and locked it. 'She's not in. Come on, let's go to the market and have a cup of tea. I'm due a break. You can tell me all about it.'

I looked up and down the street. There was no sign of the men or their car and *Boadicea* was sitting there waiting. I remembered Cookie's desperation to become a Bluebottle. I was sure those two were connected to the police so I mustn't let him get involved. 'Thanks, Joe, but I've got to get back to school.'

'Hang on. You can't ignore this. We should report it to the town hall. We can't have people being grabbed like that off the streets.'

'It's okay. I'll report it later but I must get back.'

'You make sure you do, now.' His broad face wrinkled with concern. 'You're not involved in any criminal activity, are you?'

I had to laugh. 'Of course not. They must have mistaken me for someone else. Don't worry, I'll report it.'

He didn't look convinced. 'You'd tell me if you were in trouble, wouldn't you?'

I wanted to hug him. I knew I could trust him but getting involved with my uncle could ruin his chances of escaping from a job he hated. 'I'm fine. Just a bit surprised, that's all.'

He reached into the back then slammed the doors closed. 'This your hat?'

I nodded and he handed me the battered panama. 'Nice.' He strode towards the front of the van. 'Take care, now.'

I watched him leave in a cloud of blue exhaust then hurried towards the bike.

27

'No thank you, Malita, I have had sufficient, *Gracias, no más.*' What Malita had described as a *tortilla de huevo*, or Spanish Omelette, had been rather more than my stomach could handle. The pooled olive oil on its surface had almost defeated my ability to pretend I was enjoying the meal. Fred had literally lapped it up and I supposed that he had long ago decided to smile or starve. The pungent smell of the cooking hung in the air of the small kitchen.

'Good, Jack, you're learning.' Fred grinned at me while Malita turned back to the range then shovelled the remains of my omelette onto his own plate.

She returned to the table and picked up my plate with a satisfied smile as Fred splashed more of the *vino tinto* into my tumbler.

'I'm pleased to see you've joined the ranks of the afflicted at last, young Jack.'

The way my head still ached from the Calvados, I guessed I was more than a recruit. But the alcohol hadn't loosened my tongue and I'd kept the secret of the diamonds to myself for the moment.

'Uncle, when are you going to tell me what you've discovered?'

Fred reached back to the carved dresser and retrieved the photographs he had printed in his makeshift darkroom. His own equipment had been smashed by the intruders so he'd borrowed some from another comrade, whose name he declined to reveal. The quality wasn't good but the faces were clear enough.

'My dear Watson, what we have here is a small mystery but nevertheless we have the tools to solve it.'

'Okay, Uncle Sherlock, spill the beans.'

'Lita, stop crashing about and come and sit with us. Emilio has done well. You must thank him.'

'He is clever man, waste time in this place. He need money, hate these people. I give him your thanks.'

'Now, Jack, you recognise Hurel as well as your friend Kohler's uncle and your possible father in law Hayden-Brown.'

I spat out a mouthful of the raw *tinto*. 'For Christ's sake, Uncle, he'd rather she married Saul than me.'

'You may be right but I think he would find the wedding challenging, having to wear a black cap and dance in circles with a bunch of sweaty Hebrews.'

'*Bastardo!*' Malita rounded on Fred, whipping him with dozens of abrasive Spanish words.

He reeled back in surprise then apologised for his gaffe.

Malita glowered at him and continued to mutter to herself while he tapped the photos.

'Kohler's friends are as yet unknown. These two are also a mystery though I have a suspicion that one of them is Sir Edward Fairfield. We'll know more when Eric arrives.' He glanced up at the clock. 'He should be here soon if the *Saint Julian* is on time.

If these three are German,' I stabbed at Kohler and his two older companions, 'do we inform the authorities?'

'No! That's the last thing we do. This isn't about the law, Jack. This is about gathering information and passing it on to those who know how best to use it.'

'But, if they are breaking the law – using illegal passports, conspiring against Britain – shouldn't we do something?'

'I thought I'd explained that before. Even though we are not yet officially at war with the Germans, a secret war has been going on for some time. But this isn't about territory or culture or race, it's about the class struggle –'

'Oh, Uncle, not the Red Fred manifesto.' I wanted to bite my tongue but the words were out.

Malita gasped. 'Jack, you no understand –'

'Of course he doesn't, Malita.' Fred was quite calm. 'It's never been explained to him. It's not something that is taught at Victoria College and it certainly doesn't get broadcast on the BBC or printed in the *Morning News* or the *Evening Post*. He would have to make a special effort to find out about such things. I'm not even sure I am the best one to explain.'

It was a mixture of drink and exasperation but I blurted out, 'Oh, do try, Uncle. Do try and convert this simple capitalist to your world view.' My rather childish sarcasm prompted another sharp intake of breath from Malita.

Fred waited a couple of beats before responding. 'Are you religious, Jack?'

'If you mean do I go to church, the answer is occasionally... but I do believe in Christ, and in goodness.'

'But do you believe in the Devil?'

I hesitated, my father would kill me if he heard what I was about to say. War had reinforced his Christian beliefs as much as it had destroyed my uncle's. 'Not in the way the church portrays him. Of course there is evil in the world but I don't believe the Devil is there trying to trip us up all the time and stop us going to Heaven.'

'Oh, "Heaven"? Where is that, Jack?'

'I don't think it exists as a place as such. It's perhaps an everlasting peace for those who achieve goodness in their lives.'

'And the reverse for those who don't is Hell?'

'I don't know.' I was floundering. These were not issues that were discussed openly. It was accepted that Christianity was the norm but that God forgave those who sinned, if they repented in time. What that meant, I had never attempted to understand – as I had never begun to address the issue of death. 'I'm only eighteen, Uncle. It's not something I've really thought about.'

'Only eighteen? Three of your relatives were slaughtered in the trenches in France before they reached your ripe old age, Jack. They looked like men to me and your father.' He was angry now.

'I'm sorry. I didn't mean to imply that I'm too young to –'

'To what? Make a contribution to your society? Fight for your king? For your country? Kill other men who are fighting for theirs? But what are they fighting for, Jack?'

'Well you should know, you went to Spain to fight. What was that for? For your king? For your country?'

Fred looked shaken. 'In truth, Jack, it was for neither. It was for my beliefs and for my comrades. I could say it was in the mistaken hope that, by fighting the fascists there, we might be able to prevent more bloodshed later. But that isn't true. We answered a call, the call of the working man, if you like, though he was hardly organised enough to make it.'

He paused, thoughtful, and emptied the bottle into his cracked glass. 'Who do you admire most, Jack? Who is your hero?'

I was tempted to say, 'You, Uncle', but didn't want to be accused of being facetious, though I did admire him more than anyone else I knew. From history I could choose Henry V, Nelson, Wellington. All those who had fought against the odds. Rather like my uncle. 'No one. I suppose there are more I despise, more I distrust, than admire.'

'I understand, Jack. You are a strong person, you are self-sufficient, you will fight for the underdog and put yourself in harm's way. But you must understand that there are multitudes out there who need strong men to offer them models, to provide leadership, because they are not happy with their lives. Think of the millions who worship Adolf Hitler. It's not rational, is it? But he provides leadership, offers solutions, takes the burden of thinking off their shoulders. I'm sorry to throw a quotation at you but it was Marx who said "It's not consciousness that determines being, but social being that determines consciousness".'

'What does that mean?'

'Well, in the past, for example, in feudal society, a man worked for himself and produced all he needed for his family. He traded any surplus with other men for necessities he couldn't make. So he was largely self-sufficient and this gave him a sense of identity and purpose, an independence, if you like. You with me?'

From the little I'd read of Marxism, that sounded like an oversimplification but I nodded like a good pupil, though my mind was still wrestling with Caroline, Rachel, diamonds and sabotage.

He sipped his wine. 'You will stop me if you think I'm being patronising, won't you? You can find all this in the public library, if you dig deep enough. And, yes, it's only an opinion.'

It had taken me long enough to find out about Lawrence.

Listening to his opinions was preferable to excavating the library. I couldn't resist. 'Should I be taking notes, Uncle?'

He ignored the sarcasm, got up, rummaged around in a drawer and returned with a writing pad and a thick pencil. He placed them both with exaggerated care in front of me. 'If you wish.' His voice was frosty again.

I picked up the pencil as he continued.

'Now, in the capitalistic system in Marx's time, a man didn't work to produce all he needed, but instead worked for another man in order to obtain a wage to purchase from other men all his needs. This made him feel detached from himself and all things around him and he felt a loss of purpose. The worker was now in a position whereby he did not produce an entire item, had no control over what he produced and was in competition with other men for his livelihood.'

He paused and looked at my pad, which was covered in scrawl. He grinned and continued. 'Capitalism is basically competition and it forces the members of society into two groups: workers, the *proletariat,* and capitalists, the *bourgeoisie.* Marx explained that the worker, because he was now valuable only for his ability to earn wages, sank to the level of a commodity. He maintained that the whole of society must fall into two classes: the property owners and *propertyless* workers.'

'Okay, I get some of it. You're talking about a new form of slavery.'

'That's it – wage slavery. Despite your education, your mind is still open enough to understand.'

'Uncle, we had an inter-school debate at college earlier this year. It was on the best type of social organisation. The girl's college proposed fascism, the intermediate school proposed democracy, and we championed Communism. You didn't know about that, did you?'

'No, but if we'd seen you more often, you might have told us.' Disappointment underscored his words. 'Tell me, did you take part?'

'I asked some questions.'

'And let me guess who won.'

'I think we won the debate on our arguments but the audience voted for democracy. Communism came a poor third.'

'So why am I not surprised that our educated elite prefer the status quo?'

His sarcasm was getting to me. 'The fear expressed by members of the audience and the other debating teams was that Communism is an ideal but doesn't work in practice. Perhaps it would have been more successful in a less backward country than Russia.'

He flared up. 'That's the bloody problem. It's capitalist propaganda that's promoted this canard that it doesn't work in Russia. The oppressed are frightened by change –'

'It's bloody revolution they're frightened of,' I snapped back. 'The majority view was that the state is for *man*, and not *man* for the state.' For once I felt I was holding my own with him.

He smiled. 'Let me tell you the truth about Russia and the revolution –'

He was interrupted by a sharp knock on the door.

28

Malita tugged at his arm and pointed to the clock.

'I hope that's Eric.' He gestured to her to check the window. 'Please don't mention this discussion to him. You will have gathered that I'm not always a true believer in the official party line.'

This was too deep for me. I felt sorry for Fred and sad for Malita. I'd agreed to help and he was treating me like a recruit who needed indoctrination. Now I was going to have to meet Eric, who was higher in the party than my uncle, and be very careful what I said. I'd also have to decide whether to reveal what I knew about the diamonds. Before I did, I wanted to gauge their likely reaction.

Eric didn't fit my expectation of a scruffy Communist as he was dressed like a banker. Fred introduced him as "my comrade, from London".

After the usual tea routine, Eric studied the photographs from the United Club. He pointed to the tall patrician figure who was discussing something with Hurel.

'That's Sir Edward Fairfield, a pillar of the establishment.' He laughed. 'Cheating, conniving, fascist; definitely one for the little red book, Fred.'

Fred scrutinised his class enemy. 'Thought so. Smug-looking bastard. What's he do?'

'Not a lot. If memory serves me correctly, he's a non-executive director of the Bank of England, has massive estates in Ulster. Some think he's going to be ennobled and brought into government via the Lords. Hates the Jews with a vengeance.'

'So, he's collected a few enemies.'

Eric laughed. 'He still has powerful friends. He was at Winchester College with Oswald Mosley. We believe he helped to finance the establishment of his British Union of Fascists. Even though Mosley and his Blackshirts are a spent force, his ideas are still revered by the inner core of the establishment. Hitler is an admirer and probably has him pencilled in for a major role once he conquers us. He just loves English gentlemen who share his world view.'

He pointed to a shorter, slightly-built man who was standing by Fairfield's side. 'Don't know about this creature, though. He looks German but I can't help there. I do recognise that fat fellow next to him. Monsieur Georges Sleeman. He's a Belgian diamond dealer. Works from London where that rat Oppenheimer has his stockpile. We hear that someone has been nibbling at the De Beers mines in the Congo – it could be him.'

He rubbed his finger over another tall figure. 'Can't place him either but he also looks German.'

'He is. Jack's found out that he's here with his nephew, Rudi Kohler, though we don't believe that's his real name. They're definitely German though.' Fred paused. 'So, what do you think? Why are all these buggers meeting States members and lawyers on our little island?'

Eric shrugged. 'Until we identify the Germans, we're just guessing.'

I spoke up. 'Excuse me but I have a question.'

Eric glanced at Fred and raised his eyebrows at me.

'I don't recall inviting questions, young man.'

'You didn't, but I have one.' *Patronising bastard.* 'How much would six million carats of industrial diamonds weigh?'

I was pleased to see the surprise on their faces. Fred responded first. 'Is this a trick question? You're not in class now.'

'No trick. I know the answer and wondered if you might see the connection.'

'Right, clever clogs. Tell us,' Fred said.

'Six million is approximately what an industrialised nation needs for one year's supply for its factories. 3,000 carats weighs about one and half pounds. Ergo, six million would weigh round about 3,000 pounds.'

Fred still looked puzzled.

'How much does a load of our Jersey Royals weigh?' I asked.

The light dawned. 'So you could get the entire supply of diamonds into two of your farm lorries?'

'Yes and with room to spare. So, they're not too difficult to hide or transport.'

Eric looked less than delighted. 'So, are you suggesting that all these secret meetings are about smuggling diamonds?'

'I'm not sure but I believe that Hitler would pay over £18 million for that amount of good quality industrials. But they cost less than half a million to purchase directly from the mines.'

'That's chicken feed as the Yanks say. Have you any idea how much money our capitalist friends have thrown Hitler's way?' Eric asked.

It was my turn to look puzzled.

'That's right. We've been paying for the Nazis to rearm. It seems we prefer their brand of socialism to what Russia has to offer. Have you heard of the Bank for International Settlements, sometimes known as BIS?'

'Caroline mentioned that acronym. It came up over dinner but she didn't know what it stood for.'

'Well it might surprise you to hear that it was set up by the world's central banks back in 1930. It was initiated by the Reichsbank but the American Federal Reserve and the Bank of England took over. It was meant to bring stability to the banking system but its real purpose was to establish a massive fund to fight Communism. The driving force is a group who are pleased to call themselves The Fraternity. How quaint, but it shows that fascism is alive and well in America as well as Europe. Now that Funk and his little lapdog, Pohl, are running the Reichsbank –'

'I've heard those two names before. That's right. Caroline said they were also discussed at that dinner party with the other Germans and the two you claim are Fairfield and Sleeman.'

Eric sighed at my interruption. 'Quite possibly but to date we believe this BIS has provided Germany with nearly one hundred times the amount you think those diamonds are worth.'

It was a staggering sum and I must have look amazed.

'That's right, young man. And the irony is that most of these bankers are Jewish. If it wasn't so sad, it might even be amusing. Even if your diamonds cost Hitler fifty times their face value, they're still only a minor part of the picture –'

Fred interrupted. 'Minor they might be but think of the profit if Hitler has to pay a premium like that. The middlemen will be fighting each other for the privilege of filling that order.'

'There is one major flaw in your reasoning. De Beers won't sell to Hitler and they control all the mines in Africa.' Eric responded.

'Not if they were smuggled out of mines in the Belgian Congo,' I suggested.

'Where did you get all this information, young man?'

'I asked a few questions of a friend –'

'That would be Saul, I suppose,' Fred interrupted. 'He's a Jew from South Africa. I believe his father is involved in the diamond trade.' He looked at me sternly. 'Why didn't you mention this before?'

'It's only speculation. Your comrade mentioned this Belgian diamond dealer. He's here with a known British fascist, there are Germans involved and Hayden-Brown lives for profit. It's not a big leap, Uncle.'

Fred seemed pensive. 'But I don't see the Jersey connection. It's a bloody long way round.'

'As you've told me, Uncle, it's also a sleepy backwater where customs officials aren't on the alert. They may even be on the take.' I hesitated. 'While I was following the Germans this morning, they entered the offices of Du Bois & Legard. I examined the brass plates on the wall. One of the companies listed was the Société Générale Belgique, or SGB.' Saul had been right.

Eric coughed. 'Before you two get carried away, I think you should look at the geography. There's more to this than diamonds.'

'Possibly, but if Jack is correct and there's a plan to smuggle that quantity of diamonds then we need to get some help to stop them. Think of the blow that would be to Hitler's war preparations.'

Eric snorted. 'You may be right but, for the sort of profit you've described, there'll be no shortage of capitalists fighting to get their snouts in that trough.'

He seemed to be on the same wavelength as Saul. Too big a problem to be dealt with. I toyed with telling them about the sample quantities nestling only a couple of miles away but decided to keep quiet for the moment. I was still working on my own plan.

Fred seemed more engaged. 'Right, we need to find out more about these Germans. Do you think Hélène might be able to help?'

'Probably but you'll have to go to her.' Eric said

'There's a daily boat to St Malo. I could take the photographs tomorrow, be back by the evening and telephone you – unless you want to come with me, or are you planning to stay?'

'No, I need to –'

I interrupted again. 'Who's Hélène?'

Eric shrugged. 'You don't need to know.'

'It's alright, Eric. He knows I've been to St Malo. I can trust him to keep quiet about this, can't I, Jack?'

At least someone trusted me. I nodded.

'She's a comrade who is very well placed. I'm sure she can get these creatures identified,' Fred continued.

'Fine. But what are we going to do? Surely we need to report this and get these bastards kicked off the island.'

Eric responded with irritation. 'You must be patient with us, young man.'

I suspected that Fred would be severely reprimanded for involving me once I was out of earshot.

'We do have a job to do and it does not involve alerting the authorities. This information is very important in the right hands and we cannot risk beating these pheasants out into the open just yet. You have –'

Fred spoke over him. 'Jack, you must also take into account that we are small fry. These are very big issues. There is little we can do directly, so we must accept that. Besides...' he hesitated, 'you've already discovered there is considerable personal danger involved. We are not the only ones observing this – despite what your German friends might think about the sleepiness of this island. The two who followed you today are probably Special Branch but they could be –'

'What's this? Who followed him?' Eric broke in.

'The two I told you about on the phone, the ones who've been keeping watch on this house –'

'They're not here now, are they?' He hurried to the window, peering through the curtains.

'Can you see any cars?'

'No, the road is clear.'

'Well they're probably having a cup of tea at the town hall. Relax, they were just trying to intimidate the lad.' Fred looked at me and touched his finger to his lips.

'Well you'd better be extra careful.' Eric turned and sat down again. He stared at me. 'You've done some sterling work, Jack, but now I must ask you to stand back. Try to forget about all of this. I think I can speak for the party when I say how grateful we are for your help. Without it we wouldn't have this information and –'

'And what? I just don't see how my helping with all this has any point unless you do something about it.'

'And what would you have us do, young man?' Eric snapped. 'Who would we inform? You've already confirmed that your own politicians are aware of what is happening. They might even be involved in it. There is some financial advantage for this island in any arrangements that might be made. Some of your leaders have realised that you need to have more than pretty cows and ugly tourists to keep this island solvent.'

'But I think I know someone who should be informed. After all, it's his committee members who –'

'No, Jack. You must not tell anyone about this – especially Ralph!' Fred exploded and thumped his fist so hard on the table that his mug of tea fell onto the tiled floor with a splintering crash.

Malita jumped up and fetched a brush, pan and cloth while Fred simmered in his seat. 'It is too dangerous for you. I forbid you to mention this to anyone. Do you understand?'

I nodded my understanding even though I disagreed. These Communists were all talk. Marxist theory wasn't going to stop Hitler. Once Eric was out of the way, I might tell Fred about my plan, though the more I thought about it, the more risky a venture it appeared. The best solution was to get the lot of them thrown off the island. What to do?

Is this what Hamlet felt as he agonised over action versus inaction? I believed I could see the right course to take, but the strong pull of Fred's tide of disapproval was sweeping me backwards.

29

Wednesday

As a symbol of Hamlet's dilemma, I thought the ceiling fan, whose hesitant rotation failed to stir the thick air in Jurat Poingdestre's oak-panelled office, was almost perfect. Even though it was active, it was moving in a small circle – just like Eric and Fred.

For such a senior politician, Uncle Ralph's limp handshake held little promise, so I wasn't surprised that inaction seemed to be the order of the day. If only those labourers drilling a road through my head would understand that. Fred's *vino tinto* would be better used for cleaning the silver.

I'd decided not to mention diamonds but as soon as I had started the story about Germans pretending to be Dutchmen, the good jurat had interrupted and asked if Red Fred was involved. I'd glossed over my uncle's role and focused on the issue of their meeting with members of the Finance Committee, but its president didn't seem concerned. Perhaps, as Fred had suggested, he had approved it.

Why were Eric and Fred so determined that I shouldn't try to get the Germans thrown off the island?

Couldn't they see that with them out of the way, the diamond deal would collapse and Hayden-Brown would be stuck with his samples? That way I wouldn't have betrayed Caroline's secret, nor would I have risked my neck to make a tiny dent in Hitler's plans.

My head throbbed with frustration. Was I just angry with Kohler, wanting to hurt him because of his involvement with Caroline? Or because I felt an intense dislike for his sneering attitude and disdainful superiority?

Ralph looked alarmed. 'Are you feeling alright, Jack?'

I realised I'd been staring at the fan while punching Kohler about in my mind.

'Not really. I think it's wrong to let these Germans get away with lying like this.' My anger was beginning to rise, swamping my sense of stupidity, fuelled by the deliberate, bureaucratic calmness of my uncle.

A sequence from the *Merchant of Venice* started to play in my head. Gratiano, crimson with anger shouts at me across the stage, "*Can no prayers pierce thee?*" Playing Shylock, in a scene where everyone was against him, I'd always derived great pleasure from my line in response, especially as the loquacious Gratiano was played by that racist, Surcouf. "*No, none that thou has wit enough to make!*"

I felt like the desperate Gratiano now, even though I wasn't pleading for my friend's life. I wanted to be listened to but didn't have the "wit" to convince these cynical adults who couldn't see right from wrong.

'I'm sorry, Jack, but this isn't any of your business, and my idiot cousin shouldn't have got you involved.' He leant back in his chair and squinted over half-moon spectacles at me. 'I see you are in school uniform – shouldn't you be in lessons?'

The ultimate adult put-down. I stood up and turned towards the door. 'Yes, Jurat Poingdestre, I should be in school, but I asked to be excused so that I could come to the States Building to work in the library. I wanted to see you because I thought this matter was important. It seems that I was wrong.'

I opened the door but stopped on the threshold. 'Perhaps the police might be interested in illegal entry into the island. I think I'll find out.'

'Jack! That would be most unwise.' Uncle Ralph lurched forward in his seat, his eyes blazing.

I closed the door, wondering if the fan would be able to cope with the sudden rise in temperature. I had no intention of speaking to the police but Uncle Ralph didn't know that.

I crossed the corridor and took my pounding head into the canyon of bookshelves. Perhaps an hour or so checking up on Fred's beliefs would give me a new perspective. In truth I felt like vomiting over the issue desk – or would that be classified as a "return"?

An hour trying to unravel the capitalist plot to "crush the workers" had turned into a whole morning and my head was spinning as fast as the wheels of *Boadicea* as I urged her through the lanes. Each piston slap reverberated in my head. I would take the pledge, write my name in blood if necessary, and never touch the Devil's brew again.

It was oppressively hot so I stopped briefly at Five Oaks to remove my blazer and strap it to the pillion so that I could enjoy the cooling breeze of the big bike's passage.

I turned into the sunken lane bordering the farm. The hawthorne and willow sprouting from the hedgerows was out of control. Grasses and ferns tried to reach each other across the narrow divide, guarded at intervals by robust oaks and sycamores. It was beautiful, but in need of the biannual haircut known locally as the *branchage*. There would be an inspection the following week and my father would be fined by the parish if he didn't get our Breton workers out there with their scythes and sickles soon.

I was so preoccupied with the scenery and swerving to escape the grasping weeds that I had to brake hard to avoid a car blocking the end of the lane. There was no room to turn the eight-foot long beast so I dismounted and pulled her onto her main stand.

Two men were poking about in the boot of a black Talbot 105 saloon and looked up when they heard me. One was wearing a cream linen suit and a panama hat. The other had rolled up his shirtsleeves, and his jacket was draped over the boot floor and rear bumper, obscuring the number plate. I stopped by the handlebars as the one in the suit moved towards me.

He tipped his hat and I nodded in return. 'We have a problem with a flat tyre and can't find the right tools to change the wheel. Do you know where we might get some help? Is there a farm nearby?'

His speech sounded unnatural to me, as though he was trying hard to speak polite English and disguise an accent. There were faint echoes of Saul in his inflections.

As he had taken off his hat, I had caught a glimpse of a balding head with some scraggly hair over rather neat little ears. His eyes were a dull blue, his mouth twisted to the left, his nose red-veined, and bearing the signs of several collisions. His voice was soft but he looked anything but.

The other, shorter, man stood up and looked at *Boadicea*. 'That's a fine motorcycle. Do you mind if I have a look?'

The accent was harsh, as though English wasn't his first language. I nodded as the wiry fellow, with a well-lined, feral face and broad grin, slid past me to examine *Boadicea,* like a fox on his way to the hen house.

'Eh, look at this.'

I turned and felt the older man at my shoulder.

'It's an SS 100. Didn't that Arab lover get killed on one of these?' He looked at his companion. 'It couldn't be the same one, now could it?'

The older man's mouth twisted into a sly smile, revealing stained teeth.

Not again. What was it about this bike? My head was already clanging so much, I hadn't heard the alarm bells. Who were these two? What did they know about *Boadicea* and what the hell were they doing in the lane?

I moved to the side and peered through the shade at the front left of the car. The tyre was fine, the rear was as well. I moved to the right. There was another man sitting in the driver's seat. He tipped his hat and grinned at me. I ignored him and started forward to look at the other front tyre closely but found the bulk of the older man blocking my path.

'There's nothing wrong with your car,' I pointed out.

'Steady now, Jack.'

I shrugged off the restraining hand and took a step backwards. 'How do you know my name?'

'Excuse me if I don't introduce myself but we know a lot more about you than your name, Renouf. We just want to have a quiet word with you, give you a message.'

I sensed the younger man moving in behind me. I was alone this time – no chance of Cookie arriving on a white charger. These men exuded more confidence and sly menace than the two in the Jaguar. Were they connected?

I stood my ground and tried to keep my voice firm. 'What message?'

It was so sudden I didn't even have time to react. I crumpled to the ground, clutching my back, my whole being focused on the burning pain in my side.

'That's a problem with being young and skinny, not much fat to protect your kidneys.' The younger man stood over me. 'Just a small tap, but you'll be pissing blood for a couple a days.'

The older one doffed his hat again. 'Well, that's the message. Keep your nose out of other people's affairs.'

'I think he's got it, Alf. Let's get him on his bike, now, tidy things up a bit.'

They bent down and, with surprising ease, pulled me upright and frogmarched me to *Boadicea*. I was gasping in agony, trying to twist away from the pain but it was unrelenting. They hauled me onto the bike, forcing my legs astride the tank. Alf held on to the front brake while the other man pushed the bike off its stand. They supported it while I gritted my teeth to swallow the pulsing pain.

Alf leant in close, his breath a mixture of stale tobacco and other unhealthy habits. 'Just so there is no misunderstanding, or any attempt to make a complaint.' He reached into his jacket and pulled out a leather wallet. He let the flap drop in front of my face. Shafts of sunlight, filtering through the trees, highlighted the metal badge.

My eyes could barely focus but I recognised a crown and royal crest before the wallet was whipped away again. Alf nodded and they stepped away from the bike.

I was too slow to react and it toppled over, trapping me underneath it, the pain from my left kidney overwhelmed by a panic rush as the full weight of the machine collapsed onto my left leg.

They inspected the scene.

'Unlucky accident. You should be more careful with a powerful bike like that. Still, no real damage done.' Alf wrinkled his nose at the smell of petrol as it seeped out of the carburettors and along my leg. 'You know, Carl, I think I fancy a cigarette.' He patted his pocket and withdrew a sliver case. He extracted a cigarette and slipped it between his lips. He patted his pockets again in a pantomime. I heard a match strike.

Carl leant forward and lit his fag for him.

He turned back to me and held the lit match close to my face. 'Now wouldn't it be a shame if I dropped this?'

My teeth were chattering with fear.

He laughed and tossed the match into the hedge – away from the petrol. 'Take care now, young man.' He patted my head.

They both laughed and, without a backward glance, strolled to their car, closed the boot and drove off.

I lay still, fighting the waves of nausea as they broke over me. I tried flexing my left leg and relief surged through my body as I realised that all my muscles responded. *Boadicea's* tank had taken most of the weight of the fall and the sturdy rear forks had absorbed the shock. It was very awkward and painful but I could move the leg a few inches left and right. I would have to use my hands to lever it out from under the frame.

I could wait but it was unlikely anyone would use this road for hours unless they were going to the farm.

I was worried about the petrol. Eventually it would evaporate but, until then, any spark could set me alight. I had to make the effort now.

I bent my right leg and manoeuvred my knee until it was pressed against the petrol tank. Burning pain shot through me again as I twisted my arms to get some leverage on the frame.

I took a deep breath, pushed hard with my right knee, scrambled out from under the bike and fell backwards into a patch of stinging nettles. *Boadicea* groaned in protest and slumped into the hollow I had left behind.

My left trouser leg was ripped from thigh to ankle and soaked in petrol. I undid my black college shoes and struggled out of the ruined pants. A quick examination of *Boadicea* revealed that the handlebars were bent and there were scratches on her tank but there was no serious damage.

Did I have the strength to lift her? I had to try. I crouched down under her bruised flank and tried to push her up but couldn't balance the weight. She slumped, wounded, to the ground again.

I got my breath back and tried from the other side. If I used my own body weight as a counterbalance, I might be able to pull her up. On the third attempt, gasping for breath, knuckles bruised and running out of swear words, I got her balanced. I pulled her on to her main stand before she could collapse again and gave her a thorough inspection.

She was battered but unbowed and, like me, looked just as though she had been in a careless accident. After I tickled the carburettors to get some fuel back into their chambers, she started on the fifth kick. I let her engine tick over while I tried to make some sense of the situation.

How had Alf and his vicious sidekick known I was going to be riding along the lane at that time? Had they been following me all day? If they had been waiting while I struggled to unravel Marxism in the library, how had they arrived before me? It could only have been when I stopped to remove my blazer but I couldn't recall a black Talbot overtaking on the road. Nevertheless, it had and they'd delivered their message. But who had sent it?

Uncle Ralph seemed unlikely. Too much action. A stiff letter was more his style. I'd love to blame Kohler and it was possible they were German, trying to disguise their accents. Surely Eric and Fred wouldn't play this rough to frighten me off?

Apart from the message, Alf and his little bastard also seemed to suspect that Lawrence had been connected to this Brough Superior. But was this really the bike?

Fred had always maintained that it was special and Malita had said something about it killing before. What about the others that Eric had mentioned? Were the UK security services involved? Perhaps they were just business rivals but that badge had looked official. Their menace had been real enough. Perhaps I should just go home, count my bruises and follow the advice I'd been given.

I mounted up and snicked her into gear. My face blossomed with heat. How dare they? I'd never given in to bullies. Why should I start now? I'd find them and – well, I didn't know what I'd do. I needed to know more about them first and I wouldn't find that by trailing home with my tail between my legs. Besides, turning up in this condition would provoke questions I didn't want to answer. I couldn't ride without trousers though – I didn't want to be arrested for indecent exposure. That left the contents of my holdall.

30

'I didn't know you played cricket.' Caroline's initial amusement at my outfit turned to anger as she examined me. 'I thought I told you not to come here.'

My lack of smile matched hers.

'Something's happened, hasn't it?'

I didn't even know why I was there. *Boadicea* had brought me and she hadn't explained.

Caroline sighed in exasperation. 'I suppose you had better come in – but you're not staying.' She opened the door wider.

'Who's that?' Hayden-Brown's voice boomed from his study to the right of the tiled hallway.

'It's Jack.'

'Jack, who?'

'Jack Renouf, from the swimming club.' She rolled her eyes and pulled me along the corridor and into the kitchen.

I was expecting her father to come storming in and give me a lecture on keeping my nose out of other people's affairs. However, there was no further response, though we could hear him talking on the telephone as his cigar smoke leached into the hall.

There was still that awkwardness between us and I waited for a sign that she wanted a hug but she moved around the oak table and indicated that I should sit opposite her.

'Lemonade? It's fresh. Or perhaps you want something stronger?'

'Give me a pen I want to sign the pledge.'

'What have you been drinking? Don't tell me. I bet it was cheap red wine. Here, drink this. Christine prepared a jug before she left.'

The pert little Frenchwoman acted as a live-out maid and housekeeper and, I suspected, attended to more than her father's dietary needs. I allowed Caroline to pour me a glassful but, as I was reaching across the table to pick it up, such an intense pain shot up from my bruised kidney that I dropped the glass.

'Clumsy.' She was turning to get a cloth from the sink when she stopped. 'Christ, Jack, what's wrong? You look white.' She moved round the table and examined my face.

I felt like retching and tried to suppress the nausea as she helped ease me back in the chair. I was gasping for breath, my face screwed up as the pain pulsed through me. I hadn't tested my assailant's prediction yet and didn't really want to see my blood splashing into the toilet bowl. I gulped down another wave of pain mixed with fear but, as my side touched the wooden back of the chair, I clutched at it with my left hand.

Caroline grasped my shoulders, pushed me forward and pulled my shirttails from my trouser band.

She gasped. 'What happened?'

'Nothing. I fell off the bike, that's all.'

'Jack, you are a hopeless liar. Now tell me the truth or I'll start playing nasty nurse on you.'

I was surprised by the tenderness in her voice and let her press a cold wet cloth to my back while I tried to explain what had happened and my guesses about who might have given the orders.

When I finished, she kissed me softly on my head. She wandered over to the sink, under the leaded window, and gazed out over the lawn. 'I think you've got it wrong. My father wouldn't hire thugs like those. It's your uncle they're after. I bet it's something to do with his politics. My father and his chums are only obsessed with money.'

This was ridiculous. She knew some of his "chums" were Germans, she knew about the diamonds and how important they could be for the Nazis.

'Do you know who –'

'Shush, I'm thinking.' She was still staring out on the lawn but I could tell from the tension in her shoulders that she was struggling with something.

The antique clock ticked solemnly. I focused on my breathing and the cooling touch of the cloth. I stared gloomily at her, aware of the long pendulum swinging in the Grande Sonnerie. It seemed to be synchronised with my pulses of pain. I counted them.

After forty, she pushed herself away from the sink and turned to face me. Her eyes challenged mine. We stared at each other – an old game, which she usually won. This time she blinked first. 'There's something I need to tell you about Rudi –'

'Caroline? Ah, here you are.' Hayden-Brown filled the doorway. He gave me a cursory glance. 'You're still here I see.'

I contemplated stretching out my hand to introduce myself and ask some questions about diamonds but thought better of it.

His expression was icy. 'If you'll excuse us, John, I need to talk to my daughter.'

'Don't be so bloody rude. His name's Jack, not John. How dare you come barging in here interrupting our conversation!'

Bloody hell. If I'd spoken to my father like that, I would have woken up in hospital – if at all.

He ignored her outburst and turned to me again. 'Please leave. I apologise for any...' he struggled for a word, 'inconvenience. But I do need to talk to my daughter in private, if you don't mind.' He had sufficient mastery of sarcasm to qualify as a maths teacher. He pushed into the kitchen.

I started to leave but Caroline shouted at me.

'Stay. Don't give in to the bully. Whatever he's got to say, he can say in front of you.'

Her father exploded. 'Don't be so bloody impertinent! We are not going to discuss family business in front of a stranger.'

'Family business? That's a joke. We don't have a family, thanks to you!'

'Caroline, I've just been speaking to your mother on the telephone. We need to talk. In private.'

'What? She's still talking to you?'

'I'd better be going then.' I moved towards the door again.

'Jack, go see your uncle. That's where the answers are,' Caroline said.

I hesitated.

'It's alright. I'll be fine. He may be a foul-mouthed bully but he'd never hit me – would you, Father dear?'

God, he must have been sorely tempted though.

'Let yourself out. You know the way.' She made no move towards me so I left them to it. As I reached the front door, she called out, 'I'll be in touch – soon.'

Fred answered the door, stepped out and scanned the empty street in all directions. He spotted the damage to *Boadicea* but made no comment on that or my cricket gear before ushering me in. He was very agitated. Malita was there in her working clothes so I assumed she'd just come back for lunch. She didn't speak.

'Are you alright, Malita?' I moved towards her.

'No, she's not bloody alright. She's just been bloody sacked!'

'But why?'

'Apparently an anonymous customer complained about her. It's bloody crazy. She isn't even allowed to talk to the customers. It's just an excuse.'

'But they can't just sack her?'

Fred shot a withering look at me. 'You haven't been listening to me, have you? They can do what they bloody like. Lita is a foreign national. She's got no rights. That's why they pay her so little. Bloody slave labour.'

'But if she's living with you –'

'We're not married so it makes no difference. If we were, she would have some protection but –'

'Sit down, Yak. He is angry. Doesn't listen. I am pleased. I hate job –'

'That's not the bloody point.'

'It's probably a silly question, Uncle, but why don't you get married?'

Malita studied the table. Fred stared into space.

She got up, moved to the range and reached for the kettle. 'Is good question, Yak. The answer, not so good.'

Fred sighed. 'What she means is –'

'I still married. To bad man – in Spain.' She spat onto the hot plate. Her venom sizzled.

At this rate there'd be no more room in my mouth for my big feet. I didn't know what to say.

'It gets worse. They've taken my passport.' Fred sat down. 'I went to the *Brittany* this morning. I was going to meet Hélène in St Malo. I showed my passport as usual at the control desk but they wouldn't let me through. One of the immigration officers came out and told me there was a problem with it. An irregularity. He was apologetic but said he would have to keep it until it was checked. No passport – no boat.'

'Unbelievable, but surely you can protest. You've been using it without a problem.'

'Jack, they open my mail, tap my phone, wreck my house, stop me getting a job, sack my... they have so many ways of making life difficult. If I told them I was leaving the island for good, my passport would be fine for any outward journey. They would find a way to stop me getting back in again though. Anyway, Eric phoned. I called him back from a public box. He was stopped at Southampton, questioned for hours. He doesn't think he'll be allowed to leave the country. We're all trapped.'

Malita banged the teapot down. 'You silly. Give up too soon. Tell Jack your plan.'

'I don't want to get him involved again.'

I stood up, pulled out my shirt and turned my bruised side to them. 'It's too late, Uncle. I'm more than involved.'

I told them the story but left out my visit to Caroline's.

The silence that followed was so complete I could hear a clock ticking in the bedroom above. After what seemed like minutes, Fred rose and opened his mouth to speak but Malita gripped his arm so fiercely I could feel the pain across the table.

She spoke softly in Spanish to him until he sank into his chair. She got up and moved around the table, helped me up and hugged me tenderly.

Fred came over to us. His anger was gone, replaced by a stony demeanour that I had never seen before.

'Can you describe them?'

'The little one who hit me was about five foot four, wiry, with a lopsided grin and a guttural accent. The tall one called him Carl. He could have been Dutch or German.'

224

'They are easy to confuse – go on.'

The other, I think the younger one called him Alf, had a strange accent. It sounded as though he was trying to disguise it. He was closer to six foot, solid, balding, cold eyes, a twisted mouth. Do you know them?'

'No.'

'They seemed very interested in *Boadicea*.' I'd have to ask him now. 'Uncle, the other two questioned me about the bike as well. One of them gave me a date and a place and told me to look it up.' I sucked in a breath. 'Did *Boadicea* really belong to Lawrence of Arabia?'

He seemed lost in thought.

'Uncle?'

'Yes, it was Ned's bike.' He sounded distracted.

'Ned?'

'Yes, Ned, Ted Shaw, Thomas Edward Lawrence. We were friends. But that was all long ago. There are more pressing problems to deal with.'

'But isn't this Lawrence thing part of the problem?'

'Not anymore. It's all over. He's dead.' He looked at Malita. 'We've made sure his name is safe.'

'What do you mean?'

'Not now, Jack. It's a long story. I'll tell you sometime.'

I couldn't stand his dismissive tone. I slammed my fist onto the table, making the crockery jump. 'I want to know now. You treat me like a child but I have to take grown-up punishment. Don't you trust me?'

Malita laughed. 'How you say? Chip off old block, eh? You tell him what he wants. The plan can wait.'

He bit his lip in frustration but nodded at me. 'Go ahead then. Ask your bloody questions.'

'Okay, I've read about Lawrence, the accident –'

Fred snorted.

'Wasn't it an accident?'

'That's the verdict the coroner gave the jury – before he started the trial.'

This was going to be difficult. He'd taken refuge in an almost childish truculence. I felt like a housemaster interrogating a wayward pupil. How would I get information out of Alan? I decided to be indirect. 'How did you first meet him?'

He looked surprised. 'Green Street slipway. July 20th 1896. We were both eight.'

'That's over forty years ago yet you remember the exact date?'

'It was a rather special occasion.'

'Why?'

'He was drowning. I saved him.'

I must have looked incredulous.

'You remember when you fell off the wall at the pool and almost drowned when you were about six?'

I would never forget. It was probably the reason I was still frightened of deep water. 'I don't remember the date though.'

'Ned was always very precise about such things. We even celebrated the anniversary a couple of times.'

'What happened?'

'He slid off the slipway. I was there playing with some friends and pulled him out.' He was agitated again. 'I'm sorry, Jack, but this really isn't important now. Can't we leave it?'

My side still throbbed with pain but I pressed on. 'No. What was he doing in Jersey?'

Fred gritted his teeth. 'On holiday, with his mother. They were staying at Bramerton House, overlooking the beach. She waded in fully dressed to help pull him out.' He paused. 'She bought me an ice cream.'

It was so incongruous that I laughed.

'It was my first ice cream.' He seemed lost in time again.

I switched tack. 'How did you get the bike?'

'This is bloody silly. I got it. That's what matters – and now I wish I hadn't.'

'Why?'

'Alright, if you must. I was ordered to get reacquainted with Ned –'

'By whom?'

'The bloody party. Who else?'

'Why?'

226

'He had a certain use.' He inspected his hands. 'He knew people. Oh, bloody hell, he knew everyone. You must have read that in the paper.'

'You said reacquainted?'

'Yes, we were friends at Oxford.'

'I didn't know you went to university.'

'There's a lot you don't know and, believe me, now is not the time for my life story.'

'I understand, so just tell me about the bike.'

He rubbed his hands together and gave Malita the "more tea" look. 'After the inquest, his brother inherited the bike. I bought it from him and took it to the BUF.'

'The British Union of Fascists? I thought you said you were working for the Communist Party?'

He cracked his knuckles. 'I was. I had to join the buffers – Oswald Mosley's mob – to report on them. It's how the Nazis got the votes – jackboots on the streets. The party were worried the same might happen in England.' He leant back in his chair. 'Mosley was very keen on Ned. Thought he could save Britain – mistook his love of Arabs for a hatred of Jews. Not too many brain cells in that organisation.'

Was he trying to confuse me or had he led such a tortured existence that truth was on a long holiday? If I stuck to the essentials, I might make sense of it.

'Why did they want the bike?'

He chuckled. 'Mosley couldn't have Lawrence but he wanted his bike as a talisman. He also believed that it had been sabotaged and that certain papers might have been hidden in it.'

'What?'

'Oh, yes. That wasn't reported, was it? Ned couldn't stop writing – letters, books, diaries. After the accident, his cottage at Cloud's Hill was searched but his most recent diaries weren't found.'

'How do you know?'

'I'd already taken them.'

Was there no end to my uncle's nefarious activities? I looked askance at him. 'What was so important about them?'

'Names, places.' He was serious again. 'A few minutes before the crash, he sent a telegram to Henry Williamson to arrange a meeting with him to discuss something of importance.'

'Who's Henry Williamson?'

'I'm surprised you haven't heard of him. He wrote *Tarka the Otter* and the *Patriot's Progress*. Joined Mosley after meeting Hitler at a Nazi rally in Nuremburg. Harmless, wouldn't hurt a fly, but a true British eccentric. Also wealthy enough to be acceptable to Mosley. Great friend of Ned's. He and GBS helped buy the bike.'

'GBS?'

'George Bernard Shaw, another of Ned's friends. You must have heard of him.'

'Of course but what was that about a telegram?'

'The telegram is public knowledge. There was lots of press speculation about the purpose of the meeting.' He leant forwards again. 'Williamson was working with Mosley to arrange for Ned to meet with Adolf Hitler.'

31

I was stunned. 'Are you sure?'

'I was working for Williamson – as his chauffeur. Ned got me the job. Look, Jack, this is so complicated. Do you really want to know more?'

I wanted to know why I'd been beaten up by one group and followed and threatened by another. Both were connected by their interest in the bike.

'Let me get this straight. You bought the bike and gave it to the BUF. What happened to it then?'

'They had me strip it and check every part for sabotage. It hadn't been tampered with, though it did need a complete service. The rear brake needed relining but had worked in his emergency stop. The front brake cable had snapped though. He was in second gear and travelling at about thirty-five miles per hour at the time.'

'So it was an accident?'

'Yes, it was the most unfortunate accident.'

'How can you be so sure?'

'Williamson wanted to see Lawrence that day. I was driving. We stopped at Cloud's Hill but he wasn't there. We drove into Bovington. On the way, I saw him riding towards us.'

He stopped. The words seemed to be stuck in his throat. He looked at me, his eyes liquid. 'As we passed each other, I waved. He looked round in surprise, recognised me and smiled. Then he was gone out of sight over the rise –'

'The black car.'

'Jack, nearly all cars were black then but you're right – I was

229

driving the mystery car. There was a national appeal to find it but Williamson wouldn't come forward.'

'But didn't you stop to help Lawrence?'

'We didn't see the accident. Williamson decided he wanted a newspaper and told me to drive into Bovington before we went to see Lawrence.

When we returned, the road was closed. An ambulance shot past us. I asked a soldier what had happened. He mentioned a motorbike accident and I knew immediately.'

He exhaled deeply. 'I told Williamson but he ordered me to find another route to Cloud's Hill. He sent me in to see if I could find anything which might have been incriminating. Stupid bigot. He trusted me – not very bright for a eugenicist.'

'A what?'

'Eugenics. Breeding humans, keeping the herd healthy. We've practised it for thousands of years but only with animals. Like Hitler, Williamson believes in improving the bloodline through selective mating. More importantly, he believes in removing all contaminants. All those with a mental illness, Jews, Gypsies, homosexuals. In short, anyone who isn't of pure Aryan stock.'

'What? Aryan supermen like Himmler, Goebbels and Goering?' I'd seen their photographs. It was laughable.

'That's what I mean about brain cells. The BUF seem to have had theirs bred out of them.'

I tried to refocus. 'Did you find anything?'

He sipped his tea and looked out of the window. His face was gaunt in the reflected sunlight. He made his decision. 'The less you know about that the better.'

'Why, Uncle?'

Malita rattled her cup, spat something in Spanish at him then turned to me. 'Is reason we go to France. I tell you if he don't.'

'Right, Lita, if he's that desperate to know.' He grabbed my wrists. 'Even she doesn't know where they are and I won't tell you. If I don't survive... then the diaries will never be found, which is just as well.'

'What's in them?'

'You don't want to know. It's the connection with the bike that you're after, isn't it?'

'Yes, but this could be the reason why these men are so interested in *Boadicea* –'

'Possibly – anyway, they were written in exercise books. After I was instructed to steal the bike back by my masters, I rolled them up, slotted them into the tubular frame and sealed it. I crated the bike up, locked it in a garage in Birmingham and gave them the key. I thought the books would be safe there. And they were. The party sent me to Spain soon afterwards.'

He smiled at Malita. 'When we returned, they were so grateful they gave me the crate. And that's it, Jack. That's the story.'

'At least all you're going to tell me.' I must have sounded exasperated.

'For the moment, Jack. One day, perhaps.'

'So, when they broke into your house, they were looking for the diaries?'

'I don't really know. I have no idea how they might have guessed where they were. The only one who might have suspected I had them was Williamson.'

He picked up the photographs. 'This is what's important now. I have to meet Hélène, show her these, get her advice on the diamonds, but I can't get to France and they'll probably stop her getting in.' He scratched his wiry hair. 'I wanted to keep you out of this, Jack. You know I did but –'

'It's alright, Uncle. In for a penny, in for a pound, as they say. What do you want me to do?' I just hoped it was something violent to that little Carl bastard.

'I need you to ask a favour of your friend Saul.'

'Pardon?'

'His boat, the *Star*?'

'*Jacob's Star*.'

'Would he take me –'

'Us,' Malita interrupted. 'He take us. I go with you this time.'

'Us.' Fred rolled his eyes. 'To Les Écréhous.'

'I see. Clever thinking. Halfway to France – no active customs or immigration, only a few people staying overnight.'

'One of your relations has a cottage out there, doesn't he?'

'Yes, he goes there most weekends though.'

'How about tomorrow afternoon? Do you think he'd let you have the key?'

Thursday, half-day closing. No school. Saul would jump at the opportunity.

'Don't worry about the key, I know where it's kept. I'm sure Saul will help, any excuse to put to sea. He knows about the diamonds but not about Hélène or Lawrence. Are you prepared to tell him more?'

Fred looked at Malita who nodded. 'Do you think he'll understand?'

I tapped my nose in imitation of Saul. 'Well I'll only tell him enough to get to sea. The rest can wait until needed.'

I left *Boadicea* with Fred and retrieved my own bike, *Bessy*, from the yard. On the journey to Saul's, I tried to make sense of Fred's story. I found the information about Lawrence quite disconcerting and, should I ride her again, I would feel more wary of *Boadicea* – perhaps I should call her by her real name and change her sex.

I was way out of my depth but the anguish caused by Caroline and Kohler grated with me like a broken tooth. I had to resolve that even if the other issues were way out of my reach.

I contemplated visiting Ralph and showing him my bruised body. I rehearsed the scene in my mind.

My patronising uncle stood up to greet me. Refusing his hand, I pulled out my shirt. No explanation just a sardonic "thanks" then I marched out without waiting for a response. It was tempting, but what would it achieve?

I didn't plan to show Saul my bruises. I didn't want to frighten him. He laughed at my cricket outfit then ushered me into the kitchen and pointed to his purchases.

'I could only get six tins of Lyle's golden syrup and I tried three shops. That's twelve pounds in weight but I'm not sure it's enough. Have you got any?'

'I don't make cakes but I know my mum keeps some in the larder. I'll see what I can find. What about the bleach?'

He pulled a crate from under the table. 'Here we are, six bottles of the best. I got some strange looks buying these at the same time as the syrup.'

'You think this will work? Wouldn't it be easier to dump some seawater in the tank?'

'Much simpler but you'd need quite a lot and if the tank is nearly full, it would spill over. It's only plan B but, if you can find two more tins, that should give us nearly a gallon of sludge. Add in about the same of bleach. The tank in Hayden-Brown's boat probably holds about 200 gallons.' His eyes gleamed. 'Now, if we were to mix some ammonia in with the bleach, we would liberate some chlorine gas and have a nice little explosion.'

'Saul, surely you remember why you were removed from chemistry classes?'

'Spoilsport. The fuel mixture is plan B anyway. Don't forget that torque wrench. You have to get the injectors back on at the right tension after you've dropped the ball bearings in. Everything should appear normal so the engines have to start and run. We don't want them breaking down in the harbour.'

'I've had another thought about that. Those ball bearings will certainly bugger the engines but they may not get very far. We need them to break down way out at sea. I wonder if something smaller but more abrasive might be better –'

'Good thinking and how appropriate. I'll pick out a handful of the hardest diamonds and you can pop them in. Hoist with his own petard, as we naval folk like to say.' He was getting overexcited now.

'Calm down. We've got to sneak aboard first and hope that the key is still where it was when I was last there with Caroline. If we can't get in without breaking something then it's plan B. We mustn't forget the fuel funnel from your boat.'

'Don't worry, I've checked the tides and it's quite a big one this evening – over thirty-seven feet. It's not going to be dark until the tide is falling though so we need to wait until after eleven to make the move. I'll get a taxi to run me and the supplies down there early evening and load the tender. You meet me at the harbour at ten o'clock. Afterwards you can run me back here.'

'Hang on. Do you really think it's a good idea to get a taxi driver involved?'

'Well we can hardly carry them on your thrusting steed.' His eyes lit up. 'I know, I'll drive the MG.'

I groaned. 'Just remind me what happened last time you tried that?'

'So the roads are a bit narrow, I over corrected on a couple of corners –'

'And your father forbade you from ever driving again. He even set up an account for you with Luxicabs so you wouldn't be tempted. I've never understood why he lets you use his boat anyway.'

'Well, what his eyes don't see won't worry his wallet.'

'Wallet? My father would drown me in the bloody bilges if I defied him like that.'

'As you know, we can't choose our fathers but perhaps I've been luckier in life's lottery than you. Never mind the philosophy what are we going to do about the car?'

'How long has it been in the garage?'

'How should I know, I don't drool over it and polish its arse every week. A month or so?'

'So the battery's probably flat. Has it got any fuel? Is there a starter handle?'

'Okay, clever clogs, just because you can mate with anything mechanical, there's no need to be so bloody superior. You can drive the fucking thing, if you want.' He got up and rummaged in a cupboard then threw me a set of keys. 'Instead of asking stupid questions, go and have a look for yourself.'

I caught the bunch and let them dangle from my hand. 'I've been thinking about this all day. Have we've got this right? Get your atlas again. I'm still not convinced.'

'Never thought you'd turn into Hamlet. Remember Shylock: "*A sentence, come prepare*" – surely you've sharpened your knife?'

'But we still don't know if he's going to use the bloody boat. They could be flying directly to Berlin, freight to Cherbourg –'

'You carry on torturing yourself and looking for excuses to back out if you wish, I'll get the atlas.'

Unbelievable, the studious wit, Saul Marcks, had turned into the man of action while I dithered and prevaricated.

He dumped the atlas on the table and turned to the double-page political spread showing Africa and Europe. Over half of Africa was coloured in the red of the British Empire.

'Look, that green chunk is Belgian: Congo and Ruanda. Apart from Nigeria to the north, Gold Coast, Sierra Leone and tiny Gambia, the rest is run by the Frogs. It's a good 5,500 miles from those diamond mines by sea but once the ship is in international waters, it's safe. Try to transport diamonds by rail or road and you have to cross British or French territory. If you can get to Libya, it's possible the Italians would help but they'd want a big cut. It's possible by air but they'd have to land to refuel. No, it's much safer by sea, especially as the Portuguese control Angola which forms the southern border.'

'But why bring the cargo to Jersey?'

'You have to think like Hayden-Brown and his cronies. They can't rely on foreign customs not sniffing around. They might be able to bribe a few but they can't guarantee the cargo won't be intercepted and confiscated. I still think they will have rendezvoused somewhere outside territorial waters, unloaded their samples onto *Lorelei* and brought them ashore. They would have told harbour control they were out for a spot of fishing and didn't plan to visit France, so when they returned, there wouldn't be any customs visit.'

'Caroline did say she thought he'd been to St Malo to collect them –'

'There you are. Perfect. I bet you a pound of biltong to a pint of your sour milk that there's a cargo ship riding at anchor somewhere between Gorey and Granville.'

'But, you can't just park your ship in the channel.'

'Of course you can. The territorial waters only stretch for three miles from each coast in this area. So they would be in international waters and safe from any inspection. If some busybody did enquire, they could claim engine problems and say they were trying to fix them and waiting for a part from the opposite side.'

'So you really believe there's six million carats of diamonds sitting in the hold of some ship just out of sight.'

'Perhaps not six million, that's a lot of production, but I bet she's Portuguese.'

'If you're right, then what we are planning is worth it –'

235

'And if I'm wrong, it's still worth it. Just imagine the look on Hayden-Brown's face when his gin palace seizes up.'

'Plan A will bugger his engines, plan B might. Do we need plan C?'

'*Oy* fucking *vey*. Stop it already.'

His enthusiasm was becoming infectious. Now would be a good time. 'I've got something else to ask you.'

'Go on.'

'Fancy a trip to Les Écréhous reef tomorrow afternoon?'

'Why?'

'Uncle Fred needs to meet someone from France. Immigration have confiscated his passport.'

'What the fuck are you getting us into? Diamonds, sabotage and now some commie plot?'

'Will you do it?'

He smiled. 'Of course.'

'Are you sure? It could be dangerous.'

'Having you as a friend is dangerous but always interesting. If we're not banged up in prison, I'll get both of you out there. Hey, we could take a peek to see if I'm right about the freighter.'

'There you are, plan C. Ram the fucker!'

'That's the spirit. I'll need some help getting the boat out of the harbour though.'

I scratched my head. 'Slight problem. I'm not going to be able to get away until lunchtime.' I was going to try to find out more about Hayden-Brown's plans, sneak around his house if I could, but Saul didn't need to know that. 'What's the latest you can leave with the tide?'

'Eleven o'clock and that's pushing it. If I can get over to the main harbour, I can wait by the lifeboat landing stage but I'll need help to get the legs in.'

'I'll bring Alan to help you. He'd love an excuse to skip school for the morning.'

'What, that *meschuge* brother of yours?'

'He's fine. He's also very good with boats. He'll crew for you. Wait until midday and the rest of them can join you.'

'Rest of *them*? How many more for God's sake?'

'Only Malita. You can have a pleasant chat in Yiddish with her.'

32

After giving Fred the news and discussing arrangements, I rode back home, trying to work out how best to get Alan's cooperation.

He was in the kitchen munching on some toast while scanning the *Evening Post*. We might not have a telephone but the paper was delivered every evening.

'You're in the manure' was his greeting.

'How so?'

'You forgot, didn't you?'

'What did I forget?'

He folded the paper, wiped the crumbs away from his mouth and grinned. 'It's Wednesday isn't it, third one of the month? What's special about that?'

I groaned.

'Ah, the penny drops. White glove night for the old man. Full regalia at the temple and mum's knitting circle at the rector's. I won't even bother to repeat what Dad said. Anyway, I did your share so you owe me one.'

Normally, he'd be so cock-a-hoop that I'd messed up, he would be relentless in his teasing until I clocked him one. However, I needed him on side this evening.

'Sorry, Alan, I've been a bit preoccupied.'

'Is that the new word for it?'

'I wanted to speak to you alone.' That got his interest. 'I need your help.'

'Yuk. You got two girlfriends, surely you can manage on your own.'

'This doesn't involve either of them. Just you, me, a couple of friends and a boat trip.' I waved his question away. 'Before I tell you any more, you need to swear on whatever it is you hold dear that you will not tell a soul about this.'

A flicker of alarm crossed his face. 'Is it legal?'

'Perfectly. Now, will you swear?'

He got up and walked to the dresser. I thought for one bemused moment he was going to get the Bible but he bent down and scooped up Tonto. The little cat wriggled in his arms as he held him between us.

'I solemnly swear to keep my brother's nefarious activities secret – on Tonto's life.'

The little bundle shot free and rushed up the stairs. I always thought he understood more than he let on.

'Okay, here's the deal. Tomorrow, I want you to take the morning off school and help Saul get his father's cruiser from St Helier to St Catherine's then take a trip around the Écréhous.'

He looked puzzled. 'That's it? Hooking off school and swanning around in a boat? What's the catch? Who else is coming?'

'Uncle Fred and Malita.'

He rolled his eyes. 'They moving house?'

'No, and you will be polite. Promise?'

'Will we have time for some fishing and a swim?'

'Yes.'

'Will I have to be polite to Saul as well?'

'No, you can be as rude as you like but don't come crying to me if he rips you apart with his tongue.'

'So long as it's just his tongue.'

'Do we have a deal?'

He considered for a moment. 'Can I borrow your bike on Saturday?'

'Okay, but don't push it any further. Tomorrow, we'll leave early, straight after milking, and I'll drop you at the harbour. Saul will meet you there.'

'Okay if I bring my rod?'

'Yes, that's fine but you'll have to manage it on the pillion.'

'What about food?'

'For God's sake, stop worrying about your stomach.'

'Just because you've given up eating doesn't mean I have to.'

'Food's taken care of.' Another lie. Though there might be some syrup. 'Now, I'm going to be out for the rest of the evening so why don't you take *Smellie*, nip up to the field and get some target practice.'

'You off to practise on your two targets, are you?'

'Something like that. See you in the morning.'

While he retrieved his rifle from the gun safe, I sneaked the only two cans of golden syrup out of the larder and slipped them into my gym bag. I hid my torn trousers in my bedroom cupboard. Saul and I had decided that, if we were seen, we would bluff it out so I changed into overalls. What's more natural than a couple of mechanics fiddling about on a boat? Doing so in the dark might arouse suspicion so he was going to work out a cover story. On the way back to *Bessy*, I picked up a torque wrench and some smaller tools from the barn.

Had I gone too far by dragging my brother into this? My father would have a clear opinion and it wouldn't be delivered with his tongue. The boat trip shouldn't be dangerous and might not happen if Saul and I were caught tampering with *Lorelei*. Was I doing the right thing, or was this just plain stupid?

Hamlet's words had been ringing in my ears for much of the day but they only made me more determined that *"conscience"* wouldn't make *"cowards of us all."* And, in the total absence of any action or leadership from the adults, ruining Hayden-Brown's deal to provide Hitler with these vital industrial diamonds was the only way I had of striking a blow against the fascists for what they had done to Fred, Miko and Malita.

By ten o'clock, the Old Harbour was deserted. *Jacob's Star* rode easily on her buoy. There were lights and noise from La Folie Inn but only dim reflections on the black water. *Lorelei*, with her ghostly-white hull, stood out against the darker walls. Saul commented that it was odd her dinghy was tethered to her side rather than on its davits or tied up against the wall. It might mean nothing as there were plenty of small punts available for boat-to-shore transfers. As

Lorelei swung on her mooring, we could see faint lights peeping from three of the nine portholes on her port side. Curtains were drawn over the square windows in the main cabin under the wheelhouse but there was a perceptible glow behind them. It looked like plan A was scuppered before we began. She was moored about one hundred yards from us in a deeper part of the harbour though at low tide, like the rest of the boats, she was supported on legs to stop her toppling into the mud.

We observed for thirty minutes then the wheelhouse door opened and light spilled into her cockpit. The lamp was extinguished and a tall man lowered himself into her dinghy. The lazy sod fired up the outboard motor and chugged to the wall nearest the inn. He tied up, climbed the steps and disappeared into the noisy pub. With drinking-up time, he would be there for at least half an hour. There might still be a chance for plan A, after all.

We dropped into our dinghy and I sculled us over to the harbour wall as Saul had come up with an addition to our plans. I held us alongside *Lorelei*'s dinghy while Saul stepped aboard. We weren't going to waste golden syrup on the engine as his plan was more direct. He fiddled about in the bilges and held up a round plug. He'd pulled the bung from the drain socket. With the weight of the engine, she'd sink into the mud in minutes. I sculled us away and over to *Lorelei*. They'd be able to retrieve the dinghy when the tide went out but the outboard engine would need a complete overhaul. Saul fended us off. We were working silently, using only hand signals. We seemed to be unobserved as we rested against *Lorelei*'s steel side but the hairs on my neck prickled with the sense that we were being watched. I twisted around and scanned the harbour but couldn't spot anyone at all. Perhaps it was just nerves. Saul appeared calm enough. I hauled myself aboard then slithered into the large cockpit to search for the key. It wasn't there. Bugger, I tried a few other spots but no success. I crawled back to the side and leant over to Saul and whispered, 'No key.'

He hissed, 'Try the fucking door.'

I wormed myself back and crouched outside the door which led into the spacious cabins and engine compartment. I pushed gently and it started to open. I held onto the handle then eased it fully open before sliding in. I had a small torch but didn't want to use it until I was in the engine area below the saloon deck. There was some light filtering through the front portholes and, as my eyes adjusted, I could see the outline of the central table. I felt my way around this and moved towards the master cabin. It smelled of fried food, stale cigar smoke and acrid sweat. I held my breath and strained my ears.

There, a faint snuffling sound, an exhalation and a snore. Buggeration, there was another crewman. We hadn't thought of that. Plan A definitely down the plughole now. I backed out, secured the door and tiptoed back to Saul.

I hissed, 'Plan B. To the stern.'

He pulled the dinghy slowly around the hull until it was under the transom. He handed up the funnel and I lifted the wooden seat cover then flipped up the fuel filler cap and inserted it. I leant over and grabbed the first bottle of bleach, unscrewed the cap and glugged a quart of bleach into the funnel. I listened again, trying to sense movement below. Nothing.

Each bottle seemed to take longer and sound noisier as I emptied it. Eventually, I'd dumped over a gallon of bleach into the diesel. Now it was time for the golden syrup. We'd already emptied the eight cans into bottles, not wanting to struggle with awkward lids in the dark. I love the syrup, will lick it from the spoon until Mum pulls it away, but the smell of diesel and strong whiff of bleach disguised the sugary aroma as it slipped through the funnel.

I passed everything back to Saul and secured the filler cap. It was pure guesswork but we believed it would take several miles before the engines overheated from the new mixture and stopped working. They'd have to clean out the tank and the filters and probably the cylinders as well. *Lorelei* wouldn't be going far in the next few days.

I started to lower myself into the dinghy when I felt *Lorelei* rock. Someone was on the move. The door opened, inward fortunately, and I had enough time to duck down and drop into the dinghy. We were trapped under the stern. We crouched, praying whoever it was wouldn't look down.

Footsteps approached across the cockpit. Someone yawned and then a stream of hot liquid splashed into the water alongside us. Whoever it was obviously preferred fresh air to the claustrophobic heads for relieving himself. He yawned again then his footsteps faded. I waited for the door to creak open then motioned Saul to push off.

Once aboard *Jacob's Star*, we collapsed in the cockpit.

I didn't feel this exhausted after a hundred-yard sprint.

Saul produced his flask. '*Le'chaim!*'

As relief flooded my veins, I responded. '*Bumsen sie Hitler.*'

33

Thursday

While waiting, I calculated that I had been alive for 6,869 days, had consumed 250 pounds of roast beef – about one fifth of Victor – and had kissed four girls. I was having embarrassing difficulty with the next sum when I spotted movement across the road from the field. Nestled on a ground sheet in the damp grass, I raised my father's field glasses and trained them on the front door.

Hayden-Brown held it open, allowing the smell of cooking bacon to escape. I'd skipped breakfast again rather than face my father's anger and that succulent aroma reminded me that the rumble in my stomach wasn't just caused by emotional entanglements. Alan had stayed to stuff his face but we'd managed to get away without problems. We'd stopped when we were out of sight and changed out of our uniforms. I just hoped that Saul and Alan wouldn't start fighting before I got there.

Caroline's father glanced up the road and I refocused the glasses to follow a taxi as it approached the house. Kohler got out, followed by his uncle and the other slightly-built German who had been with him at the Palace the day I took the photographs.

Hayden-Brown provided an effusive welcome then ushered them into the house. The taxi drove off but, minutes later, another arrived. Fairfield and the chubby Belgian, Sleeman, got out and rang the bell. This time, Caroline opened the door. My binoculars vibrated in rhythm with my trembling elbows. After I steadied the glasses and refocused, she was magnified seven times and filled my entire field of vision. I could almost touch her as she greeted the fascist knight and the diamond merchant.

She led them inside and I flopped onto my back, cursing the effect she had on me, even from that distance. We'd shared this field only a few days before in the burning heat. Now the damp permeated my bones and spirit. Could I trust her? Steam rose from the grass as the sun burned through the clouds. I rolled back and raised the glasses again. There was some movement round the side of the house and Caroline appeared with Kohler in tow. Anger surged through me. I struggled to keep calm and watched them as they dried off two wooden picnic chairs on the lawn. They pulled them close together and sat down.

Wearing very little, as usual, she flicked her hair and smiled at Kohler. Would she be doing this if she knew I was watching, or would she be even more demonstrative? I just didn't know. I tried to lip read.

Christine, wearing a maid's uniform two sizes too small for her, sashayed from the house, carrying some drinks. She smiled invitingly at Kohler as she bent over him to place the tray on the grass between them. Her efforts to engage him with her cleavage appeared to have failed as he was so focused on Caroline that he ignored her. As she flounced off, she turned briefly to favour the pair of them with an aggressive pout.

The hollowness in my stomach was such that I couldn't have eaten the bacon now even if Christine had brought it over on a silver platter. Betrayal? *"Frailty, thy name is woman."* Like Shakespeare, I'd send her to a nunnery and him to Hell.

Gradually, my anger evaporated and an icy stillness gripped me. I knew now that I couldn't trust her. That whatever plan she constructed would almost certainly encompass a trap for me. I lay there calculating a cold revenge.

At eleven-fifteen, two different taxis arrived and waited until Hayden-Brown appeared on the porch with his guests. I'd already left it too late to get aboard *Jacob's Star* in the harbour. I'd have to meet them at St Catherine's. I'd forewarned Saul and asked him to wait until one o'clock if I wasn't there on time. After that, he'd have to get Fred to the rendezvous without me.

Kohler's uncle called out to his nephew. Caroline got up, moved close to Kohler and kissed his cheek. I held my breath as he hugged her in response. Reluctantly, it seemed, they separated, and he joined the others. There was much handshaking before the group split up and Kohler disappeared into the courtyard. The visitors clambered into the taxis while Hayden-Brown stood in the doorway to wave them off. So cosy, so friendly.

I mentally swapped the binoculars for the optical sights of my Lee-Enfield rifle and aimed at Caroline. I was about to pull the trigger when I heard a diesel engine clatter into life.

A Bedford lorry grunted out of the courtyard with Kohler at the wheel. Hayden-Brown waved him onto the road and hopped up into the passenger seat. The loading bay was covered with a canvas hood so I couldn't see inside. He beckoned to Caroline, who wandered over and scowled up at him. Words were exchanged and she stormed off, flapping her arms in disgust.

I rushed off to *Bessy* and kicked her into life. I caught up with them but held back, trying to keep at least one bend between us. The lorry skirted the town and I was sure they were heading for the main harbour. I followed as they chugged along.

Soon we were past the Weighbridge and moving along Commercial Buildings towards the old French harbour. We'd been right. He was going to use *Lorelei* to move the diamonds.

I pulled up, parked by La Folie Inn and scurried around to hide behind some laid-up boats and watch through my binoculars.

Lorelei seemed even larger in the bright sunlight. Saul reckoned she was only a few feet longer than *Jacob's Star*. Perhaps it was the white hull but she looked far bigger to me. Without doubt, Caroline's father had spent a lot more on this cruiser than on her piano.

I hadn't spotted it before but an Irish flag was fluttering from her masthead. I examined the transom. She was registered in Cork. The Irish Republic was no friend of Britain. Perhaps we'd got it completely wrong and they were heading there for a rendezvous. Perhaps Ireland was to be the staging post for onward shipment to Germany. But that didn't explain how the samples had arrived.

As I watched, the crewman and Kohler unloaded one crate at a time. They'd covered them in hessian but I was sure they were the same ones. They were both muscular but it took two of them to carry each crate down the slippery steps and hoist it over the side. Hayden-Brown supervised until all four were stowed below in the cabin.

From the generous handshakes as his guests had left his house, it would seem that the samples had passed the test. How long before they put to sea? Would he and Kohler be going with the boat? I couldn't imagine Caroline's father putting himself at risk. Perhaps it would be just Kohler and the crewmen. Suddenly, the engines coughed into life in a cloud of black smoke. Kohler appeared and jumped onto the harbour wall, released the stern line, re-boarded and fended off with a boat hook.

Caroline didn't think her father capable of piloting the cruiser so I wasn't surprised to see him on deck as it manoeuvred away. However, instead of chugging towards the pier heads, *Lorelei* headed towards her mooring buoy. Kohler hooked the line and started to tie her up.

The engines stopped. Surely not seized already? But neither Hayden-Brown or Kohler seemed surprised so I guessed this was planned. One crewman appeared and pulled a small tender around the hull. Their own dinghy must still be underwater or under repair. They were coming back ashore.

If Caroline had discovered any more, would she tell me? I needed to see her before these two got back.

I sneaked around to the Bedford. It was in sight from *Lorelei* so I kept low. It would be too risky to get at the engine. This model didn't have a key, just a switch for the ignition, so I couldn't pinch that either.

I examined the gutter. Some fag ends and a few spent matches. Perfect. I grabbed two and jammed them into the rear tyre valves and pressed until all the air had hissed out. That should slow them up for a while.

I looked at my watch. Twelve-thirty. I was already late. I fired *Bessy* up and headed for Caroline.

As expected, she was in the middle of a wrestling match with Beethoven. Christine was in the kitchen. I didn't want to be seen and reported so I sneaked around to the conservatory and tapped on the window.

So immersed was she in her struggle that I failed to get her attention. I tried the glass door. It was unlocked. Strangely, this was more frightening than clambering aboard to sabotage *Lorelei*.

She stopped in mid-phrase. 'What the fuck to you want?'

'Sorry. I tried knocking.'

'Yes, I bloody well heard you. Stop sneaking around and spit it out.'

'Are you still helping us?'

'No. I want nothing to do with whatever you're up to. Tell your commie uncle to bugger off.'

'He loves Puccini, you know.'

She blinked, baffled at my change of direction, then snapped. 'Well, that fucking explains it. Soppy romantic, living in some workers' paradise in his head. Wake up, Jack. Get on with your own life.'

Pleasantries over, I advanced, made room for myself on the piano stool by shoving her sideways with my hip then thumped my fists on the keyboard. The cacophony must have been hideous to a musical ear.

'Tell me where *Lorelei* is going with those diamonds, or I'm going to murder your piano.'

She stared at me for a long minute but I wouldn't look away.

'I suppose you are going to be a complete pain –'

'Your piano and your ears will suffer the pain.' I raised my fists.

'Enough. Stop. I don't know much more than I've told you already.'

'Liar.' I raised my voice to the level of my fists.

She clenched hers, ready to strike.

'Steady, don't damage your hands on my thick skull.'

Her lip trembled. She tried to suppress the giggle but it grabbed her by the throat and soon she was convulsed, rocking on the stool in hopeless mirth.

How do you get sense out of someone who's seized with laughter?

I raised my hands again then crashed them down with even more force.

She calmed immediately. 'Stop it. You know I don't care about

247

this piece of shit and it'll take more than your bare hands to make it any worse.'

She stood up. 'Come with me.'

'What about Christine?'

She pulled a face. 'Ignore her. She's only a servant.'

Well, she must have been serving elsewhere because we didn't bump into her on our way through into Hayden-Brown's study. Perhaps she was resting her ears.

Caroline stopped by her father's desk and opened a drawer. She extracted a brown cardboard file and dropped it on the desk. 'Here, help yourself but nothing leaves this room. Find me when you're finished. I've got something more interesting to do.' She flounced out.

I opened the file. It contained letters, receipts and a side-on photograph of a cargo vessel along with its details. Saul had been right. It was Portuguese and registered in Lisboa. Its name was SS *Espírito Livre,* gross tonnage, 4,500. It had a single funnel amidships and two derricks over holds fore and aft. It looked similar to the potato boats that served the island, only a bit larger.

There was nothing about its destination or port of origin so I assumed it was for identification only. Its owners were listed as Mermaid Trading of Cork, Eire. Same as *Lorelei*'s registered port. Probably not a coincidence.

I scanned the letters but they were all in German though one had a letterhead proclaiming the Reichsbank. Fred would love these. Should I steal them? I'd promised Caroline, but this was important. Hayden-Brown would miss them, suspect his daughter, perhaps get the truth out of her. I faltered. Somehow sabotaging his boat seemed less serious than invading his privacy and filching a few documents. I decided to extract what information I could and make notes on a writing pad which was nestled next to the telephone.

The receipts were in a mixture of languages. Some French but mainly what I assumed were Dutch and German. But there was no damning evidence of smuggling that I could see. No maps, no cargo manifests or even lists that I could pick out. If only I'd had Fred's small Riga Minox camera. I closed the file and replaced it in the drawer then picked up a pen and thought about what I could note down.

The top edge of the pad was ragged, as though a page had been ripped off. I felt the surface and was sure there were indentations. I knew how firm pen strokes could leave a mark on pages underneath so looked around for a pencil. In a history class we'd once carried out some rubbings over headstones to reveal the words which had worn down over the years. Once I'd shaded the page with pencil strokes, I examined it under the desk lamp. The borders seemed to be covered in little boxes. I counted twenty-two. In the centre were the letters "RM" followed by "50", which seemed to have been crossed through. Underneath was the number "20" also crossed through and followed by exclamation marks. Finally, in the centre of a large thick circle was the number "37.5" underlined several times.

Beneath this was a word which was difficult to decipher but which started with "des" and ended in "ate". Along with chess, I'd always enjoyed crossword puzzles so I scrutinised it again. There were probably nine letters. I doodled some alternatives and came up with desecrate, designate, dessicate and desperate. Of course the word might be German or even French. I removed the shaded page and my own notes. Caroline liked puzzles.

She was practising again so I followed the sound of the piano. She paused as I entered the room.

'Satisfied?'

'If I could read German, I would be.'

'Don't fret. It wouldn't help if you did. They're all in code.'

'Have you heard your father shouting in his study recently?'

'What do you mean?'

'Having a conversation about money perhaps?'

'That's all his conversations are about, but now you mention it, he did sound angry this morning when he was in there with Rudi's uncle and that Englishman. I think they were arguing about a price. He kept saying it wasn't enough. This went on for a while, with the price going up. I think it stopped at thirty-seven Reichsmarks, which is hardly worth shouting about. Anyway, he came out with a big cigar and an even bigger smile.'

'What's that in pounds sterling?'

'Don't know for certain but not much. Ask Saul, he'll probably give the price in whatever it is the Russians use as well.'

I showed her my notes. 'Nine-letter word, first three letters, d - e - s – last three a - t - e. What do you think?

She examined my writing. 'I think you need some lessons in spelling. It should be d-e-s-i-c-c-a-t-e not d-e-s-s-i-c-a-t-e – double c, not double s. As in dehydrate or perhaps lifeless, as in desiccated romance – you'd know about that.' Before I could respond, she continued, 'Anyway, not the sort of words my father would use, though he does have an air of desperation about him at times. That's probably it. In fact, I'm sure I overheard him say, "They're desperate." to the Englishman.'

That made sense. Hayden-Brown and Sir Edward trying to get the best price out of the Germans. I'd show this to Saul. He'd make sense of it.

'Tell me. How much is Kohler involved with these diamonds.'

'I've told you before. It's nothing to do with him. He is just helping his uncle.' She sighed. 'He doesn't have any choice. He controls his allowance. Rudi's just a harmless student.' She considered me. 'There's something else you should know about –'

'Caroline!' Her father's voice boomed into the room.

How the hell had he got back so quickly?

'Go. Disappear. I'll divert him.'

She leapt up and hurried into the corridor.

I crept out and, crouching down, slipped around the house and into the field where I'd left *Bessy*. A taxi was just leaving. I hadn't thought of that but then I could hardly sabotage all the island's taxis, could I?

34

'*Kaffir*, mind the paintwork!' Saul was playing the white man today. In fact, in his white shorts, white shirt and white captain's cap it was difficult to see where white ended and man began.

'What the hell is he up to, Saul? Shouldn't we be moving on?'

Alan twisted round from his position hanging over the stern of *Jacob's Star*. 'I'm fishing. What does it look like?'

'Fishing? With a boat hook?'

'I'm snagging pots, stupid.'

'I'm surprised Saul didn't push you overboard on the way here.'

'I didn't need pushing. If he'd got any closer to that rust bucket tramp ship, I'd have jumped. I thought he was going to ram her.'

Saul tugged my arm. 'See, I was right.'

'So it appears. Tell me, was it called the *Espírito Livre*, registered in Lisboa?'

His mouth hung open. 'How the hell did you know that?'

I tapped my nose. 'Tell you later.'

Clambering out of the wheelhouse, I walked along the port side and plonked myself down next to Malita.

I called out, 'Saul, press on. Let the bugger fall overboard.'

'There's no hurry, Jack. Not now we've missed the tide. It's too late to get into the lagoon so we'll have to moor in the channel anyway. Let him play. If he damages the paintwork, he's fish bait.'

'Got it!' Alan yelled, making Malita jump.

Fred peered out of the cabin and Rachel, who'd been keeping a lonely vigil in the prow, walked cautiously towards us.

Whatever Alan had snagged was masked from the shore by the

cruiser's hull. The sea was glassy and there was no wind, just an overpowering heat now that we'd stopped.

Malita and I leant over the side to inspect Alan's catch as he dragged it in. Conscious of Saul's scrutiny, he draped an old sack over the transom to protect the teak varnish before he hauled a willow crab pot over the side. It was attached to a buoy from which sprung a slender cane topped by a quartered yellow and red flag.

Releasing the trap, Fred reached into the pot and extracted a decent-sized lobster, five large male spider crabs and a lonely, curled-up female full of eggs. He tossed her back and dropped the others onto the planking. Malita jerked her bare legs up with a squeal of undoubtedly very rude Spanish. Fred laughed, picked up the black lobster and teased her with its grasping claws.

'Hang on. You can't just raid other people's pots.' I sounded like my father.

'It's Surcouf's pot. Does that make a difference?' Alan asked.

The altercation in the prefects' room had quickly spread around the college. I was now greeted with quips of "howzat?" as well as "ground belts." I looked around. There were no other boats and we couldn't be seen from the shore.

Saul hurried aft. 'Isn't there something we can dump in the bastard's pot as payment?' Ducking into the cabin, he reappeared clutching a string of sausages. 'Surcouf will like these – they're kosher.' He dropped them into the pot and shoved it overboard.

Rachel surveyed the large orange and white crabs, which had now assumed fighting positions on the deck. 'How are we going to cook those?'

'Not in my bloody galley, you're not. They'll stink it out.'

'Ignore him, it's not a problem – there's a propane stove in the cottage,' I said.

Alan dropped a galvanised bucket over the side and hauled it back full of water. He ignored the crabs' massive claws, grabbed their bodies, turned them over and dumped them into the bucket.

Fred dropped the lobster in with them. 'They'll probably eat each other if we leave them too long.'

'What, they're cannibals?' Rachel clutched her hand to her mouth. We all laughed.

Miko stuck his head out of the cabin. 'Why you all laugh?'

Fred picked up the bucket, now full of wriggling crustaceans, and held it out to him. 'Keep it in the galley, please, chef.'

Miko held it at arms length and retreated. A sudden gust of wind picked up the exhaust from the idling diesels smothering us with foul gases. Our laughter briefly turned to choking.

I felt more relaxed than I had for ages. Rachel looked stunning in her shorts and halter-top. The sun seemed to bleach the greyness out of Malita's hair and she looked radiant. Even Fred looked more sanguine than usual. The gearbox clanked as Saul engaged the twin propellers and we resumed our journey.

I could see the Écréhous clearly now, about four miles to the north. Fred, Malita and, to my very pleasant surprise, Rachel and Miko had been onboard and were anxiously waiting for me. I hadn't told anyone about my visit to Caroline, though Saul had guessed after I told him about the ship. Rachel had kept her distance, almost clinging on to Miko to avoid having to speak privately with me. We had exchanged smiles though and I felt that warmth of companionship I always felt when she was near. I just hoped we could find some time alone once we reached the reef.

I'd shared my news with Fred but hadn't mentioned our attempted sabotage or my latest visit to Caroline. He promised to raise the question with Hélène and told me to stop fretting. I lolled on the seat next to Malita, feeling the comforting throb of the engines, and surreptitiously eyed Rachel, who was chatting to Saul in the wheelhouse.

'How fast will this tub go, Saul?' Alan asked as he lowered the binoculars.

'We're running at eight knots at present but, in this calm, I could squeeze twelve out of her.'

'Would that be enough to outrun that cruiser behind us then?' Alan queried.

I looked over my shoulder. I could just make out the sharp prow of a motorboat thrusting towards us about 300 yards behind. It looked purposeful, almost as though it was pursuing us. It couldn't be *Lorelei*, could it?

I stood up and took the glasses from Alan. Even with the modest vibration from the engines, it was difficult to focus so I steadied my arms on the roof of the wheelhouse. These were Zeiss glasses and their optics were excellent. I blinked in surprise but the image remained, burned into my brain – Alf and Carl, the little bastard who had coshed me. What the buggeration were they doing here? Were they connected with Hayden-Brown and his shipment? My mouth was sandpaper as I lowered the binoculars and handed them to Fred.

'It's them. The pair from the lane.'

'What lane? What are you talking about?' Alan asked.

I called out to Saul. 'Can you outrun them?'

'Not a chance. They'll be alongside in minutes. Do you know them?'

'Blue hull, white upper decks, single mast. A bit smaller than us and less tubby.'

Saul handed the wheel over to Miko and joined us in the cockpit. He took the glasses and examined the closing boat. 'About forty-five foot, big petrol engines, probably twenty knots flat out.' He lowered them and looked closely at me. 'Why do I feel there's something you're not telling us, Jack?'

'Two of the men on board ambushed me yesterday, beat me up and left me under *Boadicea.*' I stopped and looked at Fred. He nodded.

I pulled my shirt out of my shorts and showed them my side. Rachel gasped. Alan touched the livid bruise, which made me gasp even louder.

'We don't know who they are but they're obviously following us,' I said.

Alan hurried below, emerging moments later with his long canvas fishing rod case.

I looked at him in amazement. 'What are you going to do with that? Try to hook them?'

He grunted as he unfastened the buttons. Dropping the case, he revealed *Smellie*. The oil glistened on her bolt and the sun reflected off the scope as he raised her stock to his shoulder.

Fred was the first to recover from his surprise. 'What the hell are you doing? Who told you to bring a gun on board?'

'No one. I was going to shoot at some floats once we got there.'

I reached out and pulled the barrel down. 'And now you're going to shoot at some people?'

'Only over their heads.'

I grabbed the binoculars again. The boat was less than 250 yards away, overhauling us on our port side. I could see two other men on deck now. One was looking at us through a large pair of binoculars. He couldn't fail to see the rifle.

I lowered the glasses, handed them to Fred and tugged the rifle out of my brother's hands. I stood in the open in full view of our pursuers, brought the rifle up to my shoulder and sighted it on the man with the binoculars.

'What are you doing?' Fred's breath was hot in my ear.

'Their dinghy. Alan, what's in the magazine? Your matched specials?'

'Yeah, ten beauties.'

'How much powder?'

'Enough. Nearly 3,000 feet per second so allow for the drop.'

I worked the bolt and chambered a round. The bullet sitting on top of Alan's reloaded cartridge would be supersonic for over half a mile. The dingy was only clinker-built.

Fred voice was urgent now. 'What are you thinking?'

'Blast the stern off their dinghy – that should shake it loose from the davits. What do you think?'

'I think you're on a platform moving at ten knots aiming at a target moving at twenty knots. I think you'd be lucky to hit any part of their boat. Your shots would penetrate alright but their calibre is too small to blast the wood apart.'

'We need to give them a demonstration – make them back off.'

'Demonstration, yes – laugh, no. You'd need to hit the stern post several times to dislodge the ring bolt, unless you think you're good enough to shoot through the davit line.'

I dropped to one knee and braced the stock against the port stanchion, trying to focus on the dinghy's transom. Fred was right – it was like trying to thread a needle while running. 'If Saul cuts our speed, it will be steadier.'

'Won't make much difference. We could hit a small wave at any moment and throw your aim off by fifty feet.'

'We can't do nothing, Uncle.'

'Here.' He handed me the binoculars. With their much wider field of vision, I could focus on the dinghy but it was still blurred by our relative movements. He was right. I tracked the glasses along the hull to the wheelhouse.

'*Merde!*'

The little man's sneering face snapped into focus. Then the bastard raised a black object and rested it on the cabin, pointing it towards me. I handed the glasses back. 'What's he got in his hand?'

Fred adjusted the binoculars. 'Looks like a small automatic – probably a nine millimetre Beretta. No danger at this range but if he gets alongside we could be in trouble.' Fred touched my shoulder gently. 'Perhaps we should wait – see what they want? Shooting now could start a war.'

I called to Saul, 'Throttle back – take us down to five knots. Let's see if they get any closer.'

Saul didn't argue. The revs dropped and we could now hear the gentle swish of the displaced water as the boat settled into almost a walking pace. The other boat continued to close until they were about one hundred yards away then slowed to match our speed. A much easier target now.

'I think they just want to follow us, Uncle. How important is this meeting?'

His voice was dry. 'Not enough for a life, Jack. I think they've got the point. If you stand down, I think they'll back off.'

I felt like John Mills in the film *Brown on Resolution*. He'd held a German battle cruiser and its entire crew captive with a stolen Mauser rifle. But this wasn't a film. I hated the bastard for what he'd done to me. The pain of the blow was beyond my experience but the match over my petrol-soaked body had been an act of terror. Would *he* hesitate to shoot?

I clambered onto the wheelhouse roof then took up a prone shooting position. This was much better. The relative movement was greatly reduced. I was sure I could hit something as large as their dinghy but hitting a metal tube or even a mast was far too ambitious.

'Where's their petrol tank, Saul?'

'Below the waterline aft I would guess. No, Jack. Don't even think of it. They'd blow up – literally.'

It was tempting. My kidney still ached and the bastard had been right – I had pissed blood. A shot into their engine would absorb the bullet but Saul was right – it might cause an explosion. I removed the scope and placed it by my side.

'What are you doing?' Alan seemed surprised.

'Field of vision is too narrow. I need to see the whole of the target. Iron sights are fine at this range.'

I was confident now that I could hit the dinghy. Fred was worried about starting a war? Yet he kept telling me it had been going on for years. My throat was dry but I managed to croak. 'Distance?'

'One hundred and holding.'

'Are we still alone?'

Alan answered. 'Not even a bloody seagull.'

Sweat trickled down my forehead. I blinked it away. The transom of their dinghy gyrated in my sights. We couldn't stay like this all afternoon. We had the advantage. We mustn't let it slip away.

'Saul, when I shoot, go to full speed and get us away from them.' I hesitated, running Fred's worries through my mind. Of course he was right. This would be foolish and dangerous. You couldn't recall a bullet. Bugger it. Too much thinking. I was paralysed with indecision again. Pain slapped my kidney.

The exhaust coughed but Rachel's voice – unmistakable this time – cut through my head. 'Do it, Jack!'

35

I braced my shoulder, held my breath and squeezed the trigger gently. The muzzle crack was spectacular but I'd worked another round into the chamber before the little bastard reacted. The bullet smashed through the dinghy's transom before he heard the rifle shot. He turned in surprise as my second round sliced into it again.

The cruiser's prow dropped, quickly followed by its occupants. Someone cut the throttle as my third bullet hit something metallic and ricocheted away. We could hear the gearbox screeching as he thrust it into reverse. He was too late. The dinghy's stern plummeted onto the cruiser's transom and bounced into its wake.

The splintering crash echoed towards us as the cruiser, it's engines screaming, smashed into the remains of the dinghy. As it turned away from us, I could read its name: *Morning Mist*. I scrambled back into the cockpit and handed the rifle to Alan as Saul pushed the throttles wide and the diesels hammered into life.

Rachel's eyes were wide with fear. Her mouth opened but nothing emerged. Malita wrapped her arm round her and shot Fred a withering look.

Fred's voice was strained. 'Well that's that then – stalemate. It'll buy us some time but we'll need to fox them somehow. We can't risk them seeing who we're meeting.'

'Meeting, what meeting? What's going on, Jack?' Rachel sounded desperate. 'Who told you to shoot?'

Annoyed with her change of heart, I snapped back. 'You did, you shouted out *"Do* it!" – like you did in that match.'

Her hand flew to her mouth. 'No. No. I said, *"Don't* do it!" – just as I did last time. Oh, Jack, what have you done?'

Fred filled the silence. 'He misheard you. It's done now. We have to accept that.' He looked at each of us in turn. 'Perhaps we shouldn't have – but don't blame Jack. I could have stopped him. Look, it's worked, they're keeping well back. We can be sure they won't make an official complaint. Do you want to continue, Saul?'

He nodded his agreement. Miko seemed more enthusiastic and even smiled at me. Malita shrugged. Rachel looked across at the other boat, bit her lip then turned back and held my eyes. There was accusation but understanding. Could it be trust?

Alan retrieved the three brass cartridge cases, slipped them into his pocket then aimed the rifle. 'Count me in. If she gets too close, I'll pop some more into her hull.'

'No you won't. Just look as though you might. There'll be no more shooting. Understand?' Fred sounded fierce.

Alan nodded reluctantly.

Fred grabbed my elbow and tugged me towards the cabin. 'Jack and I have to talk. We need a plan.'

Saul took the wheel back from Miko and steered us towards Marmotier, the middle islet where most of the cottages, including my cousin's, were situated.

Maître Ile was off to port and we were transiting towards the distinctive Bigorne rock before we agreed the plan. Instead of swinging through the main stream towards the lagoon, Saul would take us round to the north of the treacherous reef. Our followers had kept at least 400 yards behind and were maintaining station. We had to lead them away from the rendezvous. If they didn't know these waters well enough with this falling tide pushing hard to the northwest, we might even be able to lure them onto the rocks.

As we rounded the easternmost point, we were temporarily out of sight of our pursuers. Saul increased speed heading north then swung us round, mere yards from the closest rocks.

Fred pulled his waterproof burlap sack from the cabin and I stripped off before placing my shorts, shirt and sandals into it. I waited for him to do the same but he seemed hesitant. Malita looked at him and shrugged in her expressive way.

I'd never seen my uncle in a swimming costume before. Now I knew why. His back was as brutalised as Miko's and his chest was pitted with black holes. I managed not to gasp but Rachel looked horrified. Miko nodded in understanding. Saul was too busy holding the boat on the throttles to notice and Alan still had the rifle trained on the point where our pursuer would appear.

Fred wrapped the photos in his clothes and slipped the bundle into the bag. Grabbing one of Saul's cork fenders, he jammed that in to give it some buoyancy. Before he sealed it, he fished his revolver from his canvas bag and shoved that in as well. He hefted the package towards me. God, it felt too heavy to float.

We planned to slip over the side and swim for the rocks while Saul powered off round Les Dirouilles to the Paternosters, another four miles in the distance. We hoped Alf and his friends would chase after *Jacob's Star* and not spot us hiding in a gulley. As far as plans went, it was just on the reasonable side of desperate.

'Hurry up. I can't hold her much longer.' Saul sounded frightened.

I started to clamber over the side but Rachel grabbed my arm. 'Wait. I'm coming with you.'

'Don't be silly. It's too dangerous.'

She ignored me, slipped out of her shorts and pulled her top over her head. She was wearing that crimson swimming costume which showed her figure off to perfection. I knew she looked even better without it and hoped no one spotted the secret grin on my face.

Fred certainly didn't. He gripped her elbow. 'No, Rachel. There's no need. We can manage.'

She looked at Fred but spoke to me. 'Jack knows why I'm coming.'

He turned to me, puzzled. *She knew, she realised that I might panic in the deep water.* I glowed in the sudden warmth of a friendship I really didn't deserve. I felt a great relief.

'Come on then – you can dive for the sack if I drop it,' I said.

She unsealed the sack, folded her clothes, picked up two towels and stuffed them in.

'Get a bloody move on. They'll be in sight any second now.' Saul blipped the throttles to remind us that our plan depended on speed. We had to swim at least twenty yards before we could hide from the boat as it rounded the rocks.

I lowered myself in and paddled off with the sack. Thankfully, it floated. Fred slid alongside me and Rachel eased past, allowing Saul to engage gear and chug away.

The brown kelp, slithering about in the grip of the current, reached out for us as we neared the first granite outcrop. *Jacob's Star* was up to full speed now, exiting stage north in a cloud of diesel.

We slid behind the first group of rocks as the blue hull of our pursuer appeared. The stench of iodine was overpowering. I sucked in a lungful as we clung with the myriad of limpets to the craggy surface.

I could hear the little shit swearing profusely as he saw our boat surging away. I prayed they would chase after it but they throttled back. They were suspicious. The engines burbled as they glided towards us.

I tapped the others on their heads and pointed below. We couldn't take the sack under but it would be camouflaged amongst the rocks. I swallowed as much air as I could hold and forced my body to sink, using my arm strength to push up against the rocks.

Rachel and Fred were light-coloured blurs alongside me. I could hear the twin screws cavitating as the blue hull nudged closer to the rocks. Another thirty seconds and they would have us. Saul would be too far away to help.

Suddenly, a dark shape rushed past us and, with a flick of its fin, shot to the surface. A dolphin had found us and wanted to play.

My breath was gone but I eased myself up until my nostrils were clear. The boat was side on, only yards away. Alf was leaning over the bow, pointing at our saviour, who had broken surface and was staring at this intrusion into its territory with a pair of glassy eyes. I felt the other two alongside.

I took in another breath and pushed myself deep again and listened. The engine exhaust note changed and the burble was replaced with a buzz, then a scream as someone cracked open the throttle.

I waited until it was a distant wail before breaking surface again.

The dolphin looked curiously at me then, with an elastic quiver, was gone.

We waited until the boat was a dot on the horizon before navigating our way through the rocky outcrops. The main cluster loomed high to the south but we had to cross a wide channel first. It narrowed at the eastern end, funnelling the water through with some speed. Even though there was no swell, small wavelets broke over the granite at its entrance.

This was going to be tricky as the tide was ebbing rapidly. Combine that with the swirling currents, and the next fifty yards looked a very long way. I was thinking too much again.

Fred still had one hand on the rock and reached out with the other for the sack. Once we let go, we had to hope we could swim strongly enough to make headway as the tide and current thrust us sideways. If we missed rock fall on the other side, we would have no chance of getting to Marmotier until the tide turned. That might take another three hours. The water was deep here. I wanted that sack for its buoyancy but I couldn't fight Fred for it.

Rachel manoeuvred around the rock and nudged into me, reading my thoughts. 'You can do it. It's not that far. I've got the strongest leg kick. Give me the sack.'

Fred looked reluctant but shoved it towards her.

'You two follow.' She pushed the sack in front of her like a cork training float and kicked off. I waited to see how the cross current would affect her but she was making forward progress.

Fred pushed off and quickly caught her up. He had a strong stroke, which shouldn't have surprised me as he had played water polo in his youth.

I waited until he was alongside Rachel. I needed to sprint the distance, to fill my brain with speed to prevent myself thinking dark thoughts about the depth of the water and the lack of support if I got cramp or panicked. I curled my legs up and sprang off the rock.

I passed them within a few strokes and was into mid-stream within seconds. The push on my breathing side was getting stronger and I knew I was only making crab-like progress. I broke my stroke to look up.

My body convulsed with shock. I rationalised that it was a delay from the shooting but I couldn't control it. A small wavelet, teased by an eddy of wind, broke over my face and I panicked. I swallowed desperately, helpless in the grip of a blind terror. I could only escape by sprinting but my body was frozen. The current pushed me westwards. I was going to drown.

36

'Jack! Get your feet up. Lie on your back.' I could hear Rachel but I couldn't obey.

Fred grabbed my chin from behind and tried to pull it into his shoulder. Panicked by his grip, I fought free. All my training was boiling away in my fevered brain.

I felt a whipping sting across my left cheek. Startled, I turned towards the pain.

Rachel's face was close to mine. She slapped me again. 'Stop it. Calm down.' As her arm swung round to deliver another blow, I ducked. I could tread water. I was back in control.

Her eyes pierced mine. 'Jack Renouf, if you only knew how much I've wanted to do that.'

I glared back at her. She'd certainly woken me and, despite the slap, I wanted to hug her.

Fred had other ideas. 'Come on, you two. We're drifting. Let's pull the sack together.'

What had Miko said? *If you think, you sink.* I had misapplied his advice. It was right for a race, when I over-think everything. But this wasn't a race. It was because I had tried to avoid thinking about my fear that I'd panicked. Rachel's slap had kick-started my rational brain, made me face the reality. The depth of water was immaterial. I might be skinny but I could float, hold my breath, swim underwater and sprint faster than anyone else I knew apart from that bastard Kohler. I was certainly far stronger than Uncle Fred and Rachel so I grabbed the sack and used my power to drag them along. For once, it felt good to be swimming against the tide.

Soon we reached the main outcrop and scrambled ashore. We dried ourselves, slipped on our sandals and clambered up the steep rock face of Marmotier before heading towards the houses.

The lagoon held two sailing yachts and two motorboats captive. The yachts were flying the Red Ensign, the two boats, the Tricolour. All of them must have been there for some hours as the entrance was only passable for a couple of hours either side of high tide.

There were two families camped out on the white sand enjoying a picnic. We could hear the screech of young children from further away. I was comfortable enough in my wet costume and the other two seemed content to stay in theirs so I led the way and pointed to my cousin's cottage.

Fred stopped me as we neared the first family. 'Don't get into a conversation. Just smile and wave.'

'Is Hélène here?' I asked.

He looked around. 'We're an hour late but I expect she'll have moored in the channel anyway. Wouldn't want to risk getting trapped in the lagoon. There's probably a tender tied up somewhere. She won't know which house.' He pointed up the pathway. 'You two go up. I'll look for her.'

At last, I was going to be alone with Rachel. Her shoulder touched mine. There was so much I wanted to say to her. I reached for her hand but as we rounded the bend we almost bumped into an elegant woman wearing a yellow frock.

She smiled. *'Bonjour.'*

I smiled back. No conversation, Fred had said. We passed her, aware that she probably thought us very rude.

I heard Fred's voice and looked back. The woman was grinning in quiet amusement at us as Fred strode up the path.

'Hélène – *ça vas?*'

I gulped. She certainly didn't fit my preconception of a Communist agent. I looked more closely. She was blonde, green-eyed, slender and beautiful in the way only Frenchwomen could manage. She got up and kissed Fred on both cheeks then looked curiously at us.

'This is my nephew, Jack Renouf.'

I offered my hand. *'Je suis heureux de vous rencontrer.'*

She shook it firmly then looked me up and down carefully. 'Very polite. Your uncle has told me much about you. And who is this pretty girl?'

'My name is Rachel Vibert. Fortunately, I am not related to either of these two but I do love your dress, it's beautifully fitted.'

Hélène laughed. 'Of course, Malita has spoken about you. She seems to think you are very sensible. Your arrival with these two might seem to suggest otherwise.' She took her hands and kissed both cheeks. 'Now, perhaps it is time to talk.'

I led us on to the house and retrieved the key from its hiding place. It was cool inside. There was a propane stove and cylinders outside but we had no time for food.

Hélène scrutinised the photographs in silence and compared them to some she extracted from her bag. I wondered if she had a gun in there as well.

She only had a slight accent when she spoke English. 'This tall one is Doctor Ferdinand Kempler, chief counsellor to Emil Puhl, Director of the Reichsbank. The other, sickly-looking one is Hans Schmitz.' She read a note on the back her photograph. 'He is one of Hitler's circle, won the Iron Cross in the trenches, collected some shrapnel and now has a pronounced limp. He is a director of I.G.Farben, the Nazi's largest manufacturing firm. I have no idea why these two might be in Jersey. Perhaps they are –'

Fred interrupted. 'When we last met, I told you about the two men who were observing my house.'

'Yes, I thought they might be from the British security service.'

'Well they attacked Jack two days ago but ran off when a member of the public appeared. They mentioned something about Lawrence.'

She shrugged. 'I told you they hadn't given up.'

'There's more. Another two men with foreign accents assaulted Jack yesterday and really tried to frighten him. They warned him to keep his nose out of other people's business. They also mentioned Lawrence. He has the marks of the attack if you wish to look.'

'There is no need. I have already seen the bruise. I thought that he might have a violent girlfriend.' She gave Rachel a half-smile.

Rachel blushed but said nothing.

I also felt my cheeks warm up with the realisation that my uncle had told her about my relationship with Caroline. I wondered what else he might have revealed about me and my family.

'Fred, do you have any explanation for these two?' Hélène's query was brusque.

'Not really but Jack has an idea. Go on, share it.'

Even though she was a Communist agent and probably a lot more dangerous than she looked, there was something comforting about her presence. I felt she was a person of action rather than words, that she might actually do something, so I decided to tell her everything.

'I believe that these Germans, Kempler and Schmitz, have conspired with Hayden-Brown to defeat the embargo on industrial diamonds and supply Germany's needs for the immediate future.'

She stared at me. 'That sounds rather dramatic, and a trifle over-rehearsed if I may say. I have heard about your acting skills but –'

'Let him finish, Hélène. Best to hear the whole story. He might even provide some details.'

They both sounded so patronising that I stormed on. 'If it's details you want, the SS *Espírito Livre* left the Belgian Congo about two weeks ago, loaded with about a ton of industrial diamonds from the Forminiére mines and steamed 5,500 miles. She met Hayden-Brown's cruiser, *Lorelei*, unloaded four crates, each weighing over sixty pounds. These were taken to Les Routeurs, his house in Jersey.'

I picked up the photograph showing the group. 'This is Georges Sleeman, a Belgian diamond merchant, and this is Sir Edward Fairfield, a well-known English fascist. Both of these were verified by your comrade Eric.'

She shot my uncle a pained look.

'The other one is Rudi Kohler, Kempler's nephew, who is apparently a student and assisting because he has no choice.' I snorted at Caroline's flimsy excuse. 'During a dinner meeting on Sunday evening, Sleeman succeeded in persuading Kempler, Schmitz and Fairfield that these diamonds were of the quality needed. The Germans are paying thirty-seven point five Reichsmarks per carat which works out at 112 million for the shipment. In sterling, that's nine million pounds or nearly two billion francs.'

She looked stunned. My uncle whistled and Rachel continued to look puzzled.

Saul and I had discussed the notes I'd made from Hayden-Brown's study and agreed the figures with me. If there were twenty-two crates then we estimated at least three million carats or twelve million mixed diamonds, all suitable for cutting machine tools. So, it was with more than *acting* confidence that I continued. 'This money is to be transferred from the Reichsbank to Rothschild's in Jersey then to Hayden-Brown's holding company, Mermaid Trading, in Ireland. Doubtless he will already have agreed a means of sharing this with his associates. We believe that he only paid £450,000 to the mines. Take away his shipment and other costs and he and his little gang are going to make a profit of over eight million. And the Nazis are going to get the diamonds they need for their factories to feed their war machine. Is that enough detail?'

'That's conjecture, not detail, young man.' Hélène echoed Eric's words. Maybe all these Communists were the same.

'Well *conjecture* or not, the *Espírito Livre* is riding at anchor six miles off the coast of Jersey, roughly halfway to Granville. She's been there for several days. The four crates of industrials, which I've seen and my friend Saul, who is an expert, has verified, are at this moment in the cabin of *Lorelei* in the Old Harbour in St Helier, guarded by two men.'

She opened her mouth to speak but I charged on.

'Now you can dismiss this as theatrical invention, or you can investigate for yourself. I'm sure you Communists have as much interest in stopping Hitler getting his hands on these diamonds as we misguided believers in democracy.'

She clapped her hands. 'Bravo. He's definitely got some of your blood in him, Fred. Have no fear, we will check. Some of our comrades are customs officers. They will board this vessel, if it is still there.'

'Oh, it will be for a while longer yet.'

'How can you be so sure?'

'Simple. Saul and I sabotaged *Lorelei* last night. We dumped a gallon of golden syrup and a gallon of bleach into her diesel tank. She will never reach the *Espírito Livre* and I doubt it will leave without those sample diamonds.'

268

'You did what?' Fred sounded angry.

'Sabotaged, we hope. We would have made sure but there was a guard on board.'

'Why the bloody hell didn't you ask me first?'

'Because you would have tried to stop me. You're so tied up in procedures and reports that by the time you'd made a decision, the bloody diamonds would be long gone!'

I thought he was going to strike me but instead he launched a stream of Spanish at Hélène.

She turned to me. 'Your uncle is one of the bravest men I have ever met. He does not deserve your scorn.'

Rachel broke the silence. 'He loves you, Jack, more than you can understand. But then you are not very good at understanding love.'

All three stared at me.

My pulse was hammering and my face was burning with embarrassment.

'I'm sorry, Uncle. I didn't mean to insult you. Perhaps I don't understand love, but I know what I feel for you.' My tongue was so thick I could hardly speak but I had to blurt it out. 'You're much more of a father to me than that man who married your sister and hates me for being his son.'

Fred, the self-confessed man emptied of emotion, reached out and hugged me.

'Mind my kidney, Uncle. That hurts.'

He laughed and the others joined in.

'No more than you deserve, Jack,' Rachel said, but softened her words with a smile.

Hélène packed all the photographs into her bag then extracted a chart. 'Well, it would seem young Jack has given us something to deal with. We will investigate this ship if you will be kind enough to point to it on this map.'

Fred picked a spot midway between Gorey and Granville and she marked it with a slim pen, which she then used to make a note of the ship's name and that of Hayden-Brown's cruiser. She made a few more notes while we watched.

'I think I have enough *solid* information now.' She looked at her watch then touched my uncle's arm. 'I will contact you as soon as I have anything to report. Usual time and place.'

'But what will you do if you find the diamonds?' We all looked surprised at Rachel's question.

Hélène glanced at Fred, who nodded. 'As far as we are aware, it is only the Nazis who need these diamonds. We will put them beyond their reach.'

'How?' Rachel persisted.

'There are many secret places but don't worry about this –'

Rachel reached for her arm. 'Promise me you won't let the Germans get them.'

'We'll do our best but we do not make empty promises. Now, you must excuse me.'

She moved to Fred and embraced him then they exchanged several sentences in Spanish. She hugged Rachel and patted her back. She smiled then wrapped me in her arms and planted two soft kisses on my cheeks.

I was sure I enjoyed it more than Rachel even though her perfume overpowered my salt-encrusted nose. Clear orange overlaying something more oriental. I guessed it was Vol du Nuit, which, according to Caroline, was favoured by Marlene Deitrich. It suited Hélène perfectly.

As she pulled away, she gave me a secret smile. 'Be sure to give my regards to Doctor Pavas.'

'How do you know Miko?'

She ignored my question but spoke to Fred. 'Please remind him that our offer still stands.'

As she left the house, Rachel hurried after her. They spoke for a couple of minutes. Before Hélène moved on, they kissed cheeks again. As she rounded the bend, two burly men stepped out alongside her. She hugged them both and waved to us before disappearing towards the lagoon.

'Wow. Not what I expected, Uncle.'

'Yes, she's quite a looker, isn't she?'

Rachel joined us, catching Fred's remark. She muttered, 'Men.'

'What was that about, then?' I asked.

'Nothing. I just wanted to know if she had heard of someone from Caen.' Her look said, *Don't ask any more questions.*

Perhaps I'd have better luck with my uncle. 'How does she know Miko?'

Fred grimaced. 'That was a bit loose-tongued of her. I'm surprised. She obviously doesn't mind you knowing.'

'Knowing what?'

'I thought he'd told you two his story.'

Rachel shrugged. 'About the escape from Romania and his wife's death, he didn't mention Hélène, did he, Jack?'

'No. But how did you know he'd told us anything, Uncle?'

'Ah, I see. You'll have to excuse me. Force of habit. "Need to know" and all that. I've had to be so careful over the years. Sometimes it's difficult to remember who said what to whom, where and when. Right. I can tell you this much. I've known Miko for some time, well before he came to Jersey.'

He held up his hand to stifle my question.

'We met in Berlin, during the Olympics. He was there as an assistant coach to the Hungarian water polo team but he also helped out with the diving and swimming. I think you two know how knowledgeable he is. I was there for a different purpose. He was more successful than me. Hungary won gold medals in the water polo and the one hundred metres freestyle. You were in good hands, Jack.'

He tapped Rachel's arm. 'No luck in the diving, but then he only had men to work with.' He grinned then continued. 'A few months later, we met again in Northern Spain. I'd been sent to help organise the International Brigades, the Communist volunteers who fought to defend the Spanish Republic against Franco's fascists.'

'And that's where he met Hélène?' I interrupted. I wanted to know what Fred was doing in Berlin but couldn't face another long story. I'd ask him on another day, sure it was nothing to do with collecting medals.

'Jack will remember that I told him Miko was trying to get to an English university to pursue his specialist field in physics –'

'But they wouldn't let him in because he was a clever Jew.'

'That didn't help, but the immigration authorities also believe he is a member of the Communist Party.'

271

'Is he?' Rachel asked.

'It's complicated.' Fred rubbed his chin. 'I'm sure you understand there are some things I can't talk about but I do trust Hélène implicitly. Her husband was a political commissar in Albacete, where the International Brigades were trained. She helped to get the volunteers across the French border. That's where she met Miko. He was with the Romanian contingent. The whole camp was run by Comintern and only party members were accepted at that stage.'

He creased his forehead as if to clear his brain. 'This isn't black and white. Not all Communists were followers of Stalin and Comintern, there were a misguided number who believed in the traitor Trotsky's subversive views –'

'Stop a minute, Uncle. You're losing me here. Who's Trotsky?'

'A self-serving enemy of the Soviet people, nothing more, nothing less.'

'That sounds like the party line. But I remember reading something about this now. Didn't Lenin prefer him over Stalin?'

'Lenin was ill, wasn't thinking clearly, but enough of this. You wanted to know about Miko, didn't you?'

I was tempted to remind him that he had raised the issue but it was obviously a sore point. 'Sorry. You're right. Perhaps another time. So what happened in this camp?'

'As I was about to tell you, we were suspicious of volunteers who weren't already party members. You can't just join, you know. You have to be sponsored and vetted.'

I couldn't resist. 'So, more exclusive than the Jersey Swimming Club. No riff- raff like Trotsky or Miko allowed in then.'

He scowled. 'Trotsky is worse than riff-raff. He is a real impediment to the Permanent Revolution. Even from his lair in Mexico, he's still a menace. Do you know, the traitor applied for asylum in Jersey? I'd have put him in the bloody asylum if he set one of his manicured toes on our shore. Anyway, I thought we'd agreed not to discuss him. Now, where was I?'

'Vetting?'

'Yes. Miko was interrogated by a panel led by Hélène's husband. It was a normal procedure but Miko's not very good in interviews. He failed to show the requisite respect and they declined to accept him. I didn't know about this. It was a large camp, but Hélène told me about a disrespectful Romanian and I realised that I might know him. Cut a long story even shorter. We got together and I persuaded him to play nicely. He swallowed his pride, apologised and convinced the commissars that he would follow Stalin's orders without question. I'm sure you can imagine how easy this was.' He rolled his eyes.

'But how did you communicate? I know you and Hélène speak French and Spanish but Miko speaks Hungarian and Romanian. His English is –'

'Don't underestimate him. He also has some Russian and German and all European Jews speak Yiddish. Hélène's husband spoke Russian as well as Spanish and French. Besides, you'll find that many Communist officials have learnt the language of capitalism so they can better understand their class enemy.'

'You mean English?

'Of course. On that basis, you might be advised to learn German. Anyway, that's how they met and now she wants him to take his expertise in physics to Russia. He says he's considering the offer but I don't think he really wants to work under that sort of close supervision. Though I don't know how much longer he can wait around hoping to be allowed into England. Training you and Rachel has provided an interesting diversion for him but he's only using a tiny part of his brain and worries that he'll soon be too far behind to catch up.'

I was puzzled. 'So he's no longer a Communist?'

'I think Hitler would disagree. He won't allow Jews to relinquish their identity, neither will he allow Communists to change their spots. Once you've been a member, or associated with members, you are forever unclean, a dangerous leper. Unfortunately, many of the democracies share the same view.'

'If that's the case, how did he get at job at the Palace Hotel?'

'Ah, I'd done a favour for the owner, sorted out a union problem. He did one for me in return. Believe me, if I could get Miko to England, I would. Hélène wouldn't thank me though.'

There were still some things bothering me about this. 'You and Malita were helped to escape. How did Miko and Hélène and her husband get out?'

'Why do you always ask questions to which there are no simple answers?'

'Call it youthful ignorance, Uncle.'

'Miko fought with the Dimitrov Battalion along with the British and Americans. The brigade suffered heavy casualties but gave the fascists a bloody nose. All over Spain, we were holding the Catholic bastards and then, in late 1938, the British and French appeasers pulled the plug and forced the International Brigades to disband. That handed the victory to Franco. You see, the international capitalist community had decided that not upsetting Hitler was more important than supporting social democracy in Spain so they let the fascists have their victory.'

'So Miko went back to Romania?' Rachel asked.

'Yes, and straight into the arms of the Iron Guard. I believe he's told you the rest.'

'What about Hélène and her husband? How important are they?' Rachel asked.

'He was betrayed and captured by the fascists.' He stopped, held my gaze. 'You know what that means, I don't need to explain, do I?'

'No.' We could spare Rachel that at least.

'Let us say he was executed in such a way that his widow will never rest until the last fascist is dead… this is her life now, but it's not easy. She has had to deal with internal issues… I'm saying far too much. But you asked if she was important, Rachel. She is far more than that. She is vital and needs to be protected. As I've told Jack, I believe that the Nazis will go for a rerun of their 1914 plan but they won't get bogged down in trenches this time. They'll crash through and conquer France in weeks. Britain might hold out but she'll be isolated. The Americans will screw every last penny out of us and, when we've got nothing to sell, we'll be left to rot. The only hope is Stalin. He nearly succeeded in Spain and lessons have been learnt. Hélène and her comrades can keep that hope alive and provide a resistance to the Nazis, that's why she's vital, Jack. If she gets those diamonds, you can be sure they'll never end up in German hands.'

There was one very big "if" in his belief but, until he fell out of love with Stalin, there was no point in mentioning it. 'Thanks. I think I understand, but what should we do now?'

'As Hélène said, she will contact me as soon as she has any information. We just have to be patient.' He considered me. 'If you really want to do something then get on and send the signal to Saul.'

'Let's hope Miko and Malita are keeping watch and my brother hasn't shot himself or anyone else on *Jacob's Star* by accident then.' I picked up the sack, opened it and dug around for the flag. My hand brushed the revolver and I felt clammy again. Had that really been me shooting at that boat?

Fred helped me attach the Red Ensign to the halyard on the flagpole and I hoisted it to the top.

'How close will they need to be to see that?' asked Rachel.

'Saul could calculate that for you in a second but I know it involves square roots and some algebra, not my strong points,' I responded.

Fred looked amused at my mathematical weakness. 'About eight miles in this light. The flag looks to be at least fifty feet above sea level. With binoculars they should be able to spot it easily. We may have to wait for some time though. It's a pity we didn't bring those crabs with us. We could have cooked them up and had our own little feast.'

Food was the last thing I wanted, though we could have left Fred in charge of the crabs while we explored. I caught Rachel's eye and tried to mime the suggestion that we take a short walk.

'Are you all right, Jack? You seem to have developed a twitch.' Her voice was teasing. She knew what I meant but didn't want to talk in private.

Fred seemed oblivious to this pantomime. 'Well, we might as well enjoy the sun, I think I'm going to grab forty winks. Old soldier's trick, Jack. Grab the shuteye when you can, you never know when you'll get the next opportunity.' He fished his clothes out of the bag, bundled them into a pillow and surrendered to the sun.

At last. Now I could pull Rachel aside.

But she grabbed her bundle and lay down beside him. 'That's a great idea, Fred. I think I'll join you.'

Why didn't she want to speak to me? Bugger them. I'd had enough sun. I went inside, wriggled out of my wet costume, changed into my shorts then spent the next hour observing the horizon and brooding. Both were circular activities and only one yielded any results. While I watched *Jacob's Star* approach from the north, I realised that trying to understand women was even more frustrating than algebra.

'We had some fun, I can tell you. The *kaffirs* tried to close a couple of times. But your brother aimed the rifle and they backed off. Give him his due, he's been more sensible than I expected.' Saul kept talking as we clambered aboard and Alan stowed the dinghy. 'I swear I had this tub up to fifteen knots. We swerved around the Paternosters twice. That shook them up. Not much room for error there. Miko gave me a long explanation in Yiddish about how he would deal with them if they did attempt to board. I thought you told me he was a professor of physics. Sounded more like a professional butcher to me. Anyway, Malita suggested we head off for Carteret. They followed until we were close to port then turned tail –'

'Why didn't they keep chasing you?'

'As I explained before, Jack, it's all about engine speed and fuel consumption. Their petrol engines are like some of your older water polo players, they need pints of ale to keep them happy after a match. We more sophisticated diesel operators require mere sips of a decent wine. They must have realised that we could have kept the game going for hours.'

'So what's to stop them lying in wait for us on the return journey?' I asked.

Alan waved the rifle. 'This. Are you glad I brought it now?'

Fred pushed the barrel away. 'Be careful with that. Why don't you get up on the cabin and keep watch whilst Saul takes us back.'

Alan patted the stock. 'Locked, loaded, and at your command, sir.'

'Do you think they will be waiting for us?' Rachel asked.

Fred replied, 'Unlikely, if they are short of fuel, they'll need to get back to St Helier. I suggest we go straight to St Catherine's and

Saul moors there overnight just in case they are waiting in the harbour.'

I tapped his shoulder. 'That makes sense. What do you think, Saul?'

'Fine by me so long as we can get a lift home. Is there a phone box nearby?'

'Why?'

'Well you don't have a phone at home, you can't get us all on the back of your bike – not that I'd risk my neck anyway – so I'll have to phone for a taxi.'

'What about the bus?' suggested Rachel.

'Bus? Jack, tell her what happened the last time I used public transport.'

'It's not that he's a snob, Rachel, but having to share a bus with those who can't afford taxis brings him out in a rash. I'm not sure there's a bus anyway at this time of day. Not that it matters. I'll take Alan home and come back with our car. It'll be a squeeze but I'll take all of you back.' That would give me a chance to drop the others off and be alone with Rachel. I enjoyed that comforting thought all the way to the breakwater.

Saul moored us to a buoy as there wasn't enough water to reach the slipway. We'd have to take turns in the dinghy.

'What about the crabs? You're not planning to leave them on my boat, are you?'

'I'll take a couple home to Mum and Dad,' suggested Alan. 'They love spiders.'

Alan thinking about others? I was too dumbfounded to speak.

'I'll take the lobster and one of the spiders,' offered Fred. 'I can teach Malita some new culinary skills.'

'What about you, Rachel? You want one for your parents?' Alan's thoughtfulness was in danger of getting him strangled.

'No thanks. My father,' she shot me a look, 'hasn't got any teeth, won't wear false ones and I can't see him using his gums on those shells.'

We must have all shared the same image because we started to giggle. Even Miko found it funny.

'I take one of these spiny monsters. Give to chef. He cook for us,' Miko said.

Somehow, after an afternoon spent risking our lives, shooting at our pursuers, nearly drowning then arranging a way to deprive the Nazis of their diamonds, arguing about crabs made it seem all worthwhile.

Alan and I rode off on *Bessy* while the others waited. I dropped him, the crabs and his "fishing rod" in the yard. He could present the gifts while I borrowed our car, picked up the others and drove them back to St Helier. I didn't want to risk my father's ire so decided not to ask permission.

I returned just as a red and white S.C.S Bedford bus pulled away from the top of the slip. Saul, Fred and Malita were waving from the back window. My heart leapt. At last. I could take Rachel home and finally get to talk with her in private.

'Hey, Jerk. Over here. You have room for crabs?'

Miko stood on the slipway holding two of the spider crabs aloft.

Of Rachel there was no sign.

Double buggeration.

37

Friday

Another day, another ticking off. It was hardly worth the bother of attending college anymore. There were no classes for me and I really wasn't in the mood for digging Mrs Buezval's garden, however needy she might appear. Four cups of tea and two wheelbarrow loads of weeds later, I revised my view and promised to return to help defend her from the rampaging foliage.

Bessy took me into town on an impromptu raid on my post office savings account. After the past few days, hoarding money seemed to have less meaning. I resolved to do something useful with it instead. Flowers for Rachel would be an appropriately romantic gesture but she might plant them in my ear. A length of rope coiled into a noose for Caroline was a tempting idea.

I stopped outside Donaldson's music shop again – this time I seemed to be alone. Bjoerling stared back at me from behind the glass.

Uncle Fred was by turns amazed, grateful and then embarrassed that I should make such a gesture. I shut him up by slipping the record out of its sleeve and letting Puccini answer his reservations. Cup of tea number five was followed quickly by three slices of Battenberg cake.

He had no news from Hélène. We argued half-heartedly about my involvement but we both knew that I could hardly place adverts in the *Morning News* and *Evening Post* to advise whoever was following me that I was, henceforth, disassociating myself from all further activity. After my double dose of action the previous day, my appetite for further confrontation had diminished anyway.

Finally, we agreed that, if I was stopped or threatened again, I should tell my father and report it to the police. It was Fred's suggestion and he made it, knowing that my father's wrath would certainly fall on him like a tidal wave.

Yesterday, I could have killed a man, blown his head apart, yet I still felt unmoved. My side still ached in time with my heart, but there was little I could do to relieve either pain.

We listened to both sides of the record twice and, after my eighth cup of tea of the day, I left feeling somewhat deadened by the whole experience.

I should find Saul and arrange to return *Jacob's Star* but I was still angry with him for dragging them onto the bus and leaving me with Miko instead of Rachel. I needed to see her, wanted to slap Caroline, but went home with *Bessy* instead. I wasn't even surprised when she threw a spark plug fit and seized up after struggling up St Saviour's Hill. Rather like Saul, she had too much oil on her head. I cleaned her up and puttered back home.

Alan was in the yard pacing up and down as if he'd just fallen into a bed of nettles and couldn't ease the itch. From his first few words, it was clear that I wasn't the dock leaf he needed to rub it better either.

'Where the hell have you been? What's going on? Shouldn't we be doing something?'

'Such as?'

'I don't know, you're the spy – you tell me. Shouldn't we be following someone, reporting on their movements?'

'It's over, Alan. There's nothing more to do.'

'Don't be daft. Of course there is. Never mind what Fred says. There are crazy men out there with guns and coshes and –'

'Shut up and calm down. We have to stay out of it. I was bloody crazy yesterday. I should never have involved you and Saul and... God, I wish you hadn't brought your rifle.'

'That's right – blame me. *Smellie* jumped into your hands and fired itself, I suppose?' He poked me in the chest but I didn't react. He pressed his face into mine and hissed, 'Just tell me where we would have been without the rifle – bloody fish bait, that's what.'

I stood nose to nose with him. I couldn't blink away his anger but I waited, hands by my side, until it cooled.

He stepped back and grunted, 'Did Surcouf find you?'

'No.'

'He's upset. It seems someone emptied one of his pots and left some sausages inside. He says a crab choked to death on them.'

Typical Alan. He'd gone from outraged anger to facetious charm in the twinkling of an eye.

We were still laughing when a post office messenger arrived in a cloud of muddy spray and two-stroke smoke. Straddling his bike, he let the raucous engine tick over and thrust an envelope into my hand.

'You Jack Renouf?'

'Yes.'

'Any reply?'

'What?'

'Reply? You need to read it and tell me if you want to reply.'

I'd gone nearly nineteen years without receiving a telegram and now I'd had two in a matter of days. I stared at the brown envelope, bemused.

He blipped his throttle impatiently.

Alan grabbed the telegram and ripped it open. 'Wake up, Jack. Mister Pony Express here is in a hurry. Go on, read the bloody thing and you,' he tapped the messenger on the head, 'wait, if you want a tip.'

I unfolded the paper. "DINNER SEVEN PM TONIGHT PALACE HOTEL STOP BLACK TIE STOP BE THERE STOP LOVE C ENDS."

Alan read it over my shoulder then turned to the messenger. 'No reply.' He grinned impishly. 'And here's your tip. Don't be rude to your customers. Now bugger off.' He turned back to me. 'Still got you by the short and curlies then? You going?'

The flimsy paper shook in my hand. I might be able to hold a rifle steady even when facing another gun but she could still reach out and shake me to the core. This time, I really thought I'd escaped. It was only an illusion. My eyes were burning as I walked past Alan.

'No, you can't borrow the car and that's an end of it.'

'But –'

'You borrowed it yesterday evening without permission and don't think a couple of crabs is fair payment.'

'But –'

'No, and that's final! Why can't he understand me, Mary?'

Mum hovered the teapot over my tenth cup of the day. I felt quite light headed. 'Probably because you haven't told him why, Aubin.'

'I don't have to explain myself to him... or anyone. "No" is "No". Isn't that sufficient?'

Gulliver must have felt the same way when all the little people were tying him down. His word was law – why was I questioning it?

'Aubin, he's almost a man now and, as you always tell me, men need things explaining to them – don't they?'

He grunted but continued to sip his tea.

'What he means to say, love, is that we're going out tonight. Don't look so surprised. It does happen occasionally. We're picking the Cabots up and your father is driving so you see, it's quite simple. No need to make a fuss about it, Aubin.'

She turned her back on him and winked at me. 'Of course we could use the lorry or hitch a trailer to the tractor.' He didn't rise to the bait. She rattled the cups in the sink. 'Anyway, where are you going, love?'

'Your bloody brother's I bet,' Father said.

'What if I am? What's the problem you've got with Uncle Fred? Why can't I see him when I want? Why don't you want him coming here? It's bloody crazy.' I'd gone too far and we all knew it.

In the silence which followed my outburst, we could hear the distant crack as Alan scratched his itch on wooden targets.

My father, heavy with disappointment, got up and moved to the door. He grabbed his cap. 'Tell him if you must – it won't change anything. He won't be welcome in this house until...' he left the rest unsaid and stalked outside.

Mum dried her hands and sat down, collecting her thoughts carefully before she spoke. 'I love my brother but... he can be so difficult. I think he's changed but your father doesn't.' She looked

282

at her hands, realised they were empty, got up and lifted a can of Brasso out of a cupboard.

'What did he do to upset Father so badly? Was it during the war?'

She shook her head as she fished a rag and a duster from the drawer.

'Religion?'

She picked one of the copper pots off its hook above the range. 'Come on, Jack. What drives your father?'

'Money?'

'After Grandpa died and your father inherited the farm, we had very little – not enough to expand, barely enough to survive, especially as we had his mother and mine to look after as well. The banks weren't interested so he borrowed from a Jewish moneylender.'

She plonked the pot, which looked perfectly clean, onto the table. 'Lord knows he wasn't the only one. The interest rate was crippling but it was either that or sell the farm but we couldn't do that, not after Grandpa had nearly broken his back keeping it going during the war. Before the flu took him, he made your father promise. Anyway, we worked every waking moment and started to earn enough to pay back a little bit of the capital. You were only a baby and Alan was on the way.'

She opened the Brasso tin and released the acrid smell into the room. 'Fred came back from his adventures – you know about the Communist business. He was broke, couldn't find work because of his views. He came to me and I persuaded Aubin to help.'

She dabbed the tin onto the rag. 'It nearly finished us. Your father was devastated. He'd put everything into the farm and your uncle, who now hated everyone who owned their own business, wanted money.'

The tin wobbled as she slapped it down. 'We couldn't believe his hypocrisy but I couldn't turn him away, especially after what he'd done for us.'

Something crossed her face. Alarm? I had the feeling she hadn't meant to say that.

She inspected the pot, turning it as she spoke. 'He'd tried everywhere else. Aubin went back to the moneylender. The deal this time was five times the normal interest rate. Take it or leave it.'

'Is that why he didn't like me playing Shylock?'

'No, nothing like that. He doesn't like Shakespeare, hates the chairs in the Great Hall – they remind him too much – he loathed school you know, couldn't see any point in it once he'd learned what he needed.'

The pot was upside down now as she dabbed polish on a blemish I couldn't see. 'No, your father's not a racist. He's not too fond of your friend Saul though – finds him a bit smarmy.'

'What about Malita? Why won't he meet her?'

'Did your uncle say that?' She stopped smearing polish.

'No. Not directly but I got the impression –'

'It might be the other way round, Jack. She might not want to meet him. Have you thought of that?'

I hadn't but, as my father refused to talk about his brother-in-law, I had only ever heard one side. From Mum's tone, clearly she saw another.

'This loan you gave him, it was a long time before Malita, wasn't it?'

'Oh yes, before he went back to England.'

'So he needed it as no employers would give him a job because he was a Communist?'

'I just don't understand how things get so dirty' She rubbed vigorously with the rag. 'It wasn't quite that simple. We didn't know at the time but he used most of the money to help set up a branch of the General Workers' Union.'

'That was rather cheeky, wasn't it? Taking money from an employer to help the workers?' The ammonia was tickling my nose. I fought back a sneeze.

The once clean and shining pot was now discoloured with an opaque sheen. 'It was worse than that. He set up a new section for agricultural workers and tried to get them out on strike until employers, like us, paid them more money for their labour.'

'Could you afford to?' I couldn't watch this much longer. Either I had to start polishing with her or take the pot away.

'Not really. You know we do most of the work ourselves but need help during the potato season. If we paid more, we couldn't be sure of making enough to plough back in for the next year's crop. What with maintenance, replacements, running costs, it doesn't take much to tip us over into loss. There are only a handful of large farms that can cope with poor seasons.'

I moved closer, grabbed the duster and tried to polish the side of the pot. 'Surely Uncle Fred understood that. What's the point in driving you under? That wouldn't help anyone.'

She pulled the duster from my hand. 'Of course he understood. He knows how farms work, what a fine line it is, but he was driven by these socialist beliefs. The redistribution of wealth, I think he calls it.'

'Did they strike?'

'For a few days but their union decided not to support them and refused strike pay. They were quickly back to work and your uncle was forced to resign from the union he had borrowed from us to set up.' She held the rim in one hand and swept the duster over the surface with the other. 'Your father thought it was no more than he deserved.'

'Hasn't Uncle Fred paid you back?'

'Oh, he tried. After Spain, he came back with quite a bit of money. Wanted to give us double what we'd lent him. He didn't seem to understand that we'd paid nearly three times the amount we'd borrowed in interest alone. At one stage we had to pawn nearly everything. I'm sure my mother, bless her soul, noticed but she didn't say anything. Granny Renouf, poor thing, had stopped noticing anything by that time.'

'But we're not poor now, are we?'

'No, we've worked very hard and been fortunate with the crops but your father has never forgiven him for the pain he caused. He's very stubborn, as you know. He asked Fred where he'd got the money. He wouldn't tell him so Aubin refused to accept it. He seemed to get some pleasure in cutting off his nose to spite his face.' Her polishing hand speeded up.

'So he still hates him because he used you. And because he's a Communist as well.'

'He doesn't hate him, that wouldn't be very Christian, but he's been a big embarrassment to your father.'

She spun the pot then looked at me over its rim. 'He's also upset that you seem to be closer to Fred than to him.'

The reflection in the polished surface stared back at me accusingly.

'It's alright, love, I understand. I think he does really. He'll come round.'

The way she'd told it made sense but I still felt there was something missing. Dare I ask? 'Thanks for telling me, Mum, and there was I thinking it was just about a woman.'

She looked shocked; a deep red colour seeped from her neck into her face. I'd embarrassed her. Big mouth, both feet – again.

'Jack Renouf, whatever do you mean?'

'Sorry, I must be confusing him with me. I meant... I heard that Phillips, Father, and Uncle had a fight over a woman. I just wondered –'

'Wondered what?'

'Whether that woman was you?'

She pushed the pot away as her flush faded.

I daren't speak.

Suddenly she got up and left the kitchen. I heard her moving about upstairs in her bedroom. The pot glared at me.

Eventually she returned clutching a worn leather album. She sat next to me and placed it between us.

'Will you tell me where you're going tonight that you need the car?'

I reached into my pocket, unfolded the telegram and held it out to her.

She scanned it quickly. 'Will you do as she demands?'

'I don't know.'

'Have you thought of saying "no" to her – for once?'

She knew I was seeing her. She'd met her once. Must have known about our exchange of letters. I'd never thought of discussing it with her. How could she understand how I was feeling?

'Yes, I've thought about it... I haven't decided yet. Where are you and the Cabots going?'

'Not to the Palace, I'm sure. But really, I don't know. It's Marjorie's birthday and Edgar has planned a surprise treat. It's a bit difficult as I don't know what to wear and your father's no help...' she leant closer to me. 'Listen love, we've noticed that you haven't been sleeping well. You're not eating much. You're out at all hours,

286

secretive, impatient. We don't want to interfere in your life but we're worried about you.'

She touched the back of my hand with her slender fingers. 'I think I know something of what is happening in there.' She tapped my chest and smiled. 'Not everything though – I'm only a woman, after all.'

She fingered the book then eased it open. Inside were clippings of newspaper reports on swimming, diving, and water polo from before the war. Most were from the Havre des Pas pool but there were images from La Rocque's and St Aubin's harbours as well.

She turned the pages without comment until she reached a large glossy photograph. According to the caption, it was taken at a water gymkhana in August 1911. The background was clearly the start of the 110 yard course and there was a large crowd watching a group of girls in fancy dress preparing to dive into the water.

I spotted Mum immediately. She was laughing and looking at the camera self-consciously. I recognised Yvonne, Joan's mother. I had no idea about the rest. One, who wasn't smiling, seemed to be staring directly at my mother.

She stabbed her finger at the diving stage. 'Sometimes, you can see almost everything in a photograph.'

The boards were empty but underneath, dressed in the old-fashioned strapped water polo costumes, was a group of seven men. They were watching the girls. My father was standing next to Uncle Fred. I was sure two of the others were my father's younger brother, Raoul, and Fred's brother, Arthur, both of whom had fallen in Flanders. One was definitely Phillips, the rest were strangers. I looked quizzically at my mother.

She traced her finger back to the girls and rested it above the one who was looking at her. 'Isobelle.'

'Should I know her?'

'Everyone wanted to that summer – especially your father, and my brother.'

So that was the mystery woman that Nutty had mentioned. But there was something wrong here. 'So Phillips and Father fought over her?'

'No. She showed no interest in George Phillips. I was the apple of his eye.'

'I'm getting confused, Mum.'

'It was all very silly, really. George wanted to walk out with me but I wasn't interested in him. He thought your father was... oh this is so complicated.'

Complicated? Compared to my relationships? 'Go on, Mum, you can't stop now.'

She tapped the photograph again. 'It was all her fault. She was only here for the summer. Her father was in the army, on secondment to the militia. She was a good swimmer and joined the club but she wanted to win more than races. She set all the men against each other. It was so obvious to the rest of us girls. Fred thought your father was sweet on me and was angry that he should pay attention to her. She flirted with both of them. All very demure, but unmistakable to those with eyes to see. Unfortunately both of them seemed temporarily blinded. Fred warned him off and I heard that there was a fight over it. George thought your father wasn't being fair to me and called him something rude. That was a more public fight – in a water polo match I believe, though I didn't see it. I suppose it must seem all very trivial now but it hurt a lot then.'

'Is that why neither of you go to the club anymore?'

'Of course, the war changed everything. Somehow, swimming and socialising didn't seem so important afterwards. We did go for a while then... we had so much to do here. Too many sad memories.'

I touched the photo again. 'What happened to this Isobelle?'

'She left. Some thought she was probably unaware of the ructions she caused. I didn't think so. She knew exactly what she was doing.'

'Have you seen her since?'

My mother's face was a mask. 'Oh, yes. She came back in 1919, just after your father married me.' She shut her eyes. 'If I tell you, you must promise never to tell your father.' She opened her eyes and I saw in their depths a pain which unnerved me.

Dumbly, I nodded.

Her voice was faint. 'I'd rather tell you than let you find out from the gossips.'

288

She looked at the photo as though it was alive. 'She had an affair with your father. It broke my heart.'

Stupefied, I stared at her. She seemed calm but her eyes were misty. I felt shame for her, anger with him. 'But you're still together –'

'Yes, love. We're still together. We survived. Thanks to my brother.'

'How?'

'He confronted them. Forced your father to tell me the truth. She never forgave him but he'd seen right through her.'

'She gave up then?'

'She's not the sort to give up. She bounced off and grabbed another man.' She pointed to the photograph again. 'Him.'

I scrutinised the picture but the man's face was in shade. He was wearing an army officer's uniform, standing apart from the others, half turned towards another, older man, also in uniform. There was something familiar about his bearing. 'Who is he? Do I know him?'

She closed the album with a snap, and fiddled with her wedding ring then refolded the telegram and pressed it into my hands.

'I love your father, always have. I've forgiven him but he knows I'll never forget.'

She took in a deep breath. 'He's a good man only, where women are concerned,' her eyes bored into mine, 'somewhat bewildered.' She tapped the album. 'Her name is Isobelle Hayden. He is Wilbur Brown. Your Caroline is their daughter.'

'What's for tea?' Alan blundered into the kitchen, propped his rifle against the cupboard and marched to the range.

Mum covered the album with a tea towel and carried it over to the dresser. Alan didn't seem to notice.

'I've left you a tasty salad. Dad and I are going out.'

'Good, that's two portions for me then. Jack's out for some posh nosh – aren't you big brother?'

'That reminds me. Do either of you know anything about two tins of golden syrup which have disappeared from the larder?'

An innocent look was one acting expression I had yet to master.

'If you're hungry, Jack, just ask. I know you love it but I'd rather you ate proper food.'

Alan chirped in. 'Well it's not me. I hate the stuff. Try Dad, he's probably used them in some Masonic ritual.'

Mum fought to keep a straight face. 'You two will be death of me.'

Completely oblivious to any atmosphere he might have disrupted, Alan clattered about the kitchen and cleared a space for himself on the table. In the process, he knocked his satchel onto the floor. An assortment of exercise books fell out. Tonto sniffed at them before I shooed him away.

I picked them up and placed them on the table. A white envelope dropped from his English composition book, which seemed to be the thinnest on the pile.

'What's this?' I held it up. It had my name on it.

'Oh shit. Sorry, Mum, forgot. It was in our pigeon hole.'

'When? Today? Yesterday?'

'Bugger. Sorry, Mum. Can't remember. Think it was Monday, or it might have been Tuesday.'

I eyed the rifle. If only it had a bayonet attached. 'What's in it?'

'How do I know? I'm not a bloody magician. Sorry, Mum.'

I examined it. My name was typed. There only seemed to be a single sheet inside. It was probably a reprimand for my non-attendance. I unfolded the sheet. It was Grumpy's handwriting. I'd seen it enough times on my essays.

Renouf, An excellent swim and well-deserved record. Well played. On another matter, you might find this helpful: Venus and Adonis 799–804
   Best wishes.
   J.B.G.

This had been in Alan's bag for over a week. So I'd been right. Grumpy believed I had listened to his advice and lost the race deliberately. If only he knew half the truth, he'd be sending me a rude summons instead of a Shakespearian reference. Saul would probably know it without looking it up but I needed my *Complete Shakespeare* which was in my bedroom.

'It's a note from the headmaster. I've got to check a reference. Excuse me.' I ignored their curious stares and made for the stairs.

In my room I pulled the book from the shelf and thumbed through until I found the lines:

Love comforteth like sunshine after rain,
But Lust's effect is tempest after sun;
Love's gentle spring doth always fresh remain,
Lust's winter comes ere summer half be done;
Love surfeits not, Lust like a glutton dies;
Love is all truth, Lust full of forged lies.

My eyes burned. *"Lust full of forged lies."* How could Shakespeare, writing three centuries before, know so much about my frailty?

Tears trickled down my cheeks, some for my mother and the hurt and shame Isobelle had inflicted on her, but most were for Rachel and the pain she had suffered through my own crass stupidity.

Alan was right. I was going out tonight but not meekly in answer to Caroline's call. Like Shylock, I now wanted my pound of flesh. From somewhere closest to her heart would be best.

38

Fortunately, the showers had passed to reveal a fine, crisp evening. I rode *Bessy* off Mont Millais, along the road separating the two large fields belonging to the Palace's farm and positioned her out of sight under the trees in the corner of the large gravelled car park. I checked my watch. I was early but I wanted to examine the lie of the land. I marched up the lane and into the impressive hotel courtyard.

Skirting the entrance, I took a shortcut through the garage area and emerged on the eastern end of the veranda. The dining room was full of hotel guests and I spotted Miko serving them – our meal wouldn't be in there so I wandered through the ballroom and billiard room down to the Golden Restaurant and peeked in.

Apart from a few white-coated waiters, the room was empty. The tables were laid with crisp linen cloths and intricately folded starched napkins. Some diners were outside enjoying the unexpected clear evening, while more waiters fussed around them bearing trays of exotic drinks. The surging swell of their chatter and laughter overwhelmed even the frenzied crickets.

I looked more closely. The room had two large openings onto the long south-facing veranda. I was standing in the first doorway from the north. The south-facing wall was a series of full-length windows protected by an external sunshade, though this did little to exclude the softening rays of the evening sun. To my left was the full-length elevated bandstand with a drum kit, grand piano and music stands taking up the whole of the east wall.

There were two tables at either end of the room. The first of these was centred in front of the stage, almost as a top table, and was laid for six. There were four tall square-sectioned pillars on each side of the room and one round table was set between each of them. Most seemed to be laid for six but, in the far west corner, was one with only five settings.

Each table was ready now, complete with individual ornate menus between the cutlery. Thin blue candles had been placed in silver holders in front of each setting and the few waiters were busy lighting them. A large fresh flower display was in the centre of each table and the room was fragrant with the scent of sweet peas.

"'*Free from our feasts and banquets bloody knives.*'" I jumped as Saul poked me in the back. '*Macbeth*, in case you'd forgotten. Nice suit, waterproof this time?'

I spun round. First surprise. Saul was there, wearing a maroon velvet jacket and matching tie.

I couldn't hit someone dressed in such a ridiculous outfit. 'If you had a wig, you could be in a Restoration play, some foppish Sheridan character.'

'Why thank you, kind sir.' Saul flourished an elaborate bow. 'Allow me to introduce my companion.' He motioned behind him. Second surprise. Rachel smiled hesitantly.

I tried to keep the shock from my face but Rachel looked dazzling in a long black dress, with a plunging neckline, that clung tightly to her body. A simple silver chain with my old Saint Christopher nestled between the gentle swell of her breasts.

I reached for her hand, which felt warm and soft, breathing in the slightly musky fragrance of her eau de cologne. Her face was in shadow but I felt the challenge in her eyes. She looked so elegant. "*Love's gentle spring doth always fresh remain.*"

Confusion tripped my pulse as I fought to keep my voice level and light.

'Charmed, I'm sure. Have we met?'

'Mrs Malaprop, milord.' Saul had picked up the game. He turned to Rachel. 'Promise to forget this fellow – to *illiterate* him, I say, quite from your memory.'

She snapped, 'Stop showing off with your silly word games. I have no idea what you are talking about –'

'Neither does he, Rachel.' I poked Saul in the ribs.

Saul took both our hands and ushered us into the corridor. 'What in damnation's going on, Jack? Why's she invited us? Where the hell have you been?'

'Fighting with my father, learning more secrets. You?'

'Trying to find you so we could return *Jacob's Star*. I even traced you to that old biddy Mrs Buezval. She's the first woman I've met who's got a good word to say for you. Shame she's in her seventies. I got fed up following your trail and went to the harbour. *Lorelei* wasn't on her mooring so let's hope she's wallowing in the trough of despair somewhere at sea. I also asked around the boatyards about that blue-hulled boat, *Morning Mist*. Tracked her down and told the foreman that we'd seen her at Les Écréhous and the crew had left a picnic hamper behind that I wanted to return. He told me she was on hire to an advocate from Le Marquand & Le Sueur in Hill Street. I found their offices and checked the brass plates outside. Guess the name of one of the companies they represent?'

'No. But you must be exhausted with all that walking unless you used taxis to –'

'The Diamond Trading Company, one of De Beers. They must be working with those men who followed us.'

I was about to lecture him on his foolish bravery when I spotted Phillips, Brewster, Nelson and their respective wives moving in from the veranda, following a waiter who had placed all their current drinks on a tray. He showed them to the table between the middle pillars on the south wall.

Saul and Rachel followed my gaze. 'Oh double shit. All we need now is Grumpy and –'

The headmaster hove into view along with Martlew, Captain Knowles and three women I assumed were their wives. They were ushered to the table closest to us, near the kitchen entrance.

I was feeling nervous now. 'Oh fucking bollocks.'

Saul choked in surprise at my language but followed my eyes as Jurat Ralph Poingdestre shuffled in with his wife, the unblessed Iris, in tow. Following them was Jurat Hurel with an imperious-looking woman who was probably his wife. Another couple joined them and they all sat at the table opposite the Jersey Swimming Club contingent.

Surely Fred wouldn't turn up as well? I watched three more groups being ushered in by the waiters but didn't recognise anyone. Now there were just two unoccupied tables.

'Well, that narrows it down. We're either out on the balcony or at one of those two.' Saul seemed to be on the verge of giggles. 'This is going to be fun.'

'I think I want to go home.' Rachel sounded anxious.

'Nonsense, my dear. The party's about to begin. You can't go home until the clock strikes twelve – can't disappoint the prince and we've got to have a search for someone to fit your shoe.' Saul put his arm around her waist and whispered something.

A waiter approached Saul. 'Excuse me, sir, are you Mr Renouf?'

'Good God, man. Do I look like a peasant?'

The man, no doubt considering his tip, if not his future employment, didn't answer but turned to me and smiled, as only someone trained to deal with idiots can.

'Please follow me, sir.' He escorted us through the room to the table at the far end. I looked neither left nor right but was keenly aware of the glances from those at Uncle Ralph's table.

Saul smiled graciously in all directions, especially at Grumpy, who peered back, disbelievingly. The waiter pulled out a chair for Rachel which gave her an overall view of the room. I sat next to her with my shoulder turned away from Ralph's table.

Saul sat on her other side and grabbed the waiter's arm. 'Champagne. Now.'

The waiter went off to find something suitable for the strange-looking guest who didn't want to be taken for a peasant.

I reached out for one of the menus as a means of avoiding eye contact with anyone else. I studied the seven courses and realised I didn't have room for any of them. I hissed at Saul. 'It's Friday – shouldn't you be fasting? Hasn't your Sabbath started?'

Saul laughed. '"*I will buy with you, sell with you, talk with you, walk with you, and so following, but I will not eat with you, drink with you, nor pray with you.*" Relax and get up to date – even Shylock wasn't that orthodox. I might have to say some prayers over the candles though.'

'What are you two talking about?'

I stopped my immediate response. It was possible that she hadn't discussed her secret with Saul and probably wouldn't know much, if anything, about Jewish tradition yet. The shock of what she must have felt hit me.

'Only some silly school boy stuff – from that play we were in.'

'Oh, when you played Shylock. I thought that was very brave, Jack.'

Saul looked shocked, though his tone was mocking. 'Why? It was a privilege for him.'

Further banter was suspended when the final party entered the room from the hotel entrance. All the guests swivelled in their chairs to watch.

Hayden-Brown led in the two Germans Hélène had identified, Kempler and Schmitz. The latter did seem to have a slight limp. The overweight Sleeman bustled after them. They all waited patiently at the table while Sir Edward Fairfield made a fuss about escorting a woman through the double doors.

I'd never met her but I could see Mum's finger hovering over her photograph. The years hadn't been kind to her – she looked frail and drawn, almost haggard – but there was no doubt it was Isobelle.

The men bustled about her, arguing about where she should sit. Fairfield won and placed her between him and Kempler. Hayden-Brown bowed politely to everyone in the room, though he looked puzzled when he saw us.

He smiled uncertainly then sat down. The guests applauded politely then resumed their conversations. How long before a waiter appeared to eject us?

Saul pointed to the two empty seats at our table. There was no sign of Kohler or Caroline. Was she planning to bring Rudi to sit with us?

The adrenaline surged again and I put my menu down before it started to shake in my hands. The waiter arrived with our champagne, which Saul examined before he told him to open it.

'"Bollinger" '28. That was a good vintage. Should be fine.'

'Christ, that's eleven years old, how much will that cost?'

'Too rich for you, Jack? Don't worry. The meal's all taken care of, according to Caroline. Of course, if you don't want to accept her hospitality, you could always go "Dutch" – talk of the devil.'

I refused to look and turned to Rachel instead, but I could see it in her eyes. I watched them closely. It might have been a trick of the reflections from the sinking sun but they seemed to glow with a fire I hadn't seen before. Perhaps there was more than one score to be settled this evening.

I judged Caroline's progress to the table by the increasingly ironic smile on Rachel's face which grew in defiance of the coldness which slowly crept into her eyes, until the fire was extinguished and our hostess had arrived.

I heard the rustle of her dress before I was almost overwhelmed by her perfume – jasmine, musk and an abundance of rose so strong it seemed to encircle my throat and constrict my breathing. I remembered this one for the inherent irony. Joy, the most expensive in the world and, on Caroline, so inappropriately named.

"*Lust full of forged lies.*" Those lines would haunt me. I shut my eyes to focus better on her presence, trying to understand why I was quivering with anticipation. Trying desperately to work out what I felt for this woman who seemed to have such power over me. I hated her, wanted to humiliate her for what her mother had done, for what she had done, but when I reached for the sword of my anger, I couldn't pull it loose.

I sensed her confusion, her hesitation as she hovered behind me. I opened my eyes and looked into Rachel's. The coldness had evaporated and all I saw was sadness beyond my reach. She shut her eyes and I stood up, breathed deeply and turned slowly to face my nemesis.

39

She was dressed in white – an ice maiden pulsing with the energy and confidence of one who didn't need to look to see that every eye in the room had followed her from entrance to table. I fought to keep my face neutral and de-focused my eyes to avoid responding to hers as she searched my face for an explanation. I bowed politely. She leant forward over the back of my chair and brushed her lips gently against my right cheek. Her hair smelt of apples and cinnamon as it flicked against my face. The heat from her cheek burnt my ear as she turned away, moved around to Rachel and kissed the air beside each of her cheeks. She rustled round the table to Saul for a more intimate embrace.

Finally, she turned to Kohler, who was standing away from the table in no-man's-land. 'I know that Jack has met him, but allow me to introduce Rudi Kohler, Rachel.'

Kohler bowed but stopped short of clicking his heels.

'Saul Marcks.'

Kohler reached across, offered his hand but barely touched fingers.

Saul chuckled wryly. 'A pleasure, sir. I don't think I've met any *real* Dutchmen before.'

Caroline assumed command. 'Well, we're all here. It's a bit unbalanced with only two girls, but I'll sit between you two. Jack, you move around and sit next to Saul so Rudi can sit next to Rachel.'

I followed my instructions and just avoided bumping shoulders with Kohler, who seemed slightly unsteady as he moved past to take his seat.

'Ah, champagne. Good. Are you joining us, Jack, or are you back on the wagon?'

'I think he can handle it now he's had some experience, Caroline. I'm sure he won't spill any.' Rachel's tone was as clear as the crystal glass she waved in her rival's direction.

Kohler clapped his hands together. 'Good, let us enjoy a pleasant evening. We put bad times behind us, yes?' He reached across Caroline and offered me his hand.

Given the angle, it was impossible for me to respond without elbowing Caroline out of the way so I stood up and we shook behind her back. I was pleased to note that the "Dutchman's" nose was still slightly swollen and he seemed to have yellow bruising around his eye sockets. His cheeks were also rather red. Had he been drinking already?

I caught Brewster nodding his approval and drawing Phillips' attention to the gesture. I must have imagined it but the room seemed to draw a collective sigh of relief.

The Bollinger was poured and Saul offered a toast to "international relations" without the slightest irony in his voice.

Kohler responded with one for "European unity".

I raised my glass to "justice" at which point Caroline interrupted. 'That's enough of that – we'll be drunk before the meal starts. Well, what are we having?'

The others examined their menus in silence while the waiters hovered. I looked at Caroline surreptitiously as I pretended to study mine. Her cheeks were flushed and it wasn't from rouge. And she was worried about us getting drunk? I felt sure she had made a good start with Kohler before they arrived at the table. In his room probably and perhaps the flush wasn't just the alcohol.

I caught Rachel looking at me and thought she shook her head to tell me to stop torturing myself. I didn't feel like eating at all but settled on the remoulade of artichoke followed by consume chantilly. A selection of olives, nuts and celery would be served after the first course but I wondered if the meal would last that long.

Everyone ordered an entrée, with the men settling on a meat dish which stood little chance of living up to its lavish description.

Caroline ignored the menu and asked for a very small fresh Jersey plaice with no sauce.

Rachel expressed surprise at her lack of appetite and asked if she could have a large one in a butter sauce.

One nil to her.

Saul started a discourse on women's obsession with their figures until Caroline cut him short with an observation on his crassness and his waistline being in equal proportion to each other.

The others laughed and sipped their champagne more rapidly.

I brooded. Did Hayden-Brown know his daughter had invited us? What was Caroline's mother doing here? Did anyone else know about her and my father? Where were the diamonds?

The tension around the table was palpable. Saul looked as though he was calculating an attack, though I wasn't sure which of them was his target.

Caroline had invited Rachel for a purpose but I couldn't fathom it. Perhaps I should just wait until she made the first move. She had something planned – I was sure of that. With six more courses to come, there was no shortage of time.

During the break for queen olives and celery, I caught Saul experimenting with the discarded stones on the tip of his knife. Was he planning to launch them in the general direction of the head's table or fire them at Kohler?

Rachel quietly intervened and removed his plate before he could take his plan any further.

I leant over to Saul and whispered Shylock's famous aside: "*How like a fawning publican he looks!*'"

'Who? Not me I hope'

"*I hate him for he is a German.*'"

Saul laughed at the transposition of German for Christian. 'Don't misquote the Bard – Grumpy will excommunicate you.'

"*If I can catch him once upon the hip, I will feed fat the ancient grudge I bear him. Cursed be my tribe, if I forgive him!*'"

'What are you two talking about? It's rude to have private conversations. Come on, Jack, share your joke with us.' Caroline didn't understand the concept of whispering and her voice carried over the waiters who were now trying to serve the consommé.

'Nothing. I was just quoting some Shakespeare.'

'Ah, the English obsession with their great playwright. Tell me, Jack, why is he so popular when ninety percent of your population don't understand his language?' Kohler leant forward to speak to me over the arm of the waiter fussing over Caroline, his grey eyes slightly unfocused.

Saul bared his teeth ready to reply but I beat him to it.

'Many reasons, Rudi. I suppose the main one is he's English, he's ours. He writes about our history, has sympathy for the underdog but, most of all, he is inspiring. Not everyone may be able to read his language easily, but everyone understands his stories.'

'Most of which he stole from other writers.' Kohler smirked, his soup spoon halfway to his mouth.

'I don't suppose he translates very well into *German*, though.' Saul got his barb in just as the spoon reached Kohler's mouth.

To my satisfaction, the thrust was so unexpected that Kohler dropped the spoon into the plate, splattering his shirt. A waiter fussed over him with a napkin, which gave him time to recover.

'No, I don't suppose it does. German is a very precise language, rather like Dutch. His sloppy English is difficult to transpose. It might fit into French or Italian though.'

Saul said, 'We were actually discussing the *Merchant of Venice*. Do you know it, Rudi?'

He wiped his napkin over his mouth before replying. 'Is that the play where the Jew tries to cut a pound of flesh from the merchant?'

'That's right.'

'So, nothing changes. Only now the Hebrews want more than a pound of flesh, yes?' He laughed but no one responded.

'Actually, Shakespeare gives a more balanced view. I played Shylock in our college production. Saul, who doesn't look it with his red hair but is actually Jewish, played the Merchant, Antonio. It was a challenge for both of us.' I smiled at Saul. 'I think we both learned a lot.'

Kohler stiffened slightly but didn't change his expression. Of course Caroline might have already told him about Saul. His name was a bit of a give away so perhaps I had imagined the German's reaction.

Caroline pushed her soup away. 'It doesn't change the fact that Shylock tried to murder Antonio though, does it, Jack? I'm sorry but I didn't feel any sympathy for him. He got his just desserts in the end. Not because he was Jewish, but because he was a miserable bastard. He reminded me of someone else I know.' She glared in the general direction of her father. 'That greedy –'

Rachel interrupted. 'But it's not just about race, is it? I haven't had the privilege of a classical education like all of you but I saw the play and even I realised that the meanness of spirit which drives Shylock has nothing to do with his religion.'

We all stared in surprise at Rachel's intervention.

She continued. 'I can't quote from the play like you two but I did understand what that woman who was dressed as the lawyer, said –'

'You mean Portia,' Saul interrupted. *"The quality of mercy is not strained, it droppeth as the gentle rain from heaven upon the place beneath –"*'

'Oh stop showing off, Saul,' Rachel retorted.

She was right. The only one who spoke any sense. She would have made a far better Portia than the diva we'd borrowed from the girls' college.

'For Christ's sake, that's enough of the bloody Bard.' Caroline gulped down her glass of Chablis Grand Crux, which Saul had ordered with the first course. 'How the hell did we get started on him again?' She glared at me. 'Isn't there something more interesting to talk about?'

'How about Danzig?' volunteered Saul. 'I understand Mr Chamberlain's latest speech has gone down a bomb in Berlin. What do you think, Rudi?'

'I'm afraid your Prime Minister is talking through his top hat. Danziggers have every right to return to their fatherland. If he seriously expects the world community to believe that Danzig belongs to Poland then the world might start to believe that Gibraltar belongs to Spain.' Kohler clearly felt pleased with his overarching statement, which I thought sounded similar to something in a Goebbels speech which had been reported in the *Evening Post*.

I glimpsed a secret smile on Caroline's lips. So was this her plan?

To encourage us to provoke Kohler into defending Germany so openly he might confess his nationality in public? It couldn't be too obvious though – he might just walk away. We had to suck him in a bit more.

'You might be right there, Rudi. It is a complicated situation and we mustn't be hypocritical. Besides, international affairs are far too contentious. Why don't we talk about music?' I nudged Caroline gently with my elbow. 'What do you think? Is music international or tribal?'

'What are you talking about, Jack? Tribal music?' she asked.

'I meant, does each country have its own identity in music or is it universal? I know the Italians seem to have hijacked the language.'

'How observant of you. Are you suggesting that only Italians identify with Verdi and Puccini, that the French only love –'

'Themselves,' interrupted Saul. 'No, Jack's talking about identity in music. I think he means, can you tell the nationality of composer by the way his music sounds? Am I right, Jack?'

'Sort of. For example, Beethoven. He's Austrian. Are the emotions his music provokes really those peculiar to that nation? Are Tchaikovsky's just appropriate for the Russians? Are Chopin's for the Poles –'

Kohler interrupted. 'What about the English, Jack? Don't you have any composers of your own?'

Caroline turned on him. 'Yes, of course we do. And bloody emotional they are as well. Think of Elgar and "Land of Hope and Glory."'

Kohler pushed his chair back. 'I think I understand what Jack is talking about. The British are militaristic and so is their music. The Italians are romantic and theirs reflects that. The Germans, who I believe would lay claim to Beethoven, are strong and emotional –'

'What about the Poles, though, Rudi? Are they militaristic? Will they fight?' I spoke softly, daringly.

Kohler twisted his napkin in his hands as he looked around the room. 'I'm not a musician but perhaps I can answer that with an example. Chopin is a typical Pole, is he not?'

Caroline answered, 'Yes and a real patriot.'

Kohler pushed himself up and stood behind Caroline's chair. 'Well, let me play you a short piece by Chopin and you tell me.' He stepped out towards the bandstand, rolling slightly as if the dining room was on a cruise liner at sea.

'Can he play?' I asked Caroline.

'I have no idea. This should raise the temperature though – assuming he doesn't fall off the stool.'

'Was this your plan, to provoke him?'

'He's not as bad as you think, Jack.'

There wasn't an immediate answer to that so I changed the subject. 'Who organised this function? It's not a normal evening meal, is it?'

'My father invited a few people to celebrate his business deal. You know the people with him, Rudi's uncle, his associate, whose name I've forgotten.'

I almost interrupted with the correct name but bit my tongue just in time.

She didn't notice. 'The sleazy-looking one is from Belgium and I think you know Sir Edward.'

'Sir Edward?'

'Fairfield, the banker. I'm sure I told you.'

'Oh, yes and who's the woman with him?'

She hesitated and covered the pause by sipping her wine. 'Not sure, we haven't been introduced.'

And there it was – her first blatant lie. How many others had there been?

She carried on, oblivious to my expression. 'There are some lawyers behind you, some local bankers on the other side –'

'What about Brewster and the people from the club?'

'Oh, he's just thanking them for looking after me and being kind to Rudi... and, before you ask, I didn't know your Uncle Ralph and his hangers-on were coming.'

'So you invited us just to show off your new friend.'

She glared at me, her colour rising again. 'Grow up, Jack. Don't be so prejudiced.'

I clenched my fists under the table, not daring to ask the questions I really wanted answering as Kohler fiddled with the piano stool.

Without any warning to the other diners, he started to play. The music was slow, deliberate, precise, but lacking in emotion. It conjured up images of slow moving troops, smartly dressed but without menace – on parade.

I hissed at her, 'What's this called?'

'It's Chopin's Polonaise Number Three – "Military". He's playing reasonably well – too much pedal and the left hand is rather pedantic, but he's making his point in a ponderous way.'

'Which is?'

'Chopin and, by implication, Poland, is military. It's strong but not powerful. There's no emotion in the notes and it ends without any crescendo. He's actually a lot more subtle than I thought.'

I sensed a disagreeable measure of admiration in her tone and said, 'So he can play the piano but I'm not sure what the guests make of it.'

There was a scattering of applause as Kohler walked back to the table, though I could see that his uncle, Kempler, looked rather puzzled. Caroline's mother seemed delighted and clapped enthusiastically.

Saul stood and applauded him ironically as he took his place back at the table.

Rachel clapped politely. 'That's very good, Rudi. But what does it mean?'

'It shows the Polish temperament.' Kohler emptied his glass of Chablis and held it up for a refill.

A waiter scurried over and lifted the bottle from the ice bucket. He wrapped the napkin round the base but some of the iced water dripped onto Kohler's sleeve.

'*Arschloch*. Clumsy French oaf!'

40

In the empty silence that followed, I saw a wicked smile play over Saul's lips.

Rachel murmured something to him.

Caroline, clearly embarrassed, nudged Kohler with her elbow.

He glanced around, noted our expressions then smiled apologetically. 'Sorry. It was a surprise. Look, no damage done.'

The waiter bowed and withdrew.

I waited then fixed my eyes on Kohler. 'I think I understand, but that was quite a powerful piece. Not much emotion, granted, but strong, wouldn't you say?'

'Ah, you mustn't confuse strength with power, Jack. I do believe your Mr Chamberlain is about to make that mistake. The Polish Army is large, looks strong, very smart, lots of cavalry, good manoeuvres but it is a parade army. It lacks power. It is equipped –'

'Are you an expert on armies, Mr Kohler?' Saul interrupted. 'Is it as powerful as the Dutch Army, or the Belgian Army?'

Kohler laughed. 'I am no expert, Mr Marcks, but Poland is a long way from England. Chamberlain's armies would have to cross Germany to get there.'

Caroline tapped his arm. 'What about the French Army, Rudi? Would they fight?'

'Only if attacked. They are not an army of movement. They are equipped to fight the last war, not the next.'

'What's this got to do with music?' Rachel seemed determined to get an answer to her first question.

Kohler replied. 'It's about inspiration, as Jack said. A country needs passion to fight. The Poles, like Chopin, as you heard, march on the spot.'

I needed to probe for the button that would shatter his careful pretence and I had to needle Caroline into reacting to him. If what I'd read about Nazis was true then they had a very clear view of a woman's place in their grand scheme.

I kept the smile out of my voice. 'Tell me, Rudi, you've obviously worked hard to learn to play like that – even though you say you are not a musician. I doubt any other man in this room could get up and play a Chopin piece from memory.'

Kohler looked at me quizzically but nodded his agreement.

I ploughed on. 'You speak of passion and emotion. All the great composers, poets, writers, are men. Is it possible for a woman to convey that power, in speech, in writing, in music, do you think?'

Kohler laughed again. 'No offence to our beautiful companions, but of course not. No woman can display the passion of a man and be taken seriously. How can a mere woman harness the power of Beethoven? That is not where their strength lies.' He swallowed another mouthful. 'Some things are best left to men.'

I sensed a little volcano about to erupt as Caroline folded her napkin and pushed herself up from her chair.

Keeping a straight face, I stood up and pulled it out for her.

She leant forward and placed her face close to Kohler's. 'You shouldn't believe everything you read, Rudi. Chopin didn't just write polonaises you know. Just over a century ago, Russia invaded Poland and he wrote a little piece, which he wanted played *con fuoco*. Do you know what that means?'

Kohler glared at her. 'I'm sure you're going to tell me.'

'I'm not going to tell you – I'm bloody well going to show you.' She spun around and marched across the dance floor towards the piano.

The diners watched as Caroline raised the lid of the Steinway and settled herself on the stool. Their babble slowly ceased as they sensed the tension flowing from her. As she raised her hands to begin, the room was silent.

I had been overpowered by her playing of Beethoven's "Appassionata" but I had not been prepared for this. The piano roared

307

as she swept her left hand at incredible speed over the base notes, rolling, dramatic arpeggios thundering through the room. Her right cascaded impassioned rhythms, crashing against the base notes almost crying out in revolt. It was defiant, raging, patriotic. A bravura performance. The most intense emotion I had ever heard. Short, dynamic, it was utterly absorbing.

Her hands were a blur as she sped to the climax in a waterfall of crashing chords, which echoed throughout the stunned room. She rose from the stool and slammed the lid with such force that it sounded like a cannon shot.

There was silence, and then everyone was on their feet thundering their applause. Even the waiters, and Miko, who had emerged from the reception area, applauded as she strode back to her seat.

I watched her mother closely. She wasn't applauding and looked angrily at her husband, who seemed to be sitting on his hands. Another puzzle – did *neither* of them care for their daughter?

Caroline stood in front of me and looked straight into my eyes. Hers were on fire. Sweat beaded on her forehead.

'Sometimes, the notes need some help to speak for themselves.' She smiled at me as I eased her into her seat.

I had never been more moved by her, nor more frightened of her, than at that moment. She was indeed the *"tempest after sun"*.

She looked at Kohler. 'Chopin's Twelfth Etude – sometimes called the "Revolutionary". I'm sure you've heard of it, Rudi. It's a pity you didn't play that as an example of Polish emotion.'

I watched Kohler smile back at her in admiration and, to my horror, I realised that the German's feelings for her were every bit as strong as my own.

Kohler took her hands in his; she didn't resist. He turned them over, palm up, and inspected her fingertips. 'Such strength, such technique. Who taught you how to play like that?'

'Schnabel.'

'Of course. Such a shame.'

Saul snapped. 'A shame, oh yes, definitely a shame. The greatest pianist of his age is, unfortunately, Jewish. Such a shame, though I don't hear Adolph using that word. Eliminate them from the German economy, yes. Take all their possessions, yes. Annihilate them, yes. Remove them from history –'

'I can understand your viewpoint, Marcks.' Kohler sounded calm. 'But you have to be realistic. Germany feels betrayed by the Jews after what happened in November 1918. You must remember the Fuhrer was in the front line in an unbeaten army when the Jewish socialists destroyed them from behind. He also feels threatened by world Jewry – believes they want a war so that Europe can be Bolshevised –'

I interrupted. 'Bollocks – that's just a mealy-mouthed excuse. It's Hitler who wants to dominate Europe and probably the world as well. It's only the Bolsheviks who can stop him.'

'Jack, Jack, we mustn't fall out over these matters. I'm not an apologist for Hitler. I'm merely trying to explain the situation from, what I believe, is the German perspective. It's not mine.'

I gasped in disbelief. I was fed up with the pretence. 'Rudi, we know you are a German. It's no good pretending you're a Dutchman anymore.'

'Jack, I'm no more a German than you are a Guernseyman.'

'For God's sake, Rudi, I have a photograph of you in the German swimming team, wearing the badges. The only thing missing is the Nazi salute.'

Kohler roared with laughter and poured himself another glass. 'Jack, I swam for the Royal Navy last week. That doesn't make me an Englishman. Let's say I was an unpaid mercenary. The Germans wanted to win and we Dutch didn't have a team.'

'Caroline, for God's sake, tell him we know.'

She held Kohler's gaze but remained silent.

'But what about the diamonds? You're an economist, Rudi. Tell us about the Bank of International Settlements, tell us how you Nazis are using the money you have stolen from your Jews to rearm for war.' My voice rose as the anger gripped me.

Kohler spread his hands in an appeasing gesture. 'Shush, Jack. Don't make such accusations without evidence. There are many important people in this room. Don't offend them with this boorish behaviour, please. Calm down, have another drink.'

'Caroline, what's going on? Where's your plan? Why are you letting him get away with this?'

Rachel spoke softly. 'There is no plan, Jack, she's fooled you again. She's brought Rudi here to show us how human and pleasant he is. Can't you see what is really going on?'

Saul eased his chair back. 'I think that's enough, Rachel. There's nothing we can do. I'll take you home if you like. I'm not comfortable with the smell in here.'

'How predictable, Mr Marcks. Insults really are unnecessary. You needn't leave before the meal is over. Thank you for trying, Caroline, but I did warn you. Young Jack is too aggressive for his own good and Saul... well the less said.'

He turned to Rachel and patted her arm. 'If you will accept advice, I believe it would be in your best interests to find some new friends before these bring you down with them.'

Rachel lifted his hand and dropped it onto the table then she bent over and retrieved her small evening bag. 'Before I leave with Saul, there's something I want to show Jack.' She fumbled in her bag. 'Joan found some more photographs from Berlin and gave me one this morning. I didn't want to come to this... charade but I guessed what Caroline was up to and... Joan left it up to me whether I should show it to you or not. I wasn't going to but, in the circumstances, I don't think I have any choice, now.' She pulled out a photograph, which had been folded in two, and slipped it past Saul to me.

I looked down at the glossy print, which showed a young girl wearing a summer dress smiling broadly and looking to her left beyond the fold of the photograph. She was thinner and younger, but there was no doubt it was Caroline.

'Before you unfold it, Jack, think for a moment. It won't be something you can undo.'

I stared at the picture. The diving boards of the Schwimm Stadion were in the background, the swastikas were fluttering on their masts. Caroline's hand disappeared off the folded edge.

I turned to Caroline, who avoided my eyes and stared into space.

I examined Rachel's face. She looked sad and her expression was full of apology. I placed my left hand on the corner of the photo and

310

began to pull the fold apart until the whole photograph lay in front of me. I traced Caroline's hand and followed her eyes all the way to the face of a younger Kohler, standing proudly in the uniform of a German officer.

I turned the photo so that Caroline and Kohler could see. I felt drained, as empty as I had felt playing Shylock when I mouthed the words *"is that the law?"* as I fell into the Venetian's trap and forfeited everything. The courtiers had laughed at my misery then – my friends were silent now.

Kohler spoke a few quiet words in German to Caroline before stretching across to take the photograph.

Saul moved faster and stabbed the print with his steak knife, spearing it to the table inches from Kohler's fingers.

The German pulled back in surprise and anger.

Rachel turned to him, her eyes burning. 'I don't suppose that's the same photograph that's in your passport, now is it? I wonder if the immigration authorities would like to take a look?'

Kohler snarled, 'Oh no you don't, you little bitch.'

'Add "Jewish" to "bitch" if you wish, you lying German bastard. I have a toast for you.' Rachel stood up, raised her wine glass and tossed the contents into Kohler's face.

41

He sprung up and swung his arm at her. She ducked her head but his hand caught her shoulder and spun her onto the floor.

I shoved my chair back, rushed past Caroline and thundered into the German. We struggled for a grip on each other. Our bodies bounced off the wall then careered into the table behind us, scattering the guests, their food and their drinks.

The fall split us apart but Kohler recovered first. He waited for me to get to my knees then kicked me in the chest. I hit the floor and rolled away into the space between the tables. Kohler threw himself onto me and pinned me to the floor. He punched me in the face with his right hand, then hit my head with his left.

Rachel screamed, 'Stop!'

He ignored her and kept punching me.

She picked up the champagne bottle and swung it at Kohler's head. He saw it coming and swayed backwards but his head was still within the arc and the heavy bottle connected with his ear. It knocked him off me and onto the carpet. He shook his head and pulled himself up.

Looking around at the startled guests, he lunged for a steak knife which had fallen from the table behind him. He grabbed it and crouched – the blade pointed at me. He looked beyond reason, completely out of control.

He advanced, the tip of the knife aimed at my face.

Suddenly, massive arms crushed his chest in a bear hug and forced the knife from his grasp. My father held him like a bundle of hay he was about to pitch onto the stack.

I pulled myself up, using a chair for balance. My nose was bleeding and I grabbed a napkin to staunch the flow. Clutching the linen to my face, I slumped onto the chair.

Caroline sank to the floor.

What was my father doing here?

I looked towards the Hayden-Browns. Isobelle was holding her hand over her mouth.

Behind them, I could see my mother and the Cabots standing in the entrance. My mother was staring at Isobelle, her eyes flaming with hatred.

'I saw everything. I'm arresting you for an unprovoked assault, Renouf.' Centenier Phillips stood over me, crimson with indignation. 'You are a menace to civilised society. I'll make it my business to see you get birched or worse for this, you little hooligan.'

'Thank you, Centenier.' Jurat Poingdestre tapped the honorary policeman on the shoulder. 'You are out of your jurisdiction. The Palace Hotel is in St Saviour. You have no authority here. I suggest you resume your seat. I'll deal with this. Let him go, Aubin. I feel sure he won't be a problem now.'

My father dropped the German like a sack of spuds and straightened his jacket. 'Remember, Ralph, he pulled a knife and threatened my son. There are enough witnesses here to prove that, despite what this idiot thinks.' He pointed at the centenier, who was backing off to his table.

Mr Grumbridge's voice carried across the room. 'Yes, I agree. I saw the whole thing. This man definitely used a knife. He is the one who should be arrested. I suggest we ask the manager to call the police.'

'There's no need for that.' Hayden-Brown had crossed the room with one of his guests and was now crouching down over Caroline. 'My daughter needs some air and this young man needs some first aid. It is very regrettable but I believe this is probably her fault for leading these two men on. It's nothing new is it – two men fighting over a girl?'

His polished tones conveyed authority as he sought to control the situation. He acknowledged my father. 'Young Renouf's parents are here to look after him and Mr Kohler's uncle,' he indicated the distinguished-looking man behind him, 'will deal with his errant nephew. I will take my wilful daughter home and have some serious words with her in the morning.'

He looked around him for any dissent. No one seemed keen to send for the police and they started to melt back to their tables.

'Just one moment everyone.' Saul's voice rang out. 'It's not quite as simple as Mr Hayden-Brown would have you all believe.'

They stopped moving and turned to look at him. 'This wasn't a fight over a girl, though they both have strong feelings for her. This was about lies and deceit. Mr Hayden-Brown has been less than honest with you. Mr Kohler is no more Dutch than I am. He is in fact, and in picture,' he waved the photograph in front of him, 'a German officer.'

Silence. Then a shockwave of questions pulsed through the room as the guests absorbed the news.

Saul raised his voice above the hubbub. 'And, what is more, his uncle is Dr Ferdinand Kempler of the Reichsbank. Both of them are travelling under false passports, here on the invitation of Mr Hayden-Brown to set up a deal to sell industrial diamonds illegally to Nazi Germany.'

Saul had overdone it. The false passports would have been enough – even though we had no physical proof – but the accusations about diamonds sounded too fantastic to be true. The crowd started muttering. A couple laughed and that was enough to allow Hayden-Brown to recover from his surprise.

He clapped ironically. 'Thank you for the entertainment, but I fear your imagination has got the better of you. My friends are here on holiday – nothing else. Your headmaster is to be congratulated on the acting skills he has taught you.'

He bowed in the direction of Grumbridge. 'Perhaps he should have taught you how to hold your drink as well.' He laughed and many more joined him as he helped Caroline to her feet.

'Thank you for your patience, everyone. Please allow me to buy you all some more wine – apart from our Jewish friend here, who shouldn't be exerting himself so much on the Sabbath.'

The laughter tailed off into an embarrassed silence and Saul sat down glumly.

Rachel put her arm around him and kissed his cheek. 'Take me home, please.' She glanced at me as I held my blood spattered face in shame. 'Do you want to come with us, Jack?'

My father answered before I could. 'No. He'll be coming home with us. We need to have a talk.'

Hayden-Brown tried to lift his daughter but she shrugged him off. Her expensive white dress was smeared with my blood, which mirrored the colour of her cheeks.

She pulled herself up, dragged a chair over to me and sat down. 'It's not what you think, Jack. Please believe me.'

I nodded indifferently, completely drained, resigned like Shylock to his fate. '"*Pray you, give me leave to go from hence; I am not well: send the deed after me, And I will –*"'

Caroline cut me off. 'For fuck's sake, Jack, cut the Shakespeare. You're not Shylock and this is not a fucking play.'

She jumped up and screamed for attention. 'Listen everyone. Please listen. Father, please let me tell them the truth. I'm not ashamed –'

Isobelle shouted across the room. 'Enough, Caroline. This must stop now.'

My mother moved forward, her back towards Isobelle. 'No, Caroline. Don't stop. You tell us what is really going on here. I suspect you might be more truthful than your mother.'

Saul and Rachel looked accusingly at me. I shrugged in apology. I should have told them, but how?

Caroline looked nervously towards her father, who seemed frozen, nonplussed by my mother's intervention.

My mother had waited a long time for this and wasn't going to be denied her revenge. She stopped short and addressed Kohler. 'It would seem that you are a liar as well as a bully – characteristics of your national breeding, no doubt.'

She turned to Caroline. 'Well, young lady, what do you have to say for yourself? Your mother tried to steal my husband once. Are you punishing my son because she failed?' She addressed the final question to the whole room.

Even my mouth sagged in the silence that followed.

Caroline looked helplessly at me then at my fuming mother.

315

Hayden-Brown whispered hurriedly to Kempler, who nodded then barked in rapid German at Kohler.

He then bowed to my mother and spoke in English with barely a trace of an accent. 'Our apologies, Frau Renouf. We will leave now.'

He gestured to Kohler, who pulled himself up, straightened his clothes and followed his uncle to their table. Sleeman looked confused as Schmitz stood and prepared to leave. Fairfield hadn't moved but, as Isobelle pushed her chair back, he reached out, grabbed her wrist and shook his head. She sat down again, desperately trying to regain some of the dignity which had been punched out of her by my mother's accusation. Hayden-Brown smiled grimly then fell in step behind Kohler.

Saul started to clap slowly but Rachel pulled his hands apart. All the guests and staff watched in silence as the host squared his shoulders and, nodding politely to everyone, made his way back across the dance floor.

Saul wouldn't be denied though. 'How about Beethoven's "Funeral March", Caroline? That should win the competition.'

No one laughed so, his callowness ignored, he sat down again and reached for the Chablis.

I sensed that conversation was about to restart when the two men from the Jaguar entered and walked over to Fairfield. They were wearing dark blue suits and trilby hats. They spoke quietly to him and one pulled a badge from his pocket. Kempler listened to their conversation then his shoulders slumped and he beckoned Kohler to join him. Hayden-Brown sat down heavily on a chair.

Kohler walked back to us. He stopped in front of me. I looked up at him almost indifferently.

'This isn't over, Renouf. You'll pay for this. Not today, or tomorrow. It might not be for some time, but you will pay.'

He turned to Caroline, who kept looking at the floor. He shrugged, clicked his heels and marched towards the veranda.

Caroline lifted her eyes and watched his back as he joined his uncle and the two men, who then escorted them into the reception area. Her mother, father and his other guests followed.

My father moved towards me and reached for Mum's hand. 'We'll wait for you outside.'

The other guests stayed in their seats, bewildered by the turn of events, though I spotted one of the lawyers making notes on a menu.

Caroline pleaded with me. 'Don't go yet. Come with me. We can talk. I can explain. Please, I don't want to go home. I can't. Please, Jack.'

I twisted away, looked around for Rachel. She was standing with Saul in the shadows by the veranda. He had his arm around her shoulders. I guessed they had a lot to discuss.

I felt so tired. I didn't want to talk anymore. I knew I would have to listen but I could do that without hearing.

I got up and walked towards the door. I didn't look back. My father was waiting and, for the first time I could remember, he put his arm around me.

42

We emerged, through the four-columned portico, into the shaded courtyard. Dusk was settling but the area was well-lit from the foyer and adjacent windows. Twin floodlights on the flanking walls illuminated the Jaguar and a Wolseley parked either side of the entrance, their long black noses almost as officious as the two uniformed drivers who stood by their doors.

We waited for Mum and the Cabots to catch up and I heard Saul at reception demanding a taxi for Rachel and himself. There was no sign of Caroline or Kohler.

'Where's your bike, Jack?' My father's query was brusque. Clearly I'd had my ration of sympathy for the evening.

'In the car park, by the trees. It'll be alright for the night, I'm sure. Unless you want me to check?'

Rector Cabot edged past us and led the way to our car. He opened the rear doors for his wife and my mother. Father walked round the bonnet and waited for me to get in the passenger seat.

I looked over to where I'd left *Bessy* and gasped. Not only was *Boadicea* there but the Talbot 105, which my two assailants had driven, was parked alongside. I also spotted Caroline's Bugatti parked closer to the road. I pushed the door open again and got out.

'Where do you think you are going?'

'Sorry, but there's something I need to check.'

'Oh no you don't. Get back in the car this minute!'

I had walked only a few paces when I felt his heavy hand on my shoulder. I shrugged him off.

He grabbed me again. 'Now do as you are told, please. For your mother's sake, if not for mine.'

Just then he noticed *Boadicea*. 'What's he doing here? We agreed he would keep out of it. He can't be bloody trusted. I should have guessed. Nothing but bloody trouble. This is all his bloody fault, isn't it?'

I didn't answer but bent down to touch the bike's cylinders. Still warm. I moved to the Talbot. The bonnet was cool to my touch. So they had been here for some time. I looked around.

Bessy was still there but there was no sign of Fred or the Talbot's occupants. I turned to face my father. There wasn't time to explain about Carl and Alf.

'Please trust me – I have to find Uncle Fred. It's important.'

I thought he'd shout at me but instead he grabbed my shoulders again, pulled me towards him then twisted my body, as easily as if I were one of his scarecrows, until the thin sunlight was on my face. His was in shade so I couldn't see his expression. He stared into my eyes. I squared my shoulders and stared back until he released me.

'We've seen Fred. He's told us everything. That's why we're here. There's no need now. It's all over.'

So that's why they'd arrived. I wondered how much Fred had actually told them. I needed to find him. 'Just let me talk to him. Please.'

He swallowed – anger, pride? I wasn't sure. He nodded unwillingly. 'Go on then, but I'm coming with you.'

He called out to the car, 'We won't be a minute.'

I started walking to the courtyard with my father a few steps behind. I stopped by the corner of the field under an oak tree. I felt his breath heavy on my neck.

There was movement in the entrance and Fairfield, Kempler and Kohler emerged, escorted by the taller of the two, men who, I now assumed, were plainclothes policemen. He took them to the Wolseley on the east side of the pillars. The other prodded the diamond merchant, Sleeman, in the back with one hand. With the other he held Schmitz's elbow and hurried the limping German to the Jaguar.

Hayden-Brown burst out between the columns, shouting, 'You

don't have the authority to do this. You are completely out of order. These people are my guests. How dare you cart them off like criminals!'

Fairfield stopped and spoke calmly to Hayden-Brown, 'Wilbur, it's fine. These gentlemen know what they are doing. Don't fret, there's a good chap.'

The taller plainclothes policeman echoed his tone. 'That's right, sir. It's for their own *protection*, if you understand my meaning. We're just going to the town hall to examine some information we have received. Nothing to worry about.'

'That's not acceptable. I demand to know who provided this information. Speak up, man.' Hayden-Brown sounded as puzzled as I felt.

'I did,' a voice whispered behind me.

I whirled round to find Fred standing there. Father pushed him away and raised his fist.

I stepped between them. 'Shush. Wait a moment.' I hoped my voice hadn't carried. 'What do you mean?'

'I received a message from Hélène. The ship has disappeared. I used my phone and told the story about the Germans to my contact in England. He was furious. Kept reminding me I was on an open line. Well that was the point. I knew Special Branch would be informed. Much quicker than trying to explain to the locals. Seems they must have believed me. Then your parents arrived and I told them what they *needed* to know.'

I hoped that meant he hadn't told them or his contact about the diamonds and the shooting.

He pulled me aside gently and squared up to my father. 'I'm sorry, Aubin, but this is very important. I'll tell you everything later but for the moment please trust me.'

My father glared back. I pushed between them. Fred was still facing down my father, their two figures indistinct in the shadows.

'Stop it,' I hissed at them. 'Whatever your quarrel, put it aside until this is over, please.'

Their breathing slowed and I focused my ears on the argument in the courtyard again.

'Aubin, I think it might be best if you took Jack home now. I think this is going to get dangerous in a minute.' Then he was gone, melting back into the shadows.

My father's hand was on my shoulder again and I realised that, now Fred had abandoned me, I would have to relent.

As I started to relax against his grip, Caroline's strident voice rang from the entrance.

'You bastards, let him go. He's got nothing to do with this. Father, do something right for once in your miserable life and tell them the fucking truth!'

Hayden-Brown, far from being stunned by his daughter's outburst, turned and slapped her across the face, a blow reinforced with what I suspected were years of frustration with her spoilt behaviour.

The slap echoed across the space and I winced.

The policemen seemed perplexed. One of the uniformed officers took Fairfield's arm and escorted him to the Wolseley. Sleeman followed him, along with Schmitz. Kempler and Kohler were ushered towards the Jaguar.

During this performance, I moved forward, closer to the outbuildings on the edge of the courtyard. My father followed.

I stopped as Rachel and Saul emerged from the foyer and stood still, surveying the confusion in front of them.

The policemen were starting to pack the two groups into their respective cars when Alf and his enforcer walked around the side of the building and confronted the two plainclothes men.

'Thank you, we will take over from here, if you please.' Alf sounded very confident.

The policeman peered at him, clearly startled. 'Who are you?'

'I can't tell you that but, shall we say, I represent an authority higher than yours.'

'Nonsense. Show me some identification.' His tone was more suspicious and I noted that little Carl had moved closer.

Alf laughed. 'Fair enough. If you want to play that game. You show me yours and I'll show you mine.'

The policeman reached into his jacket pocket and pulled out a black wallet. He flipped it open and held it close to Alf's face.

Alf studied the details and made a show of checking the

photograph. 'Ah, Detective Sergeant Archibold Greaves, Metropolitan Police, Special Branch, 349625.' He turned to the other plainclothes man and held out his hand.

The man extracted his ID and held it up for inspection.

'Detective Constable Clitheroe, same branch.' Alf handed it back, reached into his pocket and drew out a snub-nosed automatic. 'Here's mine.' He pointed it at the sergeant and jerked his chin up, indicating that they should raise their hands.

Carl darted in and extracted two automatics from what must have been shoulder holsters. He pocketed them before patting both men down.

He nodded to Alf then spun on his heel and chopped the sergeant in the neck with the side of his hand. It was a vicious blow, delivered with all his force, and the policeman dropped to the ground.

Carl kicked him in the ribs then stood back and surveyed his handiwork.

Everyone had frozen when Alf pulled the gun. Now he pointed the weapon at the chubby Belgian and the English knight. 'You two, Sleeman and Fairfield – over here, or I'll set my dog on you.'

Carl growled.

At that moment, Phillips emerged from the hotel and barged his way in. 'I don't know who you people are and I don't care. None of you are local. I demand that we all go to the parish hall and get the duty centenier to deal with this.'

He stopped, aware of Alf's gun. 'Put that away. Don't you realise it is a criminal offence to point a gun in a public place?'

He sounded so offended, I thought he was going to pop.

Instead it was the gun that popped as Alf shot a bullet into the front tyre of the Jaguar. The explosion was so loud in the enclosed courtyard space that the reverberation took several seconds to dissipate.

Everyone stayed frozen except Isobelle, who strode from the portico and advanced on Alf. She held out her hand imperiously. 'Give me that gun, you silly man, and let Sir Edward go.'

Alf regarded her with surprise and disbelief.

For one moment, I thought he was going to comply then he laughed thinly and backhanded her across her face.

She staggered, blood spurting from her mouth, but didn't fall. She shook herself and, stretching out her hand, approached him again.

'Stay back, you silly bitch, or I'll shoot you and anyone else who gets in our way.'

She ignored him and moved closer.

He was raising the pistol to point at her when Fred shouted, 'No!' and rushed at him, revolver in hand.

Alf spun towards the new threat but Carl was even quicker. His black cosh swished down onto Fred's wrist. The gun clattered to the ground as the cosh swung across and slashed into his neck.

My uncle collapsed onto the tarmac with a sickening thud.

I reacted without thought and charged from the shadows, taking the little bastard in a low rugby tackle that carried him onto the bonnet of the Jaguar. Carl was dazed so I grabbed his head and banged it against the door pillar.

I heard my father shout just as a gun fired. I waited to feel the pain, the rush of blood, but there was nothing, only the hiss of another deflating tyre after the gunshot echoed into silence.

'That's enough. Now do as you are told before I shoot someone.' Alf shoved Isobelle out of his way, lifted Carl up and gestured him towards the Wolseley, indicating he should reverse it and turn to face the exit.

Disoriented, he felt the side of his head with his hand and pulled it away to show a dark sticky patch. He held it out to me as he advanced, the cosh once more in his fist.

'Oh, if you must. But hurry up. The boat won't wait for ever. And pick up that bloody gun.' Alf pointed his pistol at the others and urged Fairfield towards the car again.

Carl scooped up Fred's revolver and handed it to Alf, who slotted it into his pocket.

The two uniformed policemen were rooted to the spot. I looked at them as Carl advanced but they were in thrall to the gun.

I watched his right hand. His face was smeared with his own blood but he was grinning. I was sure my father would rush in so I screamed at him. 'Stay where you are. This is my fight.'

Carl laughed, a thin, almost girlish giggle, as he closed in.

43

Miko rushed between us with a carving knife in his hand pointed at Carl's throat. We all froze but there would be no referee's whistle this time.

Alf was the first to move. He grabbed his companion and threw him towards the car. 'Get in and drive. Take those fucking Germans with you.' He pointed to Kempler and Schmitz.

He grabbed Fairfield and pointed the gun at Sleeman. 'You two, come with me. Carl, you know the way. The breakwater. Now go.'

Carl bundled Schmitz into the back of the Wolseley and slammed the door. He shoved Kempler into the driver's seat and slid in alongside then pulled a flick knife from his pocket sprung it open and pressed the point into Kempler's neck and ordered him to drive.

I had to jump out of the way as Kempler reversed at speed, braked sharply, struggled with the gears before finding first then drove off.

I was wondering where my father was as our Standard Ten came barrelling around the corner and attempted to ram the Wolseley. Its nearside bumper made contact but he managed to accelerate and swerve away from the glancing blow. The Wolseley bounced off the wall, demolished a length of fencing then sped up the track.

Braking hard, our car lost traction and skidded into the side of the building. Father stumbled out and moved towards Alf.

By now the hotel management should have alerted the police to the gunshots but, as two of their cars were already here, I supposed it would take some time to get others mobilised.

Alf was backing away, the gun still pointed at us. Isobelle knelt down to attend to Fred as Alf, pulling Fairfield and Sleeman with him, retreated towards his Talbot in the car park.

Kohler started to follow then stopped and pointed at Rachel. 'You, come here!'

'No, don't move, Rachel.' Saul sounded desperate.

'Relax, little boy. We're not going to hurt her. Just some additional insurance.' He whispered to Alf, who listened then nodded.

'Do as he says. Now. Or I shoot your friend.' Alf pointed the gun at me.

I ignored him. 'Don't, Rachel, please.'

She looked at the gun then at me, gave a helpless shrug and walked calmly towards Kohler. She was almost within reach when Miko stepped in front of Alf, his knife glinting in the spotlight.

'You, German, Nazi. Let her go or I kill you now.'

'You are very polite, my friend, but we are not Germans.' Alf pointed at me. 'You ask him and his uncle. I think they understand.'

'They might not but I do.' Saul's voice carried across the courtyard. '*Voetsek*, you're Afrikaners. It *is* about the bloody diamonds. That's why you want the Belgian. You're working for De Beers and Oppenheimer, aren't you?'

Alf threw a stream of what I now recognised as Afrikaans at Saul.

He growled at me, 'That little shit talks through his bum hole. These two are thieves.' He spat in the gravel. 'They have some questions to answer, that's all. We will let the others go.'

'But why? What have they done?' Fred struggled to his feet and leant on Isobelle. He stood behind Miko, clutching his right wrist to his chest.

Alf laughed. 'Tell me, my commie friend, what does Stalin do with thieves? I'll tell you if you have the stomach for –'

'I know where the diamonds are!' I shouted.

That startled him.

'Make him let her go and I'll tell you.'

He recovered quickly and grinned. 'You are a strange young man. Much promise. A shame you waste it on these fantasies. There are no diamonds.'

'They're on Hayden-Brown's gin palace – his boat, *Lorelei*. It's taking them to a Portuguese freighter, the SS *Espírito Livre*.'

Now he looked annoyed.

I struck again. 'While you were chasing us around the rocks, your bloody diamonds were cruising behind you on their way to his ship. Didn't you search his boat, or his house?'

'This is nonsense.'

'You didn't find anything in my uncle's house either, did you, though you broke enough. Don't you *kaffirs* like opera music?'

He snarled and aimed the gun at my head. 'Don't use words you don't understand. I should kill you for that insult.'

I stared him down, praying that Rachel would break away but instead she stepped between us.

'Go on, shoot. I'm just a Jewish bitch – pull the trigger if you can.'

Her words echoed around the courtyard, stunning us all into silence.

Suddenly he moved and grabbed Hayden-Brown. 'You, as Stalin would say, are a "useful idiot", so come with me.' He gestured to Kohler. 'He can make his own way.'

He fired the pistol again – this time into the front nearside tyre of our Standard.

When the echoes had subsided, he had almost reached his car, shoving Fairfield, Sleeman and Caroline's father in front of him.

Before any of us could react, Kohler kicked Miko in the crotch, snatched the knife, grabbed Rachel and dragged her towards the car park.

Caroline called out, 'No, Rudi, don't. Let her go. We'll sort this out. Don't do this.'

'Sorry, Caroline, it's too late. I can't wait for the wheels of British justice to turn. I have to get away. She's my ticket.'

Saul had crept into the field alongside the car park while Caroline was pleading with Kohler and emerged now behind the Bugatti.

Kohler had his back to him and hadn't realised that he was crouching, waiting. I willed him to get out of the way. He would be no match for the German.

We followed, keeping a safe distance as he backed towards the sleek red vehicle. The policemen seemed bemused. Clitheroe was helping Greaves to his feet. They'd lost their weapons and the Bluebottles weren't armed. They followed carefully, no doubt hoping for an opportunity to catch Alf off guard.

My only concern was Rachel.

Kohler was almost there now, he would have to let Rachel go to open the door unless he made her climb over it. As soon as she turned, she would spot Saul.

I would have to wait until Kohler was close enough to Saul to give him the slightest chance before I called out something to distract him, but short of "Heil Hitler", I couldn't think of anything.

Just then, Alf's Talbot, with Hayden-Brown driving, roared off, side-swiping my bike as it spun in the gravel. It sped away and just missed a taxi that was turning into the lane. The driver blared his horn.

Kohler turned towards the noise and Saul's movement caught his eye. He twisted, deflecting the charge, and chopped Saul to the gravel with the side of his free hand.

Caroline rushed past me. 'Please, Rudi, don't hurt her.'

Kohler's eyes flamed. He screamed at her, '*Bumsen weg!*'

She stopped and he ordered her into the driver's seat, threatening to draw the knife across Rachel's throat if she didn't.

Defeated, she climbed in and started the engine. He clambered over the low door of the convertible and sat on Rachel's lap, pinning her to the seat.

Caroline let out the clutch and sped off, rear tyres spinning, struggling for grip on the dusty surface.

Fred was at my shoulder. 'Leave them. Alf will dump the Germans. He only wants Sleeman and the diamonds.'

'What about witnesses, Uncle. Does he want those as well? And what about Kohler? He's out of control. He has Rachel and Caroline. I can't leave them. My bike's wrecked. Let's follow on yours.'

'I can't ride it and I won't be able to hold on.' He dangled his damaged wrist in front of me.

'Where's the key, Uncle?'

'It's too dangerous, Jack.'

'It's too dangerous not to.'

My father strode forward, held out his hand. 'Give him the key, Fred. He has to do this. He won't be able to live with himself otherwise. You know what I mean...'

Fred stared at his brother-in-law then grimaced in submission. 'Here, you'll need these as well. Don't do anything stupid.' He used his left hand to fish his goggles and the key out of his pocket. He handed them to me. '*Mêfi'-ous.*'

I grabbed the key and rushed towards *Boadicea*. Alf had mentioned the breakwater. That could only be St Catherine's. They must have brought their cruiser around. I went through the starting routine, pleased to feel her strength under me again. The engine was ticking over when I felt her sink on her springs.

Miko had jumped on. '*Spumá!*' he shouted in my ear.

44

The three cars in front were all powerful, especially the Bugatti, but *Boadicea* had sufficient acceleration to overtake all of them. However, I didn't want to give them the opportunity to ram us so, as soon as I caught up with Caroline, I held back, trying to work out my options.

Overtaking alongside would be suicidal but, if I used the side roads, I could pass them with impunity – that's if they were actually going to St Catherine's. I couldn't think of any alternatives at this stage, though the tide would soon be high enough for Gorey harbour. Alf had shouted about the breakwater though and that's where they seemed to be heading.

Caroline obviously thought the same and the Bugatti was tearing along the road to Five Oaks. She carried on the main road to St Martin's Church, which was, theoretically, the shorter.

I turned right on to Prince's Tower Road, towards La Hougie Bie, and twisted the throttle to the stop. I couldn't see the speedometer as it was vibrating so much but we must have exceeded eighty miles per hour. Without the goggles I couldn't have managed. It was reckless but not as much as trying to overtake.

Miko clung on tightly with his hands braced against the pillion rack, moving with me as I leant *Boadicea* into the corners. We shot past the mental hospital – based on current behaviour, I would have qualified for entry – then past Faldouet.

I hesitated at the junction with the main road from Gorey but reasoned that I could meet them head-on if I rode towards St Martin's Church.

Alternatively, I could turn off before the church and go to the farm to get my rifle, though by the time I retrieved it, I would be too late to rescue Rachel. I could shoot a few people but I couldn't protect her from that distance. I had to try and grab her from them and that meant the slipway. This was my parish and I knew most of the byways intimately. I shot across the main road and into the network of lanes, which led, ever more steeply, down to the coast road.

Boadicea's brakes were squealing and beginning to fade as we plunged 200 feet down through the quarry to Archirondel, where the British had started but abandoned the second arm of their great harbour.

The breakwater was in sight now, its extremities glowed in the remnants of the sunset. This was the most dangerous bit as any or all of the three cars could now appear from my left as they descended the steep hill from St Martin's Church.

As I slowed for the junction, I realised there were no headlights. Either we were well ahead or some way behind. I accelerated along the road, which twisted past the Martello Tower and small slipway, through the cutting next to Gibraltar and into the final stretch. Too fast for the bends and suddenly the handlebars started to shake. Miko's extra weight had made the front end too light. The tyre shimmied, wobbled and *Boadicea* snaked across the road. Fred had explained the theory but, now she was biting back, it was brawn rather than brain I needed. I leant forward, tried to shift more weight over the front forks but I was too late. The rear tyre lost grip and we were out of control. I didn't even have time to scream to Miko before we started to slide. *Boadicea* was going to kill again.

We clung on as she shot towards the verge. Her stand hit the grass first as she reared up and catapulted us into the gorse. Not a soft landing but much better than ripping our flesh along the road or colliding with a tree.

I was on a bed of thorns, contemplating the punishment for my speeding, when I felt a tug on my ankle.

'You okay, Jerk?'

'Just dandy.'

'I say *spumá* not *omoara*.'

He hauled me out and we dusted ourselves down. It would take an army of tailors to repair our suits. *Boadicea* was almost buried in the roots of a gorse bush. I braved the thorns to reach in and turn off her ignition. It wasn't her fault I'd pushed too hard. We didn't have time or even the strength to pull her out. I'd need a tractor for that.

We were still a couple of hundred yards short of Verclut and the breakwater and there was still no sign of the cars. In the distance, I heard engines pulsing towards us, their exhaust notes rising and falling as their drivers worked the gears round the bends and through the cutting at Gibraltar.

I dragged Miko onto the grass and prayed they wouldn't spot us. It was the Talbot, closely followed by the Bugatti. The police Wolseley, with its tuned engine, had probably got there already.

We waited until they had passed then started to run. Dressed in our lacerated dinner jackets, we would have been quite a sight, if anyone had been watching.

Breathing heavily, we slid to a halt at the top of the slipway, which curved dramatically to the sea some forty feet below. There were three cars parked on the granite flagstones, their bonnets all angled towards a white motor cruiser swinging from a bow rope at the point where the water was rising over the slip. Further out, a larger cruiser started her engines. It was *Lorelei* – how the buggeration had she got here? She was supposed to be drifting out in the channel. From the sound of the sea sucking against the granite, I reckoned a swell was building. Her mast was beginning to gyrate.

Closer in, *Jacob's Star* was moored amongst the shadows, along with a few smaller boats. There were some dinghies parked near the top of the slip and several other small boats scattered at intervals down the nearside. I nudged Miko and indicated he should follow me, though I had no idea what we were going to do once we got close enough. We darted from boat to boat, crouching down behind the last one. Fifty yards of open space separated us from the closest car. The passengers were near to the cruiser now and, from the noise, seemed to be arguing. Miko leant into a dinghy and scooped up an oar and a length of rope. He handed me the rope then we dashed, keeping low, to the Bugatti. It was empty – no sign of the carving knife. The Talbot was also empty so we scooted across to the Wolseley.

Alf still held his gun and was keeping them at bay as Carl hustled Fairfield and Sleeman towards the cruiser. Kohler held Rachel. Caroline was standing next to her father. Schmitz and Kempler were huddled against the high granite wall.

Alf addressed them. 'Enough discussion, gentlemen, my orders are to take only Sleeman. I'm including Fairfield because he needs some fresh air and a good talking to. These have the free tickets. Others might be for sale. If you Germans wish, you may stay to discuss your affairs with the police. If not, you may pay me to take you to pastures new.'

'Wait. Whatever your employers are paying you, I will give you double.' Hayden-Brown even made that sound patronising.

'I have your pretty boat so I am already well-paid.'

'What about our diamonds?'

'They're not yours.'

'But we bought them fair and square.'

'And who did you pay for them?'

Hayden-Brown pointed at Sleeman. 'Him. We paid in full.'

'And how much did this cost you?' Alf asked.

'That's commercially sensitive. I can't reveal details like that.'

'Oh, but our friend Sleeman will. You can be sure of that. Won't he, Carl?'

Carl swung Sleeman around then jabbed him in the back. 'How much did you get for them, you thieving, fat bastard. Tell us?'

Sleeman's cheeks flapped as he shook his head.

Carl forced him to kneel, passed his gun to a crewman then flicked his knife open. He pulled Sleeman's head back and touched the blade to his throat.

'I'll ask once more.'

Sleeman whimpered. 'There was much expense and many shares.'

Carl lifted the knife and drew it across the Belgian's cheek. Sleeman screeched in horror.

'Final time. How much?'

'Two million dollars. Please don't cut me again.'

Alf whistled. 'A big price for a little thief.' He pointed his gun at Kempler. 'You, German banker, how much have you agreed to pay? No lies now.'

Kempler spoke to Hayden-Brown. 'Wilbur, you should be ashamed. Such profit. You could teach our Jews.'

'Oh come on, Ferdinand. It's a seller's market and the Reich can afford it.'

Alf interrupted. 'Look, the thieves squabble. How entertaining. Now, tell me, or do I have to get Carl to ask you the question?'

'This will not be forgotten. You are unwise to make an enemy of the Reich.'

Carl left Sleeman and approached Kempler.

'How uncivilised and brutish but, if you must know, we had agreed to purchase at thirty-seven point five Reichsmarks per carat.'

Alf looked surprised. 'And the total?'

'112.5 million.'

'I see. You are far more desperate than my employers realise. I think they might wish to have a discussion with you.' Alf smiled.

'Just a minute, you can't cut me out of the deal, Ferdinand,' Hayden-Brown called out.

Alf snapped. 'Oh, stop whining. Go home and count your losses. Play in a pond with the little fish. Stay away from ones that bite.'

'Where's the freighter?' Hayden-Brown asked.

'On its way to Rotterdam, under new ownership, the diamonds are with me,' he smirked, 'in your beautiful boat. But enough. You begin to irritate. Any more, and I will take you as well for no charge.'

Kohler dragged Rachel towards his uncle and spoke in German. Schmitz joined in.

After a few moments, Kempler addressed Alf. 'We think a discussion will be beneficial. Perhaps we can meet with your employers in the next few days to facilitate this.'

'You Germans are even bigger thieves than this Sleeman creature. I will follow my orders and take him so that he can explain himself. If you want to discuss this, make a better offer perhaps, you will join us now. No charge.' Alf laughed again.

The Germans shuffled reluctantly towards the boat, dragging Rachel with them.

Caroline shouted, 'Let Rachel go!' She lurched forward but her father pulled her back.

'We've done nothing wrong. I'll sort this out with the authorities. You go back to the car and wait for me.'

'Sod off, you bastard. This is all your fault. Rudi, let her go.'

'Sorry, Caroline, she's coming with me. Who knows what we will find on the other side? She could still be useful.'

Hayden-Brown called out, 'Ferdinand, don't forget you owe me. This could be very embarrassing for you and your country.'

Kempler stopped and faced Hayden-Brown. 'Wilbur, as you say, it's only business. Send me your account. It will be settled – one way or another.'

One crewman was on the boat's foredeck, shoving Fairfield and Sleeman towards the cabin. There was another at the wheel, trying to hold the cruiser on her engines. I read the name *Esperance* on her transom with *St Malo* painted underneath. A third crewman was knee-deep in water on the edge of the slip, holding onto a stern rope. A fourth now reached up and grabbed Fairfield and dragged him below. *Lorelei* was holding station a hundred yards out, her exhausts burbling softly.

Carl clambered off the stern again to assist Kempler over the side. He had to wait for the boat to dip in the swell. The others were watching. Kohler was turned towards the boat now with his back to us while Caroline hung helpless against her father's side.

Kohler started to push Rachel towards the boat. She kicked back at him and screamed. Miko leapt from behind our hiding place and charged Kohler with the oar.

He caught him a glancing blow on the shoulder and the knife clattered away. Kohler grabbed the end of the oar and pulled Miko towards him.

Rachel, off balance, teetered on the edge then twisted into a dive and disappeared into the swell.

She surfaced and started to swim towards the rocks fifty yards from the slipway.

Miko collided with the German, who stepped backwards and fell into the water.

Miko hung onto the oar and charged at Alf, who swung the gun towards him.

Caroline screamed, kicked her father then wrenched herself away from him and rushed towards the sea.

This distracted the South African sufficiently for Miko's oar to connect with his arm and the gun skittered away on the flag-stones.

Alf spun around and raced for the boat, knocking Schmitz out of his way. He clambered up with help from Carl then shouted at the helmsman to get them away. Schmitz leapt for the side of the boat but missed and slipped into the water. A crewmen grabbed him and dragged him aboard. The cruiser reversed away.

I looked up the slipway. There was still no sign of any pursuit. I was on my own.

Rachel screamed and I spotted Kohler closing in on her. He dived under and came up behind her, his arm around her throat.

He shouted to Alf to wait for him and started to drag her towards the cruiser, which was now turning towards the open sea.

I started to run to the water then stopped. *Assess the situation. Kohler's stronger and faster but he's fully clothed.* I stripped off, struggling with studs and laces as anger burned through me.

I teetered on the edge. *Always take an aid with you if you can.* I grabbed the rope and coiled it over my left shoulder.

Ready now, I launched myself. The cool water cleared my head and I used the momentum from my dive to glide under the inky surface towards them.

Rachel was struggling, her feet thrashing the water, as he held her under. I could just make out her face as I rose past her to the surface. Kohler had his hands on her shoulders and was pushing her down as I reached towards him.

I swung my fist and made solid contact with his nose. He spun and pulled Rachel up between us.

'Keep away, Renouf, or I'll drown her.'

I circled him but he twisted her round to force me to keep my distance. She had stopped struggling and was gasping for breath. This was not a life-saving scenario that I had practised.

I could dive under and pull him down but, while we were

wrestling, she could easily slip under and drown. The boat was about twenty yards away now.

Caroline was screeching from the slip and her father was already hurrying towards his car.

'Let her go, Kohler. Push her to me. Get to the boat while you can.'

He looked over his shoulder, measuring the distance. 'No, she's coming with me.'

'Make up your mind, German. We wait no more.' Alf was standing in the stern. 'Your uncle offer me a good deal if I pull you aboard. You come now.'

Kohler continued to pull Rachel with him. I followed, determined to grab her before she could be hauled aboard. If I got her legs, he would have to let go. Perhaps I could get some of the rope around his neck and pull him off.

Alf screamed as the oar slammed into his back. Miko had swum around the boat and got on their blind side. Surely these crewmen would have weapons. He was taking another crazy risk.

'Rope, Jerk, throw rope.'

I spotted him near the boat's stern holding onto the oar and waving at me. I shrugged the coil off my shoulder and hurled it to him.

He grabbed it and submerged, pushing the oar down with him.

Rudi was almost there now, though Alf had retreated to the cabin. The engines were throbbing quietly in neutral, their propellers still disengaged.

Miko bobbed up again without the rope or the oar. 'You go now, Alf. *Spumá.*' He cackled at his own joke.

Alf screeched at the wheelhouse, 'Get us out of here. Leave the German.'

The gearbox clunked out of neutral and the engines' beat increased but the boat didn't move. Miko ducked under and emerged close to me.

'What happened?'

'I wrap rope round propellers, jam oar into rudder. They go nowhere, only where tide take them.' He indicated the rocks behind us.

I paddled towards the German. 'Let her go now, Kohler. It's over for you.'

'*Gehen Bumsen sich*. It's over for her as well, the Jew bitch.' He grabbed her head, shoved her under and pushed her down.

I swam at and over him, punching at his face. He parried the blows using her body as a lever.

Just then, two crewmen jumped over the side and dived under the boat, probably to try to free the propeller. Miko reacted and swam after them.

Kohler and I grappled again but he still had Rachel under the water.

'Let her go, Rudi.' Caroline had dived in and was alongside him. 'Please, let her go.'

He released his legs and kicked off Rachel, sprinting for Miko. I grabbed her as she floated up. She was barely conscious but still breathing. I started to pull her to the slipway but Caroline reached out.

'I'll do that. You go and help Miko.' I stared at her disbelievingly. Could I trust her? Did I have a choice? Miko was on his own.

'Please, Jack. You have to trust me for once. I won't hurt her.'

I looked into her eyes. Whatever I thought of her, I knew she would not deliberately harm me or Rachel. I had to believe that. I nodded and turned back to the boat.

Miko had dispensed with one crewman and was fighting the other. Rudi was almost on him. I kicked my legs and sprinted after him, then clawed my way up his back and onto his shoulders.

We both submerged, struggling for a grip on each other. I'd taken the deepest breath I could and tried to get behind him and get the stranglehold I'd warned my life-saving pupils was fatal. He twisted and bucked but was weighted down by his jacket and shoes, whereas I had the full freedom of movement.

I got my arm around his neck and kicked upwards, breaking surface for a moment to gulp some air. I plunged down again so that he couldn't get a breath. I repeated this again and again until he ceased to struggle.

He was at my mercy. I could let him slip under now and within minutes he would be beyond revival. An unfortunate accident, or cold-blooded murder? Did he deserve to live? Who was I to judge?

337

My anger had melted away and now I only felt pity for him. I'd beaten him and saved Rachel. That was enough. I looked across to Miko and could see he was winning his battle so I grabbed Kohler's collar, hauled his inert body to the side of the slip and dragged him ashore.

Caroline was holding Rachel a few yards away, helping her regurgitate the salt water she had swallowed.

I rolled Kohler onto his back, checked his airways and listened for a breath. There was none.

I felt in his neck for his carotid pulse and there was a weak flutter.

I turned him onto his front, tugged his arms up, elbows out, placed his hands alongside his head and twisted it to the side. I shuffled round so that I could take an elbow in each hand but winced in pain as my bare knee scraped over the discarded carving knife. I nudged it away and settled again on the rough granite then started the Holger Neilson resuscitation drill, lifting his arms and trying to pump water out of his lungs.

A stream of water spewed from his mouth. Ignoring the mayhem around me, I kept working on him, pausing only to check his pulse and breathing. He was slowly coming around, his large muscles starting to twitch.

I felt faint. The kneeling had restricted my blood flow. I tried to stand to relieve the pressure but the aftershock of the fight, combined with the cold water and excess alcohol, overcame me. Desperately, I shook my head but midnight descended like a heavy blanket and I slid to the wet granite.

I struggled up through seams of green and black. A great weight pressed on my chest. It was Kohler. He held the carving knife in his hand. I had no strength left. It was over.

Dimly, I heard a gunshot then the engine note increased and the unmistakable sound of thrashing propellers floated over the water.

Kohler bent his mouth to my ear. 'Say goodbye to your Jew friend, Renouf. Then goodbye to everyone –'

Suddenly, a new sound, one I knew well from the ranges, choked off his words. The snap of a supersonic bullet followed almost immediately by the crack of a high velocity rifle. I turned my head

338

and saw triumph turn into confusion in Kohler's eyes.

Strength flooded back into my arms and I used the last desperate manoeuvre I had taught my students. I curled my right arm into my side and struck upwards with the palm of my hand into Kohler's jaw, following through until my arm was straight.

He fell off me, stunned, and I rolled on top of him, the knife now in my fist, its tip on his throat, my arm quivering, on the very edge of losing control.

Caroline's voice pierced the air. 'Don't, Jack. Don't!'

I raised my head and twisted my face to look at her. She was kneeling beside me, her hand reaching for the knife.

'Why not? He tried to kill Rachel. He was going to kill me. He deserves it.'

'He may do, Jack, but you can't do it.'

'Why not, Caroline? Why not?' I screamed at her. 'For Christ's sake, give me one reason why not!'

She screamed back, 'Because he's my brother!'

I let the knife drop to the granite. It rang as it struck the stone, an echo of the police bells clanging in the distance.

45

I rolled off him, picked up the knife and hurried down the slipway. I spotted the gun resting against the wall and scooped it up. It was dry. I had never used an automatic before but it couldn't be that different from a revolver. The boat was heading towards the rocks poking out from the side of the slipway. Most were hidden by the high tide but the helmsman wouldn't know that. She struck, twisted sideways then stopped, paralysed on the granite jaws.

The rifle shooting had ceased and I looked across the sea towards our farm. Couldn't be Fred, might be my father, possibly Alan. I waved then held my arms in a high cross. No more shooting please.

Lorelei was moving in to the rescue. Saul would have admired the seamanship as the helmsman swung her alongside. One of Alf's crewmen jumped first then leant back to help his boss. Carl shoved Sleeman across the gap and Alf dragged him aboard. Finally, the little bastard and the last two crewmen made the leap. They were leaving their other guests to find their own salvation.

As the stranded boat lurched sideways, Fairfield vaulted into the sea. Relief flooded through me as I spotted Miko swimming towards him. He grabbed his hair and swam for the slipway. I didn't think he'd bother to go back for the Germans.

Kempler and Schmitz were also in the water and looked to be in trouble.

I hurried back to Kohler and pointed the gun at him.

'Don't just sit there like a spavined duck, get in and rescue them before they drown.'

Rachel was on her feet. 'What about the diamonds? We can't let them get away.'

'How can we stop them?'

'Saul's boat. Can't we chase them?'

'Do you know how to run it?' I pointed to the eastern sky, which was greying rapidly. 'Do you know how to navigate?'

'No.'

Caroline spoke up. 'My father knows how. He'll want to go after them.'

I doubted it. 'Well go and ask him then.'

Twin headlights shot between us and a door slammed.

Saul ran down the slipway. 'See, Jack. Taxis can be useful. What's happening?'

'I'll fill you in later. First we need to get *Jacob's Star* running and chase after *Lorelei*.'

'What are you talking about? She's wallowing in the channel somewhere.'

'You might think so but look.' I pointed to the fast diminishing hull as it cleared the end of the breakwater.

'*Kak*.' He cast around. 'Here, let's get that dinghy, find an oar and you can scull us out.'

We dragged it down the slipway and Saul jumped in while I grabbed an oar.

'Wait for me.' Rachel was alongside, tugging my arm.

'No, it's too dangerous. They've got guns.'

'So have you.' She pointed to the automatic that I'd tucked into my pants.

'They know how to use theirs. Sorry, it's too risky.'

'So what are you going to do when you catch them?'

I hadn't thought of that. 'Follow them. See where they go. Report it.'

'To whom?'

Another fair point. 'The authorities.'

'I've got a better idea.' She looked more determined than I'd ever seen her. 'I know how to contact Hélène. She gave me a phone number after our meeting.'

So that's what they'd been discussing.

'I'll tell you why later but we're wasting time. Come on, after them.'

The police bells were getting closer. If we delayed any longer, they'd stop us. 'Okay. You wait while we get the boat.'

'No, take me.'

'There's not enough bloody room in this dinghy. Just wait. We'll come and get you. See if you can find Miko.'

She hurried off as I dropped into the dinghy and started sculling.

Minutes later, we had *Jacob's Star* alongside but *Lorelei* was out of sight. I jumped ashore and held her against the wall while Rachel rushed back with Miko. They clambered aboard and I was about to join them when Caroline grabbed my arm.

'I'm coming as well.'

I shrugged her off. 'No, you stay and look after your brother.'

'My father can do that. I'm coming with you and you're going to need these.' She thrust my clothes at me and, before I could stop her, she was aboard.

I leapt after her and Saul powered us away.

It might be a fruitless chase but at least we were doing something.

As we passed the breakwater, I scanned the horizon with Saul's binoculars, hoping to catch some reflections off the fleeing boat. I thought I saw something in the distance heading southeast. Saul passed the controls to Miko and joined me on the cabin roof.

He examined the distant speck. 'Definitely the wake of a boat. Can't be anybody else. I'm guessing she's got the diamonds, am I right?'

'So Alf said. You were spot-on about the price. Over one hundred million marks so there must be three million carats on board. Can we catch her?'

'I'm running flat out but we're not as fast. As soon as they spot us, they'll speed up. It looks like they're making for Granville. It's about thirty miles from here. Say they're two miles ahead now, running at eighteen knots, we're making fifteen. They'll get there at least thirty minutes before us.'

'But won't the weight of the diamonds and six passengers slow them down?'

'A little but they're still going to be tied up and unloaded before we get there.'

'What about French customs, les Douanes?'

'In France at this time of night? You must be joking. This lot have already got someone waiting for them. They're not amateurs, Jack.'

'They're not that clever either. What if the golden syrup starts to work?'

'Well that would change everything.'

No one seemed to want to talk. Saul consulted his charts. The girls towelled themselves dry, strung a line over the throbbing diesels, and hung their expensive dresses and, in Rachel's case, underwear over them. They found some blankets and wrapped themselves in them. I dressed but didn't bother with my bow tie. Miko found a pair of Saul's white shorts and a polo shirt and looked the most comfortable. It was a shame I didn't have Fred's camera. It would have made an entertaining picture.

Saul reckoned we were about three miles from the French coast when *Lorelei* seemed to grow in size. Minutes later we were within shouting distance. She was stationery in the water. Perhaps my favourite liquid had come to the rescue after all.

Miko checked the automatic as Saul cut our speed and held us out of accurate pistol distance. I hoped they didn't have any rifles.

I called across, 'Do you have a problem. Can we be of assistance?'

There was a pause.

'*Voetsek!*' Alf's voice slashed across the water.

'How very rude. We can take you in tow if you like but you'll have to come back to Jersey.'

Saul shouted to me, 'Leave the *kaffirs* to sink.'

'Caroline, does your father's boat have a radio?' I knew we didn't.

'No. I don't think so.'

'How long before they hit the shore, Saul?'

'For the next couple of hours the tide will take them northwesterly back to Jersey. I think they're hoping to fix the engines.'

343

'Can they do that?'

'Even if it was flat calm, they'd have little chance. If that mixture of ours has finally fouled the system, it's a job for a boatyard.' He scanned them with the binoculars. 'They've got their dinghy back but I can't see an outboard motor. They could row but, in this sea, they'd be lucky to get anywhere near the beaches. Basically, they're fucked.'

'What about flares?' I asked.

'It's too far to be seen from Jersey but they might wake up the Gendarmerie Maritime. If they can be bothered, they might send a rescue boat but, as we're outside their territorial waters, the lazy bastards are more likely to radio Jersey and ask them to send the lifeboat or States tug.'

'Are you sure?'

'It's happened before. They don't seem to like operating at night.'

'Right. Bring us in a bit closer.'

'What you do?' Miko tugged my shirt. 'We ram bastards, eh?'

Saul answered. 'Wish we could but they've got a steel hull against our timber. How close do you want to go?'

'No less than fifty yards and keep us head-on.' I cautioned.

As he opened the throttles, I crawled onto the cabin roof.

Miko passed me the automatic. 'Here. It work now. Just pull trigger.'

There was little hope of hitting anything but I could make some loud noises. I called out, 'You can't fix your engines in this sea. Would you like us to fire some flares and stand by until help arrives?'

There was a slight pause then a pistol crack.

Saul reversed rapidly.

'I told you. Let the fuckers sink and the diamonds with them. Even if they surrendered, what would we do with them?'

Another good point. 'I don't know. Take them back to Jersey, hand the crew over to the authorities. Anything to stop the diamonds getting to the Germans.'

'Think, Jack. What would happen if we turned up in Jersey with millions of pounds worth of diamonds and that bunch of crazies?' Saul asked.

'I hope we'd be thanked, might even get a reward.'

'*Kwas*. This is the real world. We'd be helping the police with their enquiries for months. Caroline's father and his friends would be pulling all the strings to get their goods back and we'd be little piggies in the middle. Our only way out of this is to make sure we aren't caught with the diamonds.'

Rachel said, 'I told you before, Jack. I've got Hélène's number. If you can get me to a French port, I'll let her know what's happened. I think we can rely on her to rescue the diamonds and make sure the Germans don't get them.' Rachel sounded convinced of her own plan. It might even work. There was only one major flaw.

'If she gets the diamonds, they'll end up with the Russians. Do we want that?' I asked.

Caroline answered. 'I don't think we have a choice. Saul's right. My father has powerful friends. We take them back and he'll find a way of getting his thieving hands on them again. I don't know who this Hélène is but if she's a Communist, that's fine. They'll make better use of them than my father.'

Caroline being sensible. I was in shock.

Miko spoke first. 'You not ram. I understand. These men will not surrender. They shoot. Is too dangerous. We go to French port, give problem away.'

'Okay, we'll go to plan D – Rachel's plan.'

I called out to *Lorelei*, 'Don't go away, we'll be back with help.'

We left in a cloud of diesel exhaust fumes and pistol shots.

Granville was in darkness. Saul had been before and motored into the harbour as quietly as he could. Rachel had changed into her ruined dress without complaint. I tried to help her up the dockside ladder but she slapped my hands away.

We found a telephone box but we didn't have any French coins. I dialled the operator and asked to make a *téléphoner en PCV* to the number Rachel provided. We waited patiently, expecting to be denied, but a different operator came on the line and asked for my name. I handed the telephone to Rachel and she spoke in English.

She listened then put her hand over the mouthpiece. 'I have to wait. I hope it's not for the police.'

Fred had mentioned that Hélène had good contacts in the telephone exchanges. Perhaps the number she had given wasn't just a normal line. How long dare we wait? Talking to the Jersey police would be infinitely more preferable than trying to explain this to the local Gendarmerie.

She started speaking. 'Hélène. Thank goodness. I'm sorry to call you like this… yes, I understand. It is urgent. A white boat called *Lorelei* has broken down off the coast about three miles from Granville on a line to Jersey but it is drifting northwards. It has that cargo we discussed on board. There are six men, at least one is armed and another man is being held against his will. We are on Saul's boat, *Jacob's Star*… yes, yes.' She listened for a few moments. 'Yes. Understood. Thank you. Goodbye.'

She replaced the instrument. 'She wants us to go back to *Lorelei* and keep watch. She says someone will be with us within the hour. They will flash a message in something called Morse Code. Do you know it?'

'Yes, but what's the message?'

'She didn't give one but said you would understand.'

We found them still drifting and wallowing in the swell. Saul kept us circling and Miko and I took turns with the handgun to watch in case they launched their dinghy and tried to board us.

We waited. In between shifts with the gun, I brooded about what had happened during the meal. I needed to talk about it but the girls were closeted in the cabin and didn't want to be disturbed until something happened. Saul was too busy at the wheel and Miko wouldn't understand.

Ninety minutes later, I spotted lights moving towards us from the dark ribbon of the French coast. Eventually they split and two motor cruisers approached from different directions. One shone a powerful searchlight in our direction and it started to blink. Short – long – short – pause – short – pause – long – short – short. Hélène had said I would understand. They'd sent the word RED. I grabbed Saul's torch and clicked out the response – FRED.

Both boats turned towards *Lorelei* and an amplified voice sounded over the waves. It spoke in French and demanded that they

346

dispose of their weapons and prepare to be boarded. Alf's men fired a couple of shots from their handguns. A fusillade of rifle shots cleaved through the air from both French boats.

I was wondering if any of Alf's crew understood the language when an irate voice shot a rapid stream of French from *Lorelei*. It accused the interlopers of piracy, claimed they were in international waters and didn't need assistance.

More rifle shots were fired and I could hear bullets pinging off *Lorelei*'s steel hull. Saul moved us further away. The French boats closed in and held *Lorelei* in cross beams of light and aimed rifles. The amplified voice repeated their previous order and one of the boats drew alongside the stricken vessel.

Through the binoculars I could see Carl holding his handgun aloft. I hoped he would shoot. But even Alf's snarling dog had the sense to realise he was impotent. He dropped the gun overboard. The rest of the crew stood helplessly in the cockpit as three men jumped aboard. The French ushered Alf's crew below then picked up a line from their cruiser and fastened it to *Lorelei*'s bow.

Within minutes they had her in tow and motored off towards Granville.

Caroline's dress was still damp, her body sticky with salt, but the essence of Joy still teased as she pressed into me and took the binoculars. 'Do you think he'll get his boat back?'

I inhaled her scent. *What the hell had happened to us?* 'I don't know. They only want the diamonds. I assume they'll hand the Afrikaners over to the Gendarmerie eventually. By the time Alf's employers can make a fuss, the cargo will be long gone. These commies may talk a lot but they're not shy of a bit of action. I'm glad we listened to Rachel. Looks like plan B and plan D both worked.'

'You're not very good at that, are you?' she asked.

'What do you mean?'

'Listening. If you'd listened to Rachel before, or even to me, you and I wouldn't be in this awful mess now.' Her voice was surprisingly soft as she stepped away.

I wanted to follow, ask what she really meant, but Miko slapped my shoulder. 'Hey, I still think ramming is best.'

Saul laughed. 'Fun over for the night. We've got to navigate back to St Catherine's. Caroline, be a dear and see if you can rustle up some coffee. There's milk in the fridge.'

'Fuck coffee, you prick. Where's the bloody brandy?'

Miko nudged my elbow. 'You think there will be reception for us?'

'Yes, but not the sort we deserve.'

46

'Right, Renouf, I'll ask you once more.' Inspector Le Feuvre was chairing my reception committee. Its other members, Detective Sergeant Greaves, still rubbing his neck, sat alongside him, and Detective Constable Clitheroe guarded the door behind me. 'Where is he?'

'The answer is still the same, Inspector, I don't bloody know.'

He sipped his coffee. The blue overalls I'd been given to wear were itching and the wooden chair in this interview room wasn't designed for comfort. 'Your uncle was last seen with you in the car park. Where did he go?'

'I don't know – and I don't care.' I leant forward and placed my hands on the scarred table. 'What I *do* want to know is what are you doing about the Germans. Why are you so interested in my uncle?'

'That's enough of your cheek, you young puppy.' Le Feuvre leant across the table until his nose was almost touching mine – his coffee breath acid in my face. 'You are in enough trouble already – don't make it worse.'

'I haven't done anything wrong.'

He laughed without humour. 'Public affray, assault with a deadly weapon, obstructing the police, withholding information, fleeing the scene of a crime, aiding and abetting felons, conspiracy to pervert the course of justice and anything else in the book that comes to mind.'

'Well charge me with something then. Get me a lawyer. Get me my clothes. Anything apart from asking me questions to which you know I don't have any answers.'

'Where had you been in that boat before you came back to St Catherine's?'

'I've told you enough times. We chased after *Lorelei* because those madmen had kidnapped someone. We wanted to see where they were going so we could report it but we lost them. We searched –'

'Your Jewish friend said something about diamonds at the hotel. Were you chasing those?'

I forced a laugh. 'He was trying to embarrass Hayden-Brown. He was angry because we'd discovered that he was assisting German spies. If you were Jewish, wouldn't you be upset? Don't you know what's going on in Germany?'

He snorted. 'You don't know what you're talking about. You've never been there. Don't believe everything the Jews and commies tell you.'

'I won't listen to the fascists either and I don't know anything about diamonds.' We'd agreed on this story. I just prayed the others would stick to it when it was their turn in this uncomfortable chair. One consolation was that Hélène had probably arranged a far more unpleasant interrogation for Alf and his crew.

'Excuse me, Inspector, perhaps I might ...' Greaves spoke softly. Even though he was only a sergeant, it was clear that he was in charge.

'As you wish but the boy is as stubborn as his uncle. He needs a bloody good birching.' Le Feuvre slumped back and eyed me with venom.

'Jack, you remember I gave you some information about that bike?'

'Yes.'

'Did you find out any more?'

'I might have, but what's that got to do with this German conspiracy?'

He ignored my question. 'Did you discover if your uncle has any papers which might have belonged to Lawrence?'

I was surprised by the sudden change in direction but managed to keep a straight face. 'I have no idea what you are talking about – who's Lawrence?'

He turned to Le Feuvre. 'He's trying to protect him. He knows a lot more than he is prepared to tell us. Isn't that right, Jack?'

I caught myself just in time before I fell into his trap. 'Sorry, I don't know what you are talking about. What about the *Germans*?'

'We'll come to that. First, tell me about your conversation with Eric.'

He was an expert and it was my first interrogation. I knew I couldn't fool them, however hard I tried to keep a straight face. But I had to play the game.

'Eric? Eric who?'

'Eric Slater, regional organiser for the South of England.'

'Organiser for what?'

'Comintern – but you knew that, didn't you?'

'I have no idea what you are talking about. What's commie turn?'

'Comintern. Communist International. Dedicated to overthrowing democracy and bringing the world's workers to Stalin's bosom. Ring any bells now?'

'No.'

'Does your uncle work?'

'He can't find any. Whenever he applies, the vacancy is already filled.'

'Does he claim Parish Relief then?'

'I have no idea.'

Le Feuvre broke in. 'If he did, we'd have him cleaning the sewers.'

Greaves ignored him. 'So how does he support himself, Jack?'

'You'd have to ask him.'

'Well, we don't need to as we already know. He is in the full-time employ of the Communist Party. They pay him more than he could earn as a skilled tradesman or even a police inspector.' Greaves smirked.

'If you say so. I'm sure he's better educated than Mr Le Feuvre.'

A half-grin spread from his lips then he changed direction again.

'Tell us about your uncle's gun.'

I didn't respond.

'Tell us who you went to meet on your little sea trip to the Écréhous.'

I didn't respond.

'Was she French?'

I didn't respond.

'Was her name Hélène Guzman by any chance?'

I didn't respond, but felt sure my face had.

'Regional organiser for Normandy and Brittany. Did your uncle give her the papers?'

I stared ahead. 'I don't know what you are talking about.'

'How many other members of the Communist Party have you been associating with?' He consulted a sheet of paper. 'Tell us about Malita Perez, Rachel Vibert and Miklos Pavas. Tell us about your friend Saul Marcks. They all have two things in common, don't they?'

I had to laugh – the thought of Saul as a commie was too much.

'What's so funny, Renouf?' Clitheroe's cockney growl underlined his lack of humour.

'You are. I'm fed up with your nonsense. Are you all members of the British Union of Fascists? Why do you and your boss, Mosley, hate the Jews so much?'

Greaves regarded me slyly. 'What about Senora Perez, Jack? Do you have any idea how many people she has shot? And what about your friend Mr Pavas? Do you know what he really did before he was deported from Romania?'

I believed what Miko had told me and was sure Fred hadn't lied about Malita. But those stories would be wasted on Greaves – he'd already made up his mind. Perhaps he should look at Miko's back, examine Malita... I felt my eyes burning again and turned away from them.

'What's wrong, Jack? The truth too strong for you?'

So this was their plan. Convince me that I had been lied to by my friends – try to turn me against them so that I would give them the information they wanted. Good plan but the major flaw was that I didn't have the information they wanted. They knew more than I did.

How the hell would I know where Fred had gone? With that broken wrist, he was hardly the shooter. He couldn't drive, couldn't ride a bike. Perhaps he had received some assistance from a comrade

– they certainly seemed to be everywhere. But Greaves would know that. I wanted to hit back – wipe the smirk off his face.

I pulled myself together and looked up again. 'No. I'm disappointed in your lies. Would you like to show me your warrant cards or did the mad Afrikaner take them?' I tensed myself for a punch from Clitheroe.

My stomach churned. I waited. Nothing. Le Feuvre continued to sip his coffee, Greaves smiled at me, Clitheroe moved closer. They waited, letting my provocative questions slither on the floor.

'Tell us about the rifle shots from Marcks' boat yesterday.'

How did they know that? Surely Rachel, Saul or Miko hadn't said anything? 'I didn't hear any.'

'Tell us about the rifle shots from your farm this evening.'

Well everyone must have heard those. I played deaf again. 'I didn't hear any.'

'Who sunk the boat then?'

'I didn't know anyone had sunk it. I thought it hit the rocks. Did you rescue the survivors?'

He didn't respond – just studied me as though weighing his options. 'Why do you want to kill the young German?'

I stared ahead.

'Is it because he's been shagging your girlfriend?'

I'd anticipated that one. 'Hardly – she's his sister.' At last I was able to reveal something they didn't know. I sat back with a smug smile.

A wicked grin crossed Le Feuvre's face. 'Well I suppose you're lucky she isn't *your* sister – given that your father was fucking her mother.'

I threw myself across the desk and stretched for Le Feuvre's throat. 'You bastard!'

Clitheroe got a chokehold around my neck, dragged me back and thrust me into the chair. 'Any more of that, sonny and we'll have to handcuff you.' Clitheroe sounded like he would enjoy the procedure. I slumped back and glowered at them.

Greaves' voice was calm. 'Jack, you recall when we met up with you in that street and you dived into the back of that van?' I nodded without looking up.

'Why was that? Were you trying to hide something?' He sounded so patient I realised they could keep this up until dawn and there was nothing I could do about it.

'I have nothing to hide.'

Le Feuvre snorted.

Greaves pulled out a little casket and tapped some snuff onto his wrist. He sniffed it loudly and offered the box to Le Feuvre, who declined.

'Fine, Jack, we'll trade. I'll answer one of your questions then you answer one of mine. Does that sound fair?'

'Like hell.'

'Give it a try – go on, ask me something.'

I considered. I could always lie but then so could he. 'Why are you persecuting my uncle?'

'We're not persecuting him but he interests us. That's our job. We collect information on terrorists, whether they're Irish, Jewish or Communist. They're all the same really. My turn –'

'What about the BUF? Are you persecuting them?' I interrupted. I wanted my money's worth first.

He laughed. 'What? That bunch of clowns. Harmless the lot of them – not that there are many left. We're only interested in real terrorists – ones who place bombs, kidnap and assassinate – not windbags like Mosley.'

'They're still there. It's just they've hidden their black shirts for the moment, swapped them for smart suits.' I remembered something Fred had told me and pointed at Le Feuvre. 'Why, I bet he's still got his in a wardrobe at home. Isn't that right, Inspector, weren't you a leading light in the local branch of the Imperial Fascisti League?'

Le Feuvre's face blossomed into the colour of the Communist flag.

Greaves frowned.

'Oh, it's true. They joined up with the local BUF a few years ago. Look at his face.'

Greaves shook his head but I'd knocked some of the wind out of his sails. 'He's not the one being questioned. You're the one in serious trouble. Just remember that. Now it's time –'

'What about Fairfield then? What do you know about him?' I sensed my questions were draining his patience to the point where he would drop his polite act. Even more reason to continue.

'Sir Edward? Pillar of the establishment. Great servant of his country.' His endorsement sounded hollow.

'And the Germans? What about them? Aren't they plotting against the government you're paid to protect?'

'We don't protect governments. We uphold the law.' He was smiling again. He wasn't going to let a schoolboy unsettle him.

I tried again. 'You still haven't answered my question. Why my uncle?'

'He has some particular information we would like to retrieve.' He hesitated. 'I think you know what that is.'

'You mean evidence about the conspiracy that your Fairfield is involved in?'

'And what would that be, Jack? Tell me about this *conspiracy*.' His voice leaked sarcasm.

'To turn England into a fascist state, appease Hitler, betray Poland –'

'Oh this is bloody ridiculous,' Le Feuvre interrupted. 'This is getting us nowhere.'

Greaves held up his hand for silence and leant forward again. This time his tone was intimate. 'Tell me, Jack, I am interested. Who is the bigger threat to the world? Hitler or Stalin?'

I eyed him back. 'Is that your question?'

'Indeed. Your answer will tell me a lot.' He waited.

He was toying with me again. Trying to suck me in. He wasn't going to tell me anything useful but by talking, he was hoping I would let something slip.

It was time to end this, even if it did mean a beating. 'Why don't you ask the Afrikaners?' I paused. Tensed myself. 'Of course you can't ask them, can you, because you are so *fucking* incompetent, you let them disarm you and get away.'

Clitheroe grabbed my hair and jerked my head back over the chair. Just as I sensed his fist swinging to strike, I heard the door open.

He released his hold as Le Feuvre leapt to his feet. Greaves looked confused.

'What is going on here?' The familiar voice of the President of the Defence Committee, Philip Tanguy QC, washed over me as he walked towards the desk. 'I hope you are not harming this young man.'

'No, sir, but he is being very difficult – refusing to answer questions and –'

'Never mind that, Inspector. I will speak to you about this later.' He turned to the door. 'In you come, Aubin.'

My God. They'd arrested my father.

Tanguy was speaking again. 'Allow me to introduce Sergeant Greaves of the Metropolitan Police – Mr Aubin Renouf.'

My father shook hands with my tormentor. I'd seen this magic handshake before and marvelled how it turned complete strangers into lifelong friends.

My father said, 'May I have a word outside, Sergeant?'

Le Feuvre smouldered. Obviously, he wasn't one of the brothers.

Tanguy left with the two men. He didn't need to shake hands – his Masonic membership was written all over his patrician face. I tried to listen but, apart from distant voices, could hear nothing.

Minutes later, the door opened and Greaves returned. He sat at the table and looked at me with a ghost of a smile on his face. 'Well thank you, Jack. You've been most helpful. We won't forget to tell your uncle *how helpful* now that we've found him.'

He stood up and indicated the door. 'You are free to leave.'

I was about to step through the threshold when he spoke again. 'Oh, excuse me, I almost forgot. I need to draw your attention to this.' He held up a booklet with a blue cover. 'It's a copy of the Official Secrets Act 1920. There's a minor amendment going through parliament at the moment but it needn't concern you.'

'What's this got to do with us?' my father asked.

'Well, quite a lot actually. I'm sure you don't want me to read you the whole thing but section two, "Communications with foreign agents" and section three, "Interfering with officers of the police" are relevant here. Section eight, "Provisions as to trial and punishment of offences", will also be of interest.'

'I'm not going to sign anything. You can't hush this up,' I said.

'No need. It's already a law. I am just making you aware of it.

Signing is irrelevant.' He paused as a thin smile crossed his face. 'I will be doing the same with all the others as well. Should you reveal any detail to a third party that you have ommitted to mention during your interview then you will almost certainly be prosecuted to the full extent of the provisions under this law.'

I absorbed this and was about to respond but my father spoke first. 'I see. I can understand your wish to cover up this whole episode but what about all the people who wintessed the events at the hotel?'

Greaves shrugged. 'The law applies to them as well and we have all their names. They will be visited and reminded. And, before you ask, none of this will be reported in your newspapers. The Lieutenant Governor's office will be issuing a D notice to their proprietors.'

My father considered this for a moment then nodded. 'It makes sense. No point in alarming people. I suppose it's for the best. Thank you, Sergeant. Is there anything else?'

I was about to suggest something when my father tugged me into the corridor.

47

Tanguy marched off and left us.

My father spoke softly. 'What a bloody awful mess.'

'Where's Alan?'

'Shush.' He tugged me away from the door. 'He's got *nothing* to do with this. *Understand?*'

So he was the shooter and Father was going to help cover up. He'd obviously been very busy already. 'Where's our section two foreign agent, Uncle Fred?'

My father's voice and expression were deadpan. 'He was in the hospital having his wrist fixed. He didn't know anyone was looking for him.'

'What happens now?'

'We go home. Your mother is very upset.'

I'd get the full story from Alan. It shouldn't be too difficult now that I'd had some interrogation training.

As we passed along the corridor, I couldn't resist peeking through the glass panel in each door. I hoped to see the Germans handcuffed and awaiting their turn with Le Feuvre and the Special Branch bullies. The first room was occupied by a group of honorary policemen talking with Phillips. I hurried on. The second was empty.

The third held Malita and Miko, who was wearing similar overalls to mine. He looked better in shorts. I glanced around the room but there were two uniformed policemen sitting with them. They were in for a long night. I couldn't imagine either of them giving Greaves anything other than a difficult time.

The next room held two women with their backs turned. I gasped in surprise. Rachel and Caroline were talking quietly. They were wearing yellow overalls. I wondered if Caroline was wearing the scratchy underwear. I peered in through the panel. An honorary policeman was staring into space.

The door opened and Saul stuck his nose in my face. 'I hope your fucking ears are burning. Come in for fuck's sake.' No Shakespearian references to unpick there then. I was pleased. The Bard hadn't been much use really.

My father's grip tightened and he hissed in my ear, 'Come on. Not now.'

Caroline and Rachel swivelled in their chairs and spotted me. Their faces were level – only inches apart. I had never seen them that close before. They looked at me as though I was a stranger. Perhaps I was.

I shrugged out of my father's grip. 'Five minutes. Please.'

He let me go.

Saul hauled me in and closed the door. I recognised the honorary policeman – the unfortunate haberdasher from Voisins. He didn't look as though he'd been attacked by Caroline yet. Then she didn't look as though she had the energy to attack anyone at present.

I stumbled in and sat next to them. Saul pulled up another chair. The haberdasher ignored us.

'Man, where have you been? I've had to listen to these two dissect you piece by piece. I had no idea women could remember so much. Everything, man – every fucking thing you've ever said or done. They don't forget anything.'

'We can forgive though, Saul, but not if you don't shut up.' Caroline held Rachel's hand. 'We've been talking, Jack. I know now isn't a good time but –'

'About me, behind my back?' I didn't want to hear this. 'Where's your brother?'

'Gone. They're all gone. It's as though they were never here.'

'What about your father and your –'

'They're here somewhere.' She waved her hand to indicate the town hall. 'They'll be taking me home soon.'

'Why, Caroline?'

'Why what?'

'Your brother. Tell me about your brother.'

She exchanged an intimate look with Rachel.

'Jack, I'm sorry. I got everything wrong. I thought... you and Rachel... I was jealous. I didn't think I could trust you.' Her cheeks had bright spots in them – she was finding this difficult. I noticed Rachel squeeze her hand. 'It was infatuation, I suppose. My own silly insecurity.' She exhaled. 'I asked Rudi to play along, pretend to be an admirer –'

'She was testing you, Jack.' Rachel spoke mechanically. 'She wanted Rudi to like you, to –'

'Approve, I suppose. I don't know what I wanted. You were so confusing, Jack.'

She let go of Rachel's hand. 'I always thought that you were just, you know... I thought you were really keen on Rachel – do you know how many times you mentioned her name in your letters? Only, I thought you didn't have the courage to tell her.' She swallowed. 'I thought that if I let you...' She stopped.

I looked quizzically at Rachel. They may have been talking intimately but I didn't think they had been telling each other the truth. I glanced at Saul. He rolled his eyes.

I felt desperately sad. Rachel's eyes were hooded, her face blank.

Saul broke the silence. 'It's like quick-sand, Jack. Stay out of it. She's told us about Rudi. I could almost feel sorry for the bastard –'

'Shut up, Saul. This has nothing to do with you.'

'Oh, really? What the fuck am I doing here then?'

'You had no choice. You're a witness like the rest of us.' Rachel sounded exasperated with him.

I pointed at the constable's officer. 'I'm sure he's been making notes, haven't you, Officer? Your bosses will be interested in everything that's been said. Make sure you get it right.'

Saul nudged me. 'Don't worry, Jack, they haven't been indiscreet. No references to Shylock and his daughter's theft.'

That was something. They'd had the sense not to mention diamonds in front of the poor man, who was looking quite bemused enough.

'Okay, I'm all ears – even if they are rather red. Tell me. Make *me* feel sorry for the German bastard.'

'Jack, that's enough.' Rachel sounded angry with me.

What *had* been going on in here?

'It's okay, Rachel.' Caroline patted her arm. 'It's just that we've all had rather a lot of secrets dragged out of us in the last few days –'

'Just tell me one thing, Caroline. You're not my sister as well – are you?'

It was a vicious slap – perhaps undeserved – but I was still very angry. Her face dissolved and she started to sob. The other two stared aghast at me. Even the haberdasher leant forward in his chair. Had her reaction confirmed it?

She balled her hands into fists. 'How could you? How could you? Do you think I would have let – you fucking cruel bastard!'

Saul couldn't handle silence. 'Well – just for the record, Jack. In case Caroline never speaks to you again. Her mother moved to Berlin in 1913 with her parents. Colonel Hayden was a military attaché. She met Tobias Kempler, had a fling, produced Rudi then buggered off to England with her parents when war broke out. Had to leave the little bastard behind because the Kemplers wouldn't let him go. In normal times it might have caused a diplomatic incident but the Germans had launched one of their own by then and there was nothing she could do. This was probably a relief to her father as having an illegitimate grandson fathered by the enemy wasn't a great career move. Tobias was killed by a British sniper in 1917.'

He paused waiting for a reaction.

Caroline's voice was flat, unemotional. 'My mother met Wilbur in Jersey before the war. It's a complicated story. I've seen photographs of Tobias. He was very handsome, came from a well-placed family. After Tobias was killed, Rudi was adopted by his uncle Ferdinand.' She tried to smile and turned to Rachel.

'It seems I'm not the only one to have family secrets kept from them.'

So they'd been sharing more than their opinion of me. Rachel's face was blank.

I waited.

Caroline looked into the distance. 'After the war, my mother met Wilbur again in Jersey, though it would seem that Jack's father got there first.'

I couldn't protest, not now my mother had broadcast the affair, so I kept silent.

'The Renouf men appear to be equally bewildered about relationships.' She sounded more sad than bitter.

I waited, again not knowing how to react.

'But he chose his wife. Love? Loyalty? Who knows. Perhaps Jack will ask his father one day.'

'He's outside. Do you want me to bring him in? You could ask him, Caroline. If you think it would –'

'That's not the best idea you've ever had, Jack.'

'Saul's right. He probably doesn't know the answer anyway.' Caroline looked towards the door. 'He's suffered enough this evening. Anyway, it's not about your parents. The question was about mine and I don't have any more answers – apart from guesswork and I'm not thinking very clearly at the moment.'

No one spoke.

Again the silence defeated Saul. 'Caroline didn't know she had a brother until she met him in Berlin. She didn't know about your father's relationship with her mother until this evening. She's got lots of questions for her mother –'

'That's enough, Saul. I think we've heard enough secrets for one day.' Caroline slumped in her chair.

Saul stopped and looked at Rachel.

She looked at me.

I looked at Caroline.

She looked at the floor.

She looked up and we all swapped the direction of our gaze.

When our eyes had settled, I was looking at Rachel. She seemed to have grown in strength as Caroline collapsed.

It struck me that Rachel's discovery about her parentage had been more devastating to her than the revelation of my father's and Isobelle's past misdemeanours to Caroline and myself. Now, I sensed that she was distancing herself from us – retreating to examine the reality of who she was.

There was nothing more to be said. I got up and walked to the door, leaving them with their silence. Father was waiting. He took me home.

Epilogue

The wreckage of the *Mauritania*'s raft is all around me. The only recognisable parts are the copper drums; the wooden planks are scattered, like matchwood, across the beach, victims to last night's unexpected storm.

I crunch through the smooth pebbles and pick up a two-foot spar, careful to avoid its jagged edges. I hurl it towards the sand, but it pitches short into the stones, bounces twice before planting itself in the seaweed deposited by this morning's tide.

I am midway between the pool and the Dicq Rock; the tide is reaching in again and will be high in a couple of hours. I sit on one of the copper drums, dented but still in one piece, and contemplate the wreckage at my feet. If there is a symbol of my summer, then I am in the middle of it.

It is a fortnight since we listened to the BBC news and discovered that we were at war with Germany once again. What none of us had wanted to believe is now the reality.

I feel particularly sorry for Uncle Fred. He had been confused and upset by Russia's pact with Germany in August and devastated today when we heard from the lunchtime broadcast of their stab in Poland's back.

His belief in the salvation that Communism offered the working man has been as badly dented as the copper drums scattered around me. But it hasn't shattered like the wood at my feet. He tried to convince us, though I feel he was trying harder to convince himself, that Stalin is just playing with Hitler and will turn on him as soon as he is ready and stamp out fascism forever. Two months ago my father would have thrown him out of the house for mouthing such sentiments but he seems more tolerant now. He even smiled sympathetically at Malita as he served the beef.

Alan turned up late. He'd been practising again at Crabbé with my rifle now that his own was in so many different parts buried around the farm.

He hadn't needed much encouragement to tell me about his part in the sinking. Fred had slipped away from the hotel, found one of his comrades who worked on the Palace Farm next door and persuaded him to drive to our house in their delivery van.

He'd roused Alan and they hurried to the field overlooking the breakwater. He'd spotted while Alan shot. My brother was disappointed he hadn't hit anyone on Alf's boat but Fred told us that he'd been spotting away from human targets. Instead the bullets had frightened the helmsman so much that he'd driven the boat onto the rocks.

They'd observed another white-hulled boat approach then spotted me waving. Fred had insisted on no more shooting so they'd watched the Afrikaners and their crew clamber aboard and drag Sleeman with them, leaving Fairfield and the Germans to their fate. As the police bells clanged past below, Fred had made Alan strip the rifle, wrap the components in oiled rags and distribute them around the farm.

When the police finally interviewed him, he confessed to firing on our range with Father's rifle. When they refloated and examined the boat, they found one bullet. It didn't match.

All of Hayden-Brown's guests, including Rudi Kohler, whose surname was actually Kempler, had flown out of the island the following morning.

After helping the police with their enquiries, *Boadicea* was returned in pieces on the back of a trailer. Fred hoped the rude note he'd left in her frame had been found.

The remainder of July and all of August have been miserable for me. I've taken part in competitions and won a few. Alan and I won the annual-life saving cup, which we privately rechristened the Kohler Trophy.

We beat Guernsey at everything, as usual, but I found no joy in any of it – even the water polo match. The "donkey" marking me gave me more than enough reason to introduce him to my elbow but I resisted the urge and spent most of the game underwater, examining the harbour floor.

I've no interest in food and, despite my mother's best efforts, have lost weight. Miko and I travelled together on the *St Julian* to Southampton so that I could take part in the SCASA one hundred yard championships. These were due to be held at the outdoor pool at St Leonards-on-sea in Sussex. We didn't get further than the customs shed as he was taken aside and refused entry to the UK.

Fred would have been proud of my action to demonstrate my solidarity when I accused the immigration official of racism and told him to shove his bloody country up his arse. We were held overnight in the police station and escorted to the boat the following morning. Miko is still working at the hotel, patiently waiting for a permit to enter England.

In the middle of August, Mr Grumbridge arrived, unexpectedly, at the house with my examination results. He spoke in private with my father. After he left, my father sat me down and asked me if I really wanted to study at university.

I didn't really want to do anything but, against all my expectations, he persuaded me to give it a try. His unspoken concern was that, with war looming, I might emulate his folly of twenty-five years before and join the army. For him, anything was preferable to that – even Shakespeare.

Almost indifferently, I agreed and Grumpy made the arrangements, including a generous bursary. Next month I will follow my uncle and Ned Lawrence and begin as an undergraduate at Oxford, Hitler permitting.

The summer is limping away now, the world has lost its colour and I'm sitting on a beach surrounded by the flotsam of my life, feeling far too sorry for myself.

I spend much of my sleepless nights thinking about Caroline and then worrying about Rachel. They have somehow transferred their insecurities to me and I feel rejected by both. In three weeks, I'll be nineteen years old but feel more ancient than these rocks.

I haven't seen either of them since that miserable evening in the town hall. Caroline returned to Switzerland with her mother the following day. Her father is probably still keeping Christine busy.

Rather naively, Saul had hoped his father wouldn't hear about our role in the affair. However, on his return from South Africa, he was interviewed about his son's behaviour at the Palace Hotel, in particular his rant about diamonds.

Following a robust exchange of views, it was decided that Saul should start work immediately in London, where he could focus his skills on the legitimate diamond trade. He and his father took *Jacob's Star* to a mooring on the Thames. Before they left, Saul had told me that rumours were circulating in the diamond community that a large quantity of industrials had disappeared from the Congo, along with a Belgian merchant called Sleeman.

Since he left, I've had several cards from him. I've only received one from Rachel but nothing from Caroline.

I've just been to see Mr and Mrs Vibert. I felt I should after Rachel's postcard. It had been as terse as a telegram. "I'm okay. Will write. Take care. Love Rachel."

It had been posted in St Lo the day after war was declared, five weeks after she had left for France to find her real parents. Mrs Vibert was surprised to see me but didn't invite me in. Her husband wasn't home.

I've come here for a swim instead. I'll try again later. I don't know why but I feel I must.

I look at the pool again. It is deserted now, closed up for the winter, perhaps forever. Brewster has resigned and rejoined the navy and will probably be commanding a desk somewhere in Portsmouth.

Nelson and several of the other lads have joined up and are scattered over England. Alan wants to join the army but he is too young. He'll have to wait a while before he can fire a rifle in anger again.

I feel as though someone has stolen my future and I don't know where to begin to look. I'm now a stranger in my own land. I look towards the Dicq Rock where Victor Hugo spent months of his life staring towards France, waiting for his own exile to end.

The tide is well over the pool. There is only a gentle swell. The air is cool but the water is at its warmest. I reach into my canvas bag and extract my costume and towel. I change slowly, feeling my skin pimple over in the evening air. I pick my way over the pebbles and shuffle down the beach.

This will be my last swim. The waves are muddy and seaweed swirls around me as I wade in until I reach my waist.

I look to my left – the pink granite of the Dicq Rock glows in the setting sun. I hold my breath and plunge in, let the water envelope me in its cool caress. I feel refreshed, cleansed.

I kick my feet, my body rises and I'm striking out for the Dicq. There's sufficient movement in the water to force my shoulders to roll. I can feel the whole weight of the Atlantic through those waves. I rise and fall with the motion until I can stretch and touch the warm granite. I tread water and think of Rachel.

A seagull looks despairingly at me then dives for a fish. I turn and look towards the pool, the Blue Terrace. I can hear the band, see the swirling dancers, but all is in shadow now. I push off from the rock and pull steadily towards the empty terraces. A mere 250 yards.

I increase my pace until I am rushing towards Caroline. My hand touches the concrete wall and I push back, floating while I recover my breath and my energy. The wall is cool, cold even. The warmth of the day long since gone – like Caroline.

I turn back. The bottom half of the Dicq Rock is in shadow but Rachel's face and hair are burnished by the dying sun. I push off the wall and pull towards the Rock, towards Rachel.

Am I doomed to swim forever between these two?

Halfway across I stop, tread water and look towards the beach. A small wave slops over my head and I swallow a mouthful of salt water. It's enough. "*Love is all truth, Lust full of forged lies.*"

Grumpy's right. This is not the time for serious relationships.

I look left, back towards Caroline once more, and nod goodbye. I do the same to Rachel then turn, with the tide, and sprint for the beach.